AFTER
the AFFAIR

AFTER the AFFAIR

Elaine Eleridge

FRIDAY'S
CHILD

First published in Great Britain in 2019 by
Friday's Child

A CIP catalogue record for this book is available from the British
Library.

PB ISBN 978-1-527236-44-8

Typeset in Swift by Orphans Press, Leominster
Cover photograph taken by Phil Harrison Photography, Worcester
Printed and bound in Great Britain by Clays Ltd, Elcograf S.p.A

This novel is dedicated to my parents – my beautiful mother, May, whose love was always unconditional, and my dear father, Eric, who inspired me with his love of Literature and of the English countryside.

ACKNOWLEDGEMENTS

First I want to thank my wonderful husband, Geoff, for his patience and understanding, for his unstinting support in this venture, and most of all, for standing by me in the dark days when my OCD and anxiety almost overwhelmed us both.

Many thanks also to my readers: Cecelia Arlett, without whose encouragement I may never have had the confidence to publish this book; Tricia Wastvedt, my lovely tutor at Bath Spa University, whose wise observations helped me add a greater depth to the story; Christine Allen whose opinions and interest have been invaluable; Suzanne Stone whose enthusiasm was inspiring, and Jane Oliver who has given me her quiet support for years. Last, but not least, I would like to thank my sister, Maureen, for her absolute faith in me.

I would also like to say a big 'thank you' to my editor, Sue Browning, for her insight and for all her positive comments, and to Emily Freer for a brilliant copy edit. I want to express my gratitude to those at Orphans Press who have given me much needed help and advice: Pete Swain and Chris Knight, for designing the cover, and special thanks to Joanna Narain for her warmth, patience and expertise.

In addition I must thank Phil Harrison for the cover photograph and my lovely little model Niamh.

Love has many faces but only
passion and obsession are blind.

May, 1972

Grace woke as Richard braked sharply.

'Where are we?' She shifted in the seat. Her clothes were sticking to her skin and she could feel drops of perspiration between her breasts. The air coming through the open windows was thick with heat.

'Sorry about that, tractor coming round the bend.' Richard patted her knee as he reached down to change gear, and for some reason the casual touch of his hand on her bare flesh annoyed her. She moved her legs quickly.

He reversed the car into a gateway and waited for the tractor to pass. Grace looked out at the unfamiliar scenery. All along the lane the hedgerows were white with hawthorn blossom, and through the dilapidated fence opposite she could see fields of buttercups that stretched as far as a line of low, wooded hills. Above, the midday sun was fierce, bleaching the blue from the sky.

'Are we nearly there?' She watched the dust drifting in the wake of the tractor.

'Not far.' Richard peered round the lace of hedge-parsley on the verge and eased the car back on to the road.

Grace contemplated the afternoon ahead without enthusiasm. At the very best it would be awkward; polite conversation over lunch while Richard's mother and stepfather sized her up, formed opinions and decided whether or not they approved of his choice of partner. She realised, with a swift tensing of her stomach muscles, that she knew hardly anything about them. Her husband rarely mentioned his family. They hadn't been at the wedding – his stepfather was recovering from a fall – and Richard had hidden his disappointment with a wry smile.

'It makes us equal,' he had said, 'no family on either side.'

The memories were painful. It had been a small wedding; just a few friends at the black-spired church in Wolverhampton where Richard was curate, followed by a buffet in the parish hall. It was appropriate, of course. Her mother had been dead less than two months. It would have been wrong to have a big celebration.

She sighed. Richard had no idea what a selfish person she was. He didn't know how she had resented being tied to the invalid mother she loved so deeply, or that fear of being alone had influenced her decision to marry him. And he certainly wasn't aware of her secret desire for an extravagant wedding. Although she didn't have a single living relative, she had wanted her special day – had imagined herself in white with bridesmaids, flowers, a reception in an expensive hotel – and been tempted to spend her mother's savings to make the dream come true. But of course she hadn't. Instead of a wedding gown she bought a cream dress from a local department store, and Cassie had been her only attendant, outrageous as ever, in a vivid pink mini skirt and jacket.

Grace searched in her handbag for a tissue, grief striking afresh. She didn't want to remember that morning; how she had ached to hear her mother's voice and feel the frail arms around her. The house had been hollow with loneliness. Even Cassie's chatter had brought no comfort.

'Are you okay?' Richard glanced sideways. 'You're quiet. Not worried about meeting my mother and Quentin are you?'

'I'm fine. Don't fuss!' As soon as the words were out she regretted them. She should be glad he cared about her. He had been her saviour during her mother's illness; his visits had given them strength, and afterwards, when there was no one else to help, he had arranged the funeral sympathetically, efficiently, always there when she needed him. She had loved him then. So why, after only two weeks of marriage, was she so short-tempered? If only he would stop trying so hard. His constant concern for her well-being was becoming wearisome.

Her face grew hotter. She shouldn't be so quick to find fault. 'Sorry. You're right, I am nervous.'

'No need to be, they'll love you,' he said.

She was silent again. Unconvinced. There was nothing exceptional about her. She was an ordinary young woman: average height – a little too skinny perhaps – mid-brown hair cut in a fashionable page boy style, large blue-grey eyes and delicate features. Would these elderly strangers think her pretty? She hoped they wouldn't ask too many questions. They certainly wouldn't approve of the way she had wasted her opportunities, leaving school at sixteen against the advice of her teachers, taking a series of mundane jobs and frittering away her wages with a group of dubious friends until her mother's illness had forced her to give up work altogether. She wiped away a tear surreptitiously.

'Here we are.' Richard indicated right and swung the car into a narrow driveway.

It was suddenly cooler, light barely filtering through dense woodland on either side. Grace leaned forward as the road began to wind steeply downwards, but it was some minutes before they crossed a bridge over a tumbling brook and the house came into view through the thinning ranks of trees. She drew in her breath. Below her stood an exquisite building of mellow grey stone; a mass of tall chimneys and gables and windows with diamond-shaped panes, the glass black now in the bright sunshine. Behind were formal flower beds, set in manicured lawns which merged into pastureland and, in the distance, the Black Mountains, today a mere smudge on the horizon.

'Beautiful isn't it?' Richard spoke quietly.

'I didn't think... When you said an old house I didn't imagine...'

'A sixteenth century manor house,' he finished for her as the tyres crunched on gravel and they pulled up in the middle of the forecourt.

'Why didn't you tell me?'

'You never asked.'

He climbed out of the car and walked round to open the passenger door for her. She clutched at his hand, her mind racing, trying to piece together what little she knew of his early life. His father, vicar of a country parish in Shropshire, had died when Richard was fourteen. Left with nothing, his mother had become a housekeeper, taking Richard with her to live near Hereford where she looked after a widower and his young son. After several years she married her employer, and a few weeks later Richard had gone away to college.

Grace swallowed, her mouth dry. Her notion of a homely couple in carpet slippers no longer fitted. She tugged at the short skirt of her dress in an attempt to smooth out the creases.

'Ready?' Richard put an arm round her.

'Hi there!'

The cry startled her. She turned to see a man emerge from the trees near the bottom of the drive.

They waited for him to catch up with them. There was a careless arrogance in the way he carried himself, the way he merely lengthened his stride but didn't appear to hurry. Grace stared at him, intrigued. He was about the same age as her husband, slim and long-limbed, as fair as Richard was dark; his hair, lightened by the sun, curling into his neck.

'I heard the car. How are you both? Congratulations, by the way.' His lips curved in an easy smile.

Richard's fingers tightened on her shoulder. 'Grace, this is Brandon.'

She was suddenly self-conscious. Why had she assumed the stepbrother would be much younger?

Brandon Calthorpe shook her hand. 'Pleased to meet you, Grace. Welcome to Dalchett House.' He stooped to kiss her cheek. 'I have to say I think Richard is a lucky man.'

'Glad you approve.' Her husband's voice had an edge to it.

Brandon's gaze lingered on her a few moments longer. 'Oh most certainly I approve,' he grinned at Richard, 'though I can't understand what she sees in you, old chap.'

In spite of his affable manner, Grace sensed he wasn't joking. She felt the colour creep across her face. He was watching them, a gleam of amusement in his pale eyes, as if he knew their marriage was doomed to failure.

'We should go in,' Richard said tersely.

'Of course,' Brandon nodded towards the house. 'They're anxious to meet you, Grace.'

Again that cool appraisal. She was relieved when they began to walk the few yards to the entrance.

Brandon Calthorpe held the studded door open for them. The hint of malice had vanished. His expression was friendly, slightly impish.

'Good luck,' he murmured. 'Don't look so scared, Grace. They won't eat you.'

Surprised, she found herself returning his smile as she stepped into the gloomy passageway.

PART ONE
Betrayals

CHAPTER 1
December 1978

The church smelt as it always did – of damp and furniture polish, of dusty fabric and candle wax. The child, not yet six years old, a thin, black-haired girl with a pale, pointed face and expressive brown eyes, paused for a moment in the doorway, looking back down the overgrown path. The light was fading, the sky smothered in a blanket of sullen grey cloud, the short December day coming to a premature close. Behind her there were already deep shadows in the alcoves.

She put her bundle on the back pew and closed the heavy door. Again she hesitated. There was no sound except the muffled thudding of the clock in the bell tower. She blew on her fingers to warm them before standing on tiptoe to reach the panel of light switches. Finding the one she wanted, she flicked it down and at once a single light illuminated the chancel, revealing the purple-clad altar with the huge golden cross in the centre.

Her feet made no sound on the frayed red carpet as she collected her bundle and walked down the nave. She lingered at the altar rail, frowning at the nativity scene set against the stone wall on her left, above the sanctuary steps. The figures were life-sized and most of them were chipped in places, exposing patches of grubby white plaster, but there was a serenity about the little tableau; an aura that was both mysterious and familiar. Only Jesus, asleep in the manger, had been irreparably damaged. His nose was missing, leaving a gaping hole which gave him the appearance of one of the gargoyles above the church porch.

The girl laid her bundle on the carpet and, bowing her head, went up the two steps to the makeshift stable. Here she stood, seemingly transfixed by the group in front of her, until with an audible sigh, she stooped to lift the baby Jesus from the straw. Shoulders hunched, she carried the broken figure to the altar and slid it behind the rich purple velvet of the altar frontal. Then she returned to her own bundle. Her hands shook as she removed the white shawl that covered it.

She held the naked doll, stroking the golden ringlets.

'You're still my favourite, Rosebud,' she whispered, 'but God needs you.'

Carefully, she positioned the doll on the choir stalls, wedging it upright between piles of hymn books. Next she took a small pair of scissors from her coat pocket and began to chop the pretty hair, cutting it close like a boy's. When the task was finished she wrapped the shorn curls in her handkerchief and crammed them into her pocket, together with the scissors. She picked up the doll again, cradling it to her.

'Don't cry,' she said, wiping her own tears from the plastic face.

Moving as if her limbs had grown weary, she laid the

doll in the crib and tucked the shawl round it, leaving the stiff little arms free. Then she stood back to assess her efforts, drying her eyes on the sleeve of her coat.

It seemed to her, in the subdued light, that the Virgin Mary was smiling. The doll lay on the straw, blue eyes open, hair a golden halo, tiny hands raised as if in blessing. The girl felt the sudden, fervent reward of sacrifice. Comforted, she turned and ran to the door, stopping only to switch off the light before she slipped out into the darkness.

The wind was like ice on her skin, but she was warm with an inner happiness as she skipped along the path and through the side gate into the rectory garden. The house looked inviting. Lights shone through the windows, making patterns on the lawn, and silver-grey smoke spiralled out of the chimney, drifting on the wind like one of her mother's filmy scarves. She began to run towards the back door.

Her mother was in the kitchen. All at once she found reasons to linger in the back yard. She took out her handkerchief and shook the doll's hair into the dustbin; she refastened her shoelaces and scraped the soles of her shoes on the doormat over and over again. Several minutes passed before she went inside.

Grace looked up as the door opened. 'Faith! What on earth have you been doing out there?'

'Nothing.'

'Well get yourself tidied up. Your father will be home

soon.' Exasperated by the closed, tight-lipped little face, Grace struggled to keep her temper.

As her daughter scurried out of the kitchen like a frightened fawn, all wide eyes and spindly legs, she put down the vegetable knife and leant against the draining board, unsettled by the familiar conflict of guilt and self-pity. She was trapped in this dreary Herefordshire village, tied just as surely to her husband and daughter as she had been to her invalid mother years before. And the feelings were exactly the same – resentment, the notion that she was missing out on life, restlessness, gratitude... love. She shook her head, disturbed by the ugly thoughts. It was all her fault. She had manipulated Richard shamelessly, encouraging him to accept the incumbency here against his own inclinations, persuading him it was better to bring up a child in the countryside than in some concrete jungle, pointing out how convenient it would be to live near his mother. At the time she had almost believed her own words, convincing herself that her motives had nothing to do with the Calthorpe wealth and Richard's attractive step-brother. Irritably she pushed a wayward strand of hair behind her ears. She had only herself to blame. It wasn't fair to take out her frustrations on Faith.

Her vision blurred. She hadn't wanted a child anyway. Not so soon. Shame made her cheeks burn. She knew her daughter had been conceived on that first visit to Dalchett House – in the big four-poster bed that dominated the Blue Bedroom – conceived while she imagined Brandon's long, slender fingers on her body, his flesh melting into hers.

But Faith was Richard's child, with her father's dark looks and brown, soulful eyes. She was too serious, too sensitive, too reserved. There were days when she seemed to prefer her own company, retreating to her bedroom for hours. But she was no trouble.

Grace flushed again, recalling her own shortcomings. After lunch she had washed the dishes and then, listless with the prospect of another empty afternoon, had fallen asleep on the sofa. It had been almost dark when she woke. Annoyed with herself, she had rushed around, making up the fire, setting the table, preparing the evening meal. She hadn't given a thought to Faith until the child walked into the kitchen.

What kind of a mother am I? The unspoken words seemed to hang in the air. With a sigh, she began to chop the vegetables, trying to appease her conscience, planning to give Faith an ice cream treat for pudding. For a few minutes she worked methodically, determined to be a better wife and mother. And then, once more, Brandon Calthorpe slid into her mind.

Her resolutions wavered. Old grievances surfaced. Why couldn't Richard be more like his stepbrother? No wonder they didn't get on. Richard had none of Brandon's dynamic vitality. Richard was honest, kind, dependable, dedicated to his work. And dull. He didn't excite her. Whereas Brandon... She had seen the way he looked at her sometimes; a look that left her weak with longing.

A pulse began to throb in her temples. This obsession with Brandon Calthorpe was dangerous and disloyal.

She despised herself for behaving like a schoolgirl with a ridiculous crush. Yet she wasn't a complete fool. She was aware of Brandon's faults, had witnessed his sullen moods, the flashes of intolerance and unmistakable boredom with country life. But he had always been kind to her. More than kind. She let herself remember: the touch of his hand, the expensive gifts he bought her from his travels abroad, the way he kissed her whenever they met, his lips lingering against her cheek.

The trill of the telephone interrupted her reverie. Another irrational surge of anger. Why was Richard always so *available* to everyone?

Wiping her hands on the tea towel, she went into the hall to answer.

'Tuston Rectory. Grace Lawson speaking.'

'Ah, Grace,' the plummy voice on the other end of the line began, 'it's Gwen Nisbett here. Is the rector at home?'

'No, he's not.'

'Oh. Well, would you ask him to ring me? It's about the date for the P.C.C. meeting in January. There's been a bit of a mix-up.'

Grace rolled her eyes. Why on earth was the stupid woman fussing about a meeting now? It was a week before Christmas, for goodness sake. Hadn't she anything better to do?

'I'll let him know you called, Mrs Nisbett,' she said, replacing the receiver as she heard Richard's key in the front door.

'Hi, Gracie.' His face was sallow beneath the tumble of black hair. He looked exhausted. 'Sorry I'm late.'

He followed her into the kitchen, his cassock flapping against his legs. She moved past him to fill the kettle at the sink, seeing his face reflected in the black mirror of the window, his eyes solemn above the thin, high-bridged nose.

'Fred Tyler has died.' Richard sat down heavily on one of the pine chairs. 'I was at the hospital with him most of the afternoon. He was unconscious. I just talked to him, you know... hoping he would realise there was someone close by who cared. He wasn't a religious man but I prayed for him anyway. It was a peaceful end.'

Grace shuddered. She hated it when her husband had been with the dead or dying. It was a part of his work she would rather not think about. She handed him a mug of tea, careful her fingers didn't come into contact with his.

The tea was hot and sweet and Richard felt it burning his throat, softening the knot of sadness in his chest. Fred Tyler had been an eccentric old man, independent, irascible, married to the land. 'A dying breed', he thought, wincing at the pun. He stood up and went to rinse his mug under the tap. Grace was busy at the stove, her back towards him. She had no idea how he longed to bury his face in her shoulder, find solace in the living warmth of her, tell her how inadequate he felt. Instead he went to the door.

'I'll have a bath,' he said. 'Don't worry. I won't use all the hot water.'

He climbed the stairs slowly. The door to Faith's bedroom was open and he could see her standing in front of the dressing table, wearing a white nightdress and an underskirt draped like a veil over her long, straight hair.

He paused for a moment in the doorway, watching her. 'Hello, darling, you look pretty.'

She smiled, running to throw herself into his arms.

'I'm Snow White in her wedding dress.'

Suddenly he was no longer so tired. He lifted her up for a kiss. 'Have you been a good girl for Mummy?'

Her smile faded. 'I did something good and bad.'

'Better tell me then, Minnie Mouse.' He adopted an earnest expression, brushing his cheek against hers before setting her back down on the floor.

'I put my best doll in the crib so she could be baby Jesus because the other one looked so scary.'

'Your best doll? Rosebud?'

She nodded, head bowed, and he saw tears glittering behind her lashes.

'Darling, that was a beautiful thing to do.' It was difficult to speak. Her simple offering of her best-loved doll affected him deeply. He wished he had the same uncomplicated faith.

'But I had to cut her hair to make her look like a boy. Mummy will be cross, won't she?'

Richard searched for the right words. The doll had

been an expensive birthday present and Faith was right – Grace *would* be cross.

'Tell you what, Minnie, I'll tell her tonight, when you're in bed. Perhaps I can explain things.' He patted her shoulder reassuringly.

'Thank you.' She hugged him, eyes shining with relief.

'Now we'd better get ready for our meal. Best keep Mummy sweet-tempered, don't you think?' He gave her a playful push towards the untidy pile of clothes on the bed.

CHAPTER 2

Faith stood outside the church, holding her mother's gloved hand and hopping from one foot to the other, anxious to return to the pile of presents she had opened earlier. Around her neighbours exchanged greetings, wishing each other a Happy Christmas, their breath making little clouds in front of them. Above the flurry of conversation the bells pealed out across the damp, grey countryside.

'Can we go in now?' She dug her heels into the thin layer of gravel, self-conscious in her new red coat and velvet bonnet. There was no answer. Her mother was chatting to Mrs Nisbett, shaking her head now and then, apparently in no hurry to get away. Faith waited impatiently. Her mother seemed different this morning; softer, prettier than usual. Beside her, Mrs Nisbett was huge, wrapped in a fur coat, rings glittering on her plump fingers, thick red lips opening and closing like the mouth of some enormous tropical fish.

The groups of friends and neighbours began to disperse, crowding into the little church, stamping their feet on the coconut matting by the door. Faith could hear the murmur of voices as everyone squeezed into the narrow pews. She looked beyond the bulk of Mrs Nisbett. The churchyard was almost deserted...

It was too late. She had seen the mound of freshly turned soil with the single wreath lying at the side. Walking up the path with her mother earlier she had kept her eyes averted; she didn't want to remember Fred Tyler's wrinkled-walnut face or the way his eyes watered and his fingers trembled on his walking stick. It was sad to think of him lying there, beneath the wet earth, even if his soul *had* gone to Heaven. She turned away quickly, but some of the joy had vanished from the morning.

Suddenly the sound of the organ spilled out through the open door.

'Oh, my goodness, I mustn't keep you any longer.' Mrs Nisbett swept past them into the church, leaving behind the smell of mothballs and Eau de Cologne. Faith felt her mother tug her hand and they followed, hurrying to their seats seconds before the choir began its procession from the vestry.

The plain little church was beautiful inside, transformed like a bride with shiny white material and flowers. Candlelight flickered across the statues in the nativity tableau, colouring the hard plaster faces so they appeared to be living flesh and blood. Faith was entranced. She held her hymn book proudly, pretending to read the words, while the air vibrated with the carol, *Once in Royal David's City*. As the final notes echoed in the rafters, there was a ripple of movement – shoes scraping on the tiled floor, stifled coughs, the rustle of service sheets – before all sounds shivered into silence and her father began the opening prayer.

It was a long service and several children grew restless, asking when they could go home, their complaints becoming louder and more disruptive with the passing minutes. Faith was upset by the noise they were making. When her father stepped into the pulpit to preach the sermon she wondered if he would be heard.

But there was no need for her to worry. He soon had everyone's attention, making the story of Christmas so real it was impossible not to imagine the Holy Family desperately seeking shelter on the crowded streets of Bethlehem. Every now and then he spoke directly to the children, painting the picture for them with his words and his hands and his facial expressions. Faith could almost feel the stillness when the sermon came to a close.

'Now we will sing the carol, *Away in a Manger*,' her father said, and she knew it was especially for her.

Once more the congregation shuffled to their feet. Bemused, Grace watched Richard walk back to the altar, tall and upright in the heavy, embroidered cope. He was like a stranger. With a snatch of guilt she realised that, on the rare occasions she attended church, she paid little heed to the sermon, except to grumble later if it had been longer than ten minutes. Today had been different. Seeing her husband in the pulpit, so eloquent and assured, she had felt an unexpected stirring of desire. He was still a handsome man. If only he would look at her with that fire in his eyes and satisfy her with such passion.

Disconcerted, she turned towards their daughter. Faith knew all the words to the well-known carol and Grace was amazed by the purity and power of her voice. She put an arm round the skinny shoulders, shaken by a sudden rush of love.

When the service was over they joined the queue of people moving towards the main door. Now and again Grace glimpsed Richard standing outside the porch, relaxed and smiling, his white surplus billowing in the breeze. He had a word with everyone, shaking each adult by the hand, joking with teenagers, stooping to speak to the younger children, and wishing them all a joyful Christmas.

'Don't wait for me, Gracie,' he touched her elbow as she steered Faith past the chattering villagers surrounding him.

She shrugged, pulling up the collar of her jacket. It had begun to rain, a thin drizzle which settled on their hair and eyelashes and made the paths slippery. As they hurried through the rectory gate they saw the lights of the Christmas tree in the hallway, splintered and multiplied by the frosted glass panels in the door.

Faith began to chant, 'I can see the Christmas tree, the Christmas tree, the Christmas tree.'

Grace caught some of her daughter's excitement, joining in with the impromptu rhyme until they arrived at the porch, laughing and breathless.

The smell of roast turkey greeted them when they went indoors. At the foot of the stairs the tree glittered with tinsel and the fairy lights made patterns of red, green and blue on the cream walls, the kaleidoscope of colour doubled by the reflection in the long, gilt-framed mirror.

'Isn't it lovely, Mummy?' Faith's eyes were wide with wonder.

Grace imagined the hall as her daughter would see it, her mood lightening further. Mentally she checked around the house. Everything was ready – vegetables prepared, table laid, fires lit, all the rooms tidy. She had been up at six to make sure nothing was left until the last moment. The rectory, which had seemed like a prison only yesterday, was festive and welcoming. It was her home; the place she loved best. With a little shock she discovered she was actually happy.

They were in the kitchen when Richard came through the back door, rainwater dripping from his hair, his surplus soaked through.

'Brrr! It's not very pleasant out there.' He shivered, rubbing his hands together vigorously.

'Coffee's ready. You look frozen.' Grace smiled at him, her heart filled with a half-forgotten tenderness.

'You're a life-saver, Gracie.' He pushed the wet hair back from his forehead. 'I'll just get changed.'

'We'll be in the lounge,' she said, her eyes misting.

In the bedroom Richard discarded his wet clothes for jeans and a navy sweater, thrusting his feet into a pair of comfortable moccasins as he fastened his belt. He was weary. The elation he experienced earlier had drained away the minute he came into the house. He combed his hair listlessly. Drops of water scattered like a broken string of beads across the walnut dressing table and he took a clean handkerchief from the drawer to dab them dry. Grace would be furious if they marked the wood. He sighed and tidied away his cassock and surplus before going downstairs, steeling himself to cope with his wife's indifference.

When he pushed open the lounge door he managed a cheery grin. 'Happy Christmas yet again to both my lovely girls.'

He noticed Grace's mouth tighten. She was sitting on one of the soft, pink chairs at the side of the fireplace, still dressed in the grey skirt and pretty white angora sweater she had worn to church. Her eyes were hard, assessing him, finding him wanting. His spirits slumped further. Obviously he should have worn something less casual.

'Coffee?' Grace asked. The word was like an accusation.

'Thank you.' He took the drink she passed to him and flopped down on the sofa. His daughter was sitting on the hearthrug, her cheeks rosy, the skirt of her pretty velvet dress gathered round her knees. She gave him a hesitant smile.

Richard stared into the fire. Grace had thrown on more logs and the flames were licking around them, flickering and dying, leaping back to life again. The clock on the mantelpiece ticked, marking each second, and the sound gradually filled the room. He began to wish he was somewhere else – the hospital perhaps, where people needed him; even Dalchett House would be preferable.

'Did you enjoy the service?' He lifted his head, regarding Grace dispassionately, seeing a thin, tense woman, her pretty face already settling into lines of discontent.

'Yes.' She was not going to be drawn into conversation.

It was difficult to cope with her mercurial moods. He knew she was unhappy, had been unhappy for a long time, but there seemed nothing he could do to make things better for her. What he had to offer wasn't enough, either physically or emotionally. She would always want more. Perhaps she had been too young when they married, though he had thought she was mature for her twenty years. He had fallen in love with a caring, capable girl only to discover a few weeks after the wedding that he didn't understand her at all. They barely communicated lately. It had been months since they made love. Sometimes his body ached for her, but it was too easy to make the wrong move, feel her grow rigid in his arms, hear her sighs of disappointment. Her responses depressed him, made him feel less of a man.

Placing his cup on the tray, he made another attempt at cheerfulness. 'I needed that. Thank you, Gracie.'

She didn't bother to reply.

Mindful that Faith was watching them, he slid to the floor beside her. 'I say it's time to try out one of those new games, don't you, Minnie Mouse?'

'Can we Mummy? *Please.*' Faith clasped her hands together.

Grace's features softened. 'Yes, of course, sweetheart.'

As Faith and Richard launched into a game of Twister, Grace couldn't help smiling at their contortions. She regretted her deliberate hostility. It was easy to make excuses for herself – she was tired, she had tried so hard to make everything perfect, Richard should have made an effort to dress for lunch – but in the end what did it matter? He looked relaxed and somehow vulnerable, his face glowing in the firelight, his dark hair dishevelled. Once again the wayward pulse of desire caught her unawares. Reluctantly, she left the fireside and went into the kitchen to check on the vegetables.

When they had eaten she lay on the sofa, head muzzy with wine, eyelids heavy, glad to relinquish the washing-up to Richard. She woke to find him reading Faith a story from a new book of fairy tales. Captivated by the picture they made, she remained still, listening as he took on the role of each character, fascinated by the changing expressions on her daughter's face, envious of their closeness.

As he put the book down she stretched, feigning a yawn. 'How long have I been asleep?'

'Ages.' Richard came to stand by her. 'Are you okay?' He put a hand on her forehead, withdrawing it almost immediately. 'We were getting worried about you, weren't we Minnie Mouse?'

Faith nodded, thumb in her mouth.

'I'm fine. I just needed a rest.' Grace rubbed her eyes, surprised to find them wet with unshed tears. She was so lucky. Even though she didn't deserve it, her husband and daughter loved her.

Outside it was growing dark and there were shadows in the corners of the room. The fire had dwindled to a pile of dull, red gleeds. Disconcerted, she switched on the lamp, which stood on the glass cabinet, and its twin appeared on the windowpane opposite. Richard went outside to fill the log basket.

'Would you believe the stars are out now?' he said on returning.

He left the door of the lounge open, letting in a wave of cold air and dappled colours from the Christmas tree. The room seemed touched with magic.

They ate tea squeezed together on the sofa, plates balanced on their laps. Afterwards, in response to Faith's pleas, the three of them sat on the hearthrug to play a game of Ludo, which seemed to Grace to go on for ages. She tried to ignore the pins and needles in her legs, shifting her position several times and glancing at the clock every few minutes, wondering if she would be able to move when the game was over. Yet it felt good to be involved.

Her daughter's delight at winning almost made up for the discomfort, but it was a relief to return to the sofa at last. Richard fetched the wine left over from lunch. He handed her a full glass and switched on the television before he sank down beside her.

'It's been a good day hasn't it?' He put his arm round her and she rested her head on his shoulder, watching the Morecambe and Wise Christmas show, dreamy and contented until Faith scrambled between them, wriggling until they moved apart to give her more space. Grace wished she hadn't promised her daughter could stay up late. Yesterday it had seemed the perfect way to avoid spending a long evening with her husband. Now all she wanted was to be alone with him.

'Is she asleep?' Grace was combing her hair at the dressing table when Richard came into their bedroom. The air was fragrant with the perfume he had given her.

'At last.' He came to stand behind her.

'Well done.' She smiled at him through the mirror, knowing she looked seductive in the lamplight, the white satin nightdress clinging to her body, her hair loose and shining, released from the clip that had held it back. Her hand trembled as she put the comb down. She wanted him to touch her, to take her small breasts in his hands and make love to her.

He didn't move. Abruptly she stood up and walked across the room, exaggerating the swing of her hips, aware her nakedness was clearly visible beneath the thin material. As she slid into bed she kept her eyes focussed on his face.

He took ages to undress, folding his clothes, checking the time, winding his watch. She tried to conceal her impatience. When, at last, he settled beneath the bedclothes, her need was not so urgent. She pressed her body to his, longing for him to caress her, kiss her, rekindle the passion that still simmered in her veins.

'I love you,' she murmured, brushing her lips over the hollow in his neck.

'And I love you. Best get some sleep now. Another big day tomorrow.' He gave her a quick kiss and rolled over to switch off the lamp.

Grace lay in the darkness, smarting with humiliation, tears of self-pity cooling on her cheeks. She reached under the pillow for her handkerchief, glaring at the solid shape of her husband's back. She didn't want him to know she was crying. He was cold and insensitive and he didn't love her.

In her heart she knew this wasn't so. Their couplings were infrequent, sometimes awkward, and it was probably as much her fault as his. But that didn't make rejection any easier to bear. Life was passing her by. She was nearly twenty-seven, locked in a passionless marriage, still waiting for some vague, girlish dream to come true.

Her tears dried, replaced by spite. He needn't think she was going to Dalchett House tomorrow, sucking up to his domineering mother, giving the impression everything was wonderful. Let him go by himself and try explaining that away. Her thoughts were bitter, circling like dust in the wind – Richard, Dalchett House, her mother-in-law, Richard, Brandon...

Brandon. He was vivid in her mind; charismatic, sexy, exciting. And she was more than a little in love with him. Her mouth twisted in a sly smile. He would be there tomorrow. Maybe she would go to Dalchett House after all.

CHAPTER 3

Dalchett House loomed ahead, an insubstantial cluster of shadows in the thick, shifting wall of fog.

'It's like something from a horror movie,' Grace muttered as they drove on to the forecourt.

Richard didn't respond. His mood matched the weather: bleak and miserable. He couldn't shake off the memories of last night – Grace flushed and provocative, his reluctance to make love to her, her pillow damp beneath his hand when he moved in the darkness.

'Are you all right, Richard?' She spoke without warmth. Evidently he hadn't been forgiven.

'Yes. Driving in this weather makes my eyes tired that's all.'

He knew she was watching him but he couldn't face her. Instead he switched off the engine and turned to his daughter. 'You're very quiet in the back.'

'I'm cold.'

'Okay, let's make a move. I'll get the presents.' He climbed out of the car, shivering in his best suit and thin shirt. He didn't want to be here, pretending a cheerfulness he didn't feel, trying to maintain the illusion that they were a happy family. As he opened the boot he glanced at the house, remembering the first time he saw it, on an overcast summer afternoon almost nineteen years ago. Then he had been dejected, missing the father he adored, afraid of the future. He had stared at the building with a kind of macabre fascination, imagining the secrets it had concealed over the centuries, impressed, in spite of himself, by its tranquility. Now he felt like that teenager again.

'Can I help, Daddy?'

'Faith...' He hadn't noticed her behind him. 'You can carry this for me if you like.' He passed his camera to her, ashamed of his maudlin self-pity. It was time to count his blessings. He had a beautiful daughter. He was healthy, still young. Surely there must be a way to make his marriage work?

With several parcels wedged under his arm, and clutching a small suitcase, he closed the boot and went to help Grace out of the car.

Holmes appeared almost as soon as they rang the bell.

'Good morning, Mr Richard. Mrs Lawson. Nice to see *you* Little Miss.' He chucked Faith beneath the chin.

'Season's Greetings to you, Holmes. How's Betty?' Richard put the suitcase down and shook hands with the sober-faced man.

'She's not too bad, thank you.'

'Give her our love, won't you. Tell her I'll be over to see her tomorrow.'

'Very good, sir. They're all in the drawing room. I'll put your case in the Blue Bedroom for you. Shall I take your coat, Mrs Lawson? And yours, Missie?'

Richard watched the middle-aged man walk with slow, measured steps down the stone-flagged passage. Holmes had aged recently; a wife prone to periods of depression and a daughter involved with a heroin addict had stolen the last of his youth and vitality.

'How does he cope?' Richard wondered, his own marital problems sliding into perspective. 'The drawing room it is then,' he said, attempting once more to shrug away the melancholy thoughts.

Grace ignored him, fussing over Faith. 'There, you'll do.'

'She's a picture,' Richard affirmed. 'And so are you,' he added, observing his wife properly for the first time that morning. Her eyes were huge, defined with smoky grey eyeliner, her pale skin glowing. She had twisted her hair into a pretty knot, leaving wispy tendrils to fall around her face, and she was wearing a new red dress which accentuated her slender waist, making her appear taller. He had never seen her look so alluring. Or so unapproachable.

A door slammed at the far end of the passage. His mother's voice reached them clearly.

'Hello. I told Quentin you'd arrived. I could feel the draught in the drawing room when Holmes opened the front door.'

She came towards them, a tall, buxom figure in a plain brown twin-set and tweed skirt; neatly permed silver hair gleaming as she passed each of the wall-lamps along the dimly lit hallway.

'How are you all?' She aimed a kiss at Grace and held out her arms to Faith. 'Give Grandma a hug.'

Faith stepped forward, lowering her head so her grandmother's kiss landed in her hair.

'Come along then, it's too chilly to stand here.' Ivy Calthorpe led the way, turning to speak to them as she walked. 'Did I tell you I've invited the Seymour-Tomson's this evening? Mildred Seymour-Tomson is secretary of the Ladies Circle and I think I have a good chance of being voted president in January. It's going to be a busy year. I've already agreed to organize the church flower festival in the summer. Reverend Gaskell, our new vicar, says he doesn't know what he'd do without me.'

Richard had a sudden vision of the old vicarage in the remote Shropshire village where he lived as a child, and his father listening patiently to similar diatribes. He took a deep breath. Though he was fond of his mother, she was not easy company. The knot of tension in his stomach tightened as they followed her through the lobby and into the drawing room. His stepbrother was lying on the sofa. Richard nodded to him, putting the parcels down on an empty seat.

Brandon stretched and stood up. 'Glad you could make it.'

The words were innocent enough and Richard suspected he was the only one to hear the hostility behind them. Resisting the urge to make a pointed retort, he went to greet his step-father. Quentin Calthorpe was sitting by the fire with the old Irish-wolfhound lying at his feet and the springer-spaniel sharing his chair, her head on his lap. The warmth of his smile was heartening.

Faith stayed by her mother, hands clenched to keep her thumb from her mouth. Visits to Dalchett House were always somewhat of an ordeal. Apart from having to be on her best behaviour, she was half-afraid of the vast, gloomy rooms and the paintings that hung on the dark panelled walls – men with stern faces and women in princess dresses who stared at her with watchful eyes. But a part of her loved the old house. She loved the great hall where her footsteps echoed and the sun made rainbow patterns through the stained glass shields in the windows. She loved the dining room with its high ceiling of arches. And she loved the way it was possible to run in a giant circle from the drawing room into the lobby, along the passageway, down the length of the great hall to the dining room, and back through the narrow side door.

The drawing room was her favourite. Here the wooden floor was mostly covered with a faded, patterned carpet and there were shabby grey armchairs by the hearth, as well as a comfortable sofa draped in worn tartan blankets coated with dog hairs. Today a fire flared and crackled in the grate, warming the air a little, and a giant Christmas tree stood at the back of the room, its coloured lights winking.

Among the crowding of dark furniture were several things that intrigued her – the grandfather clock with the sun and moon peeping out of the clouds on its golden face; the big piano, its lid usually left temptingly open; a carved, high-backed chair she sometimes pretended was her throne; and the desk with a secret drawer that sprang open when you pressed on a particular spot. Each of the three tall windows had a wooden window seat where she could sit, almost hidden by the heavy curtains, looking out over the gardens towards the distant mountains, making up stories in her head while the grown-ups talked. It was a shame there was nothing to see now except swirling, grey mist.

She listened to the conversations around her; Daddy asking after Grandad Quentin's health, shaking his hand, telling him not to get up; Mummy smiling at Uncle Brandon, wanting to know how long he was going to be at home, touching his arm, saying she hoped they would see more of him; and Grandma informing them about the new osty-something-or-other she had found to treat Grandad's bad back.

'And how is Faith?' her grandfather asked, his eyes twinkling. 'Come here and let me have a good look at you.'

She went to stand by his chair, and he brushed her cheek with a blue-veined hand. Both dogs eyed her warily but did not move.

'Prettier than ever,' he announced.

He drew her to him and suddenly everything was all right. This thin, old man with untidy white hair, whose jacket fell loosely about him as though it belonged to someone much bigger, and who smelt of aftershave and tobacco, was her friend; her protection against Grandma's sharp tongue and the ghosts of Dalchett House.

After a while the general chatter faded.

'Do come and sit down.' Her grandmother began to usher them all to places by the fire. 'Sherry everyone?'

Faith sat on the edge of the sofa while the grown-ups sipped their drinks and exchanged uninteresting gifts – a book with no pictures for Grandad, a scarf for Grandma, a silver lighter for Uncle Brandon, a cheque for her parents. From Uncle Brandon there was a handbag which seemed to please her mother, a wallet for her father and, for herself, money to put in her piggy bank. Disappointed, she began to blow bubbles into her lemonade.

Her grandmother took the glass from her. 'You've been a very patient little girl. Now would you like to see what's hidden behind my chair?'

The box was huge. Faith had to stand on tiptoe to peer into it. 'A doll's house,' she whispered. Then louder. 'Mummy! Daddy! It's a doll's house.'

Her father lifted it out. It was perfect; a white wooden house with bay windows and two chimneys. The front opened to reveal miniature furniture inside, and there were tiny figures that could be moved about. She was speechless with delight.

'What do you say?' her mother asked.

'Thank you. Thank you. Thank you!' She jumped up and, forgetting her shyness, ran to kiss both her grandparents.

'Now, what about your present for Grandma and Grandad, darling?'

'It's here.' Faith picked up her parcel. It contained a calendar she had made at school out of an old cereal box. She wanted to give it to Grandad Quentin, but her grandmother took it from her and tore off the wrapping paper.

'It's lovely, my dear. What is it?'

'A calendar.' Faith stared at the carpet.

'Let me see.' Her grandfather's voice was gentle.

Keeping her eyes downcast, she carried her gift to him and sat on his knee as he examined it.

'Well, well, well, this is wonderful.' He set the date for her. 'Do you think I can keep it in my study? It will be really useful.'

She nodded gratified, nestling closer to him, the fabric of his jacket tickling her cheek.

Once more her grandmother bustled into action, collecting the glasses and putting them on a tray. 'I'll organise lunch. No, Grace, don't get up. Everything's under control. Trudie knows what to do.'

Lunch was served in the morning room at the front of the house. Afterwards, they returned to the drawing room where Holmes had built up the fire and set out coffee on one of the small tables. Faith knelt on the carpet, absorbed with her doll's house, re-arranging the furniture, placing the plastic people in different rooms, only vaguely aware of the chink of cups and the low murmur of voices. When her knees began to ache, she moved gingerly, shifting her weight onto her bottom and leaning back against the arm of the sofa. Her mother and father were talking quietly to Grandad Quentin. Grandma Ivy had fallen asleep.

'Faith!'

She was startled. She had been staring at her uncle. Why did he look so bored? Didn't he like them? Well, she didn't like him anyway, especially as he couldn't be bothered to buy her a present.

'Faith,' her mother said, 'Grandad is speaking to you.'

'Sorry.' Her face grew hot.

Her grandfather smiled. 'Why don't you run along to the kitchen and ask Trudie for more lemonade?'

'Can I?'

'Of course. Give those legs of yours some exercise.'

A little apprehensively she made her way to the kitchen. Trudie was rolling out pastry.

'It's in the fridge,' she said in answer to Faith's question. 'The small fridge in the buttery.'

Faith ran past the room which, according to her father had once been the servants hall, and into the narrow corridor beyond. Here it was colder, and the cream-painted walls glistened with fine drops of water. The buttery was the first of the small rooms on her right. It was full of fridges and freezers, their green lights making the room eerie. She found a bottle of lemonade and carried it back to the kitchen.

The clear liquid foamed like bubble-bath over the rim of the glass as Trudie poured it out and gave it to her. She drank quickly, her fingers on the rough, sticky imprint left by Trudie's floury hand.

'What are you making?' she asked, putting the glass on the table.

'French apple tarts for the dinner party this evening. As if I 'aven't got a thousand things I'd rather be doin' today.' Trudie's plump face was red and her wiry ginger hair stuck out below the white cap that was supposed to cover it.

Faith sensed she wasn't wanted. 'Thank you for the lemonade,' she mumbled, eager to get away.

In the main passageway she hesitated, loath to return to the drawing room, tired of sitting quietly. On an impulse she turned in the opposite direction. The door to the great hall had been wedged open and she darted inside. There was no one about. It was growing dark, and although some of the wall-lamps had been switched on, the areas between them were pooled with shadow. The small leaded panes in the windows were black. Her footsteps sounded too loud on the stone floor and she slowed down, walking forward on tiptoe. The hall smelt damp, like a cave. On either side of the fireplace the enormous tapestries moved as though someone was hiding behind them.

A sudden high-pitched screech pierced the silence. Faith froze, her heart thumping as if it would leap out of her body. What was it? A werewolf? A witch perhaps? Or a ghost? The screeching came again, louder. This time she didn't stop to think. Her limbs weak and shaky, she ran back the way she had come, pushing the heavy door with her shoulder, and stumbling into the drawing room.

Her grandfather smiled at her. 'Are you all right?'

'I heard a noise... In the dining room.'

He laughed; a warm human laugh. 'It's probably Holmes with Evie and Jo. They'll be moving furniture ready for this evening. There's nothing to be scared of. Would you like me to tell you a story?'

'Yes please.' She curled up on his lap, her panic dissolving as he amused her with his tales. After a while, she rested her head on his chest and closed her eyes.

Later, after a light tea of sandwiches and cake, Grace tucked Faith into the bed in the small dressing room which adjoined the Blue Bedroom.

'Stay with me, Mummy.' The dark eyes were troubled.

'I'll just be next door, darling. I need to put on some make-up and comb my hair. You're not frightened are you?'

'The floor creaks and something bangs on the wall.'

Grace kissed the tip of her daughter's nose. 'It's only the water pipes. Nothing to worry about. Okay?'

There was no reply.

In the blue room Grace took her make-up bag out of the suitcase and sat in front of the mirror to apply lipstick and eyeshadow. She put more blusher on her cheeks, blending it with a soft brush. Then she unfastened her hair and pulled the comb through it slowly before coiling it back on top of her head and securing it with a pretty black clip. Finally, she sprayed perfume on her wrists and behind her knees and, for the first time in her life, between her breasts.

The door opened. She pushed the perfume out of sight as Richard entered the bedroom.

'You smell good,' he said appreciatively.

She stood up, smoothing the red dress over her hips. 'I'm surprised you noticed.'

He looked away. 'We'd better go down. People are arriving.'

'I need to check on Faith. I don't think she's asleep yet.'

'I'll sit with her. You go. Mum was asking for you earlier.'

'Huh!'

'She means well, Gracie. It's just her way.'

'Really?' She walked past him and let the door slam behind her.

The murmur of voices sounded hollow in the great hall. A huge log fire blazed in the fireplace and most of the guests had congregated within range of its heat. Grace searched for someone she knew.

'Ah, there you are.' Ivy pounced and steered her towards a stocky young man with thinning brown hair. 'Reverend, I'd like you to meet my daughter-in-law.'

'So you're Grace?' Reverend Gaskell smiled. 'I've heard a lot about you.'

Grace shook his hand. Was she imagining it or had the reverend actually winked at her? 'I hope it hasn't all been bad.'

'Not all of it,' he laughed.

Ivy turned to the woman at his side. 'Grace, this is Joyce, the reverend's wife...' Her gaze slid past them. 'If you don't mind, I'll leave you together for a moment. There's someone I have to speak to.' She hurried away to greet two late-comers. Her words carried across the room. 'Ah, Mildred. James. So pleased to see you both.'

Grace spent a few minutes making small-talk, and then, spying Quentin by the drinks table, excused herself and went over to him. He looked exhausted, and with sudden perception, she saw the effort he was making to cover his frailty.

'Not thinking of escape already are you?' he quipped.

'No. I didn't expect so many people though.' She helped herself to an orange juice.

'Oh when Ivy gives a dinner party she doesn't do things by halves. Still, when she's planning these little events she's not organising me.' He smiled indulgently. 'She's a wonderful woman; bags of energy. I'd be lost without her.'

Grace nodded, secretly admiring his forbearance.

His smile faded. 'Richard not with you?'

'He's trying to get Faith off to sleep. She's a bit nervous. Strange room and all that.'

'She's got a good imagination that little one. Takes life seriously. Like her father I suspect.'

'Yes.' Grace swallowed.

'Is everything all right with you two?'

Quentin's question caught her off guard. Was it so obvious, the coolness between herself and her husband?

'Everything's fine,' she assured him. 'Richard's been working too hard, that's all. He's tired.'

'And you think he's neglecting you?'

'Not really. I understand his work comes first.' She could hear the bitterness in her own voice.

Quentin squeezed her elbow gently. 'Don't be too hard on him, Grace. He loves you dearly. Anyone can see that.'

His words softened the resentment festering inside her. Appreciating his kindness, she tried to visualise him as a young man. He would have known how to keep a woman happy, she thought, seeing the glint in the observant blue eyes. *Like his son...*

'She's fast asleep.' Richard eased his way between several people refilling their glasses and put a heavy arm round her shoulders.

Aware of Quentin's concern, she smiled brightly.

'Well done. Have a drink now and relax.' She heard her husband's sigh of relief and felt a heartbeat's regret for the way she had treated him earlier.

Tactfully, Quentin invited them to join a group of his friends, a trio of florid-faced farmers, each trying to outdo the others with outrageous anecdotes. Grace paid little attention to their banter, looking beyond them, scanning the room for a glimpse of her brother-in-law. Eventually he strolled into the hall with an attractive, dark-haired woman in a low-cut black dress.

'Who's that woman with Brandon?' She was careful to make the question sound like idle curiosity.

Quentin frowned. 'Charlotte Sinclair, wife of one of our county councillors. A bit of a flighty piece by all accounts.'

Grace was surprised. She had never heard him say an unkind word about anyone before.

He changed the subject as his wife approached. 'Are we ready then?'

Ivy looked harassed. 'Yes, at last. Would you see that everyone finds the right seat?'

'Very good, Milady,' Quentin chuckled.

'We might as well go in too,' Richard said.

The dining room looked spectacular. A wide Christmas tree shimmering with silver baubles, filled one corner, its star-shaped lights flashing. The long table was a work of art, decorated with garlands of red flowers and every place laid with fine white china, a red linen napkin and an array of tall-stemmed crystal glasses. The embossed silver cutlery and napkin-rings glittered like frost in the light from dozens of candles, each of which had a ghostly replica in the night-black windows.

Grace found herself opposite Brandon. On her left, Reverend Gaskell made a charming companion; on her right, Simon Sinclair, a chinless, sandy-haired man with a long nose and a mesh of deep wrinkles around his eyes, sniffed continuously, glaring at his wife who was flirting with one of Quentin's elderly acquaintances. Further away, Richard was sitting between Joyce Gaskell and a pretty grey-haired woman who laughed a great deal. Ivy sat next to James Seymour-Tomson at one end of the table; Quentin next to the formidable Mildred at the other. And, amongst the few people Grace recognized were twenty or so others, all talking loudly, becoming more voluble as they drank the fine wine.

It was a splendid meal, supervised by Holmes and served efficiently by Evie and Jo, with the aid of Evie's two teenage daughters. Grace made an effort to charm her neighbours, giggling at Ian Gaskell's witty tales of life in his former parish, coaxing conversation out of Simon Sinclair, secretly delighted when she managed to divert his attention from the flamboyant Charlotte. Growing reckless, she allowed herself to drink too much. By the time Holmes brought in coffee she was a little tipsy. Aware that Brandon was silent, watching her, she returned his gaze boldly.

It was well after midnight before the last of the visitors left, reluctant to drag themselves away from the crackling fire in the drawing room.

'I'm off to my bed,' Quentin announced as his wife returned from escorting the Gaskells to their car. 'I thought vicars had to be up early in the mornings.'

'Well this one doesn't. Not tomorrow anyway,' Richard said. 'But I must admit I'm worn out. Thanks for a lovely evening, Mum.'

He kissed his mother's cheek. 'You ready, Gracie?'

'In a few minutes.'

'Right then.' Richard followed his stepfather out of the room.

Grace remained on the sofa, staring into the fire. She was finding it hard to breathe. Brandon sprawled in one of the fireside chairs, a glass of whisky in his hand, his eyes half-closed. But she knew he wasn't sleepy.

'Would you like another drink, my dear?' Ivy helped herself to brandy.

Grace shook her head.

It was difficult to feign interest as Ivy, elated with the success of the evening, sat down opposite her stepson and proceeded to give them a potted history of several of the guests, followed by a detailed account of her own involvement with various local societies. The grandfather clock chimed twice on the quarter-hour. The fire crumbled to a deep red core. The temperature in the room dropped.

Only when the clock struck a third time did Ivy notice how late it was. 'Well, I mustn't keep you young things any longer. You won't want to get up in the morning.' She prised herself out of the seat.

'Goodnight.' Brandon yawned.

'Are you coming, Grace?' Ivy waited expectantly.

'You must be exhausted, Ivy. I'm sure Grace can find her own way to the bedroom,' Brandon said with a solicitous smile.

Ivy shrugged and left them alone together. Grace's heart seemed to stop beating.

'And then there were two...' Brandon's blue eyes were suddenly wide open, boring into her.

She didn't speak.

'Have another drink.' He walked over to pour her a brandy and then threw a log on the fire, kicking it into place and toppling a pile of ash which collapsed silently on to the hearth.

'So?' He came to sit beside her.

She could feel the heat of his body across the space

between them. She swallowed a mouthful of brandy, spluttering as it burned the back of her throat.

'Oh, Grace, Grace, what are we going to do with you?' He retrieved the glass, putting it down on the floor.

Part of her realized he was making fun of her, but it didn't matter. She knew what he wanted; what they both wanted. Her whole body pulsed with desire.

He leaned towards her, pushing her back against the cushions, his kisses quick and light on her eyes, her mouth, her throat.

'Are you sure?' He began to unfasten the buttons at her neck.

In answer she drew him closer, gasping when his lips found her breasts, arching her back, almost crying out when she felt his hands beneath the hem of her dress, slowly inching up her thighs, teasing, touching, so that she thought she would die if he did not take her soon. Then his movements became more urgent. His fingers dug deep into her flesh, his mouth on hers was hard. For a second she remembered Richard's gentleness, before she abandoned herself to passion, forgetting everything but her own voracious need.

Afterwards she lay in Brandon's arms, satiated.

'Time to go, Grace. I need my beauty sleep.' His expression was impassive.

Grace pulled on her clothes, shivering. 'I'll see you in the morning?'

'Maybe.' His eyes gleamed in the dying firelight.

She blinked away the rush of stupid tears and heard

him laughing. 'Of course you will, Grace, my darling. Of course you will.'

Richard stirred as she crept into the bedroom. She undressed in the dark, desperate not to disturb him.

'What time is it?' He startled her.

'After two. Your mother wanted to talk. Sorry, I didn't mean to wake you.'

She slipped into bed beside him. He was warm, still drowsy.

'Night,' she mumbled.

She was sure that, if he kissed her, he would smell Brandon on her skin. She lay very still on the cold side of the bed until the rhythm of his breathing altered and she could tell he was asleep.

CHAPTER 4

It was chilly in Holmes's cottage. The small windows barely let in the weak morning light and the fire, which should have brightened the living room, was smoking sullenly. Richard settled in one of the two worn leather armchairs. Opposite him Betty Holmes sat upright, fingers constantly plucking at a loose thread in her stained woollen skirt. He was shocked by her appearance. Her eyes were dull, her cheeks hollow, the bones beneath them prominent, and her hair was lank and uncombed, grey at the roots. In the three weeks since his last visit she had become an old woman.

Faith drew her stool closer to his legs. He smiled at her, wishing she had stayed at Dalchett House.

'Betty.' He leaned forward, covering the restless hands with his own. 'Can you tell me what's troubling you?'

There was no answer, but the empty eyes flickered away from him. Richard looked round. A girl was standing in the doorway. Except for the bulk of her pregnancy beneath the plain, navy smock she was as thin as her mother.

'Mavis.' He stood up to greet her.

'So now you know,' she said, defiantly.

'The boyfriend doesn't want anything to do with her.' Betty Holmes spoke in a slow, flat voice.

'That's not true,' Mavis Holmes snapped. 'I told you there are complications. Doctor says I have to take things easy. No chance of that though while I'm running round after you all the time.'

Richard shifted his feet, embarrassed. 'Perhaps we ought to go.'

'No!' Betty Holmes clutched at his sleeve.

He sat down again, on the edge of his chair.

'I'll make coffee.' Mavis offered ungraciously.

The room seemed more oppressive without her presence. They were silent, listening to the clatter of cups and saucers in the kitchen, waiting for the kettle to whistle.

Faith stared into the fire, watching curls of smoke escape up the chimney and the little stabbing flames which appeared now and then between the coals. She couldn't look again at Betty Holmes's skull-like face.

'Would you like to go to Mummy?' Her father put his arm round her shoulders.

'Can I?'

'As long as you promise to go straight back.'

She nodded, jumping to her feet.

'Say goodbye to Betty then.'

'Bye, Mrs Holmes,' Faith whispered, sidling towards the door. In the narrow hall she almost collided with Mavis.

'You off then? Don't blame you. It's hardly a bundle of laughs here, is it?'

Faith shook her head and ran.

Outside the air was sharp and clean. She breathed in deeply to rid herself of the stale smell which lingered on her coat and in her hair. Shivering, she began to pick her way along the muddy track. Questions nagged her. Why was everything different today? Holmes's cottage had always been a cosy place, smelling of home-made cakes, and the Mrs Holmes she loved to visit was a plump lady with a cheerful smile. Her memories of Mavis were hazy, but surely she had never been so fat and ugly? It was scary the way people changed, even died, like Fred Tyler. Was Betty Holmes going to die? Or Grandad Quentin? He was old. What if her father...?

Preoccupied, she didn't see the puddle. Her feet splashed into the brown water splattering her coat with mud, soaking her clean white socks. She wanted to cry. Her mother would be so cross. The magic of Christmas seemed ages ago.

In the Blue Bedroom, Grace applied a bright red lipstick and scrutinised her face in the mirror. Excitement had heightened her colour. Her eyes were large and luminous, her mouth fuller, slightly swollen. She smiled. The nerves in her stomach fluttered with anticipation. Earlier she had felt physically sick. She had woken as dawn broke and immediately her flesh had burned with shame. She had looked at her husband as he slept, at the ruffled black hair and the long curve of his body beneath the quilt. He was a good man. How could she have betrayed him? Tormented by guilt, she had tossed and turned until he reached for her sleepily, holding her as though he, too, needed comfort. She lay in his arms, desperate for him to make love to her; to wipe away the feel of Brandon's lips, the taste of Brandon's tongue in her mouth. But, after a few minutes, he had simply kissed her forehead and climbed out of bed.

At first she had been hurt, then angry, and anger had freed her from blame. Richard didn't see her as a woman – she was his wife, his housekeeper, the mother of his child. He didn't want her in any other way. Within a short time she had convinced herself that what happened between herself and Brandon was all Richard's fault.

Now she stepped back from the dressing table, uncertain what to do. Brandon had not appeared at breakfast and, with a flash of panic, she wondered if last night had been a mistake, if she had been won too easily and he had already lost interest. Perhaps she had been fooling herself to imagine he cared about her. Maybe she should have gone to visit Holmes's wife instead of moping around like a love-sick teenager. Making a sudden decision, she lifted her anorak from the hook behind the door and shrugged it on over her sweater and jeans. The sensible thing was to avoid Brandon Calthorpe.

As she went down the stairs she saw him. He was standing in the passage dressed in a black leather jacket and cord trousers.

'Going somewhere?'

'To look for my husband and daughter.' She tried to sound indifferent.

'I've got a better idea, come with me.' He grabbed her hand.

'No! What we did last night was wrong. Richard doesn't deserve this.'

'Richard doesn't deserve you, Grace. He doesn't make you happy, does he?'

She couldn't meet his eyes. He put his forefinger beneath her chin, lifting her head, compelling her to look at him. Then he kissed her, ignoring her protests, tightening his free arm around her until his body was taut against hers, forcing her back to the wall.

'Brandon, not here.'

'Why not?' He kissed her again.

'Someone might see.' She struggled to get away. 'Please... let go.'

'Only when you agree to come outside.'

A door opened somewhere. She heard the patter of a dog's paws on the stone floor. Panic and desire leapt within her. 'Okay. But only for a little while.'

He grinned, releasing her. 'I think I can change your mind about that.'

They hurried past the morning room where Evie was clearing away the remains of breakfast.

'Good morning,' Grace smiled nervously.

Evie waved. 'Mornin', Mrs Lawson. Bit gloomy out there.'

'It might brighten up later,' Grace replied, aware of Brandon's smothered laughter.

Outside, he led her towards the stable block adjacent to the house. Leopold, Quentin's wolfhound, was lying outside the door and lifted his head hopefully.

'There's a stallion in here that might interest you,' Brandon murmured.

Grace put her hand on her chest, alarmed by the violent thumping of her heart. She knew there were no horses in the old stables. None of the Calthorpes had ridden for years. The building was used as storage space for machinery and part of it had been converted into garages.

'I'm sure you'd love to ride him.' Brandon slid the big door open.

Inside felt dry and church-like. Even in the semi-darkness, Grace could see that everything was neat and well-ordered – mowing machines, hedge cutters, a tractor partly covered by tarpaulins, wheelbarrows, watering cans, rows of implements hanging from pegs in the wall.

Brandon propelled her towards one of the empty stalls. He took off his jacket and spread it on the stone floor. Then he knelt in front of her, running his hands up her thighs, dragging her down beside him.

'I can't.' Her conscience surfaced briefly.

But he was already tugging at the zip of her anorak.

'No!' she said. 'No. Stop it.'

He slid his hands beneath her sweater.

She heard herself moaning, weak with lust. 'No,' she said again. 'I can't.' But she would. It was all part of the game. And they both knew it.

Faith arrived at the end of the track in time to see her mother go into the stables. Relieved, she began to run, taking the gravel path at the side of the house, intending to sneak in through the back door. Maybe she could get to the bedroom without being spotted and rub some of the mud off her coat.

At the bottom of the steps to the terrace she stopped, clutching her side, winded. An unwelcome memory stirred – a broken vase, the pieces discovered under the glass cabinet where she had hidden them. Her vague misgivings grew stronger. Her father always said it was better to tell the truth and not have any guilty secrets.

Troubled, she began to trudge back along the path, dragging her feet when she reached the forecourt. She didn't want to see Uncle Brandon, but maybe her mother wouldn't shout at her in front of him.

Outside the stables she hesitated. Leopold licked her hand, and as she bent to stroke him she heard her mother cry out twice; short, harsh cries, like the ones in the school playground when someone's hair was being pulled or their arm pinched.

'Mummy.' The word formed on her lips but no sound came out.

Silently, she squeezed through the gap where the stable door had not been properly closed.

At first her eyes could make out nothing but the mass of machinery, and then she saw them, a moving shadow on the floor, flesh pale in the half-light as they wrestled together. Uncle Brandon was trying to kill her mother!

'No!' She raced across and hurled herself at him. Using all her strength she pummelled his back with her fists.

'What the fuck!' Brandon Calthorpe pushed himself up onto his knees.

'Leave my Mummy alone. Get *off* her!'

He gripped her wrists, his fingers digging into her skin. 'Enough!'

For a second she was paralysed with fear. Then he loosened his hold, and sitting back on his heels, began to laugh. 'Well, well, well, who would have thought Reverend Richard could sire such a spirited filly?'

She bit her lip, confused, shocked by the sight of his naked body.

Her mother didn't look at her. Faith watched as she pulled on her sweater and stood up to wriggle into her jeans. When she spoke she sounded angry. 'It's okay, sweetheart. We were just playing.'

'I thought...' Faith shrank back.

Her mother's voice softened slightly. 'Don't look so frightened, sweetheart. There's nothing to worry about. It was a silly game that got a bit rough, that's all.'

You're telling me lies. The knowledge made Faith feel small and lonely. She edged away.

'Darling, wait, please.'

Her mother caught her, held her tightly. Behind them she heard her uncle adjusting his clothes; the rasp of the zip on his trousers, the chink of the buckle on his belt.

'You're hurting me.' She wrenched herself free.

Her uncle picked up his jacket and strode past. A shaft of cold wintry light filtered through the open doorway as he left the stable. Faith shuddered. She made no protest when her mother grasped her hand and hustled her outside. Within minutes they were out of sight of the house, hurrying along the rutted track towards the estate cottages.

'Mummy...'

'I'm sorry, darling. Am I walking too fast? I was hoping to catch Daddy before he left Betty Holmes. Give him a bit of support.'

Faith stopped, tugging her mother's arm. 'I don't want to go there again.'

'Why ever not?'

'I just don't. Can't we wait for Daddy here?'

'Here?' Her mother looked around at the dripping trees and the waterlogged lane.

'I'm not going any further.'

'All right. Don't make a fuss.'

Faith squelched some mud under her shoe, surprised to get her own way so easily.

'Darling,' her mother's smile was fixed, like in a photograph. 'I want to ask you a favour.'

'What?'

'I don't want you to tell Daddy I was with Uncle Brandon.'

'Why?'

'He may be cross. I should have gone to visit Betty with you, but I wasn't in the mood. It was selfish of me.'

'Daddy doesn't like Uncle Brandon, does he?'

'I don't know. Perhaps not. Listen, sweetheart, I don't want to upset your father. Promise me you won't say anything about the game Uncle Brandon and I were playing.'

Faith flinched when her mother touched her cheek. She nodded, as if in agreement, but she didn't promise.

Her mother seemed satisfied. 'Good girl. I know you love Daddy. We don't want to spoil his day, do we?'

'Can we go back now?'

'If you like.'

Faith walked ahead, hands clenched in her pockets, the scene in the stables replaying like a film in her head. *It was a silly game that got a bit rough, that's all.* Her mother's words. But she didn't believe them.

Everyone gathered for lunch in the morning room at one o'clock. Richard thought what a subdued group they were; only his mother was oblivious to the atmosphere, barely pausing in her monologue as she ate.

'You're looking tired, Grace,' Brandon interrupted rudely. 'Have some more vegetables to keep up your strength.'

'No thanks.' Grace blushed, and after that she seemed to avoid his gaze.

Richard witnessed the little exchange, perturbed by his wife's reaction. He sighed, thinking of the strange mood Grace had been in that morning, hoping she hadn't upset his stepbrother. But Brandon was smiling. Richard stared at him. The handsome face had assumed the same self-satisfied expression he had seen so many times; the expression which usually meant his stepbrother had scored a point over him in some way. He tried to ignore the uncomfortable memories – Brandon 'borrowing' his brand new racing bike and returning it scratched and dented; Brandon 'acquiring' his record collection only to leave half the records at some all-night party; Brandon dating Heather Leonard...

Richard caught his breath. He looked once more at the stain of colour on his wife's face, hating himself for the awful suspicion which leapt into his mind.

Faith watched her parents anxiously, wondering whether she should tell her father what she had seen. But her mother said he would be upset. He looked sad anyway and she didn't want to make things worse for him.

'Is something the matter, little one? You're not eating much.' Quentin eased his chair closer to her. 'Are you unwell?'

She put down her knife and fork. 'I'm all right thank you, Grandad. I'm just not very hungry.'

It was true. She wasn't ill. But she did have a peculiar feeling in her stomach. Like when she was at the dentists.

CHAPTER 5

The wine bar was crowded, buzzing with conversation, warm after the gusty March wind on the city streets. Grace looked round uncertainly. She hadn't expected it to be so busy. Everyone seemed to be in groups, laughing and confident, and she felt suddenly envious. It was unfair. All these people had such interesting lives, while an afternoon in Birmingham four or five times a year was her only escape from the monotony of her marriage.

Her mood lifted when she spotted Cassie at one of the tables by the window, bleached blonde hair conspicuous in the low ultra-violet light. Relieved, she began to thread her way across the room. Cassie stood up to hug her. She smelt of cigarette smoke and expensive perfume. 'Hi, Grace. How are you?'

'Fine. It's so good to see you, Cass.'

They sat down, appraising each other. It had been nearly six months since they last met.

Grace unfastened her coat. 'So, what's happening? How's the job?

'I've had enough. Same old thing every day. I need a challenge.'

'What will you do?'

'I've applied for a job with the council – secretary to one of the planning officers. I don't want to give up the bedsit. Can't think of anything worse than living with Mum and the kids again, especially since she's got another fella.'

Grace pictured the overcrowded terraced house in Wolverhampton, a few doors away from her own childhood home. 'Things haven't changed, then?'

'Only for the worse.'

Cassie's woeful expression vanished. She grinned at Grace. 'Let's drown our sorrows. A bottle of dry white?' She glanced at the menu briefly then handed it to Grace.

'Beef stroganoff sounds good to me.'

Grace was beginning to relax. 'Me too.'

The food was good, the atmosphere convivial. Grace took a few sips of wine as they reminisced about the past, discussed the strikes that had brought chaos to the country in January and February, and gave each other carefully edited versions of their lives during the last few months. Almost without realising, they slipped into the easy familiarity of former years. The restaurant emptied and began to refill with older customers; waiters changed shifts. Outside the sky darkened and a thin drizzle began to fall.

Over coffee Grace took a deep breath and leaned forward. 'Cassie, I need your advice.'

Cassie took the chocolate from her saucer and sucked the mint out of the dark coating. 'Go on.'

'I've met someone.'

'And?' Cassie licked chocolate from her fingers.

'We've been having an affair since Christmas.'

'Are you in love with him?'

'I'm not sure. No... I still love Richard. Cass, I feel awful deceiving him but I can't help myself.' Grace twisted her wedding ring nervously.

Cassie touched her hand. 'Be honest, Grace. You never really loved Richard.'

'I did... I do.'

'All right then. But you've never been *in love* with him, have you? He's never turned your bones to jelly. He's sweet and he's kind, and he bores you to tears. Go on, admit it.'

Grace shook her head, bemused. 'I don't want to hurt him, Cass.'

'Why would you? What he doesn't know can't harm him.'

The piped music faded for a moment. Grace lowered her voice. 'It's more complicated than that. This man... It's Brandon.'

'Richard's stepbrother?'

'Yes.' Grace wiped away a tear with her serviette.

Cassie's green eyes widened. 'Hey, you *are* in love with him, aren't you?'

Grace's skin burned with memories – the lingering kisses, murmured endearments, the passionate love-making. 'Oh, Cassie, I don't know. Sometimes I think if he asked me I would leave Richard, leave Faith, to be with him. He makes me so happy.'

'And Richard doesn't?'

'No.' The word was little more than a whisper, laden with guilt.

'Look, Grace, this thing with Brandon might burn itself out in a few months. Don't make any rash decisions.' Cassie slid a cigarette from the gold packet at the side of her plate.

'I have to do something,' Grace's throat was tight. 'I'm pregnant.'

'Hell!' Cassie put the cigarette down without lighting it. 'Is the baby Richard's?'

'No.' Grace covered her hot cheeks with her hands. 'I don't know what to do, Cass? If the truth comes out it will tear the family apart.'

Cassie frowned. She was quiet for a few moments, running a finger around the rim of her cup. 'Would Brandon stand by you?'

'I've no idea. I don't imagine children are high on his agenda.'

'How far gone are you?'

'Four... five weeks maybe.'

'So there's still time for you to get together with Richard. Pretend the baby is his.'

'I couldn't do that to him.'

The furrows on Cassie's forehead deepened. 'Then you'll have to tell him the truth.'

'I can't.'

'What other choice is there?'

'I could leave Tuston. Stay with you for a while.'

'Are you serious?'

'Why not? It would be like old times again. Before Mum got ill.'

'All night parties, smoking pot, the odd one-night stand?' Cassie sighed dramatically. 'Be realistic, Grace. Those days are long gone.'

'I didn't mean that. I just want some space.'

'But the problem wouldn't go away. The baby needs a father. Faith needs her mother.'

'You're right. It's a stupid idea.' Grace shrank back in the chair.

Cassie reached across for her hand, squeezed the fingers hard. 'Sorry. I'm not much help am I?'

'At least you've made me face up to things.'

'Whatever happens,' Cassie said softly, 'It's not the end of the world.'

Grace managed a weak smile. 'It feels like it.'

It was only as she was on her way back to the railway station that she realised neither of them had mentioned abortion.

'What time is it?' Faith glanced at the clock on the wall in Emily's kitchen.

Mrs Marsh smiled at her. 'Don't worry. I'm sure your mummy will be here soon.' But Faith was worried. Since Christmas there had been too many afternoons spent at Emily's at the end of the school day. Her mother was often late to collect her, and when she did arrive she seemed on edge, almost absent-minded. Or she would be extra loving, free with her hugs and kisses. Faith had begun to think her mother might be ill, that the frequent visits to town were to see a doctor and everyone was keeping the truth from her.

'Let's go to my bedroom and play schools.' Emily's chair scraped on the floor as she left the table.

'Thank you for the cake, Mrs Marsh.' Faith pushed the half-eaten cream bun to the side of her plate.

The two girls ran up the stairs. In the bedroom they were soon busy setting up the blackboard, arranging dolls on the floor to be pupils, searching for paper and pencils. Eventually Emily settled at the desk by the window. She put on an old pair of sunglasses with no lenses and spoke in a sing-song voice. 'Good morning children.'

'Good morning Miss Thomas.' Faith sat cross-legged in the middle of the row of dolls while Emily pretended to call the register.

'Wesley Baker, Claire Chapman, Sam Harris...' Emily chanted the names and Faith answered, 'Yes, Miss,' trying to make her voice sound different each time.

'Debbie Saunders,' Emily said.

Faith pulled a face.

'Debbie Saunders, come here.' Emily's straw-coloured curls shook with indignation.

'You can't make me. I'll tell my dad of you.' Faith imitated the sullen country accent perfectly. She didn't like Debbie Saunders.

For a while she was absorbed in the make-believe world, but as the room grew shadowy she became restless again. A gust of wind spattered hail against the window, sharp as a handful of grit.

Her stomach felt queasy. 'I'm going to see if Mum's coming.'

She stood by the window at the top of the stairs. The street below was deserted, the tarmac shiny as a river, and behind the bungalows opposite she could see the road from town, busy with a procession of cars slicing through the mist of rain. Lights shone out from houses in the village.

The rectory would still be in darkness. A tear dribbled down her cheek. What if her mother really was ill? What if she never came back? She knew a moment of sympathy for Debbie Saunders whose mother had left home last year. Distraught, she wiped her eyes on the edge of the curtain. She had no idea what time the last bus was due or if her mother would be on it.

It was after half-past six when Grace rushed up the path, her mind busy forming excuses.

'I'm so sorry,' she babbled as Liz Marsh opened the door, 'I missed the earlier bus. Thank you so much for looking after Faith.'

'She's been good as gold,' Liz laughed as Faith came hurtling down the stairs.

Grace smelt fried onions and realised Liz was preparing a meal. 'Hurry up and get your coat, Faith. We'll have to run. It's absolutely tipping down.'

'I'll ask Colin to drive you home,' Liz offered.

'There's no need,' Grace said firmly, ushering Faith towards the door. 'Say cheerio to Emily.'

They ran along the street, rain numbing their faces, driving horizontally into the skin like a thousand tiny anaesthetic needles. When they reached the crossroads they were gasping for breath. A car sped by, spreading a filthy wash of water over the pavement and into their shoes. Darkness chased the tail lights into the distance. Grace clutched Faith's hand. The only sounds audible above the wind were the hiss of rain and the creak of the sign outside the white-walled public house.

There was no light in the lane leading up to the church; all the houses were old and set well back, their gardens hidden by trees. Here the wind was stronger, lashing the bare branches. When they reached the rectory the night seemed even blacker, hemmed in by the overhanging bushes at the edge of the lawn and the conifers in the hedgerow.

Grace was annoyed to see that Richard wasn't home. She had been hoping to find the house warm and the kettle already boiled. Turning the key in the lock, she pushed the door open. Inside it was cold. She flicked the light on, her resentment fading. Without Richard the house seemed empty. She took off her coat and leaned against the wall, closing her eyes, afraid of the future.

'Mummy! Mummy!' Faith screamed. 'Mummy, what's the matter? I don't want you to die.'

She reached out to pull her daughter close. 'Darling,' she said, trying to speak normally, 'I'm not going to die. Whatever made you think such a thing? I won't leave you, sweetheart, not ever.'

CHAPTER 6

'Bye, Gracie,' Richard put both hands on his wife's shoulders as he bent to kiss her. He felt her body tense. Her lips were smooth and unresponsive.

'What time will you be home?' she asked.

'It depends...'

'Will you be back for lunch?'

'No.'

He saw the relief on her face and immediately the doubts surfaced, sliding into his head, sly and repulsive as snakes. Why did she want to know? Several times in the last few weeks he had come home unexpectedly to find she was out. Where did she go? What was she doing? Who was she with? He didn't believe her explanations. He hated himself, but he didn't believe her.

'I'll see you tonight.' She opened the front door for him to leave and went back inside without waving.

He drove slowly, aware his mind wasn't on the road. He couldn't ignore his suspicions. Why was his stepbrother so often at Dalchett House nowadays? Brandon usually stayed in London when he was not on some foreign jaunt in his capacity as managing director of Calthorpe Publishing. Richard thrummed his fingers on the steering wheel. Just what exactly did Brandon *do* for the excessive salary he received from the company Quentin had founded almost fifty years ago?

A car overtook him recklessly. He shook his head and made an effort to stifle his sudden jealousy. After all, he had been offered the same opportunities as Brandon. It had been his own choice to refuse Quentin's generosity and go into the church; a choice made because he felt a calling, not because he didn't want to be in competition with his stepbrother. He was happy in his work. He didn't envy Brandon in the slightest. Except perhaps for that potent sexual attraction which was irresistible to most women; possibly even to Grace. He braked at a set of traffic lights, surprised to find himself on the outskirts of Hereford. He felt sullied by his thoughts. There was no proof of any liaison between Grace and Brandon. He was probably over-sensitive at the moment, unsettled by Grace's coolness since Christmas, distressed by his own inability to discuss the problems they faced. He wound the window down and turned his attention to the forthcoming conference at the Bishop's Palace.

Grace chewed her fingernails, waiting for her call to be answered. She was taking a risk telephoning Dalchett House but she had to speak to Brandon. The line crackled.

'Dalchett House.' Holmes sounded efficient as always.

'Good morning, Holmes. It's Grace.' Her mind went blank. She had no idea what to say.

'I'm sorry, Mrs Lawson, there's no one at home. Can I pass on a message?'

'No. It's okay. When will they be back?' Her heartbeat slowed.

'Mr Quentin and his wife have appointments in Birmingham. I don't expect them until this evening. Mr Brandon is returning from London by train today but I'm afraid I can't say when exactly. Do you want me to ask one of them to ring you later?'

'No. I...' She searched for a reason that would satisfy him. 'I just wanted to ask Ivy for a recipe. It's not important. Please don't bother her this evening. She'll be tired. I'll phone her tomorrow.'

'Very well, Mrs Lawson.'

'Thank you.' Grace put the phone down, relief tempered with frustration. There were choices she had to make.

She looked along the hallway, picturing the rooms behind each closed door. Her eyes stung with tears. Did she really want to exchange this cosy existence, abandon her family, leave her home? For what? What was she to Brandon Calthorpe? Did he love her? Would he ask her to divorce Richard and marry him for the sake of the child she was carrying? Even as the thought surfaced, hope flickered and died within her. She was cold with the knowledge that Brandon would not give up his freedom to be saddled with his brother's unremarkable wife.

The clock in the lounge chimed the hour, each note thin and clear in the silent house. It stirred her into action. If she caught the ten-thirty bus she would be in Hereford by eleven. That would give her most of the day, and if she wasn't back by half-past-three Liz would collect Faith from school. She would go to the station and wait until Brandon arrived.

The bus was crowded, noisy with genial chatter; country voices, soft and lilting. Grace found a seat, smiling without warmth at several acquaintances, and then turned her head towards the window. The countryside was fresh, sparkling after the night's rain; a faint mist of green in the hedgerows, and the fields a tapestry of light and shade beneath scudding white clouds. But Grace felt no lifting of her spirits.

As they approached the city the volume of traffic increased and the bus lurched and stopped and crawled with the flow. She got off at the railway bridge, trying to ignore the fluttering in her stomach. How was she going to tell Brandon? Would he be angry? She imagined the blue eyes hardening to steel.

There were only a few people at the station, clustered mainly in the entrance hall out of the blustery wind. Grace studied the timetables. There was a train from Paddington due just before one o'clock. It seemed the most likely option. All she had to do was be patient.

It was easier said than done. As time passed she grew more nervous, walking up and down the platform, shivering in her thick coat, hands clenched and icy in her pockets. After a while the cold forced her into the buffet. She ordered coffee and sat down at one of the small tables, wrapping her numbed fingers round the chipped mug.

'We regret that the 12.57 from London Paddington, due to arrive at Platform Two, will be approximately ten minutes late. This service will terminate here.'

Grace was startled out of her reverie. She picked up her handbag and fastened her coat, pulling up the collar as she hurried outside. The wind tugged at her hair as she ran over the footbridge. There was no one else around. It seemed even colder on this side of the station, and she huddled in the doorway of the empty waiting room.

'The train now approaching Platform Two is the delayed 12.57 from Paddington. This service will terminate here', the disembodied voice informed her. She stood out of sight as the brakes hissed and the train screeched to a halt. Doors opened. The usual crush of passengers vacated each carriage. She saw him almost immediately. He stepped off the train and put his holdall on the platform before lifting down a suitcase for someone behind.

Jealousy sliced through her. The woman almost falling into Brandon's arms was Charlotte Sinclair. They embraced, a kiss on each cheek, like old friends, except that their bodies strained together and his hands crept briefly beneath the folds of her coat. Then he grinned, and, picking up his holdall, walked away without a backward glance. Grace followed him, hidden in the crowd.

On the station forecourt she watched him hail a taxi, her mind desperately seeking an alternative explanation; a reason to disbelieve what she had seen.

'Brandon.' She called after him, her voice high and unnatural.

He swung round, startled. 'Grace.'

Waving the taxi away, he strolled towards her. 'Grace, this is a surprise. What are you doing here?'

Suddenly it was imperative he didn't know she had been waiting for him, that she had been hanging around the station like some silly teenage groupie. 'I was just getting a timetable for trains to Birmingham.'

'Lucky for me then.' His kiss lacked warmth.

Anger and nausea curdled deep within her. She pushed him away. 'You bastard! I saw you with that awful woman.'

'So I take it there's no point trying to convince you I met her on the train?' He looked amused.

Grace said nothing, stunned by his indifference.

'Okay, I admit it. I spent a few days in London with the delectable Mrs Sinclair.'

'And what about us? Me and you?'

'Grace, darling, there is no me and you. It was just a bit of fun.'

'I thought I meant something to you. I thought you had feelings for me.' She heard herself whining.

'Grace, you're my stepbrother's wife. How could there be anything between us?'

'Then...Why?'

'Because you were up for it, darling. You made that very clear.'

'You bastard!' Grace said again, mortified at the truth of his words.

'Grace, you weren't happy. I just wanted to give you a good time. Living with Richard can't be easy. He's a pompous ass who hasn't a clue how to treat a woman.'

'He's worth fifty of you.'

'So my father seems to think.' Brandon's eyes glittered, bright as broken glass. 'Ever since we were teenagers I've had that sanctimonious prick held up to me as an example.'

'Perhaps you should have taken notice.'

'Why? There's nothing Richard has that I can't have if I want it, is there, Grace?' He touched her cheek and she recoiled, sickened.

'Is this what it's all been about? You and Richard? You wanted to hurt Richard?'

He shrugged.

'Are you going to tell him?' She struggled to stay calm.

'Don't worry. I won't say anything. Besides it's not a good time. I'm getting engaged next month – Helena Reece, daughter of Sir Edward Reece, owner of GLP Newspapers.'

Grace wanted to smash her fist into the smug face.

'Well? Aren't you going to congratulate me?'

'I'm sure you've already done that yourself a thousand times.' She turned her back on him and began to walk quickly along the street. The tears on her cheeks burned in the wind but she didn't wipe them away. She didn't want him to know she was crying. What a fool she had been. What a blind, pathetic fool. He had never loved her. And the man she had loved didn't exist. Beneath the superficial charm Brandon Calthorpe was cold, self-centred and vindictive. She pitied Helena Reece, whoever she was.

Out of sight of the station she began to run, desperate to get as far away as possible. She felt tainted. How could she go back to Richard and pretend nothing had happened? But what other choice did she have? Brandon must never know the child in her womb was his.

A taxi swept past. She had a fleeting glimpse of the passenger, his handsome features relaxing into a smile as he waved. She hated him then, as intensely as she had once wanted him.

It was beginning to rain. The sky had clouded over into a dull, uniform grey. Faith saw the first large spots land on the concrete and wished it was time to go back into school. She was alone, hidden from the watchful eyes of the dinner ladies, sheltering from the gritty wind behind one of the temporary huts in the playground. She could hear the shrieks and laughter of the other children, but she had no desire to join them. Instead she leaned against the wall, hoping no one would seek her out. She couldn't push the memory out of her mind – the bathroom door ajar, her mother in a pink slip, looking so small and frightened, crying like a child. She knew there was something dreadfully wrong. Her imagination painted pictures in her head of tombstones and mounds of earth and sad, wilting bouquets of flowers.

She closed her eyes. 'Dear God, please don't let my mummy die. I promise to be good and to help other people and to be kind and always tell the truth and—'

A footstep scuffed on the ground. Faith opened her eyes.

'What you starin' at?' Debbie Saunders was eating a packet of crisps, cramming them into her mouth, sucking the salt off her grimy fingers.

'Nothing.' Faith looked away. She didn't want to be involved in an argument.

'You're a fuckin' liar.' Debbie came closer. She smelt nasty, like stinky cheese. Her coat was grubby, her hair almost grey with dirt, and snot hung like a green bead from her nose. Faith took a step backwards. If only Emily was here. Emily would stick up for her. But Emily was in the classroom mixing paints for Miss Thomas.

'You fink I nicked these, don't ya?' Debbie wagged a greasy finger.

'I don't...' Faith stopped, horrified. She had promised to tell the truth. If she didn't God might let her mother die. And she *did* think Debbie had stolen the crisps. Debbie was always stealing things, particularly food. Emily's mum said it was because Mr Saunders never gave his children proper meals.

'You do, don't ya?' Debbie poked her hard in the ribs.

'Yes,' Faith muttered.

'You fuckin' bitch!'

Debbie dropped the crisp packet and grabbed her by the hair, pulling so hard that shreds of it came out at the roots. Faith screamed but no one heard. It was raining heavily now, the drops bouncing off the roof behind them. A whistle blew.

'We've got to go in,' Faith shouted. She twisted herself free and began to run. But Debbie was too quick for her, shoving her roughly against the wall of the hut. Faith lost her balance. Her head hit the corner of the building with a soft thud and she pitched forward, sprawling on the ground. The world slid out of focus. She lay still, dazed with pain, hot blood trickling into her eyes.

Grace returned home just before three o'clock. The hall was chilly. Unwelcoming. She went into the kitchen to switch on the boiler and leaned against it wearily, still wearing her wet coat. She felt like an intruder. It was as if someone else lived in the house, someone who cooked and cleaned and loved her family. She was not that person. She was a cheat and a liar. It was hard to believe what she had done, what she had been prepared to do, what she was planning even now. She rubbed a hand across her eyes, unable to face her thoughts. Out of habit she reached for the kettle – there was enough time to make a cup of tea before she had to meet Faith from school.

The telephone rang. She was tempted to ignore it. She hadn't the energy to speak to the likes of Gwen Nisbett. The caller didn't ring off. There was something in the shrill insistence of the tone that communicated itself to her, a sudden sliver of fear in her guilty mind. She ran into the hall. She knew before Liz spoke that it was bad news.

'Grace. Thank goodness you're back. I've been trying to get you all afternoon.'

'Liz. What is it?'

'It's Faith. She's had a nasty fall. They've taken her to hospital. The head let Miss Thomas go in the ambulance with her.'

'Ambulance?' Grace gripped the edge of the table. 'Liz, how badly is she hurt?'

'I'm not sure. The school couldn't get hold of you or Richard so they rang me. I said I'd let you know as soon as you came home.'

'I need to go to the hospital.'

'Stay calm, Grace. I'll ring a taxi for you. I should pack a few things in a suitcase for Faith. Try not to worry. I'm sure she'll be fine.'

'Thank you, Liz. I'll let you know how she is.'

Grace put the phone down. She sat on the stairs, her head in her hands. Last night she had held Faith, looked down into the anguished little face and promised she would never leave her. And she had lied. Now her daughter was injured, being looked after by strangers because she herself had not been there. Because she had been to meet her lover.

'Please let her be all right,' she whispered. 'Please give me another chance.'

Something seemed to melt inside her. The resentment she had carried around for so long eased a little with her tears. She stood up unsteadily, reaching for the telephone. Richard needed to know what had happened.

He was waiting at the entrance to the hospital when she arrived. Even from a distance she could see the tension in his stance, the pallor of his face, but he was smiling as he came to greet her.

'She's all right, Gracie. They've stitched her up but they want to keep her in for observation.'

'Can I see her?'

'Yes. She's in the children's ward.'

Grace followed him along endless corridors, the noise of their shoes on the tiled floor echoing in her head.

'Miss Thomas has been very kind,' Richard said. 'She wanted to wait for you, but I said you would probably rather talk to her tomorrow.'

'Thanks.' She appreciated his thoughtfulness. 'Did she say how it happened?'

'They're not sure. Apparently Debbie Saunders found her behind one of the huts.'

'Debbie Saunders?' Grace was reminded briefly of the Saunders family and Ed Saunders's taciturn misery.

'Yes,' Richard nodded, opening a door. 'In here.'

Faith was sitting up in bed, her head swathed in bandage, a dark smudge of bruising on her forehead. She began to cry when she saw them.

'There, there, my darling. Mummy's here now.' Grace wrapped her arms round her daughter, alarmed by the convulsions which shook the thin little body.

'Where were you, Mummy? Where *were* you?' Faith squirmed, elbowed herself free.

'I...' Grace couldn't speak.

'Mummy was out shopping.' Richard sat on the bed and held Faith's hand. 'She came as soon as she could.'

The sobbing continued.

He spoke gently. 'Tell you what, Minnie, if you stop crying I'll ask the nurse if you're allowed some chocolate from the hospital shop. Will that make you feel better?'

He took out a handkerchief and dabbed at her wet face.

Grace sat on the chair at the side of the bed. 'No wonder the child loves him,' she thought, 'he gives so much of himself.'

The ward was full and there was no one available to talk to them. They kept Faith occupied as best they could, reading stories from the books Grace had brought, playing I Spy, telling jokes. An auxiliary gave Faith an unappetising meal and offered them a cup of tea. Visitors came and went. Outside the clouds frayed to reveal a watery sunset.

Eventually a junior doctor made his round of the ward with a nurse at his side. He examined Faith, removing the bandage carefully.

'You're doing well, young lady.' He checked her pulse and shone a light in her eyes. 'But to be on the safe side we'll keep you here until the morning, and I'll have a look at you again.' He smiled, a quick, frazzled smile. 'The nurse will put a clean dressing on for you.'

'She will be all right, won't she?' Grace asked.

'There's really nothing to worry about,' the doctor said quietly. 'She just needs to rest. There will be a small scar, but fortunately it will be hidden by her hair.'

'Thank you.' Richard stood aside for him to pass.

'I want to go home.' Faith whimpered. 'I want to go home, Daddy.'

They stayed at their daughter's bedside long after she had fallen asleep. It was late when they left the hospital. The car park was unlit and they hurried to the car, the wind licking their faces, a hint of frost on its breath. The sky had cleared, becoming a deep, inky blue above the city lights.

Neither of them spoke as they drove through the streets and into the countryside. Here the sky was black, pocked with stars. The trees were grotesque in the glare of the headlights, the road ahead empty, the fields invisible. Grace found the loneliness almost unbearable. When they pulled up on the rectory drive she broke the long silence. 'Do you think I should have stayed with her?'

Richard shook his head. 'There was no point, Gracie. Better to get some sleep and be bright and cheerful when she comes home tomorrow.'

'I suppose so.' She stumbled out of the car after him, grasping his arm as they went up the uneven path to the front door.

In the kitchen she made toast while Richard boiled the kettle for coffee. The house seemed too quiet, as if the heart of it was missing. They moved around quietly, talking in hushed voices, as if they were afraid their daughter might hear.

'I'm going to bed,' Grace pushed her plate away, toast untouched. Richard switched off the light and followed her upstairs.

She lay awake, troubled by her conscience, reliving the shocking events of the afternoon. In the darkness Richard might have been a million miles away.

'Hold me,' she said in a small voice. 'Richard, hold me please.'

She thought he hadn't heard. Then he turned and enfolded her in his arms.

He stroked her hair, pulling her to him, trying to give her strength with the warmth of his body. She was so slight and insubstantial against his chest, wanting nothing more than comfort. When he kissed her she clung to him, her tears hot on his hand. Their need for each other was mutual. There was no flare of passion between them, but their love-making was slow and sweet and healing.

Afterwards he couldn't sleep. He listened to Grace's even breathing, his soul filled with an irrepressible joy. She had come back to him. For a long while she had been somewhere else, some place he couldn't reach. Lately he had thought her lost to him completely. In the stillness of the night his lips formed a prayer of gratitude for the safe return of his wife and daughter.

REFLECTIONS

The little finger on the church clock pointed to the six. Faith knew she ought to go home but she continued to walk round the churchyard, searching in the long grass by the wall for dandelion leaves. The mellow September sun was still high, the crumbling stones warm, and there was a faint smell of apples in the air. It was much too nice to go indoors. Besides, Cottontail would be hungry. She pictured the fluffy white rabbit, grown so plump now it was difficult to remember the tiny creature her father had brought home after she came out of hospital.

She bent to tug at a clump of crisp, green leaves, her mind slow and contented. Cottontail had been the first of all the good things that had happened in the summer. She put the leaves down, and using her fingers, began to count. There had been the holiday in Devon, a whole fortnight in a caravan high on the cliffs above the sea. Then there was the secret den she and Emily built in the field behind the church. And – she raised a fourth finger – yesterday she had been blackberrying with her mother and afterwards helped make bramble-jelly jam to store for the winter. Five, her father was teaching her to swim, taking her to the swimming baths in Hereford every Saturday morning. She smiled, thinking of her parents. They rarely argued nowadays. She counted that too.

And Debbie Saunders wanted to be her friend. She wasn't sure whether to include this in her list. But Debbie was different. She didn't smell so much lately and her hair was usually combed and tied back in a ponytail. Faith rubbed at an itch on her nose. She vaguely recalled her father saying something about Mr Saunders having help with the housework and coping better with the children.

Number eight. The most exciting thing – the very best thing of all, deliberately left until last – her mother was going to have a baby. She hugged the knowledge to herself. Soon she would have a new little brother or sister.

The trail of her thoughts faltered. Anxiety stirred for a moment. She had promised to be good if her mother didn't die, and God had heard her prayers. He had made everything all right. But sometimes that promise was hard to keep. Like now, when the sky was the colour of harebells and the last of the day's heat tingled on her bare arms and she didn't want to go in for tea.

She turned to look at the clock again. The sun had dipped behind the tower and the shadows in front of the church had lengthened. Unbidden, another image stole into her mind – her mother with Uncle Brandon in the stable at Dalchett House. She shivered. As usual the memory disturbed her, made her feel dirty, as if she had been listening to a smutty joke in the playground.

Quickly she picked up the pile of leaves and began to run towards the rectory gate.

CHAPTER 7

Grace gasped. The contraction tore through her, savage as fire. Her body was soaked with sweat. The world had dwindled to a mess of shadows, blurred faces and pain.

'Come on now, Grace. Push.' The nurse bent over her. 'You're almost there. You can do it.'

But she couldn't. After more than fifteen hours she had no strength left. She was going to die. Brandon's baby was going to kill her.

'Gracie, don't give up.' Richard's voice.

Her fingernails clawed into his hand as another wave of pain ripped her apart. This time she was too weak to scream.

'Good girl. Push now, that's it.'

Her body seemed to take over, expelling the child of its own volition. The thin bleating cry floated through her agony.

'Congratulations, my dear. You have a lovely little girl.' The nurse put the baby into her arms.

Grace kept her eyes closed as the furnace inside her subsided into a raw, quivering ache. The burden of guilt was almost unbearable. She had no love to give this slippery scrap of life her body had just voided.

'Gracie...' Richard was leaning over her, smoothing her hair back, wiping the sweat from her face.

She turned her head away.

Hours later, she woke to find Richard still at her side. Their new daughter, washed and dressed in a tiny white nightdress, lay in a crib by the bed. She was a small baby, with a tiny oval face and wisps of silvery blonde hair. And her eyes, when they were open, were the same bright blue as her father's.

'She's perfect.' Richard put his thumb into one of the miniature fists, and the little fingers curled round it like a sparrow's claw.

Grace tried to hide her irritation. 'Don't disturb her. She'll need feeding again soon.'

He came to sit on the bed.' How are you? You had such a rough time.'

'It's not something I want to go through again.' She forced a smile; her conscience troubled by the disappointment on his face. 'Go on, hold her. I can see you're longing to.'

He stood up and lifted the child into his arms. The delicate features creased momentarily, a sliver of blue showing beneath the long lashes,

'Hello, Hope. It's your daddy.' He touched the soft skin reverently. 'I take it we're still going to call her Hope?'

Grace leaned back against the pillows. 'If that's what you want.'

'That's what she's given us isn't it? Hope for a future together.' He sat on the bed again, cradling the baby against his chest. 'I thought you would leave me, you know... before Faith's accident.'

She heard the tears in his voice.

'Well, I'm still here,' she said softly, sad that she had hurt him.

They brought Hope home on a foggy morning at the end of November when the lanes were treacherous with black ice. The rectory garden was eerie, the bushes in the driveway ghostly and shapeless, the grass silver in the beam from the headlights.

'Let's get her inside.' Richard unfastened the carrycot. 'I'll come back for the suitcase later.'

The house was warm, the boiler humming reassuringly. There was a fire in the lounge, the coals still glowing although the flames had died.

'You and Hope stay in here. I'll make some tea.' Richard put the carrycot on the sofa and went out to the kitchen.

Grace sat in one of the armchairs looking around the room at the furniture she and Richard had chosen, at the ornaments she loved, at Faith's cardigan lying over the back of the sofa. What had she done? Her gaze rested on the sleeping baby. Brandon's child. A cuckoo in the nest. She rubbed her eyes wearily. Somehow she had to find the strength to keep her secret; to care for this baby, feed and clothe it, and pretend to love it for the rest of her life.

It was easier when Faith came back from school. Her excitement was infectious. She ran into the lounge ahead of Richard, coat unfastened, hair damp with mist.

'Is Hope awake, Mummy? I can't wait to see her.'

Grace yawned and shook her head. 'She's been asleep all afternoon.'

'She's beautiful. She could be a fairy baby.' Faith knelt by the carrycot, dark eyes suddenly solemn.

'You won't think that when she cries in the night,' Grace said.

Faith touched the downy curls. 'She doesn't look like me, does she?'

Grace was quick to reply. 'Babies don't really look like anyone, darling.'

'Look at her little fingers.' Faith tried to open one of the tiny fists.

'No!' Grace sat upright, her body tensing.

Faith moved her hand as if it had been burned.

Richard intervened. 'Tell you what, Minnie Mouse, how about you and I prepare the vegetables while Mummy has a rest? When Hope has been fed then perhaps you can hold her.'

'Can I, Mummy?' The dark eyes were animated again.

Grace found herself smiling. 'I think that can be arranged,' she said.

Hope woke as they were eating their meal. Faith heard the little staccato cries grow louder.

Her mother groaned. 'Talk about timing.'

'I'll go, Mummy.' Faith slid off her chair and ran to the lounge. She peered into the carrycot. Hope's doll-like face was wrinkled like a monkey's, her cheeks mottled, her eyes narrowed, glinting like chips of glass.

Instinctively, Faith put a finger into the tiny mouth and was surprised at how strongly her sister sucked on it.

'Hey,' she leaned closer, fascinated. Yet she couldn't quite banish the sudden twist of jealousy. Would her parents love Hope more than they loved her?

She looked up when her mother came into the room.

'She likes me, Mummy. She's stopped crying.'

'Well done. You've got the magic touch. I'll take her now.'

Faith watched them together. She saw her mother's breast, blue-veined, heavy with milk, and heard the snuffling noises as Hope drank, starfish fingers flexing and curling. Time began to drag. Faith shuffled nearer and settled herself against her mother's legs. The clock ticked loudly. She began counting the seconds.

'There we are. All done.' Her mother said at last.

Hope gave a loud burp. Faith giggled.

'That's better.' Her mother smiled. 'You can hold her now, Faith. Sit in the armchair. You have to be careful. Don't let her head flop.'

Faith sat well back in the chair. She felt the weight of her sister in her arms, heavier than any of her dolls but soft and warm. The sausage legs kicked weakly, the tiny feet paddled against her skin. She rubbed her cheek over the fuzz of hair, smelling soap and baby lotion and the slightly sour whiff of regurgitated milk. Her arm began to ache but she didn't move until the blue eyes closed.

'I think I'm going to love her,' she whispered.

CHAPTER 8

The letterbox clattered and a whisper of brown envelopes fell on to the mat by the front door. Grace walked past without interest. In the lounge Hope lay in the carrycot asleep. Richard had shut himself in the study to prepare Sunday's sermon and Faith was at school. It was ten o'clock and barely light outside.

For Grace, the winter days were bleak and grey, both inside her head and out. It was as though she was in a tunnel, trapped between shadowy walls; a tunnel which seemed to get narrower and darker by the hour. She felt exhausted. Guilt hounded her, day and night, until she couldn't think rationally. Every time she looked at Hope she imagined a greater resemblance to Brandon.

'Anything other than bills?' Richard came into the hall, a pencil behind his ear.

She pretended she hadn't heard.

Richard frowned. Picking up the mail, he followed her into the kitchen. She paused at the window, staring out at a garden stripped almost bare of leaves and colour.

'The first snowdrops are out,' he said quietly.

'Are they?' Her voice was thin and flat.

He put the envelopes on the table and went to stand behind her.

'There, see. Near the hedge.'

She moved away. He remained where he was, his fingers beating a faint rhythm on the tiled window ledge. He heard her behind him, filling the kettle, searching in the drawer amongst the cutlery, reaching into the cupboards for sugar and teacups. Such ordinary movements and yet made so hesitantly, with none of her former precision. He could visualise her without looking round – she was etched into his mind – her body angular, the bones on her face and neck showing only too clearly. It hurt him to see her. She reminded him of Betty Holmes. She seemed to have given up on life, struggling through each day, her face expressionless, her eyes dull or glassy with tears. He had no idea how to help. She didn't want to talk, she didn't want to leave the house, she hardly ate a thing. The doctor had diagnosed post-natal depression, but it was more than that, he was sure.

He turned towards her. 'You making tea for me?'

'If you like.'

'Thanks.' He walked across and began to sift through the post. The white envelope with its bold, unfamiliar handwriting had been hidden beneath everything else. He opened it, intrigued. The card inside was expensive, embossed with silver.

'It's from Helena Reece's parents. An invitation to the wedding.'

There was a small noise from somewhere in the back of Grace's throat.

'Mr and Mrs Edward Reece have pleasure in inviting you to the marriage of their only daughter, Helena Sophie, to Mr Brandon Calthorpe in Hereford Cathedral on Saturday, 26th April. Reception to follow at Dalchett House.'

He pulled out a chair and sat down. No one had told him his brother's wedding was to be in Herefordshire instead of at the Reece's Surrey mansion.

'Well that's a turn up for the books.' His mouth was dry.

'We don't have to go, do we?' Grace put a mug of tea on the table beside him. She hovered at his shoulder, chewing her fingernails.

'I don't see how we can get out of it. Besides... there's this.' He handed her a note which had been folded inside the card. 'It's from Helena. She wants Faith to be a bridesmaid.'

'I don't want to go to the wedding.' She sat down opposite him, perched on the edge of the chair as if ready for flight.

'Well we don't have to make a decision yet. You may feel better in a week or two if we can find someone to help with the house and the children.'

Grace shook her head, dismissing the suggestion.

He smiled. 'You haven't forgotten Miss Emerson's coming this afternoon?'

'You deal with her, Richard.'

'All right, Gracie. But I really need your opinion. You might hate her.'

'I won't.'

Richard stood up, pushing the hair back from his forehead. He rinsed his cup at the sink and left it on the draining board.

'I'd better finish this sermon,' he said, defeated.

Left on her own Grace reached across for the card and letter. The card reminded her of Brandon – showy and pretentious. She pushed it aside, shaken at the sudden spasm of hatred within her. Why, when she had felt only emptiness for weeks, should she feel anything at all for him now?

The note was written in large, flowing letters. The tone was friendly, somewhat effusive. Helena Reece was looking forward to meeting them. She would love Faith to be a bridesmaid – Ivy had told her how pretty the child was – and she just knew the little girl would look gorgeous in the pink crinoline dress. She went on to say she had decided to have the wedding in Hereford because Quentin had not been well and it would mean he didn't have to stay away from home.

Grace put the note down. *Had* Quentin been ill? She vaguely remembered Richard saying something about flu and bronchitis. What was happening to her? Quentin was one of the few people she loved. Why hadn't she even bothered to ask about him?

She began to cry silently.

The doorbell rang at exactly three o'clock. Richard sighed, straightening his collar. He had placed the advertisement in several newspapers three weeks earlier, but there had been only one reply. It wasn't surprising. Being a nanny-cum-housekeeper to a rural priest and his family was hardly a situation to appeal to many people, especially as the salary offered was not very high. The bell rang again. Obviously Grace wasn't going to answer. He waited a moment longer and then went to open the door.

She was not what he had expected. To begin with she was beautiful: tall and slim, with honey-gold hair in a single plait falling almost to her waist. She was wearing a quilted jacket over a long, floral skirt.

'Good afternoon. I'm Kate Emerson.' She sounded slightly breathless.

'Come in, please. Can I take your coat?' She smiled briefly as he helped her out of her jacket and hung it over the banister. 'Come on through.' He led the way to the study.

She sat on the high-backed chair at the side of his desk, hands folded on her lap. Her eyes fascinated him. They were the colour of new spring leaves, flecked with gold. He curled the corners of his notebook, disconcerted. In her letter she had told him she was twenty-two. She looked fifteen. But there was a calmness about her, a quiet confidence, that was not in the least adolescent.

'Miss Emerson,' he cleared his throat, 'Tell me a little about yourself. Why do you want this job?'

She looked at him coolly. 'As I explained in my letter, I lived with my grandmother for most of my life. She became ill last year, just after I qualified as a teacher. I didn't want to leave her... and after she died... It's been quite traumatic selling the house. All the legal things that have to be done. I wanted to move away from the sad memories, and I've always loved the countryside.'

It sounded convincing, but there was something not quite right, something she wasn't telling him.

'Why not look for a teaching post in a village school?'

'I've been very lonely, Mr Lawson. Most of my friends have moved away. I thought it would be nice to be part of a family.'

'But as a teacher you would be earning three times the salary I can offer.'

'I don't need the money,' she said simply. 'My grandmother left me well provided for, and there's still a large amount from the house sale to come.'

'I'm sorry, I didn't mean to pry.'

'I know.' This time her smile was warm and he noticed the dimples at the corners of her mouth.

'Would you like a cup of tea and then we can start again?' He found himself smiling back at her.

Over tea and biscuits they discussed the work she would be doing if she took the job. Richard was afraid she would be deterred by the idea of helping with the housework as well as being a companion for Grace and a nanny to the children.

'You don't mind all this?' he asked.

'Not in the least.'

He was startled when the study door opened. Grace took a step into the room. She was dressed in an old anorak and jeans, her face white and strained. 'I thought I would fetch Faith from school.'

'There's no need for you to go. Liz said she would bring her home.'

'I have to make the effort. I'll go crazy if I don't snap out of this.'

'Gracie, let me introduce you to Kate Emerson.'

'Nice to meet you,' Grace was already turning away. 'I won't be long.'

She was gone before Kate Emerson had a chance to reply.

'Grace is unwell,' Richard explained apologetically. 'That's why I need someone to help out here. I don't like to leave her alone but I have work to do.'

Kate felt sorry for this gentle man with his melancholy dark eyes. She made up her mind to take the job if he offered it to her.

'Well, I think it's about time you met daughter number two. She's in the lounge. She sleeps all day and keeps us awake most of the night.'

Richard Lawson's anxious expression dissolved into a grin, making his face look younger. 'It takes its toll, I'm afraid. I find myself nodding off at the drop of a hat.' He came round to the back of her chair, holding it steady for her with old-fashioned courtesy.

She walked behind him down the hall, absorbing the atmosphere, noticing details. The lounge was large, with a window overlooking the front garden, but it had none of the gracious proportions of the rooms in her grandmother's house. Her eyes misted. Soon, that beautiful Regency villa in Cheltenham would be consigned to memory. She bit hard on her lower lip. Gran was gone. The house was no longer a home. Taking a deep breath, she turned her thoughts to the present.

'Here she is, the little monster.' Richard Lawson indicated a carrycot on the floor at the side of the sofa.

'She's lovely.' Kate had never seen such a perfect baby. 'A little angel.'

'Hardly,' he said dryly. 'But you're right, she is beautiful. She takes after my wife, not me.'

Kate sat on the sofa while he put more logs on the fire.

'There – should be nice and warm when they get back.' He lowered himself into the armchair at the side of the fireplace. 'I think you'll like Faith. She's a quiet little thing but she has a good sense of humour.'

'Does she know about me?'

'I mentioned we might be having someone to stay with us but I didn't know how to describe the role you would be playing. That is, if you decide you want the job.'

'You do realise she may not approve? She may think I want to take her mother's place.'

He frowned. 'We'll have to cross that bridge if we come to it.'

Kate was silent, contemplating the future. The sound of logs spitting and crackling grew louder, accompanied by the steady ticking of the clock.

'Will you excuse me? I'll just put the kettle on to make Grace a drink when she comes in. They shouldn't be long now.' Richard Lawson got to his feet awkwardly.

Left alone, Kate stared at the orange flames eating into the logs. It was no use hankering after the past. This was as good a place as any to start a new life.

The fire was flaring cheerfully when she heard the murmur of voices in the hall. A door slammed somewhere. Ten more minutes passed and she began to wonder if she had been forgotten. A log shifted and a charred piece of wood fell on to the hearth, breaking into red-hot gleeds as it hit the tiles. Kate jumped up to reach the shovel from the companion stand. She scooped up the glowing embers and dropped them back on the fire before sweeping the ash away with the long, brass-handled brush. She was still on her knees when she heard the door squeak. Looking round, she saw a child standing in the narrow triangle of light from the hallway.

'Hello.' Kate spoke softly.

The girl was tall for her age, thin and long-legged, with smooth, waxy skin and huge, dark eyes beneath a heavy black fringe. Her little face was solemn.

'Hello.' Kate said again. 'You must be Faith.'

Faith remained in the doorway. The woman kneeling in the dusky room resembled pictures of the Madonna she had seen in books; her hair was golden in the firelight, shining as though it had been polished, and her face had a sweet, saint-like beauty.

'Do you know who I am?' The woman stood up, smoothing her long skirt.

Faith kept hold of the door handle. 'Daddy said your name is Kate, and you might be coming to live with us.'

'That depends.'

'On what?'

'On whether you want me to. And whether your mum and dad think I'm suitable.'

Faith shuffled from one foot to the other. She wasn't sure what to say. Her tongue found the gap where her tooth had fallen out that morning. The gum was soft like jelly, and she could taste blood.

The woman smiled. 'It's scary isn't it? Talking to someone you haven't met before? I'm nervous too. Will you come and sit by me and we can have a little chat?'

Faith nodded, curiosity overcoming her shyness.

They settled side by side on the sofa. The room was warm, and the leaping flames cast a circle of rosy light around them. Kate's voice was clear and expressive. She talked about her childhood and her grandparents and the funny little private school she had been sent to when she was seven. Fascinated, Faith moved closer to her, breathing in her perfume, enjoying the attention, answering her questions happily.

Then Hope whimpered. Faith tried to nudge the carrycot further away with her foot, relieved when her sister didn't cry. It meant she could keep Kate to herself a while longer.

She was disappointed when her father appeared.

'Sorry to leave you for so long, Miss Emerson, but I thought you might appreciate some time alone with Faith.'

'Thank you. I've enjoyed talking to her.'

'And do you think you could be happy here?'

'Does that mean you're offering me the job?'

'It's yours if you want it. Grace and I discussed things in the kitchen. We would both be happy if you accept and I'm sure Faith will be delighted.'

Faith crossed her fingers behind her back.

'I'd love to,' Kate Emerson said.

CHAPTER 9

At last the party was coming to an end. In the hall several little girls were shrugging on their coats, chattering excitedly to the mothers who had arrived to collect them. Grace acknowledged their thanks and held the front door open for them to leave.

'Bye,' Faith stood on the doorstep, waving as her friends made their way down the drive into the darkness.

Grace lingered at the door, inhaling the damp air, surprised to feel her heart stir with pleasure at the sight of a clump of yellow crocuses caught in the pool of light from the windows.

'Thanks for a great party, Mum.' Faith was flushed, her face beaded with sweat.

Grace drew her close, conscious that her daughter was growing up, becoming more worldly- wise. They went inside together. The house smelt of raspberry jelly and sausage rolls and there were streamers, sweet wrappers, crumbs, balloons and the odd party hat on the floor. Grace looked at the mess, her lips curving in a genuine smile.

'Well, it looks as if everyone had a good time.'

Faith grinned. 'I'll get Em and Debs to help tidy up,' she said, scurrying into the lounge to rejoin the two girls left behind.

In the kitchen, Kate was washing the dirty glasses and plates while Liz Marsh dried them and Richard stacked everything in the cupboards. Grace's mood darkened. She felt superfluous. She was losing her family. Kate was usurping her role as mother and wife.

'That wasn't too bad, was it?' Richard looked exhausted. 'And Kate was brilliant at organising the games.'

'I don't know *how* we managed before Kate arrived.' Grace couldn't conceal her bitterness. She knew she should be grateful – the demands on her were considerably reduced since Kate had been with them. Kate was happy to look after the children, to cook and clean, even to do the household shopping. The girl was a blessing surely, not a threat.

'Let me do that, you've done enough for today.' Grace elbowed Kate aside and plunged both hands into soapy water.

'I'll boil the kettle then. Does anyone want coffee? Kate's cheeks were pink with embarrassment.

'Me, please.' Liz dried the last few plates and put the tea towel over the radiator. She flopped down on one of the kitchen chairs. 'I ought to be going, really. I promised Ed Saunders I'd walk Debbie home.'

'I'll take you all in my car.' Kate was smiling again.

The three girls sat on the hearthrug in the lounge. They were looking through the colourful encyclopedia Faith had received from her grandmother.

'Look at this,' Emily pointed to a vivid picture of dinosaurs around a marshy pool with a sky streaked blood-red in the background. Faith shuddered and turned the page quickly.

'My mum's gonna get me one of them books fer me birfday, next month,' Debbie said.

'Is she coming home?' Emily wanted to know.

'Dunno.'

'Have you heard from her?' Emily sounded doubtful.

'No. But she'll get me one of them books. She will.'

Faith knew Debbie was lying. She could understand why. Everyone else had a mum who loved them and bought them nice things; someone who fetched them from parties and tucked them into bed at night. She touched Debbie's hand. 'I'll ask my mum to buy one for you, if you want.'

Debbie's eyes narrowed. 'Will yer?'

'Yes.' Faith smiled. She hadn't really wanted to ask Debbie Saunders to her party, but now she was pleased she had. It was the kind thing to do. And Debbie actually looked quite pretty. Her hair had been washed and she was wearing an old party frock of Emily's which Mrs Marsh had sorted out for her.

'Fanks,' Debbie said, beaming.

'Have you seen this?' Emily was leafing through the encyclopedia again. Debbie and Faith peered over her shoulder.

'Human re... repro... duction,' Faith read out. 'What's that?'

'It's all about having babies,' Emily giggled. 'Look at the pictures. Can you imagine your mum and dad doing *that*?'

Faith was curious. She knew where babies came from but she had never thought about how they got there. She stared at the illustrations. An uneasy memory stirred in her mind.

'What are they doing?'

'What does it look like?' Emily chortled with laughter. 'They're making a baby.'

'How?'

Emily stopped laughing. 'Well, I think—'

'Yer dad sticks his penis in yer mum an' all this stuff goes inside 'er and then a baby grows. Me big sister told me,' Debbie announced importantly. 'But if yer mum does it with someone else then yer dad gets mad and belts her.'

'Why?' Emily was incredulous.

'Because it's wicked to do it wiv somebody else when you're married. Me dad says so. He said me mum was a filthy fuckin' tart, so she went away.'

Faith began to tremble. She remembered Brandon's nakedness below his shirt; that brief, revolting glimpse of what the boys at school would call his dick, huge and swollen and wet. Her mother and Uncle Brandon hadn't been playing a game in the stable at Dalchett House. They had been making a baby. And her mother was married. That made her a filthy fucking tart, didn't it?

'Are you okay, Faith?' Emily was speaking to her.

'Yes.' Her thoughts were wild. *Hope wasn't Daddy's daughter at all.*

'What yer cryin' for?' Debbie put a rough hand on her arm.

'I'm not.' Faith pulled a tissue from her sleeve and blew her nose. Her father must never find out. If he did he would be angry, and then her mother would have to go away. Just like Debbie's mum. She squeezed her eyes shut. The day was ruined. Everything was different now.

CHAPTER 10

The morning of the Calthorpe wedding was perfect; warm, with a pearly blue sky, and a gentle westerly breeze. On the journey to Dalchett House, Grace found herself appreciating the freshness of the countryside, noticing that in places the hedgerows were already frothy with blossom and the grass verges golden with dandelions. She smiled at the lambs gallivanting in the fields, tails swinging like catkins as they ran.

It was the weather, she decided, that made her feel different. As the days had grown longer and brighter she had found the grey shroud of misery lifting, loosening its hold over her. There were still times when she felt low but she was aware of a world outside herself once more. She had new energy. Life was worth living.

Today though, she was nervous. She hadn't been to Dalchett House during her illness, or seen Quentin and Ivy since their brief visit to the rectory at Christmas. Ivy was bound to be hostile, unable to comprehend her behaviour. Brandon she had not set eyes on for over a year.

She tried not to think about him. But her imagination gave her no peace, inventing embarrassing scenarios, disastrous revelations. She was glad Hope was at home with Kate. At least no one would be able to comment on the child's striking resemblance to her uncle. She inhaled deeply, determined to stay calm. How would she react when she saw him? Would she be consumed by hatred? Or desire? In the last few weeks the old vague resentment had begun to nag at her again. The memory of the passion she had known with Brandon sometimes aroused a need so strong it almost took her breath away.

'Are you ready for this?' Richard asked as they approached the long drive.

He smiled at her and she blushed, ashamed of her thoughts. Faith opened a window and the scent of bluebells filtered into the car. Ahead, sunlight slanting through the bare branches of the trees mottled the tarmac with bright golden patches. Her stomach muscles clenched as the house came into view.

Three huge marquees had been erected in the grounds at the back, and an assortment of vehicles took up most of the space on the forecourt.

'It's like a film set,' Richard said, looking for a place to park. 'What a pantomime.'

Grace swallowed, her mouth dry. It was too late to turn back.

She slid out of the car, trying to move elegantly in her tight skirt, worried about scuffing the heels of her new shoes on the gravel. She gripped Richard's arm in sudden panic. Misunderstanding her apprehension, he squeezed her fingers. 'You'll be fine, Gracie. You've been so much better lately.'

They threaded their way amongst caterers' vans, trucks and station-wagons to the front door which was open. Holmes appeared immediately, the lines on his face etched deeper with exhaustion.

'I'm glad you're here, Mr Richard. Mrs Calthorpe needs a calming influence. She's in one of the marquees supervising the seating.'

'I'll see what I can do.' Richard pulled a wry face. 'I'd better get down there, Gracie. I think Holmes is trying to tell me Mum's getting in the way. You'll be okay with Faith, won't you?'

He kissed Faith's hair. 'Be good Minnie Mouse. I can't wait to see you in your bridesmaid's dress.'

Dismayed, Grace watched him hurry away.

'Miss Reece and the bridesmaids are in the King Charles bedroom waiting for the hairdressers to arrive,' Holmes informed her. 'Can I get you anything?'

'Some tea would be nice and some lemonade for Faith.'

'I'll organise that now. I'll leave it in the morning room for you.'

Holmes set off along the passage, his footsteps heavy on the flagstones. Grace took hold of Faith's hand, terrified of meeting Brandon, half expecting him to materialise from the shadows at the foot of the stairs.

The King Charles room was full of well-bred young women, all expensively dressed, their voices loud and confident. Grace stood by the door, feeling second-rate and ordinary in her smart pink suit. Why on earth had she agreed to come? And why hadn't she insisted Faith wore something other than jeans and a T-shirt?

A woman came over to them. She was dark-haired and stocky, with limpid brown eyes and a nose that was too large; a plain woman in her late twenties, who had made the best of herself with designer clothes, a flattering haircut and perfect grooming.

'Hello. You must be Grace. I'm Helena Reece. Pleased to meet you at last.'

For a second Grace was filled with a malicious satisfaction – first thing in the morning Brandon's wife would look quite unattractive. Though, of course, it wouldn't matter. He wouldn't be faithful to her. He was no more capable of fidelity than a feral tomcat.

Helena drew Faith towards her. 'Hello, sweetheart. You're as pretty as your picture. Are you looking forward to this afternoon?'

Faith nodded shyly.

'Would you like to see the dress?' Helena included Grace in her question. 'I do hope it fits. If not, the dressmaker is here somewhere.' She smiled, her eyes bright with merriment.

They crossed the room to an alcove at the side of the stone fireplace where all the bridesmaids' dresses were hanging on a metal rail. Helena reached for the smallest and shook it out carefully, letting the fine material settle into its natural folds. The dress was pure silk, dyed a rich, deep pink, the colour of old English tea-roses, and the full skirt over its crinoline was looped up in places and fastened with clusters of tiny rosebuds to reveal a frilled cream underskirt beneath. The bodice was stiffened, decorated with seed-pearls and trimmed at the neckline and sleeves with similar cream frills and buds.

'It's so pretty,' Faith touched the soft material, 'like a princess's ball gown.'

Helena turned to Grace. 'I do hope you approve. I think the colour really suits her.'

'It's lovely,' Grace replied through stiff lips. 'She's a lucky girl.'

'Shall I get changed now?' Faith asked.

'Not for a while, sweetheart. We're going to have our hair and make-up done. The stylists are due in a few minutes and it will take them absolutely ages to make us look our best.' Helena grimaced into the mirror, making fun of herself.

A tall woman with a wide, sulky mouth and cropped blonde hair interrupted their conversation. 'I'm going to pop outside for a few minutes, darling. I'm dying for a ciggie.'

Helena touched her arm. 'Let me introduce you to Grace, Brandon's stepbrother's wife. Grace, this is Lucinda Hammond, a family friend.'

'Hi.'

Grace felt insignificant as the blonde woman's pale gaze flickered over her and back to Helena.

'I won't be long. Don't start without me.' Lucinda Hammond brushed past them. The room grew quiet.

'Could I go and find Grandad Quentin?' Faith asked, before the silence had time to become uncomfortable.

'Of course you can, sweetie. Come back in about an hour.' Helena was frowning.

'I'll make sure she does.' Grace had the excuse she needed to get away.

Once they were on the landing another problem presented itself. If she went with Faith she ran the risk of bumping into Brandon...

'I think Holmes has left me some tea in the morning room. I'll wait for you in there, darling. If you see your father, tell him to come and find me.' She gnawed her bottom lip, angry with Richard for leaving her alone.

'Okay.' Faith ran ahead down the staircase.

Grace trailed after her. She had the absurd desire to walk on tiptoe, like a child wanting to avoid detection. To her relief the passageway was deserted. She opened the door of the morning room. It, too, was unoccupied. Grateful for the solitude, she poured herself some tea and sat by the window watching the activity on the forecourt. She glanced at the stables. The door at the far end was open and she looked away quickly, her face hot.

Where *was* Richard? Unable to relax, she went to the table and refilled her cup. She longed for a distraction from the chaos in her head – bitterness, repulsion, remorse... jealousy. Why did she feel like this? How could she feel anything except hatred for Brandon Calthorpe? Distressed, she returned to the window. It had been a mistake to let Faith go. She needed the company.

But Faith wouldn't want to talk to her. Faith had been different lately; reticent, almost morose, her dark eyes hard, her features deliberately expressionless. Memories trickled into Grace's mind – Faith hunched in an armchair staring at the wall, Faith shrinking away from her, Faith laughing with Kate. Always with Kate. When had all this started? Why had her daughter changed? She drew in her breath. The explanation which leapt into her mind didn't bear thinking about.

Faith wandered onto the terrace at the back of the house. The great hall had been full of strangers arranging flowers, moving furniture, setting out tables and erecting a stage. The drawing room and dining room had also been in a state of upheaval and no one could tell her where her grandfather might be. The terrace was cool, shaded by the building, but the marquees on the lawn were in sunlight and swarming with white-coated people who darted in and out of them like bees round a hive. Faith knew her grandad would not be among them. She went down the steps and hurried towards the gardens at the side of the house.

She skirted the walled kitchen garden, taking one of the broad, grassy paths through the extensive flower beds until she arrived at an area of woodland where the ground sloped steeply and a dirt track zig-zagged between the trees. Her pace scarcely slackened as she picked her way over gnarled roots and patches of crusted earth. Now and then she glimpsed the dull gleam of water, but only when she rounded the final bend at the bottom of the bank did the whole long comma-shaped lake reveal itself. A few seconds more and she reached the rustic bridge which spanned the point where a stream disappeared beneath the black surface.

Out of breath, she leaned against the wooden railings and watched the water slide below her, smooth and secretive, unlike the silvery cascade which tumbled under the bridge near the bottom of the drive. She picked up a piece of bark and let it fall over the side. It was caught by the current and, dashing to the other side of the bridge, she saw it slow down as it reached the lake, riding the little waves before it was washed to the side and left stranded. She looked about for something else to throw into the water but there was nothing except a clod of dried mud which crumbled to dust in her fingers. Reluctant to leave the bridge, she stood with her chin resting on the rail, staring at her fragmented reflection.

She knew she ought not to be here; she should have remained within sight of the house. Yet she didn't want to go back. If only she had found Grandad Quentin. Close to tears, she put her thumb in her mouth. Why was everything spoilt? She had been looking forward to today. A part of her longed to wear the beautiful pink dress and be Helena's bridesmaid. But she didn't want to see Uncle Brandon. She was afraid of him.

Once she allowed him into her thoughts she couldn't rid herself of his image. She recalled the ugly expression on his face and his hands circling her wrists, the knuckles bone-white in the gloom of the stables. Now she knew what he and her mother were really doing, her recollections of that day had sharpened, found their way, twisted and shocking, into her dreams. They lingered at the back of her mind even in the daytime.

She chewed her thumb, nibbling at the skin around the nail. There was nobody she could confide in, nor could she forget what she had seen. She hated her mother – her mother was a tart – but she didn't want anyone else to know. Especially her father.

A breeze scurried along the stream and she shivered in her thin T-shirt, suddenly conscious that she was alone. What if Uncle Brandon found her here? Sick with a new fear, she began to run back along the footpath. Her feet slithered on loose stones. Twice she tripped over exposed roots and grazed the palms of her hands as she tried to save herself. Every twist in the path, every movement, every shadowy tunnel of branches intensified her panic. Each breath scoured her throat. Gasping, she scanned the way ahead. Higher up the bank she could see daylight behind the trees. She must be nearly out of the woods.

Somewhere a wood pigeon clapped its wings. The sound startled her. Straining her ears she thought she heard the crunch of footsteps. She crouched down, out of sight.

They stopped a short distance away from her – Uncle Brandon and the woman with the spiky blonde hair.

'I'll have to go back in a minute. I only came out for a cigarette.'

'But I've only just found you.'

Their voices carried clearly in the heavy silence.

Faith peered through a veil of new leaves. Uncle Brandon pushed the woman against a tree trunk, his hands easing the sweater from her shoulder.

'No!' The woman tried to wriggle free. 'I can't. It's your wedding day.'

The words shocked Faith, igniting more memories. Her head felt as if it would burst, loaded with knowledge she didn't want. Anger fused with her panic. She wanted to scream at them. She wanted to call the woman a filthy fuckin' tart. She wanted to run and tell Helena what kind of man Uncle Brandon was. She shifted her balance slightly, dislodging a heavy stone. Petrified, she heard it ricocheting down the slope, bouncing off tree stumps, clattering over rocks. The couple sprang apart.

'What the hell was that?' The woman looked alarmed.

Faith lay flat, her body rigid, face pressed into the damp soil. But he had seen her. His feet crushed the undergrowth. She looked up and saw his hands reaching for her. For a moment the trees above seemed to spin wildly and the world darkened. Then his fingers clamped onto her wrists and she felt broken twigs and sharp-edged stones digging into her flesh as he dragged her on to the path.

'Get up.' He hauled her to her feet.

'Brandon, leave her. She's only a kid.'

He shrugged off the woman's restraining hand.

'So? Do you enjoy watching other people's games?' His voice was harsh.

Faith struggled to speak. Her throat was clogged, her face wet with tears and mucus.

'I know what you were doing,' she sobbed, 'and you weren't playing games.'

He smiled unpleasantly, bending his knees and thrusting his face close to hers. His eyes were a cold winter blue. He smelt of alcohol and stale cigarette smoke. 'If you tell Helena about this I'll make sure the whole family knows your mother is a bloody slut.' He uttered each word slowly, his teeth bared.

Faith swallowed the bile in her mouth.

'Now go on. Clear off.' He stepped aside to let her pass.

With a muffled cry she stumbled away from him. Her legs seemed too heavy, her heartbeat thumped against the wall of her chest. She was choking on her tears. Somehow she reached the top of the track and emerged into the sunlight. Even in the open, she didn't dare stop. She blundered on past the flower beds towards the lawn, desperate to find someone she could trust.

Her father appeared around a curve in the path.

'Faith, whatever's the matter?'

She hurled herself into his arms, weak with relief.

'Faith, hush now. You're all right. I'm here. How have you hurt yourself?' He squatted in front of her, dabbing her eyes and the grazes on her arms and legs with his handkerchief. 'Mummy sent me to look for you. She was beginning to worry. Let's go inside. We'll find her and get you cleaned up.'

'I can't. I can't!' Her sobs grew wilder.

'Faith, please. Stop crying, you'll make yourself ill.' He led her to a wrought-iron seat, partly hidden by a spreading magnolia. She felt his arm tighten round her shoulders as he drew her to him, resting his head on hers, holding both her hands in his own.

'Faith, my darling, what's wrong?'

His gentleness prompted a fresh flow of tears. The knowledge was too much for her to bear. 'Daddy, Hope isn't your baby.'

The words came with a rush. She told him everything.

Richard listened. He didn't doubt her story. Perhaps he had always known; perhaps he had just wanted to ignore his suspicions. Of course Hope was Brandon's child. How else could you explain the likeness? There was no blood link. Certainly she hadn't been conceived on the morning Faith discovered her mother and Brandon in the stables – the dates didn't add up – but all that winter Grace had been different; secretive and withdrawn. How long had the affair lasted? Brandon and Grace... He pressed his lips together, trying to stay calm.

'You're not cross with me are you, Daddy?' Faith was watching him fearfully.

'No, I'm not cross with you, Minnie Mouse.' He let go of her hands and wiped the fresh tears from her cheeks with his fingers. How had she managed to keep all this to herself?

He could feel anger building inside him. 'Why has all this come out today, Faith? Why are you in such a state?'

'I saw Uncle Brandon in the woods.'

'With your mother?'

'No. With one of the bridesmaids. He said if I say anything to Helena, he'll make sure everyone knows that Mummy's... Mummy is...'

She began to cry again. 'You won't tell Helena, will you?'

He shook his head but he wasn't certain. Surely Helena had a right to know the truth about her future husband?

'Uncle Brandon... he hurt me.' Faith whimpered.

'How?'

'He pulled me out from under the bushes. I scratched my tummy.'

She lifted her T-shirt and he could see the red marks on her skin. His anger exploded, a white flash in his head. 'Brandon did that?'

'Yes.'

She was so young and so vulnerable and so very, very precious. In that instant he could have killed his stepbrother.

The rest of the day was an ordeal. After a while his anger abated, congealing into a leaden mass of misery in the pit of his stomach. Against his better judgment he said nothing to Helena. As she passed him in the hallway, dressed in her bridal gown, hand on her father's arm, he couldn't bring himself to spoil her day. Instead he wished her luck.'I hope you know what you're letting yourself in for,' he murmured.

'I'm aware that Brandon's no angel,' she replied softly.

He understood then that she had no illusions about the man she was marrying. Anyway, it was none of his business. Marriage was a lottery, but this one was destined to fail.

Somehow he endured the wedding. The main body of the cathedral was packed with three hundred invited guests plus a large number of interested onlookers who had crowded in at the back to witness the wedding of Sir Edward Reece's only daughter, the woman who would one day inherit his vast fortune. Outside, television cameras were in position and newspaper reporters jostled each other for a better view. It was absurd. A piece of theatre, not a marriage.

His thoughts were ugly. He felt uncomfortable in the magnificent consecrated surroundings; unworthy of his calling. Watching Brandon make his vows at the altar, he couldn't even bring himself to pray for the couple's happiness. When the bride and groom walked together down the aisle he looked away, into the shadows beyond the lighted candles, and tried to ignore the hatred fermenting inside him. At his side, Grace reached across for the camera and he moved slightly to put a space between them. He couldn't bear to be near her.

The reception in the marquees was ostentatious; too much rich food; a full orchestra; television crew and pushy photographers everywhere; flattering, long-winded speeches and lavish, unwanted presents. In the evening most of the guests gathered in the great hall where a dance band was playing and they could mingle informally.

By nine o'clock the music had grown louder and the conversation more animated. The band was performing a selection of the latest chart hits which had most of the youngsters, and many of the not-so-young, on their feet. Ivy, red-faced and garrulous, was in her element, relishing her role in the day's proceedings. Brandon and Helena were dancing, but not with each other. Sir Edward Reece sat by the fireplace discussing the latest political scandal with Quentin while his wife moved unobtrusively among the guests ensuring everyone enjoyed themselves.

Richard interrupted a group at one of the tables.

'Will you excuse my wife? We ought to get going. I've an early communion service in the morning.' He held Grace's chair as she stood up. If she was surprised at his abruptness she made no comment.

It was difficult to speak calmly. 'You get Faith. She's in the drawing room with some of the other children. I'll say our goodbyes.'

'Okay.' She smiled briefly at the people she had been sitting with and went in search of her daughter.

Squeezing through the dancers, Richard managed to reach his mother who was at the centre of a group of elderly women. He waited for her to finish talking and then drew her aside.

'We're off now, Mum.'

'Already?' She allowed him to kiss her.

'Yes. Faith is very tired. I think she's had enough excitement for one day.' He left the hall swiftly, avoiding eye contact with anyone.

After a few minutes, Grace and Faith joined him in the passageway and he hustled them outside. The forecourt was still busy – film crew loading up equipment, caterers taking time out to smoke and chat, reporters dawdling by the stables hoping for some extra snippets of news. It was a warm, star-stippled night and no one seemed in a hurry to leave. The lights from the great hall shone out into the darkness, the sound of music drifted on the air.

Faith looked back. 'Doesn't it look beautiful?'

He couldn't help himself. 'It's a pity it's all wasted on that arrogant bastard.'

No one spoke on the way home. He didn't apologise for his outburst. He drove too fast, swerving round the bends, accelerating on any straight bit of road, relying on his brakes. Faith fell asleep on the back seat, her head jolting against the window. When they arrived at the rectory he lifted her out of the car and carried her to the porch, leaving Grace to collect their belongings.

Kate opened the door, her startled expression softening at the sight of the drowsy child in the rose-coloured dress.

'You're earlier than I expected. Did everything go well?'

Faith woke with a shudder and Richard put her down, steadying her as she looked around blearily. 'She needs her bed. She's out on her feet.'

'I'll take her up.'

'Thank you.' He went into the study, closing the door firmly against his wife's questions.

Faith woke suddenly, her heart racing. Something had disturbed her sleep. She sat up, staring into the shadows. Kate had left the door ajar and the lamp on the landing cast a thick wedge of light on the ceiling. Through the window, she could see the church tower in the moonlight. There was nothing to be scared of.

She slid out of bed and padded to the door. Her father was shouting. She had never heard him shout in anger before. And there was another noise, a soft, pathetic sound like a hedgehog snuffling. It was a second or two before she realised it was her mother crying.

In the main bedroom Grace faced her husband. Here, there was no light from the moon and his face was a pale oval in the dark. She could feel his fury although he didn't touch her.

'How could you? And with *him* of all people. Tell me, what did you see in my stepbrother? Was it his looks? His money? His charm?'

'Richard, please...' Grace scrubbed her eyes with her fists. How could she hurt him even more by revealing the truth? How could she say that Brandon had made her melt with desire; that she had lost herself in his love-making; that she had been almost senseless with a passion she had never dreamed possible.

'I need to know, Grace. I need to understand what made *my wife* behave like a bloody whore?'

She flinched. He never used swear words. What had she done to him? She wished she could see his expression. Was his rage prompted by sadness or disgust? Which? She didn't want to make things worse by saying the wrong thing.

'I don't know,' she sobbed. 'I don't know. I must have been crazy.'

'Not too crazy to lie and cheat. Not too crazy to make a bloody fool of me. How dare you pass Brandon's bastard off as my child. You didn't even have the decency to tell me the truth!'

'I'm sorry. I'm so sorry. I knew you'd be angry. I didn't want you to hate me. You don't hate me, do you?'

'I wish I'd never set eyes on you.'

Grace was icy cold. 'What are you going to do?'

'I'd like to wring your bloody neck! I want to beat my stepbrother to a pulp. I want to go away and never see you again. But I can't. I'm a priest. I shouldn't even be thinking such things.'

She sensed a slight change in his mood and was quick to take advantage. 'Will you ever be able to forgive me?'

He didn't answer. She moved closer to him. 'What about Hope? None of this is her fault. What are you going to do about Hope?'

'For goodness sake woman. What do you want me to do? I can't think straight. I don't even want to think about her.'

She clutched his hand. 'Richard, please don't tell anyone. I'll leave. I'll do anything you want.'

Her touch seemed to ignite his anger again. 'I *want* a bloody wife that loves me. Someone I can trust, not a——'

'I do love you, Richard. I do.'

He grasped her by the shoulders. 'Then why, Grace? Why him? Was it sex you wanted? Is this what makes you happy?' He shoved his knee between her legs and threw her on to the bed, his hands tearing at her blouse, his tongue thrusting deep inside her mouth, the weight of his body crushing her breasts. She fought against him but all the while there was a growing excitement within her. He took her roughly, making no effort to please her. But she was ready for him. They moved together until she cried out in climax and he lay panting on top of her, his head on her chest.

When he could speak he said, 'I'm sorry, Grace. I shouldn't have taken my anger out on you in that way.'

He lifted himself off her and she found her skin wet with his tears.

CHAPTER 11

There was something very wrong. Kate lingered in the hall, rocking a wakeful Hope in the pushchair, listening to the silence. She knew Richard was in the study and Grace in the kitchen, but there was no sound; no scrape of a chair, no rattle of cups, no rush of water filling the tank. Ever since the wedding five days ago it had been ominously quiet in the house. Even Faith was subdued, skulking home from school, shutting herself in her bedroom until meal times, sitting blank-eyed in the lounge afterwards, pretending to watch television while Richard and Grace made stilted conversation.

Kate tweaked the thin coverlet from Hope's mouth.

'Think we'd better go, little one. Time to collect your sister from school.'

Why was she whispering? It was ridiculous. She opened the door, letting in sunshine and warmth and the welcome noise of the outside world: voices from the farmyard across the road, the throb of a tractor engine, sheep bleating, birdsong.

'We're off now. See you later,' she called.

There was no answer.

Richard heard the door close. He pushed his papers aside and went to the window. Kate was wheeling the pushchair down the drive and he could see Hope's pale hair against the pillow. He looked away, despising himself for the way he felt. Hope was a baby, an innocent victim of Brandon's lust; a new and separate life with a pure untainted, soul. Nevertheless, he had lost all joy in her. And in his wife too. He had promised to forgive Grace. He *had* forgiven Grace. But he found it difficult to talk to her, didn't want to be in the same room with her, couldn't bring himself to touch her. He had prayed for help with empty words while his heart remained cold. He was unmoved by Grace's stricken face, by Hope's toothless smile, even by Faith's unhappiness. His attempts at offering comfort were made out of duty. They had nothing to do with love.

There was the slightest movement of air in the room. He turned to see his wife in the doorway.

'Can I talk to you?' She looked fragile, defenceless.

He knew he should take her in his arms, tell her everything would be all right. But it wouldn't be. Not for a long while.

'Come and sit down.'

She sat on the chair in front of the desk. The afternoon light accentuated her pallor, revealing the bruised hollows beneath her eyes.

'What is it you want?' He remained standing.

'I can't go on like this, Richard.'

'So what do you suggest we do?'

'I don't know. I hoped... when you said you would forgive me I hoped we could work together to make things right between us.'

'You have to give me time. I can't just forget what happened.'

'But you can't stand me near you, can you?'

'No. Not at the moment.' There was no point in lying to her. He saw her flinch, but she regarded him steadily.

'I think I need to go away for a while.'

'How will that help, running off?' His tone was sarcastic.

'It would give us some space... Give *you* some space to sort out how you feel about me.'

The idea was tempting. It would be easier if he didn't have to see her every day.

'Where would you go?'

'I could phone Cassie.'

'You've thought all this out haven't you? Typical Grace – look after Number One. What about your children? You can't take Faith out of school.'

'Kate can look after the children. Faith adores her. They'll be all right without me for a week or two.'

'Grace, they need their mother.'

'No they don't. Faith can hardly bear to look at me. And I'm not breast feeding Hope now so she doesn't rely on me. It's better for everyone if I go.'

He heard the sadness in her voice, the unspoken plea for reassurance that she would be missed, and he ignored it. 'If that's what you want, it's okay by me. Phone Cassie and I'll take you to the station in the morning.'

'Thank you.'

'You'd better let Faith know what's happening and check that Kate doesn't mind the extra responsibility.'

He returned to the window, waiting with his back to her until she left the room.

* * *

As the train hurtled through the countryside, taking her further every second from her home and family, Grace stared through the window, her thoughts and senses peeling apart. It felt as if she was leaving all that was dear to her forever; that there was no way back. The future was bleak and lonely. But, in spite of her misery, she was aware of the tension easing within her. There was a degree of relief to be away from Richard and a pulse of excitement making her stomach jittery. Her flesh was warm, the rhythm of the train soothing. She leaned back against the padded seat and closed her eyes.

Cassie was waiting for her by the ticket-office at Birmingham's New Street station and they followed the crush of passengers making for the car park.

'You okay?' Cassie's forehead creased with concern.

'I think so.' Grace wasn't prepared for the sudden wrench of sadness; the longing to feel Hope's solid little weight in her arms and the desperate need to hold Faith close and beg for forgiveness.

The journey to Wolverhampton was slow, queues at every set of traffic lights. Grace was unsettled by the grey landscape; endless rows of houses, concrete yards filled with scrap metal, grimy factories, smoking chimney stacks and glimpses of oily canal water. She had almost forgotten this – *the Black Country* – her home. Except that it wasn't her home. She didn't know where she belonged any more.

Wolverhampton had changed. She was shocked to see the altered roads and new buildings. Her eyes clouded with tears. She trawled through her memories, the way things used to be, mourning her mother all over again. And Richard too. He was part of her past – the handsome, dark-eyed curate she had believed herself in love with, not the man she had left behind in Tuston looking after her children.

Cassie's flat was a revelation. On the second floor of a detached Victorian house in a quiet avenue, it had spacious rooms with high ceilings and tall sash-windows. The furniture in the lounge was old-fashioned, but Cassie had thrown colourful rugs over the leather chairs and adorned every available surface with lamps and photographs and ornaments. Sunlight spread across the faded carpet and sparked rainbows in the bevelled glass on one of the ornate gilt-edged mirrors.

'It's lovely,' Grace couldn't hide her amazement. 'Like something in a magazine.'

'Nothing much belongs to me.'

'I never imagined you living somewhere like this. How can you afford it?' Grace walked across to the window.

'I'm working at the Quantum Club. A hundred quid a night, cash in hand.'

Grace whirled round, expecting to find she was being teased, but Cassie's features were composed, although there was a faint flush across her cheeks.

'You're serious?'

'I know what you're thinking, but it's all very artistic. It fits in with the day job and I can give Mum money every week now that rotten bloke's left her.'

'How... how did you get into it?'

'I met this man – Lance Burgess – at a party. He owns several clubs – two in London, one in Birmingham, and he had recently taken over the Quantum. He offered me some work. When he told me how much I'd be earning I couldn't refuse. I used to do three nights a week until I had enough money to buy a car and find the first month's rent on this place.' She examined her nails carefully. 'He stays here sometimes... Lance. His wife lives in London and he gets lonely.'

Grace voiced the first thought that came into her head. 'Won't I be in the way? I'm in the spare room.'

There was a moment's hesitation before Cassie answered. 'Lance sleeps with me. It's a relationship that's going nowhere, I know. He'll never leave his wife because of the children and I have to accept that. You'll probably meet him next week.' She lifted her head. 'Don't judge me, please. I need someone in my life.'

'I'm the last person to judge after what I've done,' Grace said.

Cassie reached for a cigarette from the packet on the coffee table. 'Well I'm glad that's out in the open. I'll get some wine and we can catch up with what's been happening.'

The wine was dry with a crisp apple sharpness. They kicked off their shoes and relaxed, the slight awkwardness between them ebbing away. Later, Cassie cooked a chicken curry, which they ate in the neat, well-equipped kitchen, before returning to the lounge where they collapsed on the sofa with the remains of a second bottle of wine.

'Thanks Cass— for everything,' Grace murmured; the ache in her heart softened by alcohol.

'They're both settled at last.' Kate found Richard sitting on the sofa in the fading light, the evening newspaper unopened beside him. He was so still she thought he was asleep. The room was chilly, the curtains still open. Colour had faded from the garden leaving the trees black against a sky streaked with aquamarine and pierced with the first stars. She stepped back, about to creep away.

'I'm sorry. I should have put them to bed. Weren't you going out tonight?' His voice startled her.

'It doesn't matter. Liz invited Grace and me to a lingerie party but I don't really want to go on my own.' She switched on the lamp. The light illuminated the side of his face and her heart seemed to miss a beat. It was insane, this infatuation she had for him. He was her boss. He had a wife and children and she would never destroy his marriage. She was lonely that was all, grieving for Gran. And he was unhappy. She needed to mix with people of her own age, find a boyfriend, have some fun. But, even as she reasoned with herself, she was staring at the back of Richard's head, wondering what it would be like to touch the thick hair which brushed his collar.

'Would you like a coffee?' She tried to sound normal.

'That would be nice.'

When she came back from the kitchen she found him on his knees attempting to light the fire.

'With a bit of luck it will catch this time,' he said, straightening up and taking the tray from her. 'Sit down. You're not cold, are you?'

Kate shook her head. It wasn't the temperature that made her shiver. She sat on one of the fireside chairs watching the thickening plumes of smoke, avoiding his eyes.

'Grace telephoned while you were upstairs.' He handed her a drink and, taking the other himself, settled on the sofa again. 'I think she was a little tipsy. She wanted to say goodnight to Faith.'

'Faith would have appreciated that.'

He made no comment and she continued impulsively.

'There's something worrying her. I think she feels responsible for her mother going away.'

Richard sighed. He leaned forward, hands on his knees, his gaze focussed somewhere behind her head.

'Kate, if you're going to stay on here, you may as well hear the truth. Grace had...' He faltered, then began again. 'Faith knows Hope isn't my daughter. Her mother had an affair with my stepbrother.'

'I had no idea.' Her face was burning.

'Why should you? Anyway, Grace and I... we need some time apart.'

'I'm so sorry.' She wanted to reach out to him but she remained where she was, unable to form any other words as the minutes ticked by. Finally he looked at her directly.

'Your coffee's going cold. I'll make another pot.'

As he left the room, smoke billowed out from the fireplace and the first flame flickered into life.

CHAPTER 12

Faith knelt in church, eyes dutifully closed, as her father intoned the familiar prayers. But the words in her head were her own: *Please God let my mummy come home and forgive me for making her unhappy.* She wriggled uncomfortably, aware of all the tiny sounds around her – the flutter of pages, occasional coughs, the steady ticking of the clock in the bell tower – and she missed her mother's light voice as the congregation chanted the responses. The air was heavy with the scent of lilies and candle wax, but there was no hint of the strong, sweet perfume her mother always wore.

During the sermon she eyed her father anxiously, wondering if he blamed her for her mother's sudden decision to leave. He had seemed cheerful enough yesterday. They had spent the whole day together; he had taken her swimming before lunch and afterwards they worked in the garden, weeding, mowing the lawn and digging out a new flower bed. In the evening they had strolled down the overgrown cart-track which wound its way from the lane at the side of the church to the river. The sun had been setting, the sky garish with orange and purple, like the dinosaur picture in her encyclopedia. A little afraid, she had caught hold of her father's hand, taking comfort from the warm, rough skin and the answering pressure of his fingers.

As the sermon came to an end she closed her eyes again. If she was truly sorry for what she had done, if she promised to be good, God would hear her prayers. He always had before.

Grace stirred on the bed. There was a red band of colour behind her eyelids and a vicious pain cleaving through her temples. Her limbs were heavy. It was an effort to open her eyes; the lashes were glued together, weighted with sleep. For a moment, she thought she was in Tuston. She turned, expecting to find Richard beside her.

Fear whipped her awake. It wasn't Richard lying naked on top of the bedclothes. Her stomach heaved. Who was it? What had she done? What had she taken last night? She couldn't remember. Nothing had mattered except to shed all her problems and have a good time. She lay motionless, her body chilled with sweat and self-disgust. The face on the pillow next to her was almost hidden beneath a tangle of long, brown hair.

She began to inch herself off the bed. How could she have been so stupid? Why on earth had she slept with this man? What if he had given her some disease? She retrieved her clothes from the floor and dressed hurriedly, fumbling with hooks and buttons, terrified that every movement she made might wake the sleeping stranger. Quietly she crossed the room, grabbing her high-heeled shoes with one hand, fastening her skirt with the other. She opened the door a little way, holding her breath as the hinges squeaked, and slipped through the gap into the hall.

There was a radio playing in Cassie's bedroom and she could hear the low murmur of voices. Lance Burgess must have stayed after the party. Barefooted, Grace padded along the soft carpet and let herself out on to the staircase. She leaned against the wall, heart fluttering wildly. Her tongue was dry, sticking like velcro to the roof of her mouth, her head muzzy. She needed fresh air. Clutching the banister, she pulled on her shoes and walked unsteadily down the stairs.

Outside the air was warm, the sun too bright. People emerged from the nearby church and the priest stood in the porch, smiling. In Tuston Richard would be doing the same. She changed direction and walked the other way, eyes smarting with tears. How could she go home now? Brandon Calthorpe had been right about her. She was a slut.

She moved like a sleep-walker, guilt and grief spinning in her mind. Every so often she stumbled, her ankles twisting on the spindly heels; every so often she stopped at the kerb before crossing a road, some instinct warning her of an approaching car. When her feet became sore she took off her shoes, carrying them by the straps. When her body became clammy with sweat she unfastened some of the buttons at the front of her blouse and rolled up the sleeves. She caught sight of herself, reflected in the window of a corner shop – last night's mascara, smudged and flaking; hair uncombed, hanging in limp, matted hanks above her shoulders. She looked what she was. A tart.

After an hour or so of walking she came to a park. There were teenagers on the swings and a group of young mothers on a seat nearby, gossiping while their toddlers splashed in a shallow paddling pool. Grace sat on the grass, aware of their curious glances. She stared into the water, watching the flow ripple into shimmering scales as it was sucked towards the filters. All she wanted was to sleep. And forget.

It was mid-afternoon when Cassie found her. 'Grace! Where the hell have you been? Lance and I have driven miles looking for you.'

'He's not here, is he?'

'No. He had to get back to London. Why on earth did you take off like that?'

'You know why.' Grace looked away.

Cassie knelt beside her. 'Come on. I'll make some lunch and you can have a bath. Things won't seem so bad then.'

'Why did you let me do it, Cass? Why didn't you stop me?'

'Do you think we didn't try? You were hell-bent on breaking all the rules, Grace. I've never seen you like that before.'

Grace put her head in her hands, the spark of anger extinguished. 'I'm sorry, Cass. I shouldn't blame you. But I had sex with a complete stranger and I don't remember. What's happening to me?'

'Nothing. You had a one-night-stand with one of Lance's friends, that's all. Put it out of your head. No one else needs to know.'

'I'm married, Cass. What about Richard? How could I have done this to him again?'

Cassie shrugged and stood up. 'Don't tell him, Grace. He won't forgive you this time. You have to keep this to yourself for his sake and the children's.' She held out her hand, 'Up you get. You'll feel better with some food inside you.'

CHAPTER 13

The slender box lay on the coffee table. It was nearly midday and Grace was still in her nightdress; she hadn't even drawn back the curtains. The flat was quiet except for the slow tick of the carriage clock on the bureau which seemed to grow louder, reminding her time was passing. She had been here too long, almost a month. The memory of Faith's last telephone call haunted her. *When are you coming home, Mummy? I miss you. I'm really sorry, Mummy. I'll be a good girl. I promise. You do still love me, don't you?*

Grace sighed. It had been heart-wrenching to hear the anguish in Faith's voice. But it wasn't Faith's fault. None of it was Faith's fault. The longing to hold both her little girls made her weak, made her want to catch the next train to Hereford and throw herself into her husband's arms. But she couldn't. Not until she was sure. The fear had lived in the back of her mind since the night she had taken a stranger into her bed. She picked up the box. It held her future. If she was pregnant she could never go back.

In the early evening Richard telephoned as usual.

'She's not here,' Cassie told him. 'She's gone.'

At first he didn't understand. 'What do you mean

'gone'? I said I would fetch her when she was ready to come home. Why didn't she ring me?'

'I don't know. I came in half an hour ago and there was no sign of her. She's taken all her clothes.'

'So she could be on her way here?'

'I don't think so.'

'Why not? What are you hiding from me, Cassie? Where is she?'

'I'm sorry, Richard, I haven't the faintest idea.' She sounded harassed.

He didn't believe her. 'But where else would she go? Did she have any money?'

'She got some cash from the bank yesterday. She said she wanted to buy presents for Faith and Hope.'

'So she intended to come home?'

'I assume she did.'

'But you think she's changed her mind?'

'Yes.'

'Why? You must have a reason. You have to tell me. Please, Cassie.'

'I can't. It's up to Grace to tell you herself.'

'And what about her children? What do I say to Faith?'

'I don't know,' Cassie voice faded.

'If she gets in touch will you ring me straight away?'

'Yes.'

'Thank you,' he put the phone down, trying to think logically. Cassie must be mistaken. Grace wouldn't go anywhere without leaving a message. She must be on her way home. Perhaps she wanted to surprise them.

He picked up the car keys from the hall table.

'Why didn't you let me talk to Mummy?' Faith came out of the lounge, her face flushed.

He tried to smile. 'That was Aunty Cass on the phone. Mummy isn't there at the moment.' He pushed her fringe out of her eyes. 'Is Kate in the lounge?'

'She's upstairs with Hope.'

'Right. I have to go out for a while so be a good girl. Tell Kate I won't be long.'

'Can I come with you?'

'Not this time, Minnie Mouse.' He kissed her cheek and she followed him to the front door. As he reversed the car he saw her watching him.

The church clock was striking half-past-eleven when he returned. He had waited at the railway station until it closed down for the night, his hopes rising with every train that arrived. But Grace had not been among the passengers. His wife was not coming back. Wearily, he locked the car and trudged towards the house. Before he reached the door it was flung open and his heart went cold when he saw Kate's troubled expression.

'What's the matter? Is it Grace? Has she had an accident?'

Kate shook her head, her eyes meeting his. 'It's not Grace. It's Quentin. Ivy phoned a while ago. He's dead, Richard. Quentin's dead.'

'No... not Quentin. Not that lovely old man.'

The floor seemed to shift beneath him and he sat down heavily on the stairs. 'I loved him, Kate. He's been like a second father to me. I can't imagine life without him.'

Wordlessly she put her arms round him. For a few minutes he clung to her. Then he released her, levering himself to his feet. 'How...?'

'A stroke. There was nothing anyone could do apparently.'

'I'll have to go to Dalchett House. To Mum. If I'm not back by the morning you'll look after my girls, won't you?'

'Of course I will.'

'Thank you, Kate. We'll need to rely on you more than ever.' He wiped a hand over his mouth. 'Grace has left us.'

'I'm so sorry.' She picked up his car keys from where they had fallen and gave them to him. 'Drive safely. I'll take care of everything here.'

CHAPTER 14

It was raining, a steady sheet of fine rain that barely made a sound against the classroom window. Outside everything looked dark and glossy, like an old photograph. Faith pictured the village church near Dalchett House with the yew trees dripping in the graveyard and the hollowed-out rectangle of earth waiting to receive her grandfather's coffin. Her face was stiff with the effort of holding back tears. The last time she had visited Grandad Quentin he had been the same as usual, telling his stories, making her laugh, his blue eyes bright. She couldn't believe she would never see him again. With a sudden wail she put her head on the desk and sobbed.

In seconds she was surrounded by children.

'Sit down, everyone!' Miss Thomas perched on the edge of her desk waiting for the class to settle. When they were quiet she smiled at them. 'Faith is going through a difficult time but we won't help her by making a fuss.'

Faith's sobs grew louder. She wanted her friends. She wanted Miss Thomas to hold her, tell her everything would be all right. She began to rock on her chair, making it thump rhythmically. Several heads turned towards her.

'Face this way please.' Once again Miss Thomas waited for silence.

The lesson continued. Faith rocked faster. Tears clogged her throat, and there was an in ache her chest that hurt each time she took a breath. Her father's whispered words that morning kept replaying in her head. *How am I going to tell her, Kate? How do you tell a child of seven her mother isn't coming home?* It was all too much to bear. She let the chair topple and looked for somewhere to hide.

Everyone began to talk at once, twisting in their seats to stare at her.

'That's enough noise. Fetch your reading books while I talk to Faith. And walk *quietly*.' Miss Thomas sounded angry.

Faith crawled beneath the nature table. She curled up, face pressed into her lap, sobs muffled by her clothes. The draught stirred her hair as the class moved about the room, and the noise of their shoes was like thunder on the wooden floor. Miss Thomas's footsteps were lighter; quick and metallic. They stopped close by.

'Faith, you must stop this. If you don't, I'm afraid I'll have to send for the headmaster.'

It was not what Faith needed to hear. She put her hands over her ears, a storm of resentment gathering inside her. 'Go away!'

There was an audible gasp from the class.

'Faith, no-one can help if you hide under there.' Miss Thomas bent down.

'I don't want *you*. I want Em. And Debbie. And Kate. I want... I want my mummy.'

The ache inside her seemed to swell. Her mother had promised she wouldn't leave but she had lied. Grandma Ivy didn't want children at the funeral, Miss Thomas didn't care...

'I wish I was dead!' Faith beat her fists on the floor, working herself into a frenzy, overcome by rage and loss and utter helplessness.

'Faith Lawson, you're making a spectacle of yourself. Come along and don't be so silly.' Miss Thomas held out her hand.

Faith bit it.

The great hall at Dalchett House was crowded yet again. Richard stood by one of the windows, his thoughts all in the past, remembering the man they had buried less than two hours ago. Behind him there was a sudden outbreak of laughter. He looked round, annoyed by the lack of respect. The mourners had been subdued at first, their voices low, but now the atmosphere had lightened and conversation flowed freely, fuelled by food and wine. Cigar smoke spiralled up into the beams, making his eyes smart. He caught sight of his stepbrother shaking hands with a tall, overweight man whose fleshy fingers glinted with gold. Even today Brandon couldn't resist the chance to further his own interests!

Richard averted his gaze, surveying the cars parked on the forecourt and along the driveway. There were several Bentleys and Jaguars, even a Rolls-Royce, all owned, he supposed, by Brandon's flash business associates. He sighed. It was difficult to recall the time when his stepfather belonged to that world. For so many years Quentin had been at Dalchett House, content in his retirement; a gentle, serene presence, as much a part of the lovely old building as the walls and furniture.

Someone touched his arm. Helena was beside him.

'Richard, please come and sit down. You should have something to eat. It's been a gruelling day.'

'I will. In a few minutes.' He didn't want to talk. He wanted to go home and shut himself in his study with a bottle of whisky and his memories.

'At least let me get you a coffee and one of Trudie's scones.' Her heavy features were softened by a tentative smile.

'Thank you.' He couldn't rebuff her. There was something sincere and unpretentious about her, despite her wealth. He watched her at the buffet, spooning clotted cream and jam into tiny pots and felt a flutter of regret. It was a shame their paths were unlikely to cross in the future. He would have liked to know her better.

She returned with coffee and scones on a small tray which she put down on the stone window ledge. They stood together, watching the rain, and he bit into one of the scones, surprised to find he could actually taste anything. 'You were right. They are good.'

He turned to face her and saw she was crying silently.

'Helena...'

'I'm going to miss him, Richard. He made me so welcome. I wish we'd had more time together.'

'If it's any consolation, I know he was very happy to have you in the family.'

She smiled through her tears. 'There was something I wanted to tell him, but I was keeping it until his birthday next month.' Her voice wavered. 'I'm expecting a baby.'

Richard swallowed. 'Congratulations. When is it due?' He couldn't be happy for her. She was already pregnant with Brandon's heir. There would be nothing to keep her husband faithful now. The honeymoon was well and truly over.

'February.' She dabbed her eyes with a handkerchief. 'I hope that somehow Quentin might... that he might know. Does that sound stupid?'

'Not at all.' He tried to think of something to say that would offer comfort, but his mind was sluggish with his own grief.

'I'm sorry. I didn't mean to get all weepy.'

'Helena, if I can help in any way, or if you ever need someone to talk to, give me a call at the rectory.'

'I will.' She stood on tiptoe to kiss him. 'I can trust you to keep it a secret for a while? About the baby?'

He nodded. She took a deep breath to compose herself and walked away from him.

He finished his coffee and checked his watch. The reading of Quentin's will was scheduled for six o'clock. He didn't want to be there. The thought of Brandon's triumphant smirk turned his stomach. He wanted nothing for himself, but the knowledge that Dalchett House would belong to his stepbrother filled him with dismay. He rubbed a hand over his eyes. There was no escape. He had to stay for his mother's sake.

Reminding himself of his priorities, he handed his tray to Holmes and crossed the room to join his mother, worried that she looked so old and ill. 'Take it easy, Mum. No one expects you to be the perfect hostess today.'

She looked up at him, her sharp, grey eyes bewildered.

'I need to keep myself occupied.'

He devoted the rest of the afternoon to her, circulating among the guests, making small talk, offering her his arm to lean on when needed. By half past five most people had gone, and the chatter and clatter of voices and footsteps sounded hollow in the emptying hall. Caterers began to clear away unobtrusively. He went to stand by the door with his mother and Brandon and Helena, thanking people as they left, wishing them well, waiting for the stragglers to follow. At exactly six o'clock Holmes appeared.

'Mr Willis, from Barnaby, Willis and Timms, is in the morning room, Mrs Calthorpe.'

'Thank you, Holmes. Would you ask the staff to assemble in the drawing room?'

'Very good, Mrs Calthorpe.'

Richard gripped his mother's arm. 'Let's get this over with.'

The solicitor was sitting at the table; a grey man in a grey suit, a folder on the polished surface in front of him. He stood up to greet them.

'Mrs Calthorpe, I'm so sorry for your loss.' His expression barely altered as he shook their hands.

They sat opposite him, the opaque light from the window falling across their faces. Richard sat between his mother and stepbrother. Brandon leaned towards him. 'This is where we part company, old boy. I don't want you on the Calthorpe Estate when it passes to me.'

'And what about my mother?'

'She's not my problem.'

Mr Willis took a sheaf of papers from his folder. Richard fought to control his anger, pressing his lips together, fixing his gaze on the pattern in the worn carpet. He missed the lawyer's preamble, only raising his head when he heard Brandon's name.

There followed a list of properties which Quentin had bequeathed to his son: an eighteenth century town house in London, a flat in Paris, a cottage in Cornwall and a villa on the Algarve. There was no mention of Dalchett House. Richard glanced at his stepbrother. Brandon's hands were clenched, the knuckles bone-white.

The solicitor's voice droned on. Brandon had been left Calthorpe Publishing and Quentin's interests in various other companies.

'And furthermore,' Mr Willis intoned, 'I leave to my only son all monies, shares, bonds, jewellery, paintings and other possessions not bequeathed elsewhere.'

There was a frozen silence. The solicitor took off his glasses and wiped them with his handkerchief before he continued.

Richard could hardly believe what he was hearing. *To my dear wife, Ivy, I leave the sum of one million pounds and the Calthorpe emeralds. To my son's wife, Helena, I leave the rest of the jewellery which belonged to my own mother. To my stepson, Richard and his wife, Grace, I leave the sum of two-hundred and fifty thousand pounds plus my old MG sports car. I also leave the sum of five hundred thousand pounds each for their daughters, Faith and Hope, to be kept in trust until their twenty-first birthdays.*

'This is a bloody farce!' Brandon leapt to his feet, shaking with barely controlled fury. He glared at the solicitor then, without another word, he left the room, slamming the door shut with such force that the walls seemed to vibrate.

Mr Willis cleared his throat. 'Perhaps you could send for the other beneficiaries now,' he said as if nothing had happened.

'I'll go.' Helena held her head high even though her cheeks were flushed.

No one spoke in her absence. When she returned she was pale but calm.

'They're just waiting for Trudie. There's been some crisis in the kitchen.' She took her place again, next to Brandon's empty chair.

Mr Willis consulted his watch pointedly and straightened the cuffs on his immaculate shirt. Richard put his hand over his mother's, squeezing her fingers when he realised she was trembling. He was relieved to hear a tap on the door. The staff of Dalchett House entered discreetly to take their places on the row of seats which had been set out for them behind the family. The reading continued. Holmes and his wife were given their cottage outright and other long-serving members of staff were bequeathed substantial sums of money. In addition, Trudie, Evie and Jo had all been left pieces of jewellery as keepsakes. Quentin hadn't forgotten anyone. There were several people in the room overcome by the old man's generosity.

And now, finally, it is my will that Dalchett House remain as it is; that no furniture, paintings or anything of value be removed from the premises. A sum of ten million pounds has been set aside for the management of the house and estate. My wife, Ivy Calthorpe, shall remain in residence for as long as she wishes. On her death the property shall pass to the oldest surviving child of my son, Brandon, and his wife, Helena, with the proviso that it remain in the family. Should there be no issue of that marriage then the said property shall be bequeathed to the National Trust...

Richard didn't hear any more. A savage pleasure flooded his veins. Brandon was not going to get Dalchett House. Quentin had known his son too well.

'Go inside, you'll get cold.' Richard said to his mother and Helena who had accompanied him to the door. It was already growing dark. The rain had stopped but the thick cloud-cover remained; ominously black in the east, thinning a little in the west. Water dripped from the eaves, gouging shallow gullies in the gravel.

He lingered on the step. 'Are you sure you won't reconsider and stay at the rectory for a while, Mum?'

'I'm not going anywhere.' Ivy held on to the door handle, her weight against the solid wood.

'Okay. I'll be over in the morning.' Richard smiled grimly. He understood why she didn't want to leave. Brandon was in Quentin's study, drinking himself into a stupor after searching fruitlessly for evidence to contradict his father's will.

'There's no need to worry about me. Evie or Jo will stay with me for a few days and tomorrow I'll put an advertisement in *The Lady* for a housekeeper. I can manage for a while on my own.' His mother folded her arms across her chest in the old formidable way.

Richard wasn't fooled. She was putting on a brave face, making herself plan for the future, just like she had when his father died all those years ago. He felt a rush of affection for her. Stooping, he gathered her to him. 'Try and get some sleep, Mum.'

'I'll look after her. We won't be going home tonight. Brandon's in no state to drive anywhere,' Helena said softly.

'Thank you.' Richard mouthed at her over his mother's shoulder.

Uncharacteristically, Ivy returned his embrace and then extricated herself from his arms, giving him a gentle push. 'Go on now. Those girls of yours need you. Mind how you drive.'

As he walked away he heard her close the door and pull the bolts across. It was a lonely sound.

He drove home slowly through the damp countryside. When he turned into the rectory drive he could see the lounge curtains were open, the lamps switched on. There was no light in Faith's bedroom. He hoped Kate hadn't allowed her to wait up for him. He didn't want to answer his daughter's questions tonight. His own emotions were too raw.

Kate came into the hall before he had chance to take his key out of the lock. She put a finger to her lips.

'Faith's asleep in the lounge. It's been a difficult day.'

'What's happened? She's not ill, is she?' He followed her into the kitchen.

She poured a whisky and passed it to him. Then she sat down, her elbows on the table, chin in her hands, deliberately avoiding his eyes. He drained the whisky and replenished his glass before sitting opposite her.

'Now, tell me what Faith has done to upset you.' He spoke tenderly and saw tears trapped between her lashes.

'She overheard us talking. She knows her mother isn't coming back.'

With a shock of guilt Richard realised he had hardly thought of Grace all day. He listened aghast to the halting account of Faith's behaviour at school and the violent tantrums which had persisted all evening. When Kate stood up to make coffee he was horrified to see purple bruises on her legs where his daughter had kicked her.

'Kate, I'm so sorry. I'll talk to her in the morning. She can't be allowed to treat you like that.'

'She didn't know what she was doing. She was distraught. I couldn't pacify her.' Kate closed her eyes, pressing her fingers over the lids. 'She kept screaming at me. Said I didn't care about her and I might as well clear off like her mother.'

'Kate...' Richard crossed the room quickly and put a hand on her shoulder. 'Thank you for keeping this from me. It would have added another burden to what was a very harrowing day.'

'How did it go? I'm sorry, I should have asked.' Her hand shook as she stirred sugar into his drink.

'It was a beautiful service. Quentin was a much-loved man.'

'What about Ivy?

'She's—' He broke off as the door was flung open.

Faith glared at them, eyes, glittering like shards of coal. She reminded him of his mother, fierce and frightened at the same time. He could see she was exhausted. Poor child, her rage was understandable – she was powerless in the adult world of lies, deceit and death.

'Where's my mummy?' she asked, her voice high-pitched and accusing.

'I don't know,' he said wearily. 'That's the truth of it, Minnie Mouse. I just don't know.'

'She's left us, hasn't she? She doesn't love us any more.'

'I'm sure she loves you, Faith.'

She shook her head. Richard held out his arms and she tumbled into them, spitting out her grief and hurt, her body shaking with tears.

'I hate her, Daddy. I hope we never see her again.'

CHAPTER 15

'I gave you a ten-pound note, luv.' The woman held out her hand for the rest of her change.

Grace opened the till and counted out the extra five pounds. It was hard to concentrate. The lights and the noise in the supermarket had given her the usual headache and the strange fluttery movements in her womb made her queasy. But it was the pain of loss that was hardest to bear, especially today. Today was Hope's birthday.

She smiled automatically at the next customer, lifting the toilet rolls and packets of cereal out of the basket. Her heart ached to be in Tuston with her two little girls. It was ironic, when they were with her she had resented them, even come close to hating Hope, but now she would have traded her life for the chance to hold them again. The same questions hounded her, day and night. Would Faith ever forgive her? Was she unhappy? Had she transferred her love to Kate? And what did Hope look like? Did she still have her pretty blonde curls? Did she sleep through the night? Blinking back tears, Grace handed over a receipt. Hope wouldn't recognise her now.

At half past four she finished her shift and hurried to the bus station. The town was eerie, shrouded in fog which had rolled in from the North Sea. The lights from the shops shone weakly through the curtain of mist and the street lamps were hazy moons suspended in mid-air. Everywhere smelt of exhaust fumes. Grace pulled her scarf over her mouth as she trudged along. In the summer, Lincoln had been tolerable, thronged with tourists who struggled up Steep Hill to the cathedral and castle; now it was an alien place.

The smell greeted her as she opened the door to the flat – the faint reek of drains together with the musty odour of rotting floorboards and mildew. She locked the door before switching on the hall light. It was not a salubrious area. Stepping back, she almost trod on a large, padded envelope lying on the frayed doormat. The label was typed, official-looking. Her pulse quickened. No one but Cassie knew where she was living. She picked up the envelope, letting it rest on the fingers of both hands for a few seconds before she went into the tiny kitchen and dropped it on the table next to her unwashed mug and dish from breakfast. Still muffled in her outdoor clothes, she sat down on the nearer of the two chairs, remembering too late that the stuffing in the torn seat cover would stick to the black coat she had bought from a charity shop to see her through the winter. Light filtered in from the hall casting deep shadows. The only sounds were the drip, drip of the cold-water tap and the wheezing of the ancient fridge. She shivered. Loneliness seemed to creep into her bones. It was a dismal place and she hated it.

Visions of the rectory at Tuston flooded her mind: the lounge with its polished furniture and crackling fire; the neat kitchen; the pretty bedrooms with their ruffled curtains and matching bedspreads. Her daughters were there. And Richard. She missed them so much. But she couldn't go back. She had run away from Cassie's as soon as she knew she was pregnant. It hadn't mattered where she went, only that she left without trace.

She explored the memory. On that sticky May afternoon she had been oddly excited. The fortnight spent in the cosy, inexpensive guest house had been a bit like a holiday and the necessity of finding a job had given purpose to her days. But then reality caught up with her. The small amount of money she had soon dwindled and the only flats she could afford were as squalid as the one she was in now. She had moved from the guest house with nothing except a few clothes and her first week's wages. Sheer misery made her ring Cassie a month later.

But Cassie had promised not to tell anyone the address or the phone number of the flat. So who had written to her? She stood up and switched on the kitchen light. Immediately the peeling wallpaper and shabby cupboards seemed to close in around her. Fingers numb with cold, she unfastened her coat and went into the hall to hang it on the solitary hook. Behind her, the telephone on the wall rang. Startled, she lifted the receiver.

'Hi, Grace. How are you?'

'Oh. Keeping busy.' It was good to hear Cassie's husky voice.

'I wanted to catch you when you got in from work. Did you get a package in the post?'

'Yes.'

'Grace, it's from Richard.'

Grace twisted the telephone cord round her fingers. Cassie must have heard her catch her breath.

'It's okay. I didn't tell him where you are. He came into the office yesterday lunch time. He was desperate to find you. Said it was important.'

'How did he look?' Grace leaned against the wall, her legs suddenly weak.

'Tired. Anxious.'

'Did he say anything about the children?'

'You don't want to hear, Grace.'

'Tell me.'

'He said Faith's having nightmares and problems at school. Hope's teething. They're all missing you. They want you to come home.'

'I wish I could,' Grace whispered, hollow with longing.

'Grace, are you all right?'

'Yes.'

'When Richard realised he wasn't going to get any information out of me he gave me an envelope and asked if I would send it to you.'

'What's in it?'

'I don't know. After he'd gone I put it in a bigger envelope and posted it on. You aren't cross are you?'

'No, of course not.'

'Good.' Cassie was obviously relieved.

Grace felt obliged to make conversation. 'How are you, Cass? How's Lance?'

There was a slight pause. 'His wife's left him. She's taken the children and wants a divorce.'

'Is that good or bad?'

'I'm not sure. He's talking about selling his clubs to find money for the divorce settlement. Then he'd like to buy a bar in Portugal.'

For a moment Grace forgot her own problems. 'I'm sorry, Cass. You'll miss him, won't you?'

Another pause. Slightly longer. 'He wants me to go with him.'

The words were like a life sentence. Grace let herself sink to the floor, stretching the plastic cord until it was almost straight.

'When?'

'Not for ages yet. Everything has to be sorted out. Don't worry, Grace, I'll keep in touch. You can come and visit us. Say you're pleased for me. Tell me I'll be doing the right thing. Please.'

'You know I'm happy for you.' Grace tried to sound sincere.

'Thanks. Listen, I have to dash now. I'll ring soon. Take care.'

'Bye, Cass.'

Grace reached up to replace the receiver. Without Cassie she hadn't a friend in the world. She rested her head on her knees, letting the silence wrap around her. When the shouting began in the flat above, she went into the kitchen and made herself a mug of tea.

The envelope lay in front of her on the table. It was a link with her past and she wondered if she had the strength to cope with what it contained. What if Richard wanted a divorce? What if he had sent photographs of the children? What if someone was ill?

She put the mug down and pulled the envelope towards her. It was already curling at the edges, tainted with the faint whiff of damp. She tore it open with clumsy fingers. Inside was another envelope, crisp and white, with the single word, *Gracie*, written on the front. The sight of the familiar handwriting caught her unawares and tears burned the back of her eyes.

In the second envelope she found a letter, neatly folded, and a sheaf of papers fastened with a paperclip. She smoothed out the letter. The words blurred, slipping in and out of focus as she read. Phrases leapt out at her: *after we lost Quentin in June... trying to keep things as normal as possible for the children... you must do what you want... only right that you should have your share of the money.* Nothing made sense. What had happened to Quentin? What money? She scrubbed her knuckles across her eyes.

I'm sorry if I forced you away. I want you to believe I am more than willing to accept Hope as our daughter. Wherever you are, Gracie, whatever you've done, I can forgive you. All my love, Richard. His voice was clear in her head, kind and compassionate. If only she could accept his forgiveness. But he didn't know she had betrayed him a second time.

She began to cry; wild, wrenching sobs that grazed her throat and scoured her insides until she could feel nothing. Her cheeks dried and grew icy. A skin formed on the tea in the mug. Someone turned on a radio in the flat next door and the bass beat thumped on the walls. She remained at the table, her mind empty. It was a while before she reached for the sheaf of papers. Her hands began to shake. Richard had sent her a copy of Quentin's will. Quentin wasn't lost. He was dead. Her heart filled with a fresh grief. Knowing he was no longer in the world made things bleaker. As she skimmed through the pages the extent of his generosity amazed her. But why did Richard want her to see this?

She turned over the last page. A small rectangle of paper had been clipped to the back. It was a cheque for one hundred and twenty-five thousand pounds. She looked at it in disbelief. There must be some mistake. But the cheque was made out to her and signed by her husband. She snatched up his letter again, the words suddenly making sense. *I feel it is only right that you should have your share of the money.* How could anyone be so honourable? He had no need to share his inheritance with her. And she had absolutely no right to accept it. Yet she would; for the sake of her unborn child. She would send her thanks via Cassie. It was a cowardly thing to do, but she couldn't risk Richard finding her.

* * *

'Careful, Mrs Calthorpe, mind you don't slip.' Kate peered into the darkness, holding Hope in her arms. The path from the front door was illuminated by the light in the hallway and she could see the sheen of water on the uneven surface.

Ivy hugged Faith and patted Hope's curls. 'Don't worry. I can't afford to twist an ankle. I'm organising a book sale at the church hall next weekend.'

She sounded like her old self, but Kate noticed that she clung to Richard's arm as she stepped down from the porch, her smile fading quickly, the lines on her face etched deeper.

Faith skipped along the path behind them, twirling the skirt of her satin party frock, careless of the puddles, oblivious to the raw cold and the damp fingers of mist at the edge of the lawn.

'Go inside, Minnie.' Richard frowned at his daughter. Faith spun round on her heel and flounced back to stand on the doorstep.

'Bye, bye, my darlings. Be good.' Ivy waved at her granddaughters. Almost regally she held out her hand, allowing Richard to settle her into the car.

Kate sighed with relief. She was glad the little birthday celebration for Hope was over. It had been a subdued affair. Faith had been irritable, tired after school. And Richard had been quiet, speaking only when necessary, his face paler than usual, his smile forced. Ivy had kept the conversation alive, discussing her plans for a new herbaceous border at Dalchett House in memory of Quentin and voicing her concerns about the upbringing of her two granddaughters. The atmosphere had lightened when Liz and Emily called round with a present for Hope, but they hadn't stayed long. No one had mentioned Grace yet she had been in everyone's mind.

The car turned into the lane, tail lights projecting dull red circles on the drifting fog. Kate put a hand on Faith's shoulder. 'Let's go in and get warm.'

Her hand was shrugged away. She shut the front door, surprised that the girl's indifference could hurt so much. Over the last five months Faith had indulged in a frustrating round of tantrums and tears, of insolence and a pathetic need for reassurance. It was easy to see her behaviour was a cry for help, but she kept her innermost thoughts secret, rejecting all attempts to win her confidence. Kate watched her run down the hall, knowing there would be no point in going after her. Instead, she carried Hope upstairs.

In the tiny fourth bedroom she changed Hope's nappy and dressed her in a clean pyjama-suit. The little limbs were pliant, unresisting. Kate lifted her off the padded mat and began to rock her, humming a half-forgotten lullaby. In minutes Hope was asleep. Reluctantly, Kate laid her in the cot and tucked the blankets loosely round her. She felt a bitter-sweet happiness. It was easy to pretend Hope was her baby; that the family at the rectory was her own. Her grandmother would tell her to pull herself together and stop pining for something she couldn't have.

As always, grief struck without warning, filling her mind with ghastly images – Gran asleep on the bed, her face hollowed like a skull, her breathing shallow; the endless nights; bottles of tablets lined up on the elegant chest-of-drawers; the peculiar smell in the bedroom.

She went downstairs, determined to hold the memories at bay by keeping busy, but her body was sluggish and unresponsive, the past too vivid. Outside the lounge she hesitated, daunted by the prospect of yet another confrontation with Faith. The blare of pop music spilled into the hall and throbbed in her head. When she opened the door she had to raise her voice to make herself heard.

'Would you help me clear the table please?'

Faith was hunched up on the sofa watching television.

Kate resisted the urge to shake her. 'Switch that rubbish off and do something useful for once!'

Faith didn't move.

Kate sat down beside her. 'I'm sorry. I didn't mean to lose my temper.'

Again there was no response.

'Faith, why are you ignoring me?'

'I don't have to do what you say. You're not my mother.'

Kate took a deep breath. 'Why can't we be friends like we used to be? I know I'll never take your mother's place, but I'm doing my best to look after you.'

Faith turned to glare at her. 'I don't need looking after.'

'Then maybe I do. I never had brothers or sisters. Most of my life there was only me and Gran. So if I get things wrong sometimes... ,' her throat tightened, 'please, forgive me.'

'Why should I?'

'Because I love you. You and Hope.'

For a moment Faith's dark eyes were troubled, then she stood up, tossing back her hair.

'I'm going to bed. Ask Dad to come and say goodnight when he gets in.'

Alone, Kate covered her face with her hands, no longer able to hold back her tears. Faith's rejection had pushed her beyond despair.

Richard found her in the kitchen when he returned.

'Fog's dense in places. It's a good job I took Mum back when I did.'

'Will she be okay?' Kate was rubbing at a patch of something on the draining board.

'Mum? Yes. Jim Manning had a fire going in the drawing room and the central heating was on. His wife said she'd put hot-water bottles in Mum's bed. They look after her well.'

'They seem very nice.' Her voice wavered.

'Is something wrong, Kate?' He took the cloth from her, letting it fall into the sink. 'You've been crying. Has Faith upset you again?'

'No.' Her face was blotched and swollen. She bent her head, avoiding his eyes.

'So what's the matter?' He led her to a chair by the table and pulled up another one so he could sit by her. 'What is it Kate? Let me help.'

She stared at the blackness beyond the window. The fingers of her right hand were over her mouth and her voice was muffled. 'It's my Gran. It will be a year tomorrow since she died.'

He was ashamed of his thoughtlessness. She always seemed so serene and sunny but that didn't mean she was happy. 'I'm sorry, Kate. I should have realised.' He prised her hand away and held it firmly. 'I've been so wrapped up in my own problems. I didn't think.'

'There's no reason why you should. It's something I have to deal with.'

'But you don't have to do it on your own.'

She was silent and he wondered what traumatic scenes she was remembering.

'Kate, I'm used to listening to problems. Can't you talk to me?'

Suddenly she began to sob, words pouring out of her in breathless, heaving gasps. 'I can't remember her as she used to be. I keep seeing her at the end... And I can't bear it.'

'Oh, my dear, I'm so sorry.' It wasn't the time for platitudes. He couldn't tell her time would heal or that she might find comfort in prayer. He didn't know enough about what had happened. He had never asked.

'It was awful. She didn't look like Gran. She looked so small and shrivelled. I was afraid of her. I had to make myself go into her room, make myself kiss her. How could I feel like that about Gran? I loved her so much.'

'You didn't stop loving her, Kate. You did everything you could for her, didn't you?'

'Yes, I suppose so.'

'Millions of people feel the way you did. But the love is still there, beneath the fear and the sadness. The love goes on forever.'

She looked at him through her tears. 'Do you think she knew I loved her?'

'I'm sure she did.'

She turned away from him, beginning to cry once more, doubled up with grief, as if his words had only increased her anguish.

'Kate, there's no need to punish yourself.'

'Isn't there?' She jumped up and the chair screeched on the floor.

In an instant he was on his feet, reaching out to catch her as she stumbled.

'Kate, tell me. Whatever it is. Just say what's in your mind.'

She slumped in his arms. He waited until she was calmer.

'I was so tired, Richard. I had hardly any sleep during those last few weeks. I don't think I knew what I was doing.'

'Go on.'

'The night Gran died, I gave her the tablets as usual but...'

Her felt the tremor run through her body.

'I'm sorry. I don't think I can do this.'

'You're doing fine, Kate.' He stroked her hair.

'I must have left them... left the tablets on the bedside table. In the morning two of the bottles were open, lying on their side, empty. Gran had taken them all.'

'What did the doctors say?'

'That Gran only had a few days to live and I mustn't blame myself. But I keep thinking what if that wasn't true? There might have been a miracle. She might have got better.'

Her body was rigid. He pulled her closer, wanting to reassure her. 'She was old, Kate. She'd had enough of pain. She was ready to go.'

'I know.'

'Then accept what she did. Forgive *her*.'

He held her until she seemed calmer. Her hair was soft against his cheek and he could feel her breath on his neck. He inhaled her perfume, a light floral fragrance, very different to the heady perfume Grace always wore. His heart began to thud. He knew that if she lifted her face to him he would be tempted to kiss her. Disturbed by the idea, he pushed her away gently. 'Sit down, Kate, and I'll get us both a drink.'

Faith lay in bed, awake and anxious. Her father was home. She had seen the beam of the car headlights sweep across the ceiling and heard the front door slam ages ago. Where was he? Why didn't he come to see her? Had Kate told him about her bad behaviour?

She buried her face in the pillow, her mind sifting through the confusion of the last few months. It had been simple enough to condemn her mother in the beginning – her mother was a tart. But then the doubts had crept in. She screwed up her eyes, trying to evade the persistent rigmarole in her head. If only she had kept silent about her mother and Uncle Brandon. If only Hope had never been born...

But now there was someone else to blame. Debbie had told her it was all over the village. They were saying Kate was the reason her mother had gone away. Her father wanted to be with Kate. But that was just village gossip. It couldn't be true. Kate wouldn't steal anyone's husband.

Her father and Kate. She didn't believe it. And yet they *were* always talking in lowered voices, keeping secrets from her. She couldn't trust Kate any more.

CHAPTER 16

It was the last Saturday of the January sales, and it seemed to Grace that the entire population of Lincoln had descended on the city centre. She was tired. Her back ached and her boots pinched her toes. She walked slowly along the slippery pavement, picking her way across patches of ice, the bulk of her pregnancy making her timid. The cold sapped her energy and each step she took required a greater effort than the one before.

She paused a moment to catch her breath and heard a muttered obscenity from someone behind. Tears blurred her eyes. There was not a soul in this city who gave a damn for her or the baby she was carrying; not one single person who cared whether she lived or died.

The moment of self-pity passed. She bought a morning paper from a news vendor and went into a nearby cafe. The place was busy, fuggy with heat. She paid for a coffee at the counter and carried it to an empty table, thankful to sit down for a while. When her hands had warmed a little she opened the newspaper.

Helena's face smiled up at her from page five. *Heiress in Lonely Vigil.* She skimmed the text in disbelief. *Helena Calthorpe, daughter of wealthy newspaper magnate, Sir Edward Reece, is spending today at the bedside of her new born son. Helena became ill at her London residence last night and was rushed into St Mary's Hospital, Paddington, where the baby was delivered in an emergency operation. Doctors are fighting to save his life. Mrs Calthorpe's parents are due to fly home from Switzerland today to be with their daughter. It is believed that her husband, Brandon Calthorpe of Calthorpe Publishing, is on holiday in America and does not yet know of his son's birth. The couple have recently separated.* There was a smaller photograph of Brandon bearing the caption, *Brandon Calthorpe, pictured in December at a London restaurant with party girl, Lucinda Hammond.*

Grace stuffed the paper in her bag. She felt sick. How could Brandon abandon his wife and child? He was a complete and utter bastard! Yet she had done worse. She wrapped both hands round her cup and stared at the stained plastic tablecloth, stricken with guilt and grief and a desperate longing for her children.

'You finished?'

Startled, Grace looked up. The waitress indicated the untouched drink.

'Yes. Thank you.' The coffee was cold, with a greasy film on top. Grace put an unnecessary tip under the ashtray and hurried outside.

Snow was falling again; sharp, pinpoints of ice, driven on the wind. She pulled up her collar and set off towards the bus station, anxious to get home. Although the bungalow she had bought on the Hykeham Road needed modernising, it had a welcoming feel and the previous owners had left her the carpets and curtains and a very ancient cooker. She half-smiled, remembering their kindness. At least her baby would have somewhere decent to live when it was born.

But Helena's baby might die. She imagined how lonely and frightened Helena must be with no husband or family at her side. Her own loneliness was sharp and constant. But it was no more than she deserved. Helena had done nothing wrong.

Grace pushed a lock of wet hair out of her eyes. A bus swept past sending a wash of icy brown water over the pavement. As she stepped back her feet slid in the mess of melting snow and she fell heavily on the wet concrete. The pain in her belly was immediate and cruel. She closed her eyes against its ferocity, dimly aware of the huddle of spectators gathering around her.

She woke in hospital and lay still while the world slowly came into focus. Her memories of the day were hazy – sounds and sensations trapped between agonising contractions and merciful oblivion. Suddenly fearful, she pushed herself upright.

'Nurse!' Her throat was dry. 'Nurse!' She tried again, feeling for the call button by the bed. A nurse hurried down the ward, her shoes squeaking on the rubber tiles.

'So, you're awake. How are you feeling?'

'My baby?' Grace whispered.

'Is a beautiful little girl,' the nurse said. 'I'm sorry, we don't know your name. We couldn't find anything in your handbag to identify you.'

'It's Grace. Grace Lawson.'

'Hello, Grace. Would you like me to telephone your husband?'

'We're not together any more.'

'A relative then, or a friend?'

'I've only recently moved to Lincoln. I don't know anyone.'

'That's tough.' The nurse's voice was sympathetic. 'Well, there's nothing to worry about, Grace, I just need to take your temperature and check your blood pressure.'

Grace wanted to yell at her to hurry yet at the same time she was filled with dread. She yearned to hold her baby, to fill the emptiness in her life. But would she be able to love it, this stranger's child? She hadn't wanted Hope, not in the beginning, not until she had thrown away the chance to be a mother to her.

'There, all done.' The nurse filled in the chart on the end of the bed. 'I'll bring your daughter to you now.'

Grace watched her walk out of the door; waited endless minutes until she saw her walk back wheeling the clear, plastic cot.

'Here she is; all five pounds ten ounces of her.'

Grace held out her arms. Her baby was warm and soft, little legs already kicking weakly in the folds of the shawl.

The nurse smiled. 'She knows who you are.'

Grace looked down at the tiny white face, the deep-set eyes, the mass of black hair. The resemblance was striking. She bent her head lower to hide the rush of tears. There was no doubt in her mind. The baby was Richard's.

I can go home. The thought caught like fire, took her breath away. She could go back to Tuston, back to Faith and Hope. They could be a family again. Richard had forgiven her the affair with Brandon. He would be overjoyed to have another daughter. This baby was her salvation.

Later, she analysed her situation more rationally. The idea of being reunited with her other two daughters was unbearably tempting. But she had betrayed Richard a second time. Didn't he deserve better than her lies? Better than *her*. Besides, Faith would never forget seeing her with Brandon. Despite those first desperate phone calls and pleas for forgiveness, her oldest daughter had already condemned her. And Hope? Hope wouldn't remember her. Maybe it was it too late to go back.

Outside the light was fading, the sky beginning to clear. Through the window Grace could see a single star above a line of dark cloud. She felt a sudden aching need for her own mother. 'Amy,' she whispered, holding her baby close, 'your name is Amy, after your grandma.'

The lounge door was partly open. Kate could see Richard sitting with Faith on the sofa, his arm round her shoulders as he read to her. The fire was blazing, the curtains drawn against the bitter January night, the lamps switched on. It was a cosy scene, intimate and exclusive. Kate stiffened. They were not her family. They would never love her as she loved them. No matter how long she stayed she would never take first place in their hearts. That would always belong to Grace.

Resolutely, she pushed the door open wider and went in. Richard looked up but she shook her head, indicating she didn't wish to interrupt. She sat on one of the fireside chairs, elbows on her knees, hands cupping her chin, listening as his expressive voice changed with each character, becoming involved with the story in spite of the heaviness in her heart. When he finished the chapter he closed the book.

'Oh, Dad, read some more. Please.' Faith tugged at his arm.

'No more tonight. It's almost bedtime and Kate might want to watch television.'

'Do you?' Faith glowered at her.

'No. But I do need to talk to you both.'

'What is it, Kate?' Richard smiled.

He looked relaxed, untroubled for once. It made what she had to say harder.

She swallowed. 'I think I need to leave.'

In the few seconds silence which followed she heard sleet brushing against the window.

'I thought you were happy here.' Richard's brow furrowed.

'I am. But you must be aware of the rumours. They're saying—'

'I know. And I'm sorry if it has upset you, Kate. Don't worry, I'll have a word in the right places; try and put a stop to it.'

'I really think it's time for me to move on. Maybe buy a flat in Cheltenham – I've still got a few friends there – and then apply for teaching posts. I won't do anything until you've found someone to take my place, of course.'

'It sounds as though you've been considering this for a while.'

She nodded. 'Yes, I have. It's for the best, Richard, you must see that. You risk alienating half your congregation if I stay and I dread to think what people are saying about me.'

'We don't want to lose you, Kate.'

'It's kind of you to say that, but my being here is causing too many problems.'

'Nothing that can't be resolved.' Richard's voice was gentle.

'I'm sorry.'

'I won't stand in your way if you're sure about this. But I don't want you driven out against your will.'

'It's the right thing to do.' She stood up quickly. 'I'll let you get on with the story now. Good night. See you both in the morning.'

'Goodnight, Kate,' he said.

It seemed to take an eternity to cross the room and every step widened the gulf between them. She realised just how much she had wanted him to persuade her to stay. If only either Richard or Faith had asked her not to go, she would have abandoned her plans in an instant, joyfully and without reservation. But they hadn't. Because they didn't care enough.

CHAPTER 17

Grace caught sight of herself in the hall mirror as she reached for the phone. Her skin was the colour of porridge, her hair badly in need of a wash, and her dressing gown crumpled, stained with baby puke. She looked away, wondering what Richard would think if he saw her now.

Richard... Her fingers gripped the receiver. She couldn't put off this conversation any longer. His daughter lay in the crib, fast asleep after yet another fretful night, and he remained unaware of her existence. In the two weeks since Amy's birth it had been easy to justify not telling him – she was exhausted, she didn't deserve his forgiveness, Amy was sickly, it was too early in the morning, too late in the evening. But all these were merely excuses to avoid the truth. She was afraid. All her hopes for the future rested on this one phone call.

Her hand shook as she dialled the familiar number. It was time to repair some of the damage she had done. Richard had been willing to take her back. She couldn't deny him the right to be a part of his child's life. And perhaps Amy would heal the rift between them.

She listened to the telephone ringing out. There would be the usual Saturday morning chaos in the rectory – Faith in a panic, searching for her swimming hat which went missing nearly every week, Richard on his second cup of coffee, frowning over his diary, gathering up the random assortment of papers that always fell out, Kate clearing away the breakfast things. And Hope...? The knot of misery tightened in her chest. Hope was no longer the baby she had left behind. She couldn't picture Hope.

'Good morning. Tuston Rectory.' A child's voice.

Her heart began to race. 'Faith?'

'Yes.'

Grace struggled for breath, gulped in air. 'Faith, it's Mummy.'

Nothing.

'Faith, are you still there?'

'What do you want?'

She wanted to say so many things – that she was sorry, that she loved and missed them all, that she hoped they would forgive her – but her daughter sounded resentful. Perhaps it would be wiser to talk to Richard first. 'I need to speak to Daddy.'

'He's not here.'

'When will he be back?'

'No idea.'

Faith's insolence shocked her. 'I'd better speak to Kate then.'

'She's upstairs, bathing Hope.'

Grace's stomach twisted with jealousy. Kate had replaced her as a mother. Had she replaced her in Richard's affections too?

'Shall I give her a message?' Again the barely concealed hostility.

'No. Not if she's busy.' Grace felt the sting of tears. Her daughters didn't need her. Maybe they didn't even miss her. She pushed the thought away, willing herself to speak normally. 'Faith...'

An exaggerated sigh. 'What?'

'I'll leave my number. Write it on the notepad and ask Daddy to call me when he comes home. Promise me you'll do that. It's very important.'

'Okay.' Another sigh and a rustle of paper.

'Ready?' Grace dictated the number slowly. 'Have you got that?'

'Yes.'

'Now read it back to me.'

Faith repeated the sequence in sullen tones. 'Can I go now?'

'Sweetheart, wait a minute—.'

'Bye.'

The phone clicked and Grace heard the hum of the disconnected line. Her throat closed over a sob as she replaced the receiver.

Faith hates me. She rubbed a hand over her forehead, overcome with love and remorse. How could she have been so utterly selfish? She had left home because she was a coward and a cheat, unable to face the consequences of her actions. Why hadn't she considered what her absence would do to her children? She had simply deserted them. No wonder her shy, sensitive little girl had become so cold and indifferent.

Memories tormented her. How many times had she ignored Faith, brushed her aside when she was busy, spoken too sharply and seen the hurt in the dark eyes? If only she could hold her now.

The need was too strong to bear. She began to cry soundlessly, the back of her hand pressed against her mouth. After a few minutes she stumbled to the lounge and collapsed on the sofa, drawing her legs beneath her, curling up in anguish.

Eventually Amy's cries roused her. With an effort she got to her feet. Her head was muzzy with shadows of the past, and she was too tired to deal with them. She had to put her trust in Richard. When he called they could discuss Amy's future rationally and make any decisions together.

Faith ripped the top sheet from the notepad and slipped it into the pocket of her jeans.

'Who was that on the phone?' Kate came down the stairs slowly, Hope in her arms.

'Some lady wanting to speak to Daddy.' Faith crossed her fingers behind her back. She had already told one lie – her father had only gone to the village shop for a newspaper – and she hoped Kate wouldn't ask if the woman had left a name or number.

'Oh.' Kate was frowning. 'I think Hope must be cutting another tooth.'

'Probably.' Faith looked away to hide the blush on her cheeks. She rushed past them. 'I'm just going to sort out my stuff for swimming.'

In her bedroom she sat on the floor, her back against the foot of the bed, consumed by the heat of her anger. She pushed her fists into her eyes and scrubbed away the tears. A stream of bitter thoughts fuelled her rage. Her mother hadn't worried about her or Daddy or Hope. She hadn't bothered with them for months. They could have died for all she cared. So what did she want now? Did she think she could just walk back into their lives as if nothing had happened? Well tough. Things had changed. They didn't need her any more.

She pulled the notepaper out of her pocket and tore the sheet into tiny pieces, screwing them up in her hand. Then, shifting onto her knees, she crawled to the pine chest at the side of the room and dropped them into the bottom drawer.

CHAPTER 18

The lights of May Fair were soon left behind. In the back of the car Faith rested her head against the window as her father drove towards Tuston. It was late, past her bedtime, and her eyes were heavy. Outside it was growing dark. She hugged the pink teddy bear her father had won on the coconut shy, only half-listening to the rise and fall of voices as he and Kate talked quietly. Beside her, Hope was asleep in the baby seat.

Her thoughts were muddled. Tonight had been fantastic; the city centre crowded and noisy, the rides and music thrilling. For a while she had forgotten to snub Kate, had held her hand as they wandered among the brightly lit stalls, afraid of getting lost in the press of people. She put her thumb in her mouth. Part of her loved Kate. It would be so easy to say sorry and make things right between them. But what was the point? Kate would be leaving soon anyway.

And then, as so often happened when she was lonely or confused, she thought of her mother. *Where was she? Did she miss them? Would they ever see her again?* There had been no word from her since that one phone call. Her conscience stirred uneasily. She had tried so many times to decipher the number on the tiny scraps of paper. It wasn't her fault her mother had never called back.

The car lurched as her father changed gear and she became aware of a difference in the tone of the conversation.

'Are you sure you've thought about this carefully?' Her father seemed angry.

She leaned forward, suddenly alert.

'I'm not a child. Of course I have. I knew you'd react like this. That's why I didn't tell you before.' Kate sounded upset. 'It's a great chance to make a difference in the world. I've got no ties. There's nothing to keep me here, is there?'

He ignored the question. 'What can I say to change your mind?'

'I won't change my mind.' Kate spoke softly but the sadness in her voice was unmistakable.

'So you'll just up and go on a whim and to hell with everyone who cares about you?'

'It's my choice,' Kate said.

'But why go flying off to Africa?'

Faith felt the hairs prickling at the back of her neck.

'What's the matter? Where are you going, Kate?'

Kate twisted round in her seat, her face pale in the fading light. 'I've decided to take a voluntary job – for two years initially – in Sudan.'

'When are you... when will you have to leave?'

'Not until August. Don't be too upset, Faith. I really want to do this. I'll write to you as often as I can, I promise. And, when I come home, I'll have so much to tell you.'

Faith closed her eyes. A fist of pain tightened around her heart. So Kate really was going. And much further away than Cheltenham. The pink teddy bear slid to the floor. She didn't bother to pick it up

* * *

From her bedroom window Faith saw her father loading suitcases into Kate's car. For some reason, the thought that she would never again see the old blue Mini parked in its place under the trees made her want to cry. She clenched her jaw, trying to whip up the anger that had sustained her after her mother's disappearance; anger which, in the last few months, had been directed at Kate. Mentally, she itemised the grudges she had nurtured for so long, but she was unable to invoke the usual hostility. Kate's smile. The warmth of Kate's arms around her. Kate's voice – *I love you. You and Hope* – kept imposing themselves on her memory. She chewed the skin around her thumb nail. If only she hadn't destroyed her mother's phone number. It had been a wicked thing to do. And she had been so unkind to Kate. Now God was punishing her. He was taking Kate away.

A door banged downstairs. She heard her father's voice.

'Faith, Kate's going in a minute.'

'No!' She couldn't bear it. Still in her pyjamas, she raced to the top of the stairs. Kate was in the hall, twisting a key off a silver key ring. The front door was open.

'Kate. Wait please.'

Kate looked up. Her mouth quivered in a strange lopsided smile. 'Good morning. I was hoping I would see you before I left.'

'Don't go. Please, Kate, don't go away. I'm sorry I've been so horrible to you.' Faith choked on the words. She ran down the stairs, bare feet slipping on the carpet, heels catching on the hem of her pyjama trousers, and fell into Kate's outstretched arms.

'Please, Kate. Please don't leave us.'

Kate held her, smoothing the hair back from her face. 'I have to go, Faith. I leave England at the end of the month. That only gives me two weeks to move into the flat in Cheltenham, and then I have to find an estate agent to rent the place out.'

'But I don't want you to go. Please, Kate. Please stay.'

Kate was crying now. 'Oh, my darling, I wish I could. But I can't let everyone down. People are relying on me.'

'*We* rely on you.' Faith wiped her nose on the back of her hand. She could feel the sadness swelling within her, thick and heavy, forming shadows in her mind. Her sobs grew louder.

'What's all this fuss, Minnie?' Her father emerged from the study.

She lifted her head, willing him to make everything all right. It didn't work. His expression was stern.

'Don't make this any harder, Minnie. Kate will write and she'll telephone us sometimes, I'm sure.'

'But it won't be the same.' Faith tightened her hold around Kate's waist.

Her father cleared his throat noisily. 'That's enough. Let go, Faith. You're being unreasonable. Kate can't change her plans, not even for you.'

She ignored his words, pressing herself closer to Kate; already lonely, already imagining a future without her. Outside, the church clock struck the half hour.

The front door slammed in a sudden draught. Hope toddled out of the kitchen followed by a grey-haired lady with a tired, lined face.

'Ka.' The little girl's face dimpled with delight. 'Ka.' she repeated, raising her arms for Kate to lift her up.

Faith released Kate with a whimper. She stepped aside, shrugging off the sting of jealousy. She envied Hope's prettiness – the wispy blonde curls, the wide blue eyes and the ready smile that charmed everyone, even the stern-looking Mrs Kemp who had arrived a few days earlier to take Kate's place. But it was her own fault if Kate loved Hope best. She had been deliberately unpleasant, rejecting Kate's friendship, wallowing in her own misery.

Kate gave Hope one last kiss and set her down on the floor. She drew in her breath, straightening her shoulders. 'If I don't go now, I never will. Cheerio you two scallywags. Be good.'

She spoke briskly but Faith noticed there were still tears on her cheeks.

'Goodbye, Richard. Take care.' Kate held out her hand.

He shook it gravely, and then, after a moment's hesitation, pulled her to him and kissed her briefly on the lips.

They went outside. The air was muggy, thick with tiny black flies. Faith watched her father help Kate into the car.

'I think we'll have thunder soon,' he said as he closed the door. 'Drive carefully.'

'I will. Bye.'

They waved as Kate negotiated the potholes in the drive. Then she was gone. All that was left was the cloud of dust churned up by the Mini's wheels and even that was slowly drifting away. Faith didn't move until she could no longer hear the sound of the engine, until the moment of ghastly silence was replaced by birdsong and the distant rhythm of a combine-harvester.

'It's time you got dressed, young lady. You'll catch a chill with no shoes on.' Mrs Kemp spoke sharply.

Faith whirled round. 'So? Who cares?'

'Faith! Don't be rude. Say sorry to Mrs Kemp and do as you're told.'

Her father put a warning hand in the middle of her back, steering her towards the door. But she wasn't prepared to listen. Mrs Kemp wasn't her mother. She wasn't Kate. She was just some stupid, ugly old woman.

'Why should I? I don't like her! She's a fuckin' interfering bitch!' They were Debbie's words, not hers, but they had the desired effect. Mrs Kemp's face crumpled like a punctured football.

Tossing her head defiantly, Faith ran upstairs. Too tense to cry, she lay on her bed, staring out of the window at the mass of thickening clouds. Her whole body ached for Kate. When the storm broke she hardly noticed. Soon there would be no trace of Kate in the house, no hint of her perfume, no scented soap in the bathroom, none of the butterfly cakes she had made yesterday...

Distraught, she heaved herself upright. She padded over to the chest and knelt to rummage through the bottom drawer. Beneath the clutter of long-discarded toys she had stuffed the things she wanted to forget. She pushed aside the framed photograph of her mother and the picture Helena had sent in a birthday card of baby Marcus who nearly died when he was born. Then she slid her hand under the encyclopedia which had revealed the awful truth about Hope, scrabbling with her fingers among the bits of paper that once formed part of her mother's telephone number until she found the small box she was searching for. Inside, on a velvet pad, was a small cross on a delicate silver chain. Kate had given it to her for her birthday. With difficulty she managed to fasten it round her neck. Then, in a frenzy of weeping, she knelt by the bed and begged God to forgive her and to keep Kate safe.

Grace filled the glass with water and swallowed the first of the new tablets the doctor had prescribed. The after-taste was bitter. Wincing, she rubbed the hollow of her back, exhausted after pushing Amy to the surgery and back in the sticky heat.

She pulled the blind down halfway and opened the window to cool the air in the kitchen. Amy was still asleep in the pram. Grace sighed, wishing her daughter would sleep as peacefully at night. She moved about aimlessly, tidying away some of the flutters, opening cupboards, forgetting what she was looking for. Eventually she sat at the table, too weary to make herself anything to eat. The cobwebby mist of depression swirled in her head, draining her energy, reducing her world to a place of shadows.

She no longer expected to hear from Richard. She assumed he had sent her half his inheritance to salve his conscience; to ensure she could survive on her own. And his offer of forgiveness? She pressed her lips together. He must have made that out of duty. She remembered bitterly that his letter hadn't actually asked her to come home.

At first she had been hurt when he didn't call, then worried, and finally resigned. He didn't want her back and neither did Faith. The hope that surfaced after Amy's birth had died, replaced by emptiness. And now everything seemed remote; the longing for her older daughters suppressed by apathy and tranquillisers, any thoughts of the future bleak. Amy was the only good thing in her life. And it took all her willpower to get up in the mornings to look after her.

A sliver of spite embedded itself in her heart. It was Richard's loss. He would never know he had another daughter.

PART TWO
Confessions

CHAPTER 19

September 1992

There was a woodpecker somewhere; the boy could hear its strange, hollow knocking. He took the field glasses his grandfather had given him out of their case and scanned the trees, searching for the tell-tale flash of red. Or perhaps it was a green woodpecker, camouflaged against a lichen-covered tree trunk? His grandfather had taught him about birds as they walked together through the woods and fields on the Dalchett Estate. Now, at thirteen, he spent his spare time watching them, making notes, sketching and, lately, taking photographs with the camera he had saved his pocket money to buy.

He adjusted the focus on the lenses to look further into the distance. There was no sign of the bird. The knocking had ceased. Disappointed, he put the glasses away and continued on down the path, savouring the sharp, spicy scent of the woodland, enjoying the solitude. It still caught him unawares sometimes – how clean the air smelt in the countryside.

His steps faltered. He remembered the smell of the last squat so distinctly he could almost taste it on his tongue. He used to stink of it – the reek of unwashed bodies, vomit and drugs. The kids at primary school had called him names: scumbag, pongo, sewer boy, smackhead. No one wanted to sit near him. More often than not he had refused to go to school, sleeping away the days in one of the flea-ridden bedrooms or wandering round the city thieving chocolate bars to appease his hunger.

The social workers had put him in a home once – a nice, clean, well-ordered place –but his mother had lied to get him back, promising they would live with her parents. For a while they had stayed with Gran and Grandad in their cottage. That had been the best time in his early life, those few months when he attended the village school, his hair shiny and free of lice; his new clothes always washed and ironed; his skinny frame beginning to fill out as a result of eating his grandmother's wholesome meals. But in the end they had had returned to the foul-mouthed Rick and yet another half-derelict house. His mother had deceived everyone, especially Gran and Grandad. If his grandfather had discovered where they were living, had seen the filth and degradation, he would have been appalled. As it was, Grandad would blame himself for the rest of his life because he hadn't realised the truth until it was too late.

The boy inhaled deeply. The dim light in the woods was stirring up the murky memories – his mother clinging to him, crying, desperate for another fix; his mother stony-eyed and distant; his mother and Rick rolling on the floor; his mother dead under the pile of ragged sheets...

He could feel the pain rising in his chest. It was hard to breathe. He stood still, sweat cold on his skin, waiting for the panic to pass, as he knew it would if he didn't give way to it. To distract himself he took out the field glasses again and trained them on the undergrowth, looking for deer.

As he grew calmer, he became aware of an unfamiliar noise. A strange, thin wailing, not quite human. He began to move stealthily along the path. He wasn't afraid, of course, but his heart was pumping madly, and when a twig snapped beneath his feet he froze, remaining in the shadows until he was sure nothing had been disturbed.

He saw her when he came to the wooden bridge; a thin, blonde girl, a little younger than himself, sitting on the bank at the edge of the lake, arms outstretched, long hair stirring in the breeze. She was gazing across the water, talking in a tormented, high-pitched whine. He recognised her at once. She was Hope Lawson, old Mrs Calthorpe's granddaughter. He had seen her several times since he came to live with his grandparents, but overcome by shyness he had always stayed out of sight, even when she visited the cottage. He had never seen her alone before.

'Father. My father, king of the sea, only call my name and I will come home to thee.'

Her words made no sense. Curious, he moved closer, keeping behind the trees. As he watched, she turned, eyes wild, and spoke as though to someone at her side.

'I beg you, let me go back to my own. I cannot stay here. My heart yearns for my father's kingdom.'

He could see tears on her cheeks and he wondered what could have made her so unhappy.

Graceful as a dancer she sprang to her feet, the skirt of her summer dress swirling round her knees. 'My children, forgive me. I must leave you and return from whence I came. You—' A frown puckered her forehead.

'Who's there?' Her eyes lost their haunted look.

Sheepishly he stepped forward. He felt a flush of heat spread across his face and neck. The girl's cheeks were scarlet too.

'Are you spying on me?'

Half a dozen thoughts slithered through his mind. He had been spying on her, sort of. What was he going to say to her? Were his face and hands clean? Why was he wearing his oldest shirt and jeans?

'Well, are you?' She glared at him. There was no sign of tears now.

'No. I... I heard you crying.'

'I wasn't actually crying. I'm practising for a play.' She sounded mollified.

'Sorry. I didn't realise.' He was embarrassed for her. 'I'm Russell Holmes by the way.'

'I know. I've seen your photograph at your grandfather's cottage.'

'It's an awful picture, isn't it?' He grinned nervously and thought he saw the hint of a smile on her lips.

'Do you know who I am?'

'You're Hope. Mrs Calthorpe's granddaughter. I've seen you around.'

'I've never seen you.'

She stared at him and he cringed, imagining himself through her eyes – tall and gawky, crinkly brown hair fluffed up by the breeze, shabby clothes. He scuffed his shoes on the grass. 'You belong up at the big house. Grandad's always telling me not to bother the Calthorpes and to mind my own business.'

'I don't belong to the big house. I live at the rectory in Tuston. But you probably know that already. So, is this something you do often? Spy on me.'

He rubbed his hands on the seat of his jeans. 'I don't spy on you. It's just that you're always with someone else and I'm not very good at talking to people.'

He saw her features soften. She appeared to be assessing him. 'So what are you doing now?'

He fingered the field glasses. 'It's okay, honestly. They're only for watching birds. The feathered ones, I mean.'

'I believe you. Thousands wouldn't.' She tossed her hair back over her shoulders.

'What about you? I've never seen you here before?'

'I wanted to be on my own. My cousin, Marcus, is visiting with Aunt Helena. He's eleven but he's so childish at times. I just needed to get away. Does that sound horrible?'

He shook his head, fascinated by the changing expressions on her face.

'Marcus isn't supposed to run around much and walking up hills makes him out of breath.'

'That's a shame.' He didn't know what else to say. His brain seemed to have slowed down. She would think he was stupid. Any minute now she would go away and he might never have the courage to speak to her again. He stuck his hands in his pockets and narrowed his eyes against the sun, watching the breeze skid over the surface of the water and the little waves rippling into a million sparkling points.

That was when he caught sight of it, a flash of metallic blue. Without thinking, he grabbed her arm. 'Look! Over there.' He pointed to the right, beneath the trees.

'What?' She shrugged his hand away, a note of alarm in her voice.

'Sorry,' He handed the field glasses to her. 'It's a kingfisher. You're lucky to see one.'

She followed the bird with the glasses as it veered in its flight to settle on an overhanging branch.

'It's beautiful,' she said, 'like a jewel.'

The bird was almost too far away to see with the naked eye. He was longing to observe it more closely, but it gave him an odd little sensation of pleasure to see her so absorbed.

'If we stay quiet we may see it dive for food.' He was standing so close he could smell the soapy fragrance on her skin.

'What does it eat?'

'Sticklebacks and minnows mainly. Any small fish it can find.'

They remained without moving for a few seconds but, as if it sensed they were watching, the bird opened its wings and flew upwards, disappearing into the tree tops.

With a sigh, she handed the glasses back to him.

'That was amazing.'

'Yes. There's a pair of them here somewhere. Maybe even young.'

'Do they nest in the woods?' She was surveying the trees with keen eyes.

'No. They make a tunnel in the bank, above the waterline.'

'Shall we walk along and look for it?'

'If you like.' His heart leapt with joy.

They didn't find the kingfisher's nest. But it didn't matter. For a while they looked and then abandoned the search to amble along the pathway side by side. Hope found herself enjoying his company. He told her he often came down to the lake to sketch the water birds. They chatted easily, light-hearted banter at first, and then more seriously, touching on shades of the past. They walked all the way round the lake, past the reed beds on the far side, over the stepping stones where a stream ran into the valley, through more woods and across another bridge – little more than two planks spanning the brook which rushed down the hillside – and finally they arrived at the grassy promontory where the back of the house was visible at the top of the rise. Hope glanced up at the building. The walk had taken them at least an hour. It was probably quite late. Time for afternoon tea.

She didn't want to be seen with Russell Holmes. Not that anyone would object but because she wanted to keep their encounter a secret. She wanted to be able to meet him again, as often as possible, and she didn't want to share his company with Marcus or Faith or even her father. She hesitated. 'I think I'd better go this way. Dad will be wondering where I am.'

'I'll walk with you,' Russell offered.

'I'd rather you didn't. Someone might see us.'

'Will you get into trouble for being with me?'

'No,' she realised she had hurt him. 'I just think it would be fun if no one knows about us. We could do what we liked then, without any awkward questions.'

'So you want us to meet again?'

'Yes. I want to see your sketches and I want you to teach me about birds. And I want to learn how to fish and to follow animal tracks. You know such a lot of things.'

He beamed. 'When will you be over next?'

She pulled a face. 'Next Saturday. Grandma Ivy's organising a garden party to raise money for the church. I'll meet you in the same place as today. About three o'clock.'

'I'll be there.'

'Good.' She didn't want to be the first to leave, to break the spell. But he didn't move.

'Bye.' Reluctantly, she started to make her way up the slope. She turned once and saw him watching her.

Holmes was hurrying down the passageway when she let herself into the back of the house.

'They're taking tea in the garden room, Miss Hope. Mrs Calthorpe thought it was too breezy to sit outside.'

'Thank you,' she smiled, seeing him differently now; noticing his eyes were the same clear grey as his grandson's. He followed her into the sunlit room.

'You rang, madam?' He waited by the door.

'Yes, Holmes. Could we have more tea? I'm afraid this has gone quite cold.'

Hope was disconcerted. Did her grandmother always sound so haughty? Did Holmes *mind* the way she spoke to him?

'Certainly, madam.' He collected the dirty cups, stacking them on a tray with the teapot and jugs. Hope took advantage of his presence to slip onto a seat by the window. There was a small silence after Holmes left the room. Hope pushed the toe of her sandal into a piece of threadbare carpet, sensing disapproval.

'Where have you been, young lady?' Her father spoke quietly but she could tell he was angry. It didn't take much to make him cross with her.

'I was down by the lake. I forgot the time. I'm sorry.' She heard Marcus cough and felt guilty.

'It isn't me you should be apologising to.'

'Sorry, Grandma,' Hope responded dutifully, avoiding her grandmother's steely glare.

Helena interrupted tactfully. 'Now you *are* here, Hope, would you like to pass the plates around?'

'Of course, Aunt Helena.' Hope stood up, anxious to redeem herself. She was glad to hear normal conversation resume: her grandmother wondering whether Holmes had gone to China to find the tea, Faith telling Aunt Helena about some book that had just been published, her father asking Marcus how many more weeks before he returned to boarding school. When Holmes returned she sat by the window again, nibbling a cucumber sandwich and gazing out over the lawns to where the lake lay hidden in the hollow of the land.

After tea she followed Marcus into the garden, determined to be extra nice to him. She suggested playing croquet, and as neither of them had more than a vague idea of the rules, the game soon degenerated into farce. Marcus's serious, heavy-jowled face relaxed into smiles, revealing the dimples in his fleshy cheeks. He looked up triumphantly after hitting the ball with a hefty thwack. 'How's that?'

The ball sailed across the lawn and into a rose bed. Hope watched him trying to avoid the thorns as he tried to retrieve it. He came back rubbing his arms ruefully.

'Trust me.'

'He's a good sport,' she thought, with a stab of remorse for ignoring him earlier.

'Will this do?' Richard dragged two cast-iron chairs along the terrace, siting them closer to the house, out of the warm, restless breeze.

'Lovely.' Helena sat down, pushing her hands through her hair and lifting her face to the sun. 'I hope

Ivy doesn't mind us coming out here but I was longing for some fresh air.'

'I've a sneaky feeling she'll be glad of half an hour's rest. And Faith wanted to research something in the library, so I'm sure we won't be missed.' He settled down beside her companionably.

Minutes passed and neither of them spoke, content to savour the sunlight and the fragrance of the honeysuckle on the wall behind them. Richard leaned back, letting the heat soothe his tension. The sound of children's laughter seemed a long way away.

'Richard, can I ask you something?' Helena's voice was husky.

He turned towards her drowsily. Her dark eyes were lustrous, scrutinising his face. As usual, he was aware of her quiet attraction. If only they had met in another time, another place. He could have loved her and she would have loved him. They both knew that.

'Of course. What's on your mind?' He took her hand, keeping it in his own resting on her lap.

'What are your views on divorce?'

'I've nothing against it, Helena. If a marriage has broken down irretrievably then sometimes it seems the only sensible choice.

'Why didn't you? Get a divorce, I mean.'

'I don't know. I guess it was because I took my marriage vows in church and I'm old-fashioned in my ideas.'

'Then you *do* believe divorce is wrong?'

'No. Only perhaps for myself. For others it can be a blessing.'

'What about for me?'

'For you especially.' He tightened his hold on her hand. 'So, is there someone else?' It was hard to ignore the little niggle of jealousy that taunted him.

'Possibly. It's early days yet. I just wanted to know how you felt before I even contemplate the idea.'

'Whoever gets you, Helena, will be a lucky man,' he said.

Her face was suddenly beautiful as she smiled at him, and he thought what a fool his brother was to let her go.

They remained together, talking quietly, for half an hour or so before they were joined by Hope and Marcus, both in high-spirits and oblivious to any hints that their presence was unwelcome. However their levity was infectious. In spite of his strange mood, Richard was amused by their anecdotes and innocent humour. He was pleased to see Marcus looking so well. The boy's skin had a healthy glow and his eyes, beneath the tousled black hair, were bright with mischief. Helena's son was a fighter he thought with approval.

No one wanted to go indoors. The breeze had dropped and it was pleasant on the terrace. The house would be cold in comparison.

Helena glanced at her watch. 'It's nearly half past six. I'd better go and get changed.' She stood up, yawning. 'Time for your medicine, Marcus. We'll see you later, Richard.'

'I'll stay out a while longer.' Richard stretched his legs, contemplating the evening with irritation. His mother had invited the Gaskells for a meal. It wasn't that he didn't like the Gaskells, and he was certainly pleased his mother hadn't given up the little dinner parties she so enjoyed, but... He closed his eyes. The conversation with Helena had left him faintly depressed.

'I'll get ready too, Daddy.'

He had forgotten Hope was there.

At dinner he found himself abstracted, reflecting on his life, wondering why it was he felt bound to a woman he hadn't seen for over twelve years, a woman who had cheated on him and left him to bring up two young children on his own. And he wasn't doing a very good job of that. His elder daughter was toying with her food, her face red, wine glass empty for the third time. She had wanted to go into Hereford with Debbie, and he knew she was hating every minute spent at the table with people either too old or too young to have much in common with her. Lately, her weekend visits from university in Cardiff had been more frequent, and he was aware she had been seeing Debbie's brother, a young man of twenty-seven with a powerful motorbike and a dubious reputation. It was something he had meant to discuss with Helena – his daughter's wayward behaviour – until the talk of divorce wiped the subject from his mind. He was finding it difficult to cope with Faith's unpredictable temper. Since living away from home she had changed. She wore her skirts far too short, put too much make-up round her eyes and her hair was long and untidy, with straggly plaits woven into it. He hardly recognised her any more

And his other daughter? She was an enigma – clever, secretive, obstinate, and a constant reminder of his brother. It was hard to forget whose child she was. Perhaps he didn't always give her the love she needed but God knows he tried.

While coffee was being served, he slipped outside to the terrace. Bats were swooping over the lawn, and there were owls in the woods, their cries eerie in the gathering darkness. In the west, the last of the light was fading above the black line of the mountains. He could feel the melancholy settling on his shoulders.

'Daddy.'

Hope was standing in the doorway.

'What?'

'Grandma says your coffee's getting cold.'

'Tell her I'll be there in a minute.' He spoke sharply, annoyed at being disturbed.

His daughter turned and ran into the house, leaving him alone in the dusk, feeling guilty and small-minded.

* * *

It was nearly midnight. In the rectory Hope lay in bed listening to the raised voices downstairs. She couldn't hear what her father was saying, but she knew he was furious because Faith had drunk too much wine at the dinner party, making what he called *a spectacle* of herself. She wasn't quite sure what he meant. Faith hadn't done anything dreadful; she hadn't fallen over or made herself sick or knocked something flying across the table. She had been bright-eyed and talkative but no one seemed to mind. In fact, her opinions had livened up the evening.

After a few minutes she heard Faith run up the stairs and a bedroom door slam. Then there were more noises – lights clicking off, the scrape of a bolt being pushed into place, her father's footsteps on the landing. She waited, holding her breath, but he didn't come to see her.

Switching off the lamp, she turned on to her side, staring out of the window at the blue-black sky. She hated it when no one came to wish her goodnight. It made her feel lonely. She longed for the nights when Mrs Kemp used to tuck her into bed. Bedtimes had been cosy then. And she had a hazy memory of Kate's warm hugs, though the figure in her mind was recreated from pictures in an old photograph album.

Sighing, she closed her eyes and relived her meeting with Russell Holmes. It had been mortifying to be discovered talking to herself. She hadn't dared admit that this was something she often did – make up plays to fill the solitary hours. She wished she hadn't lied though. He had been so easy to talk to, and he would probably have understood anyway. It was amazing the things she had told him. She had spoken about her longing to find her mother, about the bullies at school and about the way she felt left out when Faith was with

Emily and Deb. She had even told him how strict her father was and how he could be unfair sometimes.

And then Russell had confided in her. She tried to imagine his life in the squat and how it would feel to find your mother dead, killed by the drugs she had taken. It made her own problems seem nothing in comparison.

CHAPTER 20

The beach was almost deserted, and above the low cliffs the old town of Albufeira shimmered in the midday heat. It was the end of the holiday season. Many of the gift stalls that lined the cobbled streets had closed, and though the bars still pumped out music, most of them were empty.

Grace and Cassie lay sprawled on beach towels, their bodies moulded into the soft sand. The smell of grilled sardines drifted across from the hotel terrace behind them where a few late holiday makers were dining alfresco in the unexpectedly warm October sunshine.

Cassie stretched and rolled on to her side. 'What's the matter with Amy? She's been very quiet the last couple of days.'

'I'm not sure.' Grace lifted her head, resting on her elbows. Amy was sitting apart from them, shoulders hunched, her expression hidden by large tortoiseshell-framed sunglasses. 'She's at a funny age. She has these strange moods sometimes.'

'Does she? She usually seems so sunny and well-balanced.' Cassie made patterns in the sand with a polished fingernail.

'Not always. She has her moments, like all kids.' Grace glanced at Amy again. There was a vulnerability about the skinny adolescent body, despite the tan and the boldly striped bikini.

'There's something you're not telling me, isn't there? Is it to do with Alex?' Cassie asked quietly.

Grace felt the flush spreading across her cheeks. 'I can't keep anything from you, can I, Cass?'

Cassie grinned. 'Nope.'

'Still the same old Cassie.' Grace found herself grinning back.

Cassie had scarcely altered over the years; her face was a little plumper, the contours not so well defined, and she had the hint of a double chin, but her hair was still a defiant bleached blonde and, if her curves were slightly more voluptuous, the extra weight suited her. In comparison Grace felt scrawny and insipid.

'So?' Cassie prompted.

'I don't want to bother you with my problems. You and Lance have enough to do if you want the new bar to be open for Christmas. Amy and I shouldn't have come out this half-term.'

'Rubbish!' Cassie sat up and swept her hair back from her face. 'I depend on you. It gives me an excuse to have a rest. So come on, tell Auntie Cass what's wrong.'

'I don't know that anything *is* wrong.' Grace pushed herself upright, edging a little closer to her friend and lowering her voice. 'But remember I mentioned on the phone that I was thinking about asking Alex to come and live with us...'

Cassie nodded.

'Well, I don't think Amy's keen on the idea.'

'She could be jealous. She's never had to compete for your attention before.'

Grace was not convinced. 'What should I do, Cass? I don't want to make her unhappy.'

Cassie frowned. 'How many years have you been on your own?'

'Over twelve. I've had a few dates, that's all. Nothing serious.'

'And you want to live with Alex?'

'I think so. At least I'd like to give it a go.'

Cassie sifted sand through her fingers. 'Perhaps you should ask him, Grace. Amy's eleven years old. She can handle it. She may not like it at first. In fact she won't – she's been the only person in your life for such a long time – but she'll get used to it.'

'You reckon?'

'Yes, I do. And I also reckon it's time you forgave yourself for the past. You made mistakes, Grace, but you've paid for them ten times over. You've devoted your life to Amy. You've worked hard to become manager of that travel agents. Isn't it time to think about yourself now?'

'But I owe such a lot to Richard – the money and everything. It's my duty to put his daughter first.'

'The daughter he doesn't even know he has?' Cassie's voice was soft.

Grace ignored the comment. This was dangerous ground, something she and Cassie had never agreed on. She spoke instead to Amy. 'You okay, sweetheart?'

'Yes thanks.' The curt answer didn't reassure her.

'Is he worth the hassle, this Alex?' Cassie raised an eyebrow. 'Are you in love with him?'

'Very much. He's the best thing that's happened to me in years. He's handsome and clever and generous. He makes me laugh. He's kind—'

'And he helps old ladies across the road,' Cassie laughed. 'When do I get to meet him?'

'Next time you come to stay, I hope.'

Cassie was suddenly serious. 'Be careful, Grace. You said his wife left him after they'd only been married a year and he hasn't long broken up from another girlfriend. Are you sure he's ready to settle down?'

'He says that's all he really wants. He runs a successful business, he's got a lovely flat and a big car, but he's tired of playing the field, tired of women trying to take him for what they can get.'

'Will you marry him?'

'No. He knows I won't do that.'

'Because?'

'Because I'm not free. I don't want to upset Richard... or Faith and Hope.' They were there, always there, in the back of her mind.

'And if Richard wanted a divorce?'

'That would be different.'

'What if he wanted you back?'

'He doesn't. In all these years he's made no effort to find me. I've accepted that. Don't rake it all up again, Cass.'

For a moment there was tension between them, then Cassie smiled. 'Let's get something to eat. I'm starving.' She knelt on her towel and wrapped a pink, silky sarong round her waist, knotting it neatly.

Grace stood up, brushing the sand from her legs before pulling a skirt over her swimsuit. She patted her daughter's shoulder. 'Come on, Little Miss Moody. We're going to lunch.'

Amy stood up, taking off her sunglasses and dropping them into the beach bag by her feet. Grace's thoughts were touched with sadness. Amy wasn't a child any more. And she was so pretty; not classically beautiful – her mouth was too full and her nose had a slight bump in the middle – but her eyes were arresting, deep brown like her father's, her cheek bones high, and her hair, no longer jet black, framed her face perfectly, falling in loose dark curls to her shoulders. Although she was thin and not very tall for her age, her legs were shapely and her breasts already well formed. She had a loving nature and a generous spirit. She was a daughter Richard would be proud of.

'What d'you fancy? Your choice, sweetheart.' Grace made another attempt at conciliation.

Amy began to pick up her belongings. 'I'm not bothered,' she said, with a shrug of her shoulders.

* * *

The streets were swarming with black-coated youngsters making their way home after school. Amongst the tide of students, a cluster of younger girls straggled down the hill towards the city centre, their voices growing shrill as they tried to outdo one another with snippets of gossip. Hope was at the edge of this group, trailing in their wake. She had no special friends and no interest in the raucous conversation. These girls tolerated her. With them she felt less exposed.

'Cheer up, Hope, it may never happen.' One of them nudged her playfully.

She forced herself to smile. It had happened already. It happened every day, and there was nothing to smile about. Her cheeks grew hot with remembered humiliation. This afternoon, in the creative dance lesson, Vanessa Greaves had deliberately barged into her, sending her sprawling to the floor. She had lain winded, knees and elbows stinging, while the other girls tittered at her clumsiness and Vanessa whirled away, hazel eyes gleaming with malice. Yesterday her sandwiches had been ruined when Vanessa tipped a jug of water into her lunch box, and the day before Vanessa had stamped on her fountain pen when it rolled off the desk, and the day before that...

Hope stared at the pavement unhappily. She was afraid of Vanessa Greaves. Afraid and jealous. Part of her longed to be as spirited and confident as the other girl. Vanessa was attractive – tall, with a long mane of tawny-brown hair and clear skin, the colour of pale honey. Her eyes were wide, almond-shaped, deceptively innocent. But there was something intimidating about her. She chose her friends, singled out her enemies, ruled her peer-group like a queen bee; always the most fashionable, the first in the queue, the one the others didn't want to upset.

'Why aren't you on the school bus?'

Hope was startled by Li's question. 'I've got some stuff to get,' she said, alarmed to hear her voice sounding sharp and unfriendly. Li was just trying to be sociable. She sighed, wishing she could conquer her shyness and make friends.

In the town the girls separated, some to catch buses to outlying villages, several to wander round the shops, others to make their way home on foot.

'Bye.' Hope touched Li's arm.

The other girl ignored her. Mortified, Hope darted up the narrow alley which led to the cathedral. In the corner cafe she ordered a banana milkshake and sat at one of the small tables contemplating her life. She would be thirteen in two weeks. Her body was changing, her emotions were volatile, her hormones all over the place. There was no one she could ask for advice. Her father wouldn't understand, her mother wasn't around, and Faith had no time for her. And at school she was insignificant, a nobody.

She stirred the plastic straw round, making patterns in the froth like she used to as a child. But she wasn't a child any more. She had to stand on her own two feet, look out for herself.

'Hi.'

'Hiya, Russ.' She hadn't seen him come in. He looked windswept. He must have cycled from his school which was on the other side of the city. He dropped his school bag beneath the seat opposite her and went to order a drink. She watched him delve into his pockets for the right change, saw him counting the coins carefully before he handed them over to the girl behind the counter. His hair was longer she noticed. His blazer seemed too big for his angular frame yet the sleeves were short, exposing thin, bony wrists. He stooped a little, head bent forward, and she could see the flush of embarrassment creeping round the back of his neck. She smiled with affection. He was as insecure as she was; a misfit, an underdog. Was that why there was such a bond between them?

'You at choir practice tonight then?' He sat down, wiping the base of his glass with a serviette before putting it on the table.

'Yup.'

He shook his head with mock gravity and she giggled. She didn't feel in the least bit guilty about deceiving her father. He never took much interest in what she did anyway. She stayed for choir practice after school on some Wednesdays, on others she met Russell. She didn't lie about it. She just let her father believe what he wanted to believe.

'You'll never go to heaven,' Russell said with his funny lopsided grin.

'Probably not,' she agreed.

'So,' his grin faded, 'how's school?'

She told him. All the hurtful things, the sarcasm, the mockery. He listened, frowning, his long fingers playing with the salt cellar.

'You should tell someone.'

'It would only make things worse. Vanessa would get me back somehow.'

'I guess so.'

He was quiet, thinking. Then he pushed the salt cellar away. 'Whatever you do, you mustn't let them break your spirit, Hope. Those girls are scum. You're worth fifty of them.'

She grimaced, unconvinced.

'Okay. Tell me something good about today,' he said, changing the mood.

'Meeting you.'

'No. I mean at school. Something good must have happened, surely?'

It was uncanny. He always made her feel better.

'We were studying *The Merchant of Venice* in English this morning and Mr Morgan asked me to read the part of Portia.'

'And?'

'He said "well done".' She recalled her small triumph. It had been so much more than just the teacher's emphatic praise. While she was reading the whole class had stayed silent, listening to her, hanging on to every word. She had them spellbound – all of them, even Vanessa Greaves. When she finished there had been a moment of silence before the classroom became normal again, filled with rustles, whispers, and the creaking of chairs. For a few minutes she had been empowered.

Russell's eyes widened. 'You weren't fazed at having to read in front of the whole class?'

'Not at all. It's as if I'm a different person when I'm acting. I forget about everything else.'

'Why don't you pretend to be someone else when Vanessa and her mates get on at you?'

She shook her head. 'It wouldn't work. Because then I'm just me.'

Once more he endeavoured to cheer her. He soon had her laughing with an account of how he had been sent off the football pitch in a games lesson for not paying attention.

'There was a kestrel hovering at the side of the field. I admit I took my eye off the ball quite a bit. A ball or a bird? I know which I find the most interesting. Anyway, I only let in three goals.'

She didn't ask him about afterwards, when he would have been the butt of some cruel remarks from the other boys. Instead she told him about the arguments caused by Faith's continuing friendship with Wayne Saunders, about the bats her father had discovered in the church roof, and about the birthday party her grandmother wanted to organise for her.

'She wanted me to invite some of my friends. But I told her I was too old for parties. I really don't want anyone at school to know about Dalchett House, Russ. They think I'm too posh anyway because my dad's a vicar.'

Time passed quickly. Waitresses began to stack chairs and wipe the tables. Outside the sky was black, the alley illuminated by lights from the shops.

Hope looked at her watch. 'It's nearly six o'clock. I'll have to go.'

'Me too. Grandad worries when I cycle home in the dark.'

He walked with her to the bus stop, wheeling his bike with one hand. The bus was ready to leave, the engine running.

'See you.' Hope jumped on board. She handed her ticket to the driver and the bus pulled away before she had a chance to wave goodbye.

The casserole was beginning to smell burnt. Richard opened the oven door and steam blasted him in the face. He reached for the oven gloves and took out the heavy dish, putting it on the work top. After waiting a few minutes he lifted the lid. He had just about saved their evening meal, providing Hope wasn't too much longer. He paced the kitchen irritably. Everything was ready. The least she could do was be here to eat it.

The clock in the hall chimed half past six. It sounded loud in the empty house. He went into the lounge to look out of the window. There was no sign of Hope. Anxiety flickered at the back of his mind.

He pressed his forehead against the glass, heavy with regret, wondering if Grace missed her children. After she left, he had spent weeks trying to trace her, sick with worry, until he finally accepted she didn't want to be found. But could he have done more? Even now he questioned himself. Had he really wanted Grace to come home? Or had his growing feelings for Kate affected his decisions?

He turned away from the window. Kate's letter was lying on the coffee table. He picked it up and read it again, in case there was something he had missed, some trace of the old Kate. It was impersonal; a letter to an acquaintance informing him she was well, asking after Faith and Hope, describing her work, drawing his attention to the desperate need for medicines and money.

He tried to picture the beautiful young woman he remembered; picture her living with poverty and disease, working in conditions of famine and war. She had been home only once and then just for a few weeks to sort out some financial problems. That had been four years ago. At the time she had hardly changed in appearance. She was thinner of course, her skin bronzed, her hair dry and flyaway, bleached by the sun. But she had been different. There had been no animation in her eyes and her smile, when it came, was tentative, as if she felt it wrong to experience happiness.

Richard put the letter down. It made him feel a failure. Why did all the women in his life desert him? First Grace, then Kate. Even Helena had a new man. Faith was away most of the time and Hope...

He heard the back door slam and hurried into the hall. Hope was already shedding her school coat, smoothing her long hair with her fingers. He was ridiculously pleased to see her. It was moments like these when he knew he loved her, knew she was woven inextricably into the fabric of his life.

'I hope you're hungry.' He fought to control his emotions. 'I've made enough chicken casserole to feed an army.'

She looked up and he saw the relief on her face. She had expected him to be angry.

CHAPTER 21

It was like stepping into another world. The clamour of voices was too loud, the lights too bright, the sound of footsteps deafening. Kate gripped the handles of the trolley. It was New Year's Eve and there were hundreds of people in the Arrivals Hall, waiting for friends or family, surging forward ready to give and receive hugs, waving balloons and placards, shouting, singing, laughing. She had forgotten all this. The ramshackle airport at Khartoum had been chaotic, bodies pressed together in heaving queues, but Noah had been there, easing a way through for her, his black face set in a fixed, polite smile. She had hardly been in a state to notice the confusion. It was only the final, tearful goodbye that had registered in her exhausted mind.

And now she was here. Heathrow. England. Home. Yet she felt like an alien. She stood bewildered among the cheerful, reunited groups. What did she have to do? Where should she go? Maybe she could get a taxi to take her back to Cheltenham?

Her thoughts were fractured, slipping away before she could latch on to them. She willed herself forward, stopping every so often to lean on the unwieldy trolley, waiting for the spinning in her head to slow down. If she could only make it outside, breathe in some cold air, she would feel better.

She could see the automatic doors, and beyond them, the sprawl of airport buildings against the disturbed, lead-coloured sky. The crowds were thinning. The expanse of floor grew wider, rising up like a billowing blanket.

'Steady on!' An elderly man grabbed her before she could fall. 'Come and sit down for a while, lassie. You look all in.'

He took command of the trolley and led her to a row of seats. 'Will you be all right? Would you like me to ask someone to help you?'

'No!' Kate was alarmed. 'No, thank you. I'll be fine in a few minutes.'

'Well, if you're sure.' He seemed relieved and shambled away to join his wife.

Kate closed her eyes. It had been a mistake to come back. What was there for her here? A few friends in Cheltenham whose lives had moved on without her. And Richard.

The telephone rang and rang. Faith picked up the receiver, glowering at her reflection in the hall mirror. She had better things to do than answer her father's calls. She needed to wash her hair for tonight and iron her new dress which was still folded in its bag.

'Tuston Rectory.'

There was a crackle on the line and the murmur of people talking. She could hear an announcement in the background as if the caller was in a supermarket or a railway station. Then an intake of breath. It was probably some nutter, half drunk. She was about to put the phone down.

'Faith?' It was a little choking sound.

'Yes.'

Silence.

'Who is it? Can I help you?' she asked.

'It's Kate.'

There was a rapid beeping and the clatter of money falling into a coin box. Faith covered the mouthpiece with her fingers. 'Dad. Come quick! It's Kate. She's on a pay phone.'

Her father came out of the kitchen, rubbing his wet hands on his jeans. He took the phone from her. 'Kate. What's the matter? Where are you?'

Faith stood behind him, trying to piece together the gist of the conversation from his words.

'Kate, don't cry. Listen. Stay where you are. I'll be as quick as I can. It's not a problem. Don't worry. Go and get something to eat. I'll be about four hours. Kate? Kate? Are you still there?'

He put the receiver down and Faith saw his hands were shaking.

'What's wrong, Dad?'

'I don't know. She's in London. At the airport. I'm going to fetch her. If you go out later you'll have to find someone to look after Hope.' He was already pulling on his anorak.

'That's okay, Dad. I'll drop her off at Em's.'

'Right.' He frowned. 'Car keys?'

'I'll get them.'

She went into the lounge. Her sister was lying on the sofa watching television in the gathering dusk.

'Dad's got to go out. Kate's back.' Faith switched on the light.

'Kate?' Hope sat upright. 'Where is she?'

'In London. He's going to get her.'

'Can I go with him?'

Faith hesitated. Kate had sounded really strange. 'I think it would be better if he went by himself.'

Hope huddled back against the cushions, excitement fading from her eyes.

Richard put his head round the door. 'Bye girls. See you later.'

Faith handed him the keys and followed him to the front door. She watched him run across the path. He climbed into the car without looking round and roared off, tyres spraying muddy water in his wake as they churned up the puddles.

It took three and a half hours to reach the airport, and another thirty minutes to park, make enquiries, and catch the bus to the right terminal. Inside the Arrivals Hall he scanned the mass of people swarming round the shops and bars. He walked swiftly, the length of the building and back again, beginning to panic, wondering if Kate hadn't waited. He found her eventually, asleep on a row of chairs, her head resting on a shabby holdall.

She looked so frail. Her skin was almost transparent, her body scarecrow thin. He pushed the hair back from her face gently. 'Kate. Oh, my dearest Kate.'

She opened her eyes, struggling to sit up. 'Richard. I'm sorry—'

He sat beside her and pulled her to him. 'There's nothing to be sorry about, Kate. I'm just glad you're home.'

She shuddered, crying soundlessly as he held her, tremor after tremor convulsing her skinny frame. When she was calmer he telephoned for a taxi to take them to the car park. She seemed hardly aware of what was happening. Even when the taxi driver helped him lift her into the car she barely opened her eyes. Richard folded his anorak and placed it beneath her head. She was asleep before he fastened the seat belt around her.

The motorway was quiet. He kept to a steady seventy miles per hour, glancing at Kate every now and then, worried by her pallor. Once off the motorway he drove through the vast blackness of the Cotswolds, letting his speed drop to avoid braking at the bends on the winding road. As they approached the outskirts of Gloucester church bells were ringing in the new year. He wound the window down a fraction to listen and Kate stirred, opening her eyes for a moment.

'Happy New Year, Kate,' he said, but he didn't think she heard him.

It was after one o'clock when they arrived at Tuston. There were lights on in the house and both Faith and

Hope appeared in the porch the minute he pulled on to the drive. He carried Kate to the house while Hope held the door open.

'We've built the fire up in the lounge,' she said.

Richard murmured his gratitude, staggering a little as he went up the step, lifting Kate higher in his arms. He settled her on the sofa while Faith brought in the holdall. 'Is this everything?'

He nodded, a remote part of his mind noting with disapproval his daughter's low-cut dress and heavy make-up.

They talked in whispers. Faith made him coffee laced with whisky; Hope filled hot-water bottles and fetched blankets to wrap round Kate. Wearily, he sank into his usual armchair, touched by their thoughtfulness.

'You go to bed now, you're both tired.' He smiled at them. 'I'll stay down here with her. We'll see how she is in the morning.'

They left him and he heard them chattering on their way up the stairs. He got up stiffly to switch off the lamp, and in the firelight Kate seemed to have a little more colour. He stood looking at her for a few moments. Then he bent to kiss her, tasting the salt of her tears on his lips.

CHAPTER 22

Rhys Morgan glanced at his watch. Girls were still filing through the doors of the school hall and already the first three rows of chairs were full. It was going to take a while to audition everyone. He spotted several nubile, Italian-looking beauties who fitted his image of Juliet perfectly. The question was, could any of them act?

He stood on the edge of the stage in a patch of late-afternoon sunlight. Fastened to his clipboard were the sheets of paper he had pinned on the main notice board two weeks ago and on which each young hopeful had signed her name. He fingered the list nervously. This was his first year as head of the English department, and *Romeo and Juliet* would be his first production. He was concerned because the older pupils were embroiled in exams so his choice of actors was restricted to boys and girls of fifteen and younger. That might pose a problem. He wanted to make a good impression, make his mark among the established staff. He couldn't afford to produce something second-rate.

There was a minor disturbance and he saw a group of second-years pushing their way into an empty row of seats. He recognised Vanessa Greaves with her acolytes. Annoyed, he found himself blushing. It wasn't amusing to be fancied by lustful, adolescent schoolgirls. Then again, he thought wryly, he should be flattered that at thirty-six he still had whatever it was that made their little teenage hearts flutter.

He clapped his hands and waited for silence. 'Good afternoon girls. First, I'd like to thank you for coming. I'm pleased to see so many of you interested in Shakespeare. It proves your teachers have been doing something right.'

There was a ripple of laughter after which he continued.

'I'm quite sure that finding our Juliet is going to be a difficult task, so I've asked Miss Spencer and Mrs Lloyd-James to help me.' He turned to the colourless young woman beside him with a smile. 'Miss Spencer has very generously agreed to assist me with this production.'

There was some polite applause.

'And Mrs Lloyd-James has kindly offered to help us choreograph the fight scenes and the dances.' There was a spontaneous cheer and he grinned at the creative dance teacher, struck, as always, by her elegance and dramatic looks. She was a popular ally.

'Okay, girls, let's not waste any more time. I'd like to be finished by five. I know your parents wonder what you get up to after dark.'

More laughter.

'When I call your name I want you to go up to the stage. Miss Spencer will give you the book and the speech is highlighted – Juliet's speech from the balcony as I explained on the notice.'

He took a seat near the back of the hall and Mrs Lloyd-James joined him. Miss Spencer positioned herself at the side of the stage, looking as though she would rather be elsewhere. The auditions began.

By quarter past four he was beginning to despair. Not one girl had come close to his expectations. Most of them were too aware of their own attraction, trying to be sexy and seductive when what he wanted was innocence and passion. Some read the passage as though it was poetry, some as though they were at elocution lessons. There were girls who were too stiff, too self-conscious; girls whose country accent was too strong; girls whose voices did not carry; girls whose reading was monotonous. It was impossible. The whole thing was doomed to failure. He scraped his chair back. 'Right, those of you who have already auditioned may go now, if you wish, and we'll let you know our decision tomorrow. The rest of you take a few minutes rest and we'll continue at half past.'

He eyed the door, longing to slip away for a cup of coffee, but he was promptly surrounded by a group of chattering girls and the fifteen minutes break disappeared. At half past four he ushered the group back to their seats. 'We'll begin now with...' he consulted his list, 'Hope Lawson.'

She had been sitting by the window. From his vantage point at the back he watched her walk up the side aisle, a pale butterfly of a girl. He sighed. She would be much too shy. And then, suddenly alert, he remembered her reading Portia one morning last November, and the way she had made his skin prickle with excitement. She climbed the steps onto the stage and he felt his heart beat a little faster. There was a rude comment from somewhere and he spotted Vanessa Greaves spluttering into her handkerchief.

'Hush, please or go outside,' he said sharply.

The room was quiet again.

Hope Lawson ignored the interruptions. She shook her head when Miss Spencer offered her the book and went to the centre of the apron. Rhys sat upright. Could she do it? She was the right age. Juliet was thirteen. She didn't fit his original picture of the tragic heroine, it was true, but...

She stood with her hands by her sides, her eyes looking into the distance, wide and wistful. Her shoulders drooped, she tilted her head slightly, but there was a tension in her body and immediately he could see the anguish of a young girl in love. She uttered the first words, *Aye me*, though they were more like a sigh. He was captivated from that moment. She had learnt the passage by heart. She said the words so naturally, as if they were her own. 'Romeo, Romeo, wherefore art thou Romeo?' There was longing in her voice, and distress, but she didn't overplay the part; instead she reasoned with herself, speaking slowly, thoughtfully, building the passion little by little. She was so assured, so confident. And he couldn't take his eyes off her. When she finished the silence was almost reverent.

'Thank you, Hope,' he said.

She blushed and hurried down the steps out of the limelight. He was bemused. He had never heard the speech make such absolute sense before. Even professional actresses got it wrong, misinterpreted the words. The girl had a brilliant future ahead of her.

He was aware of a shuffling and he called out the next name on the list. But it was all academic now. There wouldn't be anyone who could hold a candle to Hope Lawson.

CHAPTER 23

Snow had fallen in the night and a layer of white covered the fields around Dalchett House.

'At least it's melting,' Richard said as he steered the car over the narrow bridge. There had been a run of bad winters in the past few years – snow, gales, floods – and the weather had affected him, making him feel old and tired. Had he just been lonely, looking inwards? Why was it that today the snow sparkled with a virginal beauty; that the house in front of him looked like a fine old oil-painting and the grey sky was milky and unthreatening? Was it because Kate was back in his life?

'Whose car is that?' Beside him Hope leaned forward as they came to a halt on the forecourt.

'I've no idea.' Richard eyed the dark blue Mercedes. 'I hope whoever it is doesn't delay lunch. I want to get back to Kate as soon as possible. She looked worse again this morning.'

He frowned. In the five weeks Kate had been with them her health had improved slowly, but there were still days when she was too weak to get out of bed; when her eyes were dull, her face without expression, and her thoughts, if she had any, far away. The doctor had diagnosed extreme nervous exhaustion and malnutrition, prescribing tablets which made her sleepy, often confused. On some days she scarcely spoke at all.

'Do you think she'll be well enough to watch me in the play at the end of March?' Hope asked.

'Can't you think of anyone except yourself?' Richard switched off the ignition, exasperated.

'Sorry.'

He heard the flatness in her voice and regretted his short temper. Why did she always manage to rile him?

'Are you two going to sit there all day?' Faith opened the back door, letting in the raw, damp air. 'I hope Grandma's got coffee on the go.'

Richard watched her trudging across the gravel. She hadn't wanted to come with them but he had insisted. If she was determined to waste her weekends with Wayne Saunders then the very least she could do was visit her grandmother on a Saturday morning.

'Okay?' He raised an eyebrow at Hope and she nodded.

They clambered out and Richard unlocked the boot to collect the flowers he had bought for his mother.

'Dad!'

He heard Faith's footsteps behind him.

'Dad, it must be Uncle Brandon's car. The number plate... it's personalised. His initials.' For an instant she was his little girl again, wide-eyed and frightened. His body tensed.

'What's he doing here after all these years? I hope he hasn't upset your grandmother,' he said grimly. 'Do you want to stay in the car, Faith?'

She shook her head, closing the boot for him. 'No. I'll come with you.'

'Let's get inside then.' He tried to sound reassuring. His daughters seemed so vulnerable – Faith shivering, pale as a ghost, and Hope waiting patiently, her face pinched with cold, oblivious to her controversial history. He put an arm round both of them and they walked to the house together.

They spoke briefly with Holmes who took their coats before they went along to the drawing room, shoes clattering on the stone floor. Richard was apprehensive, wondering how he would react when he saw his stepbrother. Would he be able to keep his temper? Taking a deep breath he pushed open the door.

His mother and Helena were the only people in the room, sitting on the sofa in front of a cheery fire. For a moment he was taken aback. He had been poised for conflict, his nerves on edge. Now he blinked, suddenly without purpose, drained of energy, like a burst balloon.

'Richard, how thoughtful.' His mother came across to take the flowers from him. She put them on a nearby stool and turned to hug his daughters. 'Faith. Hope. Come and get warm.' Her gaze flickered towards the hearth. 'Helena has been waiting for you, haven't you, my dear?'

Helena stood up, the semblance of a smile on her lips. 'It's good to see you.'

Richard kissed her on both cheeks. 'Helena. This is an unexpected pleasure.'

She made no response. He stepped back, his hands still on her shoulders. 'Is something wrong?'

There was a tap on the door and Holmes entered with coffee. They were silent while he put down the tray and set out the crockery.

'Helena has some bad news,' Ivy said when he had gone.

'It's not Marcus?' Richard swallowed, dreading the answer.

'No. It's not Marcus. He's here somewhere. I think he was going to see Russell Holmes.' Helena's eyes were shadowed with distress.

'So, if it isn't Marcus—?'

'Richard, let Helena sit down.' Ivy bustled between them.

Richard bit his lip to curb his irritation, but Helena accepted the drink his mother poured and sat at the far end of the sofa, the china cup and saucer rattling in her hands. He went to stand by her.

'What is it, Helena?' he asked again.

She put the cup on the floor and laced her fingers together. 'It's Brandon. He's ill. It's lung cancer. He has to go for more tests on Monday and then, if they can, they'll operate.'

Her words rang in his ears. He detested his stepbrother but he had never wished him any harm. Except the once. After Faith had been assaulted. 'How's he taking it?'

'He's worried sick. Apparently he's been ill for some time but he refused to see a doctor.'

'Is he here?'

'Yes. He wanted to revisit his old home. I thought it best to humour him.' She looked up apologetically. 'I couldn't let him go through this alone, Richard. He's still my husband.'

'Are you back together?'

'No. Well, sort of. He came down to Surrey last week. He's staying with me at present.'

'Where is he now?'

'Gone for a walk round the estate, with Jim Manning.'

Richard took the coffee his mother offered. He drank it in one go and handed her the empty cup. His mind was in shock, his thoughts fragmented. 'I don't know what to say, Helena. I'll pray for him, of course, and for you.' He wished he could offer more. 'There's not much else I can do. I don't suppose he will want to talk to me.'

She sighed, her mouth twisting as though she was in pain. 'I don't suppose he will.'

Faith was appalled. How could Helena take Brandon back after everything he had done? After all the humiliation and the gossip, the snide little articles in the press? Over the rim of her cup she studied the woman she had always regarded as her aunt. Helena Calthorpe was one of those plain women who improve with age. Experience had taught her how to make the best of herself. She had learned how to accentuate her huge dark eyes, to highlight her cheekbones and to wear her glossy hair in a soft, forgiving style. She had lost weight which made her appear taller. And she had been lucky. Her oily skin had remained smooth, almost wrinkle-free. Faith thought, with a flutter of satisfaction, of Lucinda Hammond, twice divorced, and looking much older than her forty-three years in photographs featured in glossy magazines, and of Charlotte Sinclair who had grown fat, wore too much make-up and dressed like a teenager. She wondered if Brandon ever made comparisons; if he appreciated the fact that his ugly duckling had turned into a swan.

Helena glanced at the clock. 'He's been gone ages.'

'Don't worry. Jim Manning would keep him talking all day given the chance. Now you will join us for lunch, won't you?' Ivy asked solicitously.

Faith suddenly needed to get out of the room. She didn't want to see Brandon. The house was tainted by his presence. She finished her coffee quickly. 'Thank you, Grandma. Would you mind if I went to the library for a while?'

Without waiting for an answer, she left her cup on the tray and went out into the passage. She hesitated, listening, half expecting to hear Brandon's steely voice. Somewhere nearby a door slammed. Startled, she ran up the stairs.

In the library the air was stale, thick with the musty smell of old books. Dust covered the long table in the centre of the room and dead moths littered the window ledge. She felt safer here. Since Grandad Quentin died the room was hardly ever used. She wiped the condensation from one of the small windowpanes with her hand

and peered down at the snow-speckled garden below. Memories rekindled, sharpened. Her hands became sticky with sweat. Where was Brandon? Was he in the wood? By the lake? Would he be having lunch with them later? Surely her father couldn't expect that of her? To sit at the table with her uncle and make polite conversation.

The heavy door was flung open. She twisted round.

'Who the hell are you?' Brandon Calthorpe glared at her, spittle frothing between his lips.

He was not the man who had haunted her childhood dreams. He was even more frightening. His face was ashen, the flesh stretched so tightly over his cheeks that she could see the bones outlined beneath. His eyes were faded and bloodshot, sunk deep into their sockets, and his mouth, curling in a sneer, was thin, blue-tinged, reptilian.

There was no escape. He took a few paces towards her, the breath rattling in his throat. Then his steps faltered and, gasping for breath, he clutched at one of the carved wooden chairs.

'Uncle Brandon... Are you all right? Shall I fetch Aunt Helena?' She heard herself speaking in a strange, hoarse voice.

'Faith?' He laughed; a guttural, unpleasant sound. 'I might have known my sins would return to haunt me. No I don't want my wife. I want some bloody peace and quiet. Get out!'

She bolted then, scurrying past him into the corridor. Weak with terror, she locked herself in the nearest bathroom and, bending over the sink, was violently sick.

For a while she leaned against the cold porcelain, panic-stricken; every muscle in her body pulsing, a band of pain tightening in her chest. Then a thrust of fear cleared the chaos in her head. *Was Brandon Calthorpe still in the library?* She had to get past before he came out. Galvanised into action, she rinsed her mouth and ran the water to clean the old-fashioned bowl. Her one thought was to get back to her father.

There was no sign of anyone when she peered into the corridor. She took off her boots so there would be no sound as she ran past the library and down the stairs. In the passageway she paused, taking several deep breaths to quell another wave of nausea. Behind her, the front door creaked suddenly and her heart lurched as a shaft of light appeared on the stone flags.

'Are you okay?'

'Marcus!' Relief reduced her to tears.

'Hey, what's the matter? Come into the morning room. There's no one there.'

She followed him gratefully, not yet ready to face Helena.

'Sit down.' Marcus took a match from a pot on the mantelpiece and knelt to light the fire which had already been laid in the grate.

Faith sat on the sofa, watching him as the wood caught and began to flame. She rubbed her eyes, wondering how this gentle boy could possibly be the son of Brandon Calthorpe. Marcus was so thoughtful, so caring. Ever since he was a toddler he had brought such joy to everyone. And she loved him.

'Are you okay?' He stood up, wiping his hands on his jeans.

She thought how much older he looked than when she had seen him four months ago. Perhaps it was his father's illness that had changed him or the new private school he had been sent to in September. Managing a smile, she said. 'I'm fine now. Seeing your dad... it was such a shock.'

'Yes.' He sat next to her, his expression serious. 'Mum's in bits. His illness has hit her hard. I'm so worried about her.'

'You need to stay positive,' she found herself comforting him, 'she'll need your support. You're the best thing in her life, Marcus.'

'She doesn't want Dad to die.' He spoke quietly, his dark eyes troubled.

She'd be better off without him. Faith kept the thought to herself.

'And I don't want to lose him either. In spite of everything, he's still my dad.'

Faith realised he was fighting for control. She wanted to hug him but wasn't sure how he would react. Instead she squeezed his arm sympathetically. 'It's amazing what surgeons can do nowadays. He'll be in good hands.'

He seemed to brighten at the words and she changed the tone of the conversation quickly. Soon they were discussing school and university; new friends, strict teachers, trendy lecturers and the homesickness they both felt at times.

Silently, she reproached herself for not having his generous nature. She would never forgive Brandon Calthorpe for what he had done.

In the drawing room, Hope was growing restless. The conversation was subdued – all about illness and hospitals and operations. For a while she had closed her ears to it, rehearsing some of Juliet's speeches in her head. Sitting on one of the window seats, it was easy to imagine living in another age. She held her head high, her back straight, her hands arranged prettily on her lap. The words formed silently on her lips. When she moved she could almost feel the heavy folds of material swirling round her legs, the high Elizabethan ruff scratching her neck.

Now she looked out at the garden, frustrated to see emerging patches of green and brown, searching for an excuse to leave the adults. She had arranged to meet Russell at half past eleven, and the grandfather clock was ticking away the minutes alarmingly. Marcus still hadn't returned either. Where on earth was he? She didn't want him hanging around with them. In desperation she began rapping the wooden seat with her knuckles, beating out different rhythms.

'Hope, stop that! Haven't you got anything better to do?' Her father frowned at her.

'Can I go outside before all the snow disappears?' she asked meekly.

'Well, make sure you're back in an hour.'

'Thanks, Dad.' Smothering a grin, she ran out of the room. Easy-peasy! He hadn't even remembered she was wearing her best clothes.

Russell was waiting for her at their secret place in the woods – an old lean-to with a corrugated iron roof. There was no sign of Marcus.

'Hi. I thought you might not come over today when I saw the snow.'

'It's nearly all gone, worse luck.' Hope leaned her elbows on a pile of damp logs stored in the shelter.

'There's plenty in the valley,' he said, 'D'you want to go down there?'

'I've got to be back by half past twelve. Is there time?'

'If we get a move on.'

'Okay. Race you!' She pushed past him, skidding on the muddy track.

Laughing, he followed, soon catching up with her. They were both breathless and their pace slackened to a brisk walk as they tried to speak.

'How's the play going?'

'Fine. We were measured for our costumes this week.' She skipped a little, excited. 'I've got five costume changes.'

'Rather you than me. Gran has a job to get me to change my socks.'

She chuckled. 'You idiot, Russ.' After the atmosphere in the house his company was as refreshing as the clean, wintry air.

They walked round the far end of the lake, over the stepping stones, through a wicket gate and into open fields. Here, there was more white than green.

'There's enough to make a snowman.' Russell bent down, gathering snow into a little mound.

Quickly shaping a snowball, Hope crept up behind him. She thrust it inside the collar of his jacket. 'Gotcha!'

He yelled, taken by surprise as the melting ice trickled down his back, and she was convulsed with giggles.

'You'll pay for that, Hope Lawson.' He swung round to grab her.

Trying to evade him, she slipped and clutched his arm to save herself, pulling him on top of her in the snow.

'Who's in trouble now?' He held her down. 'Just let me get some...'

'No! No, Russ,' she screamed in mock terror.

He held a handful of snow above her head.

'You wouldn't dare!' She tried to push him off. His face was inches away from hers, his grey eyes glinting with mischief. She could feel his breath on her cheek. Her heartbeat quickened. She was suddenly exhilarated and afraid; shivering yet suffused with heat; wanting their relationship to stay the same, wanting it to be different.

'Russ?' It was a whisper, a plea. She saw his expression change, grow serious. The snow slid out of his hand. He touched her face gently, his fingers cold on her skin. She closed her eyes.

His lips were firm and smooth on hers and the whole of her body quivered in response. She put her arms round his neck, holding him close, inhaling the smell of his skin, pressing herself against him. There was no snow, no grass, no light, no sound. Only herself and Russell, and the warm, dark kiss that seemed to go on forever.

No one commented on the state of her clothes when she got back to the house. Her father and Faith were ready to leave and they said their goodbyes quickly, hurrying her out to the car without any explanation for their early departure. Of the uncle she had never seen there was no sign.

CHAPTER 24

Richard put the phone down and went into the lounge. The fire had burnt up well and the room felt warm, despite the draught blowing under the door. Kate was lying on the sofa, a blanket tucked round her legs.

'Was that Helena?' She rubbed the sleep out of her eyes.

'Yes. Brandon's taken a turn for the worse. The operation's been scheduled for tomorrow, but there's only a fifty-fifty chance he'll survive. There's a problem with his heart. Something to do with him having rheumatic fever as a child. I'm going up to London early in the morning. Will you be all right on your own? I'll ask Liz to organise some lunch for you.'

Kate sat up, pulling the blanket round her like an old woman. 'You mustn't worry about me. I can manage. Helena needs you more.' Her smile was forced but her eyes were clear and focussed.

He looked down at her, remembering the fresh-faced girl who had come into his life twelve – no thirteen – years ago. Such a lot had happened to her since. He doubted if he would ever know what horrors lurked in the shadows of her mind.

'I'm not sure when I'll be back.' His thoughts raced ahead. If Brandon's operation was successful it might be possible to be home by midnight. He didn't want to think about the alternative.

And there was something else he didn't want to think about. Another nightmare to confront. He sat on the end of the sofa, hands clenched, staring at the carpet.

'You don't know what to do about Hope, do you?' Kate asked.

'What are you? A mind-reader?'

She shrugged. 'Will you tell her?'

He leaned back with a groan. 'He's her father. This may be her only chance to see him alive. She has a right to know the truth. But she believes she's my daughter. What will this do to her?'

'Perhaps you should leave things as they are.'

'But wouldn't that be wrong?'

Kate stifled a yawn. 'I can't advise you, Richard. If it was my decision, I'd be inclined to say nothing, but whether that would be right or wrong I have no idea.'

Leaning across, he kissed the top of her head. 'Thanks for listening anyway. I might nip over to the church for a while before Hope comes home from school. You go back to sleep.'

He left the room quietly. In the hall he put on his waterproof jacket and collected his keys from the telephone table. Then he let himself out of the house. It was mid-afternoon but the skies were already darkening. The wind was keen, stinging his face as he hurried across the garden and into the churchyard. He was thankful to reach the shelter of the porch.

Inside the church the air was colder still. He knelt in one of the pews and closed his eyes. He prayed first for his brother's recovery, then for Helena and Marcus, and, finally, for guidance in the choice he had to make. When he finished he remained on his knees, weighing one course of action against another, finding none of them satisfactory. Surely it was a sin to keep something so precious from his brother? And if he didn't tell Brandon about Hope was he keeping silent to protect his daughter? Or himself? Was he afraid Brandon would take Hope from him? Was this why he had kept the truth a secret? And there was Helena to consider as well.

The thoughts wheeled round in his head until he was weary, until he realised he was trying to twist them, to ignore the obvious. Hope was a gift from God. But she was Brandon's gift as well as his own. Sighing, he stood up. Of course he had known from the outset what he should do.

Hope sat quite still, her face tight and stiff, as though carved from stone. She couldn't move her lips; couldn't speak or cry. There was something wrong with her stomach. It felt heavy, like it did when she had eaten something that didn't agree with her.

Her father was saying he loved her, that she would always be his little girl. But he wasn't her father and she wasn't his little girl. She belonged to the wicked uncle, the one who had been so horrible to Aunt Helena, the one who had abandoned his own son; the man who terrified Faith for some unknown reason. She stared at a space on the wall above the fireplace. Her father – the man she had always believed to be her father – had never loved her the way he loved Faith and now she knew why.

'Hope, sweetheart, I didn't want to tell you all this until you were older, but Brandon is seriously ill and I have no choice. It won't make any difference to you. Nothing's really changed.'

But it had. Things would never be the same again.

'Will I have to live with him?' The words forced themselves out of her mouth.

'No. I would never let that happen, sweetheart. Your home is here, with me and Faith. We love you. We couldn't bear to lose you.'

She wanted to believe him, but something inside her had been damaged. She couldn't function properly. Her thoughts drifted, her limbs were rigid and her eyes saw the room in a strange and frightening way, as if she was looking through the wrong end of a telescope. Her father was a remote, unfamiliar figure beside her on the sofa.

He brushed her cheek with his fingers. 'Hope, listen, my darling. I'm going to London tomorrow. Uncle Brandon is having an operation. Would you come with me? Just so that he can meet you before—'

'No! I don't want to see him. Not ever. I hope he dies. I don't want anything to do with him. I won't go. You can't make me.'

Horrified, she ran from the room. Desperate to get away, she wrenched open the front door and rushed out into the darkness.

She found herself in the churchyard, the cold gnawing her skin through the flimsy material of her school blouse. Shivering, she stood among the gravestones, fear bringing the world sharply back into focus; fragments of ghost stories and horror movies, suddenly vivid in her mind. All around were shapes blacker than the night itself, shapes that moved and changed form, each one sending a jolt of panic through her until she identified them – the bush near the dark mouth of the porch, the plastic bin-bag trapped in an old tree stump, the fallen metal urn rolling drunkenly along the path.

The noise of the wind filled the air. A branch in one of the trees creaked. It was a branch, wasn't it? Not one of the old tombs sliding open? She froze. There was a smaller sound, like bony fingers clawing their way out of a grave. Her heart leapt, hammered against her ribs. She began to run again, her throat painful and dry, her eyes burning like ice where the wind caught her tears.

As she turned the corner at the side of the church she saw a body, bloodless and grey, hovering above the grass. She heard the scream in her head. Then her vision dimmed and she slid to the ground.

'Hope.'

Her father crouched down beside her. She clung to him, light-headed with relief.

'Hope, I'm so sorry. I've handled this all wrong. Please, sweetheart, come back inside. You'll catch your death of cold out here.'

He held her until the fear dissolved and she sobbed out her pain and bewilderment. Glancing over his shoulder she saw no ghostly figure, only the ancient statue of an angel next to an overgrown grave.

'I love you, Hope. You are as dear to me as if you were my own daughter. I want you to understand that.'

She heard it in his voice for the first time – the love she had always craved. But it was too late.

'I shouldn't have asked you to come with me tomorrow. This has all been too much for you. Forgive me, please, Hope.'

He helped her to her feet, wrapping his jacket round her, pulling her into the shelter of his arms. She didn't resist when he led her home. In the house he made her a milky drink and tucked her into bed as if she was a child of six.

'Try to get some sleep, sweetheart.' He stooped to kiss her, smoothing the hair back from her forehead. It was the closeness she had longed for but now it gave her no comfort. She lay mute and motionless, unable to look at him.

'Goodnight, Hope. And don't worry. I'll make sure everything will be all right.'

She slept fitfully, tormented by bitter thoughts. When she heard him go downstairs in the early morning she washed and dressed quietly. She waited for him in the hall, cold and hollow inside. It was time to face up to who she was. To meet the man who was her real father.

CHAPTER 25

It didn't begin to grow light until they reached the Cotswolds, and even then the cloud was so thick that the slow brightening in the east was hardly noticeable. By the time they joined the motorway it was raining heavily. Richard was quiet, concentrating on the road, straining his eyes to see through the spray thrown up by the never-ending stream of lorries, checking his mirror as he pulled out to overtake again and again. He hated driving in these conditions.

Next to him, Hope sat hunched in her black school coat. He knew she wasn't asleep, but it was easier for them both to pretend. There was nothing he could say that would make this ordeal easier for her, no way to undo what he had set in motion. She was so young and so innocent. How was she going to cope with whatever she had to confront today?

As they got closer to London the traffic slowed, tail lights tapering into the distance, a hazy red line in the drifting mist of rain. Richard tapped his fingers against the steering- wheel.

'How much longer from here?' Hope's voice startled him.

'About another hour I think, depending on the traffic.'

She was silent again. He looked across at her, but her expression was concealed by a veil of blonde hair.

'You needn't see him, you know.' He touched her hand briefly.

She didn't reply. Sighing, he inched the car forward, closing the gap between them and the dirty white van in front.

It was a few minutes after nine when he reversed the car into a parking bay among the neat evergreen bushes in the grounds of Weavers' Brook Hospital. It was a large, two-storey building of concrete and glass; unprepossessing, almost ugly, on the outside.

'Okay, let's make a dash for it,' he said.

They ran to the entrance, shoes squelching on the wet concrete, and shook the rain from their hair before going inside.

Richard looked around. The entrance hall was vast, furnished with white leather sofas, and glass-topped coffee tables, each with an arrangement of fresh flowers in the centre. It was unlike any of the hospitals he visited. The air smelt perfumed and piped music filtered through invisible speakers. An elegant receptionist eyed them haughtily from behind the curved wooden desk as they approached.

'We're relatives of Brandon Calthorpe. His wife is expecting us.'

Richard noted the woman's sudden change of expression.

'I'll ring and tell her you're here,' she flashed a smile at him.

He found himself mesmerised by the sight of her

immaculately groomed fingernails; blood red against the white telephone. Red and white. Blood and bone. Life and death.

The receptionist interrupted his thoughts. 'Mrs Calthorpe will be down in a few minutes. Shall I put your wet things in the cloakroom?'

They handed over their coats. Before they had time to sit down the lift doors purred open and Helena emerged.

'Richard. I'm so glad to see you.'

It was obvious she had been crying. Her eyes looked sore, the flesh beneath them puffy and red. Otherwise her skin was grey with fatigue, the faint lines around her mouth etched deeper than they had been a few days before.

'How is he?' He held her, willing her to take comfort from his presence.

'Resigned. And somehow that's harder to bear than when he was angry with everyone. It's not like Brandon, is it? To accept things?'

In spite of the old enmity he felt a deep sadness at her words. 'Will he see me?'

'I think so.' Helena nodded wearily. She turned towards Hope. 'I'm sorry. I didn't mean to ignore you, darling.'

'You stay here, Hope.' Richard was worried by his daughter's pallor. 'I'll be back as soon as I can.'

'Are you going to tell him about me?' Her eyes were huge, accusing.

'I have to, sweetheart.' He kissed the top of her head and walked away swiftly, trying to ignore the notion that after today the course of his daughter's life would change forever. He followed Helena to the lift. His mouth was dry and he ran his tongue over his teeth nervously. How would she react when she knew the truth about Hope?

'So, she really is Brandon's daughter?' Helena pressed the button for the second floor.

He was disconcerted. 'How did you guess?'

'Why else would she be here? I must admit I've often wondered about her. She's nothing like you, is she?'

The lift stopped, the doors opened.

'Helena, you never cease to amaze me. How can you take this so calmly?'

'Nothing Brandon has done surprises me. But he doesn't have the power to hurt me any more. Except that I can't bear the thought of him dying.'

She led the way along a wide corridor. Again it seemed to Richard more like a hotel than a hospital, although there were several nurses in evidence. On his left, the wall was virtually all glass. He glanced outside, looking down at a paved courtyard with a circular pool and a marble fountain. To his right there were private wards and between them huge works of modern art hung on the walls, each illuminated by a brass-covered light. Helena stopped at one of the doors. It was open. A young nurse was sitting by the bed, studying a sheaf of charts attached to a clipboard.

'You can come in,' she said with a smile, 'I'll only be a minute.'

Richard thought he was prepared for the worst, but the first glimpse of his stepbrother was harrowing.

He found himself looking at an old man – emaciated, hollow-eyed, skull-faced – a parody of the person he remembered. Shock left him speechless. He watched Brandon attempt to flirt with the nurse. The sight was grotesque. Obscene. Heart-rending.

'Sit down, Richard.' Helena nudged him gently.

Hardly aware of her, he went to the window and stared at the street beyond the car park, mindful of the need to hide his true feelings. Behind him, in the bright, white-walled room, death was stiflingly close; outside, despite the gloomy skies, the busy streets teemed with life. He watched the raindrops slithering down the glass. For some reason they reminded him of people – some tiny and insignificant, hardly moving at all, like himself; some bigger, proceeding cautiously, a little at a time; some running straight and fast, sweeping others along with them. Like his stepbrother.

'All done.' The nurse stood up, her starched skirt rustling. She left the room, avoiding their eyes. Richard took her place at the side of the bed. Helena sat opposite him.

'What are you doing here?' Brandon's bloodshot eyes rolled alarmingly. 'I suppose my wife persuaded you to come. She thinks the sun shines out of your backside.'

Richard felt the old anger stirring. He took a deep breath. 'I came because Helena asked me, but also because I wanted to put an end to the animosity between us. I came to pray with you, if you want me to.'

'It's too late for that.' Brandon's features seemed to collapse. He lay back on the pillow, his face a death mask.

'There's something else too.' Richard swallowed painfully, the words sticking in his throat. He looked down at his hands. 'You have a daughter. Hope is not my child. She's yours. Yours and Grace's.'

For a long moment the only sound was the rain on the window. Richard thought his stepbrother hadn't understood.

Then Brandon raised his head, his smile slow and cruel. 'And she's been a thorn in your flesh all these years. Why are you telling me now?'

'Because she's here, if you want to see her. I don't know if she'll be able to face you – that's up to her – but I can ask.'

'You don't want this, do you?' Brandon struggled to sit up.

'No. I'm afraid of the effect it will have on her.'

'She knows about me?'

'She's only just learnt the truth. She hasn't had time to come to terms with it yet.'

'So we're in the same boat, me and my daughter?'

'Yes.'

'Very well, I'll see her,' Brandon said abruptly. 'At least she has the guts to visit me. Unlike my so-called son.'

Helena leaned over to straighten the sheet. 'Marcus is with my parents. He's too upset. I wouldn't allow him to come today.'

'Even though it might be...' Brandon caught hold of her hand.

Richard excused himself quickly, knowing his stepbrother would hate him to witness such naked terror.

In the reception hall Hope flicked through a glossy magazine, every muscle inside her taut, sweating one minute, cold the next. It was an effort to stop herself visibly shaking.

'Hope.'

'Dad!' She scrambled to her feet and the magazine slipped from her lap. He stooped to pick it up. She watched him put it back on the table, smoothing the creased pages with the flat of his hand. Her eyes smarted with tears. He would always be her dad. The man in the ward upstairs would never take his place.

'Do you want to meet him, Hope?'

'Yes.' She had to know what he was like. She needed to hate him so that she could shut him out of her life.

The lift made her stomach heave. Her father held her hand as they went along a corridor that felt cool and clinical; all white walls, glass and marble floor tiles. His grip tightened when they stopped outside one of the many doors.

'Are you sure about this?'

She nodded, her heart beating violently.

Inside, the room was large. Fluorescent lights erased all shadows. Bile rose in her throat. The man in the bed seemed barely alive. She shrank back, terrified of his yellow, skeletal face, his glassy stare, the ghastly smile that was forming on his lips.

'This is my daughter. Our daughter. This is Hope.' Her father's voice sounded hollow.

'Come closer, Hope,' Brandon Calthorpe croaked, 'I won't bite.'

She took a few steps forward. It wasn't enough.

'Closer.'

Two more steps. He reached out and touched her. His hands were clammy, trembling against her skin. It took all her will-power to remain where she was, to hide the revulsion she felt.

'You have the face of an angel.' He traced the curve of her jawbone.

She held her breath.

'An angel called Hope. D'you think that could be an omen? That perhaps I will survive after all?'

There was no mistaking his fear. A shiver of pity moved within her. She tried to speak but could only manage a strange, choking sound. A brisk knock on the door drew his attention away from her and a nurse entered, a woman with a stern expression, large and efficient.

'I will have to ask you all to go now,' she said firmly. 'We need to prepare Mr Calthorpe for surgery.'

The room felt suddenly colder. Hope hurried into the corridor. The ordeal was over.

The day seemed endless. She watched her father and Aunt Helena consume numerous cups of coffee, their faces drawn and anxious. When the rain eased, the three of them walked along the embankment. The fresh air was welcome but water dripped from the bare trees, and although her father pointed out various sites, Hope thought everywhere looked grey and depressing. She was glad when they began to make their way back.

Marcus was waiting at the hospital, a lone figure sitting on one of the sofas, head bowed, twisting the cord of his anorak round his fingers. He leapt up, catching his knee on the corner of a low table, and hurried across to them. Hope saw he had lost weight. His cheeks were no longer fleshy and his face was pale beneath the mop of black hair.

'I'm sorry, Mum.' He spoke quietly. 'I couldn't stay away. Grandad dropped me here. Don't be cross.'

Hope was relieved when his mother merely nodded and folded him into her arms.

'I'm glad you're here.' Helena glanced over his shoulder at the receptionist.

'He's still in theatre, Mrs Calthorpe.' The woman answered her unspoken question.

The waiting continued. None of them were hungry, but Helena said they must eat something so they helped themselves to complimentary soup and pre-packed sandwiches from the well-appointed hospitality suite. Afterwards they sat in the reception area pretending to read magazines, as if they had run out of things to say to each other. There was no news of Brandon. Hope tried not to think of him. She didn't want him to die... But if he did, she would have nothing more to worry about.

The fingers on the clock above the reception desk moved round slowly. She began to recognise the same melodies emanating from the speakers on the wall. It was impossible to relax. Each time the telephone rang, and whenever a nurse came down the stairs or out of the lift, she looked up nervously, reading the dread in her aunt's eyes. Another thirty minutes crept by. She wriggled, stretching her legs, letting her head rest in the angle between the arm and the back of the leather sofa. The room was too hot. The music painted pictures in her mind. Her eyelids grew heavy.

She woke with a start. Her father was holding Aunt Helena and she was sobbing. A white-coated doctor walked away across the hall. *He was dead then. The man upstairs.* She didn't think she would care, wasn't prepared for the emptiness within her, the sudden perverse wish that she had been given the chance to get to know him.

'What's happened?' she turned to Marcus, not wanting to hear the answer.

His face was beaded with sweat and tears. 'The operation was successful. The disease hasn't spread. Dad is in intensive care, but he's over the worst.'

'So why is Aunt Helena crying?'

Her father smiled at her. 'It's just reaction to the stress, sweetheart. She'll be all right.'

Hope sat on the edge of her seat pinching her lip with her thumb and forefinger. Her real father was still alive, but the future now was full of uncertainty.

Marcus nudged her gently. 'Are you okay?'

She nodded, becoming aware of the murmured conversation between her father and Helena.

'I'm so grateful, Richard. I couldn't have got through this alone.'

'Do you want us to stay with you?'

'No, you go home. You must be worried about Kate, and Hope's had enough of hospitals for one day. We'll be all right here tonight, and tomorrow I'll open up the flat in Kensington.'

'Don't let Brandon ruin your life again, Helena. What about this fellow? The one you've been seeing?'

Hope saw Helena shake her head.

'I think perhaps we were never meant to be. I have a duty, Richard. You of all people should understand that. Now, don't keep this daughter of yours hanging around any longer. You'll get stuck in the rush hour traffic as it is.'

They said their goodbyes. Outside the rain had finally stopped and a watery sunset bathed everything in golden light. The air smelt fresh, like newly laundered clothes. Hope tilted her face upwards, trying to clear her head, rid herself of the cloying scent of the hospital. She felt somehow contaminated and she couldn't wait to get away.

CHAPTER 26

Outside it was still dark. Grace poured herself a mug of tea and sat at the kitchen table, shivering in her fleecy dressing gown. As always in late February, she was low in spirits. And this year the haze of depression had clouded her mind again. It was hard to come to terms with the fact that her firstborn would be twenty tomorrow. She felt the loss of the intervening years keenly; a hollow ache that never really went away. For her, Faith would always be a skinny girl of seven. What was she like now? Was she tall? Pretty? Clever? Did she have a boyfriend? Maybe she was married already. Maybe she had a child. Grace wiped her eyes on her sleeve. She would never know.

With an effort she steered her thoughts back to the present. Her hands were freezing. She wrapped them round the mug for warmth, afraid to switch on the central heating in case it woke Alex. He needed his sleep. Things were not going well for him. Since he moved in with them at the end of November he had been plagued with problems. The small engineering factory he owned with his business partner, Nigel, was in trouble and Alex had been relying on money from the sale of his flat to tide them over. Then, two weeks ago, the prospective buyers pulled out. The flat was on the market again but there had been no further offers.

Yesterday Alex had decided to sell his Jaguar. Grace sipped her tea, considering the options. The car was his pride and joy. It was important, he said, to impress new clients – if he had an expensive car they assumed he was successful. It generated business. The dilemma had kept her awake most of the night. Alex's problems should be her problems too. And she had the means to help him. Over half of Quentin's money remained in the bank, plus some savings from her job with the travel agency. But that money was for Amy's future…

Grace put the mug down. Why was she hesitating? Alex hadn't asked her for anything. She didn't need to get involved. On the other hand, it seemed mean not to offer him a loan to see him through the next few months. He would pay her back when things improved. She smiled, remembering the warmth of him in the bed next to her; his blond hair tousled, his features relaxed and boyish as he slept.

He's not Brandon Calthorpe. The words were as clear as if she had spoken them aloud. The conflict in her head resolved itself. She walked to the dresser and spent a frantic few seconds rummaging in the top drawer for her chequebook and a pen. By the time she found them she was breathless, caught up in a fever of enthusiasm. Before she could change her mind, she wrote out a cheque for thirty-thousand pounds, made payable to Alexander Graham Walsh.

Faith slumped in the nearest armchair, throwing a carrier bag down on the floor beside her.

Hope followed her into the room. 'Did you find a dress for tonight?'

'Yes. Eventually.' Faith kicked off her shoes and stretched her legs. 'I'd forgotten how manic Hereford can be on a Saturday.'

'Can I see?' Without waiting for an answer, Hope took the skimpy black dress out of the bag and held it in front of her, moulding it to the curves of her body, posing like a model.

'It's gorgeous.'

Faith froze, gripped by a sudden, raw jealousy. Her sister would look stunning in the dress.

'Put it down, you'll crease it.' She couldn't keep the bitterness out of her voice.

Hope dropped the dress on the sofa, her eyes filling with tears.

'Sorry. I didn't mean to snap.' Faith was immediately contrite. 'Hope, wait—'

The lounge door slammed. Faith sighed. Why could she never hide her feelings? Her sister had enough to contend with and she had just made things worse. She leaned forward, elbows on knees, annoyed that her own spitefulness had soured her good humour. Happiness was so tenuous. It didn't last. There were too many black days. Days when music made her sad, when certain lines of poetry haunted her, when even cheesy pop songs could reduce her to tears. She wished she could be different; kinder, less self-centred and moody. Rajat teased her sometimes in his quaint, dignified way.

He said she was like the weather. Unpredictable.

Her face grew hot. She touched the silver dolphin that rested against her throat, threaded onto the chain with the cross that had been a gift from Kate. Rajat had given her the dolphin after lectures yesterday, an early present for tomorrow. She remembered the feel of his hands when he refastened the chain round her neck and his breath, fresh and sweet-scented against her cheek. He hadn't kissed her, although a part of her had wanted him to. *Be happy, Faith*, he had whispered.

She had almost asked him to come home with her for the weekend. Now she was relieved she hadn't. Rajat Dasari had been born in England, but his parents were Indian and Grandma Ivy wouldn't approve. Anyway, lunch at Dalchett House tomorrow would be a bore. It would be much more fun at *Illusions* tonight, with Debbie and Em... And Wayne.

Once more heat spread across her cheeks. Was that the real reason she didn't want Rajat here? Because he would never be as exciting as Wayne Saunders. Unsettled by the thought, she picked up the dress and ran upstairs. She really wasn't a nice person.

Later, as she applied her make-up, she studied herself anxiously. Tonight she was pretty. Her pale skin was flushed, her dark eyes bright. She tilted her head, feeling the movement of the smooth, shoulder-length bob. The new hairstyle framed her face perfectly. And she looked sophisticated, even sexy, in the black dress. She could hardly wait to see the effect on Wayne Saunders.

With a shiver of anticipation, she recalled his probing fingers and passionate kisses. Debbie had warned her about him, that he was only after one thing and he dumped girls as soon as he got what he wanted. But he was different with her.

In the back of the car Debbie and Em chattered like schoolgirls, catching up with each other's lives. Debbie still lived at home, working as a barmaid in the local pub, looking after her father and two brothers between shifts. Emily was studying to be a midwife, based in Barnet, and rarely able to get back to Tuston.

Faith was only half-listening to their conversation; the usual gossip about boys and family and mutual friends. She couldn't ask about Wayne while her father was with them and she didn't want to tell them about Rajat – mainly because there was nothing to tell. They were just good friends, that was all. She smiled in the dark, thinking about their first meeting when she had been lost in one of the university buildings, trying to find her study group. A fresher like herself, Rajat had stopped to help, taking out his folder in which all the groups and venues were listed. She had recognised the name of the tutor, and Rajat had insisted on escorting her along the maze of corridors to the correct room before he hurried off to a lecture. After that they met regularly in the student's union bar and once or twice they had been to the cinema together. There was nothing more between them. He knew she had a boyfriend at home.

Wayne Saunders. She was obsessed with him. The intensity of her feelings scared her sometimes. It was as if she was only really alive when she was with him. Excitement made her impatient and the last few miles of the journey into town seemed to take forever. She was glad when her father dropped them outside the nightclub.

By half past eleven the place was pulsing; strobe lights freezing the dancers into statues momentarily before releasing them, over and over again. Faith could feel the bass beat hitting the wall of her chest as she followed Emily off the dance floor. Debbie was already at the bar, clicking her fingers to attract attention, dyed blonde hair changing colour under the flashing lights. Faith envied her confidence. Deb reminded her of someone... *Her mother's friend, Cassie.*

Emily turned, pointing. 'Let's grab that table. Deb will find us.'

They sat down. Faith's vision wavered as the memories unfolded: her mother and Cassie on a visit to Birmingham, holding her hands in the huge stores, waving to her as she sat astride a painted horse on a little roundabout, sharing her ice cream when it began to melt. It had been one of those perfect days in the summer before Hope was born. Before everything changed.

'Here we are. Bacardi and coke all round' Debbie's voice cut into her thoughts. 'And, by the way, my brother's here.'

The past receded, leaving Faith strangely light-headed.

'Be careful,' Emily muttered, 'I wouldn't trust him as far as I could throw him.'

'That's because you don't know him.' Faith glared at her oldest friend. Sometimes Emily seemed aloof; slim and elegant, the corkscrew curls of her childhood tamed and shining. Did she think she was too good for them now? But there was no hint of smugness on Emily's face. Her smooth, high forehead was puckered with concern.

Faith felt ashamed of her uncharitable thoughts.

'Don't worry about me. I won't do anything stupid.'

Wayne Saunders sauntered across. As usual he wore black: black leather trousers, a designer shirt and jacket, black silk tie. She trembled inside when he smiled at her. He was handsome in a brooding, sullen way; thin with angular features and light brown hair slicked back from his face. His eyes were a deeper blue than his sister's, his skin paler. He wasn't tall but there was a vitality about him, a defiant swagger, which attracted attention.

'Dance, Faith?'

He hauled her to her feet. Emily's warning was wiped away by the touch of his hand. A wild, crazy energy flooded her veins. As the mist of dry ice swirled round her she had the strangest notion that she was walking on clouds. When the tempo changed to a slow, dreamy ballad he pulled her to him, his cheek against hers, his breath hot on her skin.

'I've got Dad's car. I'll give you a lift home later.'

She closed her eyes and wound her arms round his neck.

The lights dimmed and brightened. The DJ turned the volume down.

'It's midnight folks,' he said in a mock American drawl, 'and time to say *Happy Birthday* to a very special lady. Faith Lawson this is for you. From Wayne.'

There was a ripple of applause. Faith put her hands over her face to hide her blushes. The song was treacle-sweet but the words seemed to hold a promise. For a second she was afraid. She was too happy.

By the time they left the nightclub she was high on champagne. Ignoring the anxious glances between her friends, she dismissed the suggestion that she went home in a taxi with them. All she wanted was to be alone with Wayne.

She remembered little of the journey back to Tuston, aware only of his dark shape beside her and a mounting excitement that made her nauseous. Just before the village he turned off the road onto a farm track, as she knew he would. It was their special place. He reversed the car into a gateway. A barn owl fluttered above the hedgerow, white and ghostly. Wayne turned off the lights and the engine. The darkness was impenetrable. A flicker of fear caught her unawares.

'Happy Birthday, sweetheart.' His lips brushed hers. 'There's nothing to be afraid of, Faith. Trust me.'

Gradually the night revealed itself – a scattering of stars through the bare canopy of trees; heavy, fast-moving clouds; outlines of branches and tree trunks; a bend in the muddy track. She relaxed a little.

At first his kisses were slow and teasing, his touch on her skin light. It was sensuous and arousing. Yet, even as she responded, she was conscious that he was too sure of himself; that he had done this many times before. But it didn't matter. Nothing mattered if he loved her.

He shifted in the seat so that his body covered hers. Slowly, deliberately, he unbuttoned her coat and slipped the straps of the black dress over her shoulders. She gasped when he took the weight of her breasts in his hands. His lips found her nipple and she felt the sharp edge of his teeth; the moist warmth of the inside of his mouth. She was lost in him, helpless.

His breathing grew faster. He moved rhythmically, his kisses rough and urgent, his body hard against hers. With a grunt he lifted her hips, pushing the skirt of her dress up to her waist, parting her legs with his knee. The passion died instantly.

'No!' Images surfaced in her head: a thread of wintry light on half-naked bodies, discarded clothes on the stone floor of the stable; Brandon Calthorpe, revolting in his aroused state.

'No, Wayne. Please.' She tried to wriggle free, but he pinned her against the seat.

'You know you want this, sweetheart.' His voice was thick, without tenderness. She had been a fool not to listen to Debbie and Em.

'Get off me!' She tugged at his hair, yanking his head backwards with all her strength.

'Bitch!' He let go of her. 'Bloody, fuckin' cock-teaser!'

She rolled from under him, pulling her clothes back in place, groping for her coat, feeling for the handle on the door. All the time he watched her, his eyes hard as granite.

'What are you doing? He reached across, holding the door shut.

'Let me go.'

'Faith, baby, I thought this was what you wanted.' He cupped his fingers under her chin. 'You must know I'm crazy about you. You do know that, don't you?'

'Don't.' She jerked her head away.

He grabbed her wrists, his fingers encircling them like handcuffs, digging into her flesh. Instinct told her not to cross him again.

'I feel sick,' she said weakly.

His eyes narrowed and she was afraid he was going to hit her.

'I must have had too much to drink.' She searched desperately for the right words to placate him. Abruptly he released her.

'Another time then, sweetheart.'

To her relief he started the engine. The car roared into life, the headlights illuminated the track.

She tried not to recoil from his kiss when he left her at the rectory gate.

Once inside the house, she bolted the door and leaned against it, breathless. The hall mirror reflected her panic. Gone was the radiant young woman of a few hours earlier. The vision that stared back at her was a harridan: wild, tangled hair, streaky make-up, dark eyes luminous with tears. Turning away, she hurried up the stairs to her room. She felt humiliated and dirty and stupid. Why hadn't she listened to Debbie? Wayne Saunders could easily have raped her.

Her skin burned with shame. She was her mother's daughter after all – a fool for a handsome face and a tissue of lies.

* * *

Hope returned from morning service ahead of her father and found Kate in the kitchen spooning coffee granules into four mugs. The kettle was boiling.

'I'll do that, Kate. You need to rest or you'll be too tired to enjoy lunch.'

Kate relinquished the task without protest and sat down by the kitchen table. Hope put a mug of coffee in front of her. Kate's face was lined with fatigue. Her hair had been drawn back through an elastic band and she was wearing an old navy dress of Faith's which was too big, emphasising her frailty. The sad pile of clothes she had with her when she arrived had all been thrown away. Everything she wore now was borrowed. Hope felt desperately sorry for her. She couldn't remember her as a young woman but she could see that she would once have been beautiful.

'Morning.' Faith appeared in the kitchen, still in her dressing gown.

'Happy Birthday.' Hope smiled uncertainly. Her sister didn't look at all happy. *Hangover*, she thought.

'Happy Birthday,' Kate echoed as Faith sat opposite her. 'Many happy returns.'

Hope made another coffee and handed it to Faith.

'You'll have to wait for your presents. Dad thinks you should open them at Grandma's.'

'Whatever.' Faith didn't seem interested.

Hope shrugged. Something must have happened last night to put her sister in a bad mood – probably something to do with the sleazy Wayne Saunders. She scooped extra sugar into her drink and thought about Russell.

The telephone began to ring just as her father came through the back door.

'It's probably for me.' He hurried into the hall. His voice carried clearly. 'Helena! What is it?'

The spoon slipped from Hope's fingers and clattered on to the work top.

'Just a minute.' Her father put the phone down and closed the kitchen door.

Hope shivered. *What had happened? Had Brandon Calthorpe suffered a relapse? Was he out of hospital?*

'I need to get changed for Grandma's.' It was the first excuse she could think of. She left the kitchen quickly, the taste of coffee bitter in her mouth. Her father lowered his voice when he saw her.

'He wouldn't do that, surely?' His expression was grave.

With a sense of foreboding Hope rushed past him and ran up the stairs. *What were they talking about?* She felt sure it had something to do with her. On the landing she hesitated. Then she went into Kate's bedroom and picked up the extension phone that had been installed there.

'You can tell him I won't agree to a DNA test and that's final. He can employ as many lawyers as he wants. As far as I'm concerned Hope is my daughter. He's got no damn right!' Her father's anger reverberated down the line.

'But he has,' Helena sounded tearful, 'and he's planning to take her from you.'

'Over my dead body! You can tell him he'll have a fight on his hands.'

'I'll do my best to make him see sense. He can't do much at the moment. But I thought you should know. Prepare you.'

'Thank you, Helena. How is he anyway?'

'He's doing well. They may let him come home next week. The doctors say he stands a good chance of living a fairly normal life.'

'I really am glad about that, Helena.'

Hope didn't listen to any more. She replaced the receiver, sick with dread. Lately there had been a lot of talk about DNA testing on the television. A DNA test would prove Brandon Calthorpe was her real father and then he would take her away from everything and everyone she loved.

Lunch seemed interminable. As there were only five of them, they were in the morning room, but Grandma Ivy had organised a full Sunday roast with beef and Yorkshire puddings and an array of winter vegetables. Hope ate little. She could see her father, too, was struggling to maintain some semblance of normality and Faith was quieter than usual. Kate was doing her best to keep conversation flowing but she was visibly tiring. However, Grandma Ivy didn't appear to notice anything amiss. She sat at the head of the table regarding them with busy grey eyes, urging them all to take second helpings. When they had eaten as much as they could manage and Holmes had cleared away the plates she clapped her hands for attention.

'Faith, my dear, I know your think you're too old for a birthday cake so I've asked Trudie to make something special for dessert.'

Holmes held the door open as Trudie, her face almost as red as her hair, brought in a magnificent gateau, topped with twenty flaring candles, which she placed in the centre of the table.

'Trudie, it's amazing.' Faith jumped up to hug the sturdy cook whose waistline had expanded disproportionately with age. 'Thank you so much.'

Trudie's blushes grew more fiery. 'You make sure you have a lovely birthday,' she mumbled, retreating hastily.

'Thank you, Grandma.' Faith smiled, a little too brightly.

'Well now, you must blow the candles out, dear, and then we can all have a piece.'

Faith did as she was asked and Hope applauded dutifully with everyone else. Her grandmother cut a slice of gateau for each of them.

'This is delicious,' Kate said politely.

Hope, took a tentative mouthful, and found, to her relief, that it was light and fluffy.

In the drawing room Holmes poured coffee and put more logs on the fire. Hope wondered what he would say if he knew his grandson was waiting in the woods for her. When he left the room she was impatient to follow. If only Faith would hurry up and open her presents. But there was a pile of cards on her sister's lap. Each one had to be read and passed round, then returned.

'Presents now,' her father said at last, fetching the pile of small packages which had been left on top of the piano. He sat down again, heavily, and Hope leaned forward to pick up several envelopes which had fallen on to the floor. Faith looked at the label on the first parcel, then removed the wrapping paper carefully. Inside was a pretty green chiffon scarf.

'I'm sorry it's not much. Liz got it for me. I hope you like it.' Kate sounded anxious.

'It's lovely!' Faith unfolded the scarf to examine it and Hope saw that this time her smile was genuine.

'Now mine, dear.' Ivy indicated a tiny white box. Faith unfastened the catch to reveal an exquisite gold ring fashioned like a knot and studded with tiny diamonds.

'Grandma, I don't know what to say. It's beautiful.'

'It was one of the rings Quentin gave me and I know he would be pleased for you to have it.'

Hope noticed Faith's eyes suddenly glisten with tears. Her sister had loved Quentin Calthorpe. Everyone had loved Quentin Calthorpe. Surely his son couldn't be so very wicked?

'Is this from you?' Faith lifted the chunky little package.

'Yes.' Hope had been preoccupied with her own thoughts. She waited nervously for Faith to pull off the wrappings.

'Oh, it's so cute!' Faith held up the cut-glass owl. 'Thanks, Hope. I love it.'

'And that's from me. I don't know if I've done the right thing,' her father said as Faith picked up a gold envelope; the last of the presents.

Faith took out the single sheet of paper. 'Dad! You're brilliant! Driving lessons. Thank you.' She wrapped her arms round him.

Hope tensed. Faith was his real daughter and he loved her best. She stared at the carpet, close to tears.

Her father put an arm round her shoulders. 'You'll have to start dropping hints for your birthday, Hope. I know it isn't until November but it takes me a long time to get the message, doesn't it, Faith?'

Just for a second Hope rested her cheek against his chest, then she wriggled away.

The rain suddenly ceased. Russell put down his sketchbook and stepped out from the shelter through the beaded curtain of water dripping from the corrugated roof. He walked up the path for a short distance, but there was no sign of Hope. He checked his watch. She was over half an hour late. It didn't matter. He didn't mind waiting. He loved it out in the woods. Besides the atmosphere at home was miserable – Gran was uncommunicative, suffering with her nerves again, and the cottage seemed to change in character when she was ill. He sighed. Gran would be better when the winter was over, she always was. And already he could see signs of spring. There was a scattering of white anemones between the trees and he had spotted clumps of primroses in the valley.

A gleam of sunlight filtered through the lacework of branches, lifting the gloom, turning some of the suspended raindrops into sparkling crystals. He stopped in his tracks, appreciating the stark beauty. After a few minutes he returned to the shelter and resumed his drawing.

But now he couldn't concentrate. He listened for any sound – the clap of a wood pigeon's wings, the snap of a twig, a displaced stone – which might mean Hope was near. It was hard to contain his excitement. Since that first kiss almost three weeks ago their relationship had become more physical. They had contrived to meet often after school; playfully finding excuses to touch at first, then walking openly with their arms around each other, oblivious as to who might see them. They walked by the river, or in the castle gardens, searching out places where they could be alone in the early darkness.

Their kisses had grown passionate. The last time they met he had felt the curve of her breast beneath her school blouse and she had allowed him to undo the buttons so that he could kiss the soft, white, rounded flesh. He grew hot remembering.

Where was she? Their time together was precious. He looked at his watch again, counting the minutes lost.

'Russ.'

He heard her voice. Dropping his sketchbook and pencil on the logs, he went out to meet her and she came into his arms without hesitation. Her face was blotched, as if she had been crying.

'What is it, Hope? Is it something to do with Brandon Calthorpe?' He held her close. She had told him about her real father the day after she came back from London, spilling out the jumble of her emotions in the dark and the rain.

'Yes.' She reached for his hand. 'Let's walk.'

He didn't ask any more questions. She would confide in him when she was ready. They talked about trivial things as they followed the steep path to the lake, walking briskly along its edge until they reached the place where the stream flowed under the rustic bridge to merge with the glassy grey water. Here, the density of the bare trees on the slope above offered some protection and the ground was drier. Russell took off his fleecy jacket, kneeling to spread it beneath a massive oak.

'Let's sit for a few minutes.' He pulled Hope down and leaned back against the rough tree trunk. She sat a little apart from him, drawing her legs up, resting her chin on her knees. The wind had died down but the air was chilly. She was shivering in her best coat and through the sheer tights she was wearing he could see goose-flesh stippling her legs.

'Hope.'

She lifted her head. Her eyes were bleak, blind with suffering. He had seen that look on his grandmother's face and it made him want to cry.

'Hope, can you tell me?'

'I hate him,' she whimpered. 'I wish he had died'

'What's happened? I thought you were coming to terms with things.'

'He wants me to have a DNA test to prove I'm his daughter. He... he wants to take me away from Dad – from Richard. Oh Russ, I don't even know what to call him now. I don't know who I am any more.'

'You're the same person you've always been, Hope. You haven't changed.'

'But who do I belong to?'

'You don't belong to anyone. Your father – Mr Lawson – he loves you but he doesn't own you. You're a free agent. Free to love your family and friends. Brandon Calthorpe can't stop you doing that.'

'But he can take me away from them.'

Russell was silent, contemplating the idea of life without her.

'I need to belong to someone. I need someone of my own that nobody can take from me.' She clenched her fists, her body shaking with the tears she had been holding back.

'Come here.' Russell slid forward and put both arms round her, stroking her hair, trying to comfort her in the way his grandmother had comforted him years ago.

'Make me belong to you, Russ,' she murmured.

'I'll always be here when you need me, you know that.'

'Then make me yours.' She opened her coat and pressed herself against him, her mouth finding his.

He felt the impact of her words throughout his body. Suddenly she was beneath him and he was undoing the buttons on her cardigan, pulling up her sweater, unfastening the stupid hooks at the back of her bra. His head was buzzing, his body out of control. His hands closed around her breasts.

Hope didn't think about what she had implied. As usual she was making a drama of her life. It was her way of coping. Russell's fingers were cold on her skin, caressing her, creating sensations in her groin she had never experienced before. The rhythm of his body excited her. It was wrong, what they were doing. She was too young. Yet Juliet had been thirteen when she married Romeo; when they lay together in their marriage bed waiting for that fatal dawn. A line from the play slid into her mind. *He jests at scars who never felt a wound*. Russell had been wounded by his parents. He understood her. She was closer to him than she had been to anyone in her life. She wanted to bind him to her, to infiltrate his mind, his body and soul, so he would never be able to forget her, whatever the distance between them.

'Hope, we mustn't!' He let go of her, pushing her away, sitting up on his heels.

The space where he had been felt cold and lonely.

'Russ, please.' She tugged at his arms until he bent to embrace her, exultant when his body covered hers again. This time his kisses were rougher. Her flesh burned where his lips touched her. Her mind soared. She was Hope Lawson; she was Juliet Capulet; she was some strange, wild creature intent on coupling with her mate. It was bewildering and thrilling and forbidden. She began removing her underclothes impatiently.

'Hope... What if I come... inside you?'

She was too aroused to understand the significance of his words.

'Don't worry. Lots of girls my age do it. I've heard them boasting at school.' She opened her legs wider.

And then it was too late. The pain was excruciating, like a knife scraping, ripping her apart, and Russell was thrusting into her again and again. She cried out.

'I'm not hurting you, am I?' he gasped. 'I don't want to hurt you.'

'It's okay.' She bit her lip and lay still, wanting it to end. When he shuddered and released her she curled up on her side, bruised and disillusioned, covering herself with her coat. *Was that it then? Was that what sex was all about?*

'Are you all right, Hope?' Russell was sobbing, his breath coming in shallow gulps. 'I'm sorry. I shouldn't have let it happen.'

She couldn't look at him. Her face would betray her disappointment and she didn't want him to see.

'I've never done it before, Hope. They say it always hurts the first time.'

'Do they?' She turned towards him, half expecting him to have changed in some indefinable way. But he was still Russ, her Russ, his narrow face flushed, his eyes wide with fear, darkening to the colour of the lake as he waited for her to speak.

She touched his hand. 'It's not your fault. You tried to stop me.'

His face cleared. 'You're not going to finish with me then?'

'You don't get rid of me that easily, Russell Holmes.'

The moment of awkwardness passed. They dressed quickly, trembling as the sweat cooled on their bodies. When they were ready to leave Russell picked up his jacket and wrapped it round them both.

'Hope, what we just did... I don't think we should do it again. Not until we're older at any rate. It's not that I don't want to. Because I do. But I respect you, Hope. I don't want to use you. Do you understand?'

She nodded, relieved.

'I love you, Hope.'

He sounded diffident and she could tell he was embarrassed. She lifted her head and smiled at him. 'I love you too.'

CHAPTER 27

It was Friday evening, thirty minutes before the final performance of *Romeo and Juliet* was due to start. The changing room was crammed with temperamental girls, some in a state of undress, others preening in front of mirrors or fiddling with their costumes, the remainder chattering animatedly. A mist of hairspray drifted in the air, its fragrance mingling with an assortment of cheap perfumes, greasepaint and a hint of chemical cleaner. The atmosphere was volatile, charged with tension, underscored with petty jealousy and grievances.

Hope stood in front of a long mirror at the far end of the room, an island of space all around her. She was hardly aware of her isolation, of the malice implicit in the actions of the other girls – the averted faces, the shared whispers, the occasional guffaw of spiteful laughter. Her thoughts were mercurial, darting through her head like arrows. She was sad that this would be her last appearance as Juliet, elated because Mr Morgan had told her she should think about a career as an actress, and apprehensive because her family was coming to see her tonight. Grandma Ivy was bringing half of the Dalchett Estate with her – Dot Manning, Evie and Evie's daughter who had recently divorced, two of the gardeners with their wives, Holmes... And Russell. The nerves in her stomach tightened.

Unexpectedly she thought of Brandon Calthorpe. What would *he* think of her? Alarmed, she tried to shut him out. Why was he in her head now? He had gone abroad to convalesce and nothing more had been said about DNA tests. She took several deep breaths to calm herself. Her life had not altered, only shifted in aspect. This wasn't the time to worry about the future.

She adjusted her headdress. The person who looked out from the glass was a familiar stranger; a figure in a painting by a mediaeval Italian master, neither child nor woman. Her eyes were wide, shining with anticipation, her hair silky and loose about her shoulders, her breasts and slender waist accentuated by the close-fitting bodice of the sage-green velvet dress.

'Are you going to hog that mirror all night, Lawson?'

Hope didn't respond. The present was fading to another time, another place. She stepped backwards and felt the heavy skirt swirl about her ankles. The transformation was complete. She *was* Juliet.

There was no sound in the auditorium as Juliet knelt by Romeo's body, the empty phial in her hands. She bent to kiss him, to taste the poison on his lips. Her grief was harrowing to witness. Richard found it hard to believe it was really his little girl on the stage, portraying a suffering close to madness. Beside him, Kate wept silently, and glancing around he saw other women surreptitiously dabbing at their eyes. His daughter had touched the hearts of everyone. They had smiled at Juliet's innocent high spirits, sympathised with her impetuous love, shared her fear of dying and finally, as if they had been dragged into some hellish nightmare, found her anguish almost unbearable to watch. Hope was a revelation!

Richard swallowed, bewildered by his emotions. She was nothing to do with him, this incredibly talented and beautiful girl. She was his brother's bastard, his wife's secret shame, a burden he had been forced to shoulder. And now she was his joy, infinitely precious. He couldn't let her go. He would spend every last penny he had in the fight to keep her. She would never belong to his stepbrother.

A glint of metal caught in the spotlight. He held his breath. Juliet's cry when the dagger pierced her heart made the hairs rise on the back of his neck. He saw her clutch at her chest for a moment, saw her absolute terror before she became too weak to draw breath and fell beside her beloved. He heard the sigh from the audience and knew that, like himself, others had been deeply affected by Hope's performance.

The last few minutes of the play were unexceptional. It was as if a light had gone out on stage. All eyes were focussed on the still figures lying at the centre of the action and it seemed to Richard that, even here, Hope dominated the scene. When the curtain closed at the end of the play he felt disorientated, like someone waking in a strange place.

There followed curtain call after curtain call and each time, when Romeo led Juliet to the front of the stage, the applause grew louder until finally Mr Morgan signalled for her to come forward alone. The audience rose to its feet.

Kate's fingers dug into his arm. 'She's a star. There are thousands of actresses who couldn't do what she's done tonight. You must be so proud of her.'

He nodded, unable to speak, his throat tight with tears.

The actors gathered on stage behind the closed curtains listening to the scraping of chairs and the rumble of footsteps in the hall. Rhys Morgan put a finger to his lips. Like his pupils he was exhilarated, light-headed with the thrill of success. He knew they wanted to let off steam, and in a few minutes it would be impossible to restrain their exuberance

'Well done. I'm very proud of you all. I think everyone excelled themselves tonight.'

There was a clamour of half-whispered responses.

'Sir, I missed two lines in the third scene.'

'Sir, did you see the handle fly off Luke Watson's sword when he was fighting with Jason?'

'I was late with one of my entrances, Sir. The zip on my skirt came undone and Mrs Lloyd-James had to pin me up.'

'I'm sure no one noticed.' Rhys grinned at their eager faces. Then, judging that most of the audience would have left, he said, 'Now, if you can get changed without causing a riot, there's a party to go to – refreshments in the canteen for you and any of your parents and friends who care to join us.'

There was no subduing the cheer that followed this news.

'That went down well,' he remarked to Miss Spencer who emerged from the prompt corner, book in hand, as the teenagers surged through the wings and into the corridor.

'Yes. You must be very pleased.' She gave him her reluctant half-smile, scurrying past to supervise the girls and make sure they hung their costumes on the appropriate rails.

Rhys looked round for Olivia Lloyd-James. He saw her collecting discarded props.

'Great show,' she flashed her eyes in his direction.

His heartbeat quickened. She was seductive, exotic. And he had always been attracted to dark-haired, dark-eyed women.

'Carry these for me would you and I'll get the rest.' She thrust a pile of velvet drapes at him.

'Are you ready for the party?'

She pulled a face. 'I suppose so, though I can't say it's my idea of fun.'

'I'd like to buy you a drink sometime – thank you for all your help. Would you be free one night next week?' He knew he sounded awkward, like a schoolboy. He was out of practice. There hadn't been a woman in his life for a long time. Not since Susannah. For a moment she danced in his memory, laughing, black hair burnished by the sunlight as they walked in Hyde Park. Before she fell out of love with him.

'That would be nice.' Olivia Lloyd-James smiled. 'Maybe next Tuesday?'

'I'll look forward to it. He hoisted the drapes higher in his arms, relegating Susannah, and the five years they had lived together in London, to the back of his mind.

He heard the noise in the canteen from the far end of the corridor – the thump of the bass beat, the resonance of a hundred or so voices – and anticipated the congratulations of the parents, the flattering comments, the adulation of the cast. It was a pleasant feeling. But there was something he had to do first. He turned his back on the revelry and hurried towards the foyer, concerned that he might be too late. Hope Lawson would not be at the party; she was by far the youngest in the cast and it had not escaped his notice that the other girls resented her. He needed to talk to her mother and father. If he hadn't missed them, they would be waiting for her near the main entrance.

There were a number of adults lingering by the glass doors. Rhys hesitated. He had no idea what Hope's parents looked like. Someone had told him her father was a vicar but there didn't appear to be anyone wearing a clerical collar.

Almost immediately he found himself the centre of attention. He accepted praise gracefully, answering questions, mentally matching parents to pupils, trying to think of something positive to say about each child. There was no sign of Hope.

The entrance hall emptied slowly until there was only one couple left –a tall man with black hair, greying at the temples, and a woman who could possibly be Hope's mother because of her fair complexion. He decided to approach them.

'Excuse me, you wouldn't be Mr and Mrs Lawson by any chance?'

The woman's pale face flushed with colour.

'I'm Richard Lawson and this is a friend of the family, Kate Emerson.'

'Rhys Morgan.' He shook hands with them both. 'I wanted to talk to you about your daughter. You're not in a rush are you?'

Richard Lawson smiled. 'It's just as well we're not. We seem to have lost Hope.'

'Please, take a seat.' Rhys indicated a line of chairs. The couple sat down and he moved his chair to face them. He thought the woman looked tired. Her skin was dry and dull but her eyes were alert, intelligent; the most amazing green. He was disarmed by the sweetness of her smile and the intriguing little dimples which appeared as her lips curved upwards. Disconcerted, he turned to the man beside her. 'What did you think of your daughter's performance?'

'Well,' Richard Lawson cleared his throat. 'I know I'm probably biased but I thought she was outstanding.'

'She was, Mr Lawson, and that's what I wanted to talk to you about. I believe Hope has a rare talent. She's already an accomplished actress.'

'I could see that tonight. I have to admit it's taken me by surprise. I didn't know she had this gift. I've no idea where she gets it from.'

Rhys leaned forward. 'I think you should consider sending her to a stage school. I have a friend who teaches at the Lucy Valentine School in London. I could send her a copy of the video made in rehearsal. That alone would probably be enough to secure Hope a place. If not it would most certainly gain her an audition.'

'I'm not sure I want her to live away from home while she's still so young. You haven't mentioned this to her?'

'No. I wouldn't do that without talking to you first but I think we should offer her the opportunity. She has something very special.'

'Surely it would be better if she got some good exam results behind her before considering her career? I'm not at all happy about filling her head with dreams at this stage in her life.'

'She could do all her studying at LVS. And I think you might find acting is her life.' Rhys tried not to sound too dramatic, conscious of Kate Emerson's green eyes watching him. She spoke for the first time. Her voice was pleasing; clear and confident with a mellow, lilting quality.

'Hope has had a traumatic time recently, Mr Morgan. Perhaps it would be kinder not to make things more complicated for her at present.'

'It's your decision, of course,' Rhys conceded. He didn't want them to see his disappointment. How could they be so blind? Couldn't they understand that they were denying Hope the chance to fulfil her potential? He stood up, holding out his hand. 'All I ask is that you think it over. It was nice to meet you both. I'll go and chase up that daughter of yours.'

He walked away quickly. His footsteps sounded hollow on the tiled floor. The corridors were deserted; by now most of the pupils left in school would be at the party. His own pleasure in the evening had soured a little. He was a fool to let Mr Lawson's response upset him but he couldn't help it. He felt deflated. Hope Lawson was his discovery. He wanted to be instrumental in launching her career.

With sudden insight, he wondered if his ambitions for Hope were inextricably linked with the past. Susannah Knight was his contact at LVS. Wasn't this just an excuse to see her again? Was he so lonely that he had to resort to chasing married women like Olivia Lloyd-James or trying to rekindle the flames of a love that died long ago?

He pushed open the fire doors which led into the arts annex. Hope Lawson was coming towards him, little more than a shadow at the far end of the dimly lit corridor. She looked vulnerable, childlike. Perhaps her father was right and she was too young to be separated from her family.

'Hope, I'm glad I've caught you.' He spoke as she drew close.

She seemed startled.

'I didn't want to single you out for extra praise in front of the others but I think you know, don't you, that you carried the play? You were superb.'

'Thank you, sir.' Her smile was radiant.

'I meant what I said about becoming an actress. I think you have a great future ahead of you. Tonight will be the first of many triumphs. However, right now I should run along – your father is waiting. Where have you been anyway?'

'Helping Miss Spencer with the costumes. No one else bothered.'

'Thank you for that, Hope. Have a good weekend and I'll see you on Monday.'

Feeling vaguely annoyed with himself, he watched her run up the corridor. It wasn't his place to interfere in her life. He should never have spoken to her father about stage school. What he should have done instead was ensure that members of the cast had been on hand to help Miss Spencer before they all dashed off to their party.

In the foyer a caretaker appeared jangling a set of keys. Richard and Kate exchanged glances. The man didn't look happy to be working late. Somewhere in the distance a door banged.

'Dad! Kate!' Hope clattered across to them. 'I'm sorry I'm late. What did you think of the play?'

Richard leapt to his feet and folded her into his arms. 'The play was good; you were sensational! I'm so proud of you, Hope.'

His voice was gruff and Kate realised he was striving for self-control. She said nothing, happy to see them so close. If only Brandon Calthorpe would leave them alone...

'Kate. Thank you for coming. Did you enjoy it?'

'I loved every minute of it. But you were most definitely the star.' Kate grinned as Hope hugged her. 'I wouldn't have missed it for the world.'

'What did Grandma think? And Mr Holmes? And Evie? Do you think they liked it? Have you had chance to speak to them?'

Hope seemed almost delirious with success; unable to stand still, effervescent with energy.

Kate tried to listen, to make the right comments, but her own energy was failing, seeping away like water into sand. She found it difficult to stay focussed. This was the first time she had been out at night since her return to England. Normally she was asleep by nine o'clock.

'Are you sure you don't want to go along to the party?' Richard managed to get a word in when his daughter paused for breath.

'No!' Hope shook her head emphatically. 'But...'

'But what?'

She tilted her head, eyes slanting up at him. 'I wondered whether we might go to Giovani's, if we could get a table. Could we, Dad? For a treat?'

'I don't know, sweetheart. What do you think, Kate? Will it be too much for you?'

Kate hesitated. Her body was screaming for rest, but she could see it would be such an anti-climax for Hope to go home when others were partying. Resolutely she straightened her shoulders and stretched her lips into a smile. 'No. I think it's a great idea.'

Giovani's was busy but he found them a corner table, setting the menus before them with a flourish. Kate sat down shakily. The sudden warmth and noise made her head ache. Colours blurred. Richard ordered a bottle of Barolo and poured her some while they made their selections. The wine made her feel slightly sick.

Somehow she ate and drank and made conversation. Her movements were slow and uncoordinated; her voice reverberated strangely in her ears. The whole restaurant took on a distant, dream like quality. For an hour or so the food and wine gave her a false vitality before her speech grew slurred and her eyelids became too heavy to stay open. As they left she was aware of Richard holding her arm, guiding her past the tables, while Hope giggled irrepressibly. In the car she leaned back in her seat and the night revolved around her. She was glad when they reached the rectory.

* * *

She struggled in her sleep. Gran was standing by the side of the bed. But it wasn't Gran. It was a vile thing, part flesh, part bone, its empty eye sockets welling with blood and tears. In one claw-like hand it held an empty phial, in the other a silver dagger.

'No!' She shrank back against the pillows, trembling, her screams becoming part of the nightmare.

'Kate! Kate, what is it? What's the matter?'

She tried to sit up, to get away.

'It's all right, Kate. Nothing's going to hurt you.'

Her eyes flickered open and closed again, dazzled by the bedroom light. Richard's arms were round her. She could feel the heat of his body and the steady beat of his heart as he cradled her to him. But the fear did not subside. The terrifying image was imprinted on her mind. She clung to him, sobbing.

'It was a dream, Kate. Only a dream.' He smoothed her hair and wiped her tears with gentle fingers.

The trembling would not stop. She was afraid to open her eyes, afraid the apparition might still be in the room.

'There's nothing to be scared of, Kate, I promise you.'

His voice was calm, reassuring. She wanted to fall asleep in his arms and forget.

'What was it that frightened you?'

She tried to tell him. The words were jumbled, the explanation halting and out of sequence, but he seemed to understand. She felt his breath moving strands of her hair.

'It was because of the play, Kate – the phial, the dagger – Hope made it so real. It played on your mind, that's all.'

His words made sense. She looked up at him, weak with relief, and he bent to kiss away the last of her tears. His lips brushed her eyes, her cheeks, and finally, her mouth. With a little groan he pulled her closer.

'Oh, Kate, how I missed you. All those years you were away.'

What was he saying? Her heart began to race again. The blood pulsed in her ears. She had wanted him for so long. There had never been anyone else. She was a virgin still, had resigned herself to remaining so. Her body responded immediately. She wound her arms round his neck, returning his kisses, blanking all other thoughts.

But it was only an illusion of happiness. Her conscience was too strong. The memories came flooding back against her will. She couldn't live a lie. If he loved her, he loved the woman he believed her to be. And that woman didn't exist.

'Richard, don't.' She pushed him away.

'Kate, I'm sorry.'

She covered her face with her hands. 'There's something you have to know about me. Something I did.'

His arms enfolded her once more. 'Whatever it is, it can't be that bad.'

'It's unforgivable.'

'Nothing is unforgivable, Kate.' He was speaking like a priest now.

'Will you just listen!' She was suddenly angry, desperate to rid herself of the burden she had carried for years. She didn't want his platitudes.

'Okay. I'm listening.' His arms tightened round her.

'You remember I told you about Gran?' Her voice faltered.

'I remember. You don't still blame yourself for her death?'

'I killed her.'

'Kate, she took the tablets while you were asleep.'

'No.' She shook her head. Tears oozed through her fingers. The words spewed out of her mouth, swift and shocking as vomit; the sickening, gut-wrenching truth.

'I gave them to her. She begged me. Over and over. I couldn't bear it.'

Her voice was muffled behind her hands, lost in harsh, grating sobs, and she wondered if he had heard.

'I loved her, Richard. I loved her so much and I didn't want her to suffer any longer. So I did what she asked. I gave her the tablets. I put the glass of water to her mouth and I tilted her head back so she could swallow. And then I held her hand until she was gone.'

She stopped, her throat constricted, her breath coming in short, sharp gasps, the weight of her guilt too great to bear.

Richard waited until she was calmer then he said, 'Tell me everything.'

She recounted in detail what she had seen and what she had done, speaking in a halting monotone, eyes focussed inward. She did not spare herself, examining her motives with a scrupulous honesty. She told him about her lonely vigil, watching over her grandmother's body; about her desire for punishment and her certainty that the family doctor had protected her, giving his own version of events, making a confession impossible. When she had finished he didn't speak. She wiped a limp hand across her face and looked up at him. 'Do you still feel the same about me now?'

Even as she asked the question she knew the answer. She could sense it in the tension of his arms which still held her; hear it in his silence. A Kate who had made a mistake he could accept. A Kate who had taken a life was different. He would forgive her, pray for her, console her – love her even – because it was his duty to care for sinners. But he would never desire her again.

She moved away from him, scrambling back under the sheet and he tucked the blankets round her.

'We'll talk in the morning. You're worn out. Try to get some sleep now.' He kissed her briefly on the cheek. 'Shall I leave the light on?'

She shook her head.

'Goodnight, Kate.'

She turned away as he left the room.

In the darkness she wept. Her secret was out in the open at last. She had lost the only man she would ever love and she didn't know if she could stand the pain. Yet, beneath the numbness of grief, there was something else. A sense of release, a tranquillity, as if her mind had been scrubbed clean.

CHAPTER 28

Grace peered through the gap in the bedroom curtains as Alex left for work. She could still taste his kisses on her lips, see the place where his tears had marked her nightdress, feel the bruises on her back where she had fallen against the wardrobe. *What had she done to upset him? What had triggered that sudden violence?* Even now she was unsure whether he had knocked her over or if she lost her balance when he hit her. It had happened so quickly. All she could remember was his face – white with anger, his eyes wild.

Her thoughts were cloudy as she watched him reverse down the drive. He had said he loved her, begged her to forgive him, swore he would never hurt her again, and she had held him while he cried, but she hadn't been convinced. She had been withdrawn, silenced by a reaction which felt strangely like grief. He was a different person to the man she thought she knew.

She moved away from the window and sat on the edge of the bed, pressing her hands to her temples, trying to recall what she had done to provoke him. Alex had been lying beside her, head propped on his arm, as she talked about Cassie, excited at the prospect of seeing her friend again. She gnawed her lip, concentrating, piecing together the conversation in her head. Alex had teased her, wondering if he would be safe with two women under the same roof. They had both laughed. Then she had grown serious, describing Cassie and Lance's early struggles to establish their business, the eventual fruition of their dreams and the spectacular success of their latest venture.

Her hands went to her mouth. That was it! That was when his attitude changed. He had tossed back the bedclothes and swung his feet to the floor saying, 'I'm glad things are going well for somebody!' It should have been her warning. She had missed the sarcasm in his voice; hadn't given a thought to the fact that his own company was still having problems. While he searched for his slippers and bathrobe she had continued to reminisce about holidays spent at the villa on the clifftops in Albufeira and Cassie's increasingly luxurious life style. Even when he had muttered, 'Change the record, Grace,' she hadn't taken the hint. She had left the bed and wrapped her arms around him, babbling like a child. 'I can't wait for you to meet her, Alex. She's such a lovely person. Money hasn't changed her a bit.'

His words, and the look on his face as he turned on her, were trapped forever in her mind. *Why don't you shut up you fucking bitch?* After that her memory was hazy – the blow to her chest, the pain as the handle of the wardrobe rammed into her back, and then Alex kneeling by her, holding her, telling her how sorry he was.

She began to cry quietly. It was her own fault, of course. She was selfish and insensitive. She always had been. Alex was worried about the future and she had been too preoccupied with her own life to notice.

'Mum, is there any more soap?' Amy shouted from the bathroom.

Grace glanced at the alarm clock. If she didn't make a move her daughter would be late for school and there would be no chance of getting to Newark in time to meet Cassie at the railway station. She stood up shakily. Her limbs seemed to have no strength in them, but she went to the mirror and dragged a comb through her hair before she left the bedroom. She had to pretend everything was normal.

It was easy to spot Cassie. With her bleached blonde hair and bright pink jacket, she looked faintly ridiculous in the midst of the drab suits and anoraks. Grace found herself smiling as she hurried across the station forecourt.

'Hi, Cass. Sorry I wasn't here to meet the train. It's been one of those mornings.' She hugged her friend.

Cassie returned the hug with a grin. 'No apologies. I've only just arrived. It's good to see you, Grace. It's been too long.'

'Let's put your things in the boot and find somewhere to have coffee.'

Grace picked up the yellow suitcase, ignoring the pain in her back and its unwelcome reminder of the ugly scene earlier. Somehow the warmth of Cassie's greeting put everything into perspective. Alex wasn't a violent man. He was going through a rough patch that was all. There was nothing they couldn't work out between them.

Over coffee and scones Grace began to relax. Cassie talked enthusiastically about the new bar and regaled her with anecdotes of dogmatic builders, temperamental artistes and inebriated customers.

'You never have a dull moment, do you?' Amused, Grace pictured the scenarios.

Cassie spooned the froth from the bottom of her cup.

'There are some things I could do without, Grace. I must admit I'd rather confront an irate Spanish builder than Lance's daughter. Staying with her is an ordeal.' She sighed. 'Both his children still blame me for breaking up their parents' marriage, but at least his son is more polite. I'm glad to get away from London and the pair of them for a while.'

'I thought, after all these years...'

'No way.' Cassie shook her head ruefully. 'Anyhow, enough about me. What about you and Alex? When am I going to meet this paragon of virtue?'

Grace felt her face stiffen.

'There's nothing wrong is there?' Cassie raised a perfectly shaped eyebrow.

'Of course not. He's looking forward to meeting you.'

'The feeling's mutual,' Cassie murmured. 'Has Amy accepted him now?'

'I think so.' Grace looked down. She wasn't ready to talk about Amy's unpredictable behaviour.

'And work?'

'Is good, though I'm glad I managed to get a few days off to spend with you. Shall we have a wander round

Newark and then find somewhere for lunch?' Grace picked up the bill.

'That would be lovely. Here, let me get that.' Cassie took charge, paying at the counter and leaving an extravagant tip.

It was as if they had never been apart. They spent an hour window-shopping in the narrow streets and in the beautiful mediaeval square they found an inviting bistro where they treated themselves to a leisurely meal. By the time they returned to the car it was mid-afternoon.

Amy was waiting by the school gates, her expression sullen. Grace drew up at the kerb, prepared for the usual complaints.

'It's my fault we're late, honey,' Cassie said, opening the passenger door and sliding out. 'I kept your mother gossiping at lunch.'

Amy's face softened into a smile. 'Aunty Cass! How are you?'

'All the better for seeing you!'

Grace experienced a twist of jealousy as she watched them kiss each other on both cheeks. It had been a long time since her daughter had shown her any affection. Amy had grown distant during the last few months, often churlish when spoken to, spending hours in her bedroom with her stereo turned up to full volume.

'Okay, let's go home. Have you got much homework tonight, sweetheart?'

Amy ignored the question, climbing into the back seat and leaning forward to talk to Cassie, eager to tell her about the sheer awfulness of life at school. Grace took a deep breath and indicated right, pulling out into the traffic. Amy's rudeness unnerved her. Her mouth was dry and the thought of the evening to come filled her with dread. She had absolutely no idea what kind of mood Alex would be in when he came back from work.

He was early. Grace was stirring milk into a mushroom sauce when she heard his key in the door. Her fingers tightened round the spoon. She pulled the saucepan off the heat, splashing some of the hot liquid over the side.

'Are you all right?' Cassie looked up from the sink where she was chipping potatoes.

'It's okay. I'll run some cold water on it.' Grace stared at the three bright red spots on the back of her hand, her fear almost obliterated by the sharp sting of pain.

'Something smells good.' Alex came into the kitchen carrying an elaborate bouquet of red roses and a bottle of champagne.

'For you,' he held out the flowers and stooped to kiss her, 'to say sorry for my bad temper this morning.'

'Thank you.' She took them from him, gratified to see his smile.

'And you must be Cassie,' Alex proffered the champagne. 'I've heard so much about you.'

Cassie's smile was impish. 'Likewise. You've got a lot to live up to, Alex Walsh. Grace makes you sound like a saint.'

'I'm hardly that,' Alex twinkled at her, 'though I do try.'

Grace turned back towards the stove. It was going to be okay.

The evening meal was a success. Alex had obviously set out to charm, and being the accomplished flirt she was, Cassie responded with wit and flattery. Beside her, as usual, Grace felt overshadowed. But she didn't mind, content for once to sit back and observe them – Cassie, Amy and Alex – the three most important people in her life. She didn't want to think of the others; the two daughters who waited in the shadows for the times when she was alone.

'You're very quiet, darling?' Alex rubbed his thumb gently over the burn marks on her skin. 'You're sure you're okay?'

'I'm fine.' She stood up to collect the dinner plates. 'I'll fetch dessert.'

'I'll help,' Cassie said without much enthusiasm.

'No, I'll go, Aunty Cass. You've drunk far too much wine. You'd probably drop all the best china.' Amy began to stack the serving dishes.

'Cheeky madam!' Cassie said.

Amy giggled and followed Grace into the kitchen.

'What can I do?' she asked, piling plates into the sink.

'Well I made an apple pie yesterday and there's fruit salad if anyone wants it, but I don't feel in an apple pie mood, do you? How about we make Knickerbocker Glories? There's jelly in the fridge which was meant for a trifle tomorrow. It's got cake in it but that won't matter. What d'you think?'

'Great!'

They worked together, Grace ladling fruit and jelly into tall glasses, Amy topping each layer with vanilla ice cream. When the glasses were almost full Grace swirled thick cream on the top.

'Chopped nuts and glacé cherries,' Amy said, pulling things out of the cupboards to find what she needed.

Grace brushed away the stupid tears of happiness. It was like having the old Amy again; the same easy-going, loving relationship they had shared before Alex came into their lives.

'How's that?' Amy asked triumphantly.

'It's a work of art!' Grace said with mock reverence.

Amy spluttered with laughter. 'I do love you, Mum.'

Grace felt the skinny arms round her. She almost lost her composure. 'I love you too, sweetheart, more than anything in this world. Don't ever forget that.'

The evening passed pleasantly. The desserts were consumed with relish and Alex opened the champagne, filling their glasses for a toast to friendship. Afterwards, he made coffee and carried it into the lounge where they sprawled in the comfortable chairs and passed round chocolates which everyone said they couldn't possibly eat, but which were demolished in minutes.

Much later Grace and Cassie tackled the washing-up while Amy went into her bedroom to plan an essay for school. Alex remained in the lounge watching the late evening news.

'Does he lose his temper often?'

The sud-covered plate slipped through Grace's fingers, sliding back into the bowl. Cassie's question was completely unexpected.

'What d'you mean?'

'I may be tipsy but I'm not blind, Grace. You were walking on egg shells when he came home. You're afraid of him, aren't you?'

'No! Of course not.' Grace gripped the edge of the sink, wishing she hadn't drunk so much wine. 'I take it you don't approve of him then?'

'I didn't say that. I think he's absolutely charming.'

'But?'

'But I've met men like him before and they're not always what they seem. Are you certain he loves you?'

'Yes.' Grace picked up the dish cloth again. She was seething with fury but there was a cold, hollow sensation in her stomach. Cassie had come too close to the truth.

'Good. Then I'm made up for you. Don't be angry with me, Grace. I didn't mean to pry, but you're my best friend and I need to know you're happy.'

'Well now you do.' Grace said frostily, aware that her attitude was building a barrier between them. She rinsed her hands under the tap and dried them. Making an effort to smile, she said, 'Let's leave this until morning. We're both tired. What we need is a good night's sleep.'

REFLECTIONS

It was nearly midnight. Hope switched off the lamp and sat upright in the middle of the king-sized bed. Through the arched windows she could see Leicester Square where, even at this late hour, people were milling around, silhouetted like matchstick men against the illuminated buildings. It was a magical world of neon lights and non-stop activity. She shivered with excitement. Soon it would be her world – the theatres, the bustle, the vibrant atmosphere. This afternoon she had been accepted as a pupil at the Lucy Valentine School.

Kate had given her this chance. If it hadn't been for Kate she might have remained unaware of Mr Morgan's suggestion that she apply for a place at drama school. Apparently her father had refused to consider the idea at first, but somehow Kate had persuaded him. Since then he had been unstinting in his support. And today he had been with her to witness her success. She hugged herself in delight. It was really happening. She was going to be an actress.

The faint throb of music echoed in her head. In the multi coloured glow from outside the huge room looked strange and exotic, the flashing lights reflected in the ornate mirrors and on the lacquered oriental furniture. Aunt Helena had arranged for them to stay at the Hampshire Hotel in this luxurious suite...

Her thoughts skimmed away from Helena and, by association, Brandon Calthorpe. She didn't want to think about him. He was still in south of France, and the longer he stayed away the better.

She lay back against the pillows, her body taut with energy. Sleep seemed impossible. She wondered if her father was lying awake in the other bedroom. He had been very quiet all day, sitting with her throughout the morning and afternoon, listening to the interviews, watching her perform, accompanying her on a tour of the classrooms.

Remembering the bleak look on his face, she realised how much she was going to miss him. Until this moment she had only thought of drama school in positive terms, but now other considerations crept into her mind. *How could she leave them – her father, Kate, Faith, Russell? What if she made no friends? What if something happened to her father while she was away and she never saw him again?* She pulled the duvet up to her chin, suddenly overwhelmed by the momentum of the changes in her life.

'Dad,' she called softly.

There was no answer. She wanted to go to him, throw her arms round him and tell him how much she loved him. But she didn't. The inhibitions of a lifetime prevented her.

CHAPTER 29

The church clock struck six, its mellow tones drifting through the open window. Hope opened her eyes reluctantly. She had slept badly, tossing and turning, waking every hour or so saturated in sweat, her brain too active for rest. Now she was exhausted. For a few hazy seconds she lay still, thoughts sluggish, limbs heavy, oppressed by a sense of foreboding. Then suddenly she was wide awake, the vague terrors of the night clarifying, sweeping aside all other possibilities, leaving the truth exposed and undeniable.

She scrambled out of bed to stand in front of the full-length mirror. The frightened child in baggy cotton pyjamas who frowned back at her had nothing in common with the sensuous Juliet of two months ago. She pulled up the loose pink top and smoothed the crumpled trousers over her stomach. Turning to the side she could see the change in her body; the slight bulge beneath the patterned material. She was pregnant!

Why hadn't she realised before? She had mentioned her first missed period to Kate who told her it was probably due to the shock of finding out about her real father and the stress of the school play. Naively, she had attributed the slight queasiness she felt in the mornings to the same causes. Last month she had been nervous about the audition for drama school so she hadn't worried when she failed to menstruate again. But it was the middle of May now and her monthly cycle had not resumed. She should have known something was wrong. Her skirts had been growing tighter over the last few weeks, yet other than making a half-hearted resolution to diet, she had thought nothing of it. How could she have been such a fool?

She padded across to the window and leaned out, breathing in the cool air. The garden below was spiced with the scents of early morning, the grass glistening with dew. Beyond, the fields and woods wore the vibrant greens of spring and the hedgerows were powdered with blossom. The sun was low in a sky of pristine blue. Somehow all that beauty only made things seem worse.

Her eyes smarted with tears. She didn't want a baby. She wanted to go to drama school. It wasn't fair. There were girls at school who went with boys all the time. She had only ever done it once. Why was she the one to get pregnant? She was thirteen, far too young to be a mother. Perhaps she could get rid of it, have an abortion before anyone found out...

Her stomach heaved. How could she even contemplate such a terrible thing? Abruptly her emotions subsided into a leaden acceptance. There would be no abortion and no career in the theatre. Her life was over.

She threw herself down on the bed. How could she tell her father? He would be mortified. She couldn't face him; couldn't bear to lose the warmth of his love; to return to the old, uneasy relationship. Her mind seethed with images of the future and she buried her head in the pillow, shaken by a violent outburst of weeping. What was she going to do? Who would help her?

She sat up, wiping her eyes on the sheet. She would speak to Kate this morning, before going to school. Kate would know what to do.

Richard came downstairs to find Kate sitting at the kitchen table in her dressing gown, her slender fingers curled round a mug of coffee.

'You're down early.' He was worried by her pallid complexion.

'I wanted to talk to you.' She put the drink down, pushing it away almost angrily.

'Kate, what is it? You sound upset.' He sat opposite her, putting his hands over one of hers. 'Are you worried about something?'

'No.' She freed her hand and went to empty her mug in the sink. She remained by the window, her back to him. 'It's time I went back to Cheltenham, Richard.'

He was on his feet instantly. 'That's ridiculous. You're not strong enough.'

'Yes I am.' Her voice was low.

Her quiet determination alarmed him. 'What are you going to live on? You told me most of your grandmother's money had gone to the project in Sudan.'

'There's enough to tide me over.'

He moved to stand behind her. 'Kate, are you sure this is what you really want?'

She turned to face him, eyes cloudy as sea glass. 'You know it's not.'

'Then why?' He didn't want to hear the answer.

'Nothing's the same is it? There's no future for us.'

'I still care about you, Kate.'

'But you don't love me?'

He hesitated, wondering how to respond. She was very dear to him and the last thing he wanted was to hurt her any more.

'It's all right. You don't need to explain.' She pressed her fingers to his lips. 'It's just that I can't go on living with you. Being near you. Don't ask me to do that, Richard.'

Something in him recoiled from her touch although he tried not to show it. How could he be so fickle? *Love is not love that alters when it alteration finds.* The words trickled through his head. He was troubled by his reaction; the way his feelings for her had changed. Yet the image of a young Kate feeding her grandmother a lethal dose of tablets lingered in his consciousness. Though he could forgive, he could not condone what she had done.

'I'm sorry.' He bent his head to kiss her hair. He felt no desire, only a desperate sadness. Devotion, dedication, empathy, tenderness – all these he could give her – but not what she wanted. He put his arms round her and held her to him for the last time, inhaling the scent of her skin, a hint of perfume, the smell of the familiar shampoo in her hair. She was so thin; there was hardly any flesh on her bones, even after almost five months of convalescence. He wished she would stay and let him look after her. But he knew he had to let her go.

Neither Kate nor Richard noticed Hope come into the kitchen. She stayed close to the door, embarrassed by their intimacy. It seemed ages before her father raised his head. His face was paler than usual, the lines round his eyes prominent in the strong, morning light.

'Kate is leaving us.'

Hope was aghast. A sick dread settled in her stomach. How could she cope without Kate?

'When?' She asked the obvious question.

'At the weekend. I need to be independent again.' Kate spoke firmly.

Hope stared at her, fighting for control. She wished she was younger, wished she could run to Kate, tell her how much she needed her. Instead she said, 'We'll miss you. You will write to us, won't you?'

'Cheltenham's not the end of the world, you know.' Kate was smiling but the green eyes were dull, without animation.

'Better get some breakfast or you'll be late.'

Hope felt her father's hand on her shoulder. She had forgotten about school. The three of them moved around each other, setting out plates and dishes, refilling the kettle, making toast; little ordinary activities which meant they didn't have to talk. The clatter of china and cutlery filled the silence. Hope wanted to scream. It was hard to behave normally when all she could think about was the baby in her womb, taking over her body like an alien.

The smell of burning startled her. It was too late to rescue the toast. She threw the blackened slices into the pedal bin and put fresh bread in the toaster, expecting her father's criticism. She squinted at him through lowered lashes. He was standing by the table, a jar of coffee in one hand, a spoon in the other, gazing into space as if he couldn't remember what he was doing.

Kate was watching him too. The expression on her face made Hope ache with pity. She was becoming aware that there were secrets other than her own in the room and she looked away hastily, a new and undefined fear quickening inside her. There was too much unhappiness already. She couldn't tell Kate about the baby now.

Miss Spencer perched on the edge of her desk reading poetry aloud. Her thin, monotonous voice made the words dreary and the class was inattentive, whispering, exchanging notes. Hope felt sorry for the teacher, but this afternoon she couldn't concentrate. She glanced at her watch. It was nearly the end of the lesson; the end of a school day which had seemed interminable. She leaned on her elbows, thoughts skidding in different directions, swamped by the nightmare of her pregnancy. She checked her watch again. Less than five minutes to go. She was meeting Russell in the coffee bar at four o'clock and her stomach was queasy with apprehension. She had to confide in him. There was no one else. After all, it was his child too.

Someone kicked her in the small of her back and she heard a smothered giggle. Warily, she looked over her shoulder. There was a sharp pull on her scalp and the giggles erupted into barely muffled laughter. Her cheeks burned. *What was wrong?* Bending her arm behind her, she felt along the back of her chair and found her hair had been stuck to the plastic with blobs of chewing gum. Unobtrusively, she tried to release a few strands but her efforts only made things worse.

'Oh dear, Goldilocks, we are in a state aren't we?' Vanessa Greaves hissed and several other girls tittered in response.

Hope was saved from further taunts by the clamour of the bell. Immediately there was uproar – books thrown down, catcalls, whistles, scraping of chairs – and most of the pupils were on their feet before Miss Spencer had chance to dismiss them.

'See you later,' was Vanessa's final jibe on her way out of the classroom. At the door she stood aside politely, allowing Miss Spencer to pass, and then pulled a hideous face behind her retreating figure.

In moments everyone had gone. Hope sighed in frustration. She had meant to leave school early; now she would be walking with the masses, unable to hurry among the dawdling groups of teenagers. Twisting in her seat she picked at the gum. It was glutinous, difficult to reach, sticking her fingers together. Eventually she had no option but to grit her teeth and, holding a section at a time, tug her hair free, leaving tufts of it behind. Almost crying with relief she gathered up her things and rushed out of the room.

Outside the sun made her blink, its brilliance magnified through her unshed tears. She was so late the street outside the gates was almost deserted. Relieved, she hurried towards the main road into town. As she rounded the corner she could see Vanessa Greaves leaning against a wall, apparently deep in conversation with two friends.

Hope's heart began to flutter wildly. She didn't want any more trouble; she had almost reached breaking point. For a moment she considered turning back, taking a longer route, but she hadn't got time. Russell would be waiting for her.

'Watch out, it's Lawson!'

Vanessa's words were evidently intended to reach her.

The chanting began. 'Juliet. Teacher's pet!'

Hope tried to ignore it. Keeping her head down, she walked faster.

'What's happened to your hair, Lawson? Looks like you've got the mange.' Vanessa's eyes narrowed with spite.

The three girls formed a line across the footpath. There was no escape. The grassy bank at the side of the road was steep, the stream of traffic barely slowing to the speed limit.

'Let me pass.' Hope lifted her head defiantly.

'Oo-ooh. Who d'you think you're talking to, mangy cat?'

'Please. I have to meet someone.'

'Oh yeh? Some randy little ginger-tom? Come on, Lawson, let's hear you meow.'

'Here, kitty-kitty. Here, kitty-kitty.' The other girls took their cue from their leader.

'I said meow, Lawson!'

Hope swallowed back her fear. Instinctively, she turned to run towards the school. When they followed, she darted sideways, stumbling down the bank, slipping and sliding on the uneven surface. Their laughter followed her, making her careless of her own safety. The heel of her shoe caught in a crevice and she pitched forward, hurtling full-length to the ground, unable to stop herself slithering closer to the road.

The laughter became screams. The terrible squeal of brakes seemed to go on forever and the air was thick with the smell of burning rubber. The world slowed. She saw the sky, the stems of grass, the stones in the tarmac and the white van coming towards her slowly, inexorably, as if she was watching a film at half-speed. Seconds became eternity before she bounced off the bumper and into darkness.

CHAPTER 30

'I'm off, Gran.' Russell peered round the kitchen door. His grandmother was standing by the sink, turning the taps on and off, again and again.

'Gran!' Dropping his school bag, he went across and pressed his hands firmly over hers, feeling the strength in the calloused fingers as he tried to prise them free. The water was already overflowing, slopping onto the flagstones, soaking her feet.

'Let go, Gran, you'll flood the place.'

Her grip tightened. 'I can't. I have to—'

'Gran, you have to let go. Please. I'll clean up the mess and make you a nice cup of tea. Come and sit down.' He lowered his voice, soothing her in the tone he used when he talked to an injured animal. Her hold loosened. She slumped against him, suddenly limp. Keeping one arm around her, he took the plug out of the sink and twisted the taps until the water stopped running. Then he led her into the living room.

She sat obediently in her chair, staring into the sooty, black hole of the fireplace. He fetched a blanket to wrap round her and then lingered uncertainly in the gloomy room, afraid to leave her alone. The atmosphere in the cottage was tainted with sadness. It seemed to congeal in his veins, sapping his strength and depressing his spirits.

He felt heavy with grief; for his grandmother, a brittle bundle of bones trapped within the darkness of her own mind; and for Hope, lying in hospital, barely alive. And then, inevitably, he recalled his own mother's death.

His mood lifted a little when he heard footsteps in the hall.

'In here, Gramps.'

His grandfather came into the room having just finished a round of early morning tasks at the big house. He threw a copy of the *Hereford Times* down on the bookcase and unfastened his collar wearily. The skin on his face was sallow with exhaustion.

'Shouldn't you be on your way to school?'

Russell spoke in a whisper. 'It's Gran. She's been acting strange again. I didn't want to leave her.'

'You're a good lad. You get along and don't worry. I'll look after her.'

'Will she be all right?' Russell was close to tears. His grandmother appeared to be asleep, her head lolling against the arm of the chair. This spring had seen no improvement in her health. She had grown increasingly disturbed, her behaviour more and more bizarre, and he was worried she might have to go into an institution for the mentally ill.

'She's recovered before. We'll see her though this. You just forget about us old folks and concentrate on your studies.' His grandfather gave him a shaky smile.

'Okay. I'll see you later.' Russell made for the door and then casually, as if it was an afterthought, turned to ask the question that hung like a great, brooding shadow over every day.

'Is there any news about Mrs Calthorpe's granddaughter?'

'She's out of intensive care. According to the paper, it seems she may have been pushed, and as if that wasn't enough the poor girl was pregnant. Lost the baby.'

Russell grabbed the door handle to steady himself. *Hope, pregnant?* He swallowed hard, trying to remain calm. 'How awful.' The words sounded strangled. He was sure his grandfather would guess his secret.

'You can't believe everything you read in print.' Another sad smile.

'No, I suppose not.' Russell sidled towards the bookcase. He picked up the newspaper. The headline was blazoned across the front page – *Injured Schoolgirl May Have Been the Victim of Bullying.* He read on, aghast. *Schoolgirl, Hope Lawson, who was seriously injured two weeks ago, may have been the victim of school bullies. A passenger in a car travelling out of the city reported seeing an altercation between a group of girls. The witness saw Hope Lawson fall down the bank but was unsure whether or not she was pushed.* His eyes scanned the article until he came to the final paragraph. *A spokesman for the hospital confirmed that Hope Lawson was pregnant at the time of the accident.*

Sweat ran down the back of his neck. It was there, in black and white: Hope had been carrying his baby. *Why hadn't she told him?* He dropped the paper on the sofa and pushed his fingers through his hair; frightened, out of his depth in a hostile, adult world. He was tempted to blurt out the truth. He even uttered the first few words. 'Gramps, I'm so sorry...' But his grandfather was kneeling in front of Gran, chafing her hands gently. It wouldn't be fair to burden him with more problems.

Russell left them, quietly closing the door on their suffering.

* * *

A nurse adjusted the flow on the saline drip. Beside the bed in the small side ward electrical monitors throbbed and sighed, but beneath the sheet Hope's body was inert, the rise and fall of her chest hardly perceptible. Kate watched anxiously.

'Is everything all right?'

'She's doing well,' the nurse answered brightly.

Kate smiled at her. Two weeks ago Hope's condition had been critical. She had sustained multiple internal injuries and the loss of the baby she was carrying had weakened her further. Surgeons had fought to save her life but they warned that she might never walk again. Since then she had undergone a further three successful operations. The prognosis now was more optimistic.

The nurse turned to leave. 'Why don't you get some rest, Miss Emerson? She'll be asleep for another few hours.'

Kate nodded. 'I might.'

The room was stiflingly hot. She felt as if she had spent a lifetime in the hospital; the peculiar odour of disinfectant and illness seemed to be on her clothes and in her hair. The temptation to be outside in the sunshine was strong. There was nothing she could do here. Heavily sedated, Hope slept most of the time. And, when she did wake, she would turn away, unwilling – or unable – to speak to anyone. Once she had cried for her baby, fierce, bitter tears, punctuated with an almost incoherent babbling about guilt and punishment, but since then, in her brief periods of wakefulness, she had been silent and stony-eyed.

Kate shuffled uncomfortably on the hard seat. Surely it wouldn't hurt to go into town for a coffee? She had stayed at the hospital all the while Hope lay in intensive care, sitting at Richard's side throughout endless days and nights, willing his daughter to live with every ounce of strength she possessed. She had abandoned her plans to return to Cheltenham, knowing she would be needed in Tuston for the foreseeable future. Now she was spending as much time as possible with Hope, allowing Richard to resume his duties. But the strain was taking its toll. She was worn out. Other memories, never laid to rest, haunted her. She re- lived the horrors of war-torn Sudan – the makeshift hospitals, the stench of putrefying wounds and dried blood, the sight of bodies covered with flies and maggots – and, always waiting in the shadows, there was an old woman, beloved and dying.

She rubbed a hand across her eyes. The sterile ward had become a place of torture. Leaning forward, she said clearly, 'I'm going to stretch my legs, sweetheart. I won't be long.'

There was no flicker of response. Abruptly, she stood up, her chair screeching on the polished floor. She had to get away.

There was almost half an hour until the end of visiting time but the lift was crowded, people pressed together, avoiding each other's eyes. No one spoke until the doors opened on the ground floor and everyone surged forward, hurrying in the direction of the exit.

Kate almost ran.

'Sorry.' She side-stepped, narrowly avoiding a tall, dark-haired man in a grey suit.

'Miss Emerson?'

For an instant she was confused.

'Rhys Morgan. Hope's drama teacher.'

Of course, she recognised him now. 'Mr Morgan. I'm sorry. I didn't mean to ignore you. What are you doing here?'

'I came to inquire after Hope. I heard she was out of intensive care. Is she improving?'

'The doctors say so but...' The walls seemed to be spinning.

'Are you unwell, Miss Emerson?' Rhys Morgan touched her arm.

She shook her head. 'I'm just a bit dizzy. It's so hot in there. I was going to walk into town.'

'Can I give you a lift then? Perhaps I could buy you coffee?'

She hesitated, unsure whether she wanted company.

'Or, if you'd rather be by yourself, I'll drop you by the town hall.'

'No. I'd be glad of the chance to talk to someone.' It seemed churlish to refuse his kindness.

In the air-conditioned restaurant Kate drank her coffee gratefully. Rhys Morgan ordered scones with jam and clotted cream, and, to her amazement, she found she was hungry.

'This is very kind of you, Mr Morgan. Thank you.'

'Please, call me Rhys,' he smiled at her. 'And do you think I might call you Kate?'

'Yes.' She was surprised he remembered her name.

'I'd like to talk about Hope, if it won't upset you.'

She looked at him directly for the first time. He was unconventional, despite the suit. His wavy, brown hair was slightly dishevelled, cut in what was almost a feminine style, making a dark halo round his face. But there was nothing feminine about him. His shoulders were broad, his jaw line square with dark stubble visible beneath the skin, his mouth wide and generous.

'What did you want to say?' She saw his eyes were brown, like Richard's. Perhaps a shade lighter.

He spread his hands on the table, palms down. 'I've spoken to my contact at LVS. The school will take Hope next year, or whenever she's well enough to attend. I wanted her to know that. I thought it might give her something to aim for.'

'It's a lovely idea but maybe it's best not to mention it yet. We're not certain she will be able to walk unaided. It would be cruel to promise her a dream that might never come true.'

'I didn't realise.'

Kate saw the heightened colour on his cheeks. 'You weren't to know.'

They were quiet for a few moments. Kate searched for something to say.

'So, how are things with you?' They spoke in unison and then laughed. It was enough to dispel the awkwardness between them.

Russell waited outside the orthopaedic ward, sitting on one of the chairs he had found piled up in an alcove, his head bent over a science book. He wasn't reading but the book gave him an excuse to hide his face. He knew Hope was in one of the small rooms just inside the ward, but the door was shut and he was afraid there might be someone with her, even though he had seen Kate Emerson come out earlier.

The minutes crawled by. He heard the rattle of a tea trolley and glanced up as an auxiliary wheeled it along. People came and went. A bell rang to signify the end of visiting time. There was an immediate flurry of activity as relatives and friends of patients made their way to the lift. He wondered if he ought to leave as well, but nobody appeared to take any notice of him so he stayed, sitting alone in the empty corridor. The main doors to the ward were left open and he could hear the nurses complaining about the heat. He watched as they began to make a round of the beds, carrying out routine checks, dispensing medication, their voices deliberately cheerful. Yet the door to Hope's room remained closed.

Pushing the textbook back into his school bag, he went to look out of the window. Although there were a lot of empty spaces in the car park, it was impossible to be sure Richard Lawson's car wasn't out there. Sighing, he returned to his chair and resumed his vigil.

It was nearly five o'clock when one of the nurses came to check on Hope.

'You all alone, precious? I'll get someone to bring you a drink in a few minutes. Is there anything you want?'

He heard the woman's words clearly. His hands were wet with perspiration. Now the opportunity had presented itself, he didn't know if he had the courage to take it. Everything that had happened to Hope was his fault. The bullies had turned on her because she was pregnant. How could he ever put right the wrong he had done? What could he say to her? His tongue flicked over his lips but there was no saliva in his mouth to moisten them. He watched the nurse walk back up the main ward, his resolve wavering. But this was his only chance. He had to make his move now.

Hope could feel the warmth on her face through the half-closed blinds. It was almost unbearable to imagine the blue sky, to know the world outside went on without her and she might never be part of it again. She shut her eyes. What was there to live for? She couldn't bring herself to look at her father – at Richard – she was too ashamed. And who else cared about her? Her real father was abroad, Kate was leaving anyway, and Russell – Russell wouldn't want a cripple for a girlfriend.

'Hope.'

Her thoughts, scrambled and drug-induced, mocked her. She could hear Russell calling her and she pictured him by the lake at Dalchett House, his serious expression breaking into the warm lopsided smile.

'Hope.'

Again a memory stirred, this time savage and painful: Russell chasing after her in the valley alongside the stream, skinny and strong, faster than she was by miles, laughing as he caught her to him. Tears stung behind her eyelids. Never again. She would never run again. And she would never be an actress. Never even live a normal life, never be anything other than an invalid.

'Hope, are you awake?'

The voice was insistent. She opened her eyes unwillingly. 'Russ?'

'Hope, I'm so sorry.'

He was crying. She didn't want his tears or his pity. He would never understand how it felt to be lying here without a future. How could he? It was she who had been damaged; she who had been pregnant; she who had lost the baby. He was unscathed.

For a moment something pricked at the numbness within her, something dark and vicious, close to hatred.

'Go away, Russ,' she said. 'And don't tell anyone about us. I don't want to see you. Not now. Not ever.'

CHAPTER 31

Hope sighed, snuggling deeper into her padded jacket.

'Don't worry. We won't stay long.' Her father manoeuvred the car into the long driveway.

'I'm okay.' She stared out of the window at the murky December morning. A thin mist hung over the countryside making the woodland melancholy and she was overwhelmed with self-pity, envisaging a life filled with similar dreary days; a future as grey and illusory as the shreds of vapour among the trees.

She knew she should be thankful. Two months ago, on her last visit to Dalchett House, she had been in a wheelchair, lifted out of the car by her father, pushed along the passageway by Kate and fussed over interminably by her grandmother. Now she could even manage to walk a short distance if she leaned heavily on the sticks provided by the hospital. But everything was such an effort; the daily agony of washing and dressing, the exercises Kate made her work at each morning, physiotherapy three times a week. Sometimes it all seemed too much to bear; a pointless waste of energy.

They crossed the stone bridge and she heard the sound of rushing water before the gravel on the forecourt crackled beneath the tyres.

'Russell Holmes is in a hurry! Something must be wrong.' Her father slammed on the brakes and leapt out of the car.

Hope leaned forward. Russell was running towards the house and she could see his clothes were soaking wet, his thick, springy hair plastered like seal skin to his head. He reached the door and hammered on it with both hands. Hope wound the window down as her father hurried to catch up with him.

When Holmes appeared Russell almost fell into his arms. 'It's Gran! She's not at the cottage. She must have gone out and left every tap in the house full on. The ceiling in the kitchen's collapsed. There's a hell of a mess!'

'You're sure your grandmother's not there?'

'I searched every room after I'd turned the taps off.'

'Heaven help us. What now?' Holmes seemed suddenly old. He put his hand on Russell's shoulders but whether it was to support himself or to give comfort Hope could not tell.

Her father wasted no time. She heard him giving orders.

'Holmes, get Jim Manning. Russell, gather as many of the estate workers together as you can. We'll organise a search party. Betty won't have got far. I'll just let my mother know what's happening.' He disappeared into the house followed by Holmes.

Hope watched Russell sprint past, racing back the way he had come. If he knew she was in the car he gave no sign. She chewed her lip, reasoning with herself. Even if he had seen her, he could hardly have stopped to speak without betraying their secret. And he must be desperately worried about his grandmother. But she was hurt just the same. He hadn't even glanced in her direction. She closed the window, shivering. If Russell hated her it was her own fault. She had turned him away each time he came to the hospital after the accident and she had thrown his letters into the wastebin without even reading them. Why should she expect any acknowledgement from him now?

It was hard to understand why she had been so unkind. At first she had been too weak to care about anyone, bewildered by her feelings for the baby she hadn't wanted, and she had resented Russell, blaming him for everything. Then, as the weeks slipped by, guilt began to torment her. She had wished their child dead and it had been impossible to face him with such bitter knowledge in her heart. Her fingers played with the cord on her jacket. If only she could talk to him, try to explain. She missed him. He was the one person on earth who understood her.

'Hope, sorry I've been so long. Come on. Let's get you into the house.' Her father opened the passenger door. Obediently, she wriggled towards the edge of the seat, swinging her legs out of the car while he rummaged among the clutter in the boot for her sticks.

'Here you are.' He held them out for her and hoisted her upright with an encouraging smile. 'You'll soon be able to manage without these.'

She clung to his arm, longing to confide in him, free herself from the tangle of lies and half-truths. He had been so kind over the last few months, especially about her pregnancy. He had accepted her diffident excuses – that she only had sex once, that she had been distraught over the revelations about Brandon Calthorpe, that she hadn't really known what she was doing – and, when she refused to reveal the identity of the boy concerned, he hadn't forced the issue. He was the best father in the whole world and she had learned to love him without reservation.

'Did you hear what happened?' His expression grew serious.

She nodded.

'You don't mind if I leave you with Grandma? I ought to help Holmes find his wife. She's in a bad way by all accounts. Her grandson was very upset. He's a nice lad. Been a blessing to them both.'

'I don't really know him,' Hope flushed at the deception.

'No, I suppose not.' Her father kissed the top of her head. 'Ready?

'Yes,' she replied, well aware that now was not the moment to unburden herself.

He released her and locked the car. She began to walk slowly across the expanse of gravel, reassured because he was at her side, ready to help if she needed him.

They had just reached the house when two Land Rovers pulled up and she saw Russell among the men who climbed out. Her grandmother was waiting anxiously on the doorstep with Jim Manning and Holmes.

'I can manage from here, Dad. You go. I'll be fine.'

'Good girl.' He patted her shoulder and gestured to Holmes. 'The sooner we make a start, the better.'

For a few minutes, Hope stood with her grandmother, watching as the men consulted plans of the estate and set off in different directions, some on foot, some in the vehicles. When the forecourt had emptied they went indoors to wait for news.

Hope woke with a start. It was almost dark in the panelled room. The fire was crusty with ash, only the centre of it still pulsed with red-hot embers. She sat up in the shabby armchair, pushing aside the tartan rug which someone had tucked round her, rubbing her eyes as the layers of sleep peeled away. *What time was it?* She looked up at the face of the grandfather clock, just discernible in the last of the daylight filtering through the tall windows. The golden fingers pointed to ten past four.

It had been a long afternoon. She had spent most of it by herself, sitting in the drawing room with only a pile of old-fashioned magazines for entertainment, and eventually she had fallen asleep. She remembered her father rousing her to say that Betty Holmes was safe, but she couldn't recollect much of the conversation.

Stretching her legs, she winced at the sharp reminder of pain. The house was eerily quiet. The creaks and bumps, which she used to fancy were the ghosts of benign ancestors, had momentarily ceased and she felt completely alone. The slow heartbeat of the clock grew louder. It was no longer soothing but sad and sombre, ticking away the minutes of her life.

Unnerved, she reached for her sticks and, with some difficulty, managed to negotiate a path across the room in the semi-darkness. Once in the hallway she stood still, undecided. She had no idea where her grandmother was but Trudie would surely be in the kitchen and Dot Manning in the flat upstairs. Yet there was no sound. It was as though she was in a parallel world, separated from the living by an invisible wall.

Frightened by her own vivid imagination, she began the trek along the dimly lit passage. The stone slabs were slippery, worn smooth over the centuries, and several times she nearly lost her balance. The front door proved a problem. She tugged at the latch. It was too stiff for her to lift up with one hand, impossible to turn the iron ring at the same time. Finally, she relinquished both sticks, propping them against the wall while she grappled with the heavy door. She was grateful when it rasped open. Grabbing her sticks, she stepped back as it swung inwards letting a draught of moist, cold air into the hall.

She was unprepared for the vast emptiness of the encroaching night. For some stupid reason she had expected her father to be outside with the returning search party. But the forecourt was deserted, and beyond it the slopes of the hill were black, the mass of trees invisible except for those on the ridge, where the bare branches touched the smudge of grey sky. There were no stars, no hint of the moon, no lights visible, other than from the passageway behind her. Once again she experienced a feeling of panic. Where was everyone? Why had they left her?

Somewhere close by a fox barked. A shadow moved in the darkness at the bottom of the driveway and she heard the unmistakable crunch of feet on the gravel. She held her breath, rigid with terror.

'Hope.'

She breathed again, her panic receding. He stepped into the narrow pathway of light and she was seized by a different fear.

'Russ!'

His face was taut, expressionless. 'Mr Lawson told me to come over. He said to ask Mrs Calthorpe if she can arrange somewhere for me and Grandad to stay for a few days.'

Mr Lawson. He had said Mr Lawson and not 'your father'. He had spoken to her as if she was a stranger.

'I don't know where Grandma is,' she was determined not to cry. 'Please, come inside. I'll see if I can get someone to find her.' She hesitated, turning awkwardly, hampered by her sticks. 'Your grandmother... how is she?'

'As if you care.'

His words were sharp and ruthless. She lowered her gaze, mortified.

'I'm sorry. You don't deserve that,' he said quietly. 'They've taken her to hospital.'

'Where did they find her?'

Hope looked up at him. His face was the colour of candlewax.

'I went down to the lake after the first group of men came back. They hadn't seen her but I remembered something Gran said...' his voice faltered. 'She has this thing about water.'

'And you found her there?'

'Yes, near the place where I first met you. She was standing in the lake, water up to her armpits. I waded in and pulled her out. She kept saying she had to cleanse her soul.' He began to cry, snivelling like a child, wiping his sleeve over the mucus running from his nose. 'I put my jacket round her and rubbed her arms and legs to get some warmth into her body and then I sort of half-carried and half-dragged her back to the cottages. I didn't dare leave her on her own.'

'Russ—' Hope put a hand on his arm and flinched when he shrugged her away.

'I don't need your sympathy. Just give the message to your grandmother. I'd better go. Mr Lawson won't be back for a while. He's helping clean up our cottage while Grandad's at the hospital.'

His eyes glittered with grief and scorn.

'Oh, and by the way, I'll keep your secret. About the baby. I'm not good enough for you, am I? That's why you don't want anyone to know about us. Well, you needn't worry. I won't bother you again.'

The door slammed behind him like a gun shot. Hope was left reeling from his accusation. How could he be so cruel? He had been her only friend; they had made a child together. Now he didn't want her any more.

PART THREE
Homecomings

CHAPTER 32

July 1996

There were no cars outside the bungalow. Amy yanked the bulky haversack from her shoulders as she ran up the path. Hands sticky with sweat, she felt for the key, scrabbling among the biscuit crumbs, sweet wrappers and crumpled tissues which had accumulated beneath her homework books over the last year. The July sun was unusually hot on the back of her neck and her stomach muscles constricted with a sudden snatch of fear. *Perhaps she had gone too far this time.* She looked back along the road, expecting to see her mother's battered green hatchback or Alex's silver Jaguar at any moment. Relieved there was no sign of either, she let herself into the hall and closed the door.

It was cool after the heat outside. She dropped the haversack on the floor and rubbed her arms, surprised to feel pin-pricks of gooseflesh. Her fear dissolved into misery. The place didn't feel like home any more. She longed to run away; as far away from Alex as possible. Instead she hurried along the corridor, passing the open doors of rooms that were no longer welcoming.

The whole place smelt of him. The scent of his aftershave lingered in the bathroom, the stale reek of cigars clung to the fabrics in the lounge, and in the kitchen the stink of kippers made her heave. Wrinkling her nose, she took a bottle of vodka from the cupboard in the dresser and swallowed a couple of mouthfuls of the clear liquid. It made her gasp, burning her parched throat. She wiped the rim of the bottle and replaced it carefully.

In her bedroom she smoothed her cropped hair, pulling a face at herself in the mirror. It had been a mistake to have it cut so short and the bright red streaks didn't suit her. She looked different, almost ugly. Her mother would be furious. *Good! It serves her right.* She pressed her hands over her eyes. Why was nothing the same? Ever since Alex came to live with them things had altered. Gradually their lives had begun to revolve around him until the special relationship she had enjoyed with her mother disintegrated, breaking down under the force of his personality. She hated him.

Her mother had changed too. She even looked different. Younger. She had blonde highlights in her hair, dressed in expensive clothes and never went anywhere without wearing make-up. When Alex first moved in she had been irritatingly coquettish, flirting like a schoolgirl, full of energy; lately she seemed sad, her face pale in the mornings, the shadows under her eyes pronounced until she covered them with concealer. Amy blinked back angry tears. A perverse part of her wanted her mother to be unhappy.

Troubled, she glanced at the photograph on her dressing table. It was hard to believe the tall, young man with floppy black hair and a clerical collar was her father. As a child she never asked about him. Her mother had been enough for her until Alex came into their lives. Alex had made her feel insecure – jealous if she was honest – no longer certain she came first in her mother's affections. And that was when she wanted to know her own history. Her mother had produced the photograph reluctantly, asking her to keep it in her bedroom out of Alex's sight, answering her questions briefly, as if she didn't want to talk about the past.

Distracted, Amy picked up the photograph. What was he really like, this man? He would be much older now, of course, but would he still have that twinkle in his dark eyes? Would he want to see her if he knew she existed? She sighed, abandoning the fruitless speculation. Her mother had explained that the marriage had been unhappy and it would only open old wounds if they tried to find him.

Turning back to the mirror she considered the problem of her hair. If she was going to get into trouble she might as well make an impact. She wriggled out of her school dress and hunted in the wardrobe for the cheap black skirt she had bought in the summer sales. It was short and tight, revealing too much thigh, and her mother didn't like her wearing it. She stepped into the scrap of material and hitched it up over her hips, slipping her feet into a pair of high-heeled black mules at the same time. Next she put on a low-cut black T-shirt. Then, squinting into the glass, she leaned forward to accentuate her eyes with purple shadow, mascara and thick black eyeliner.

Pleased with her efforts, she reached into her jewellery box and fished out a black enamel heart threaded on a lace and a pair of black hoop earrings. She stood back to assess her appearance. The effect was startling. Her mother would definitely be shocked. *So what?* At least she would get some attention and she had precious little of that nowadays.

The front door slammed. Alex was back.

Grace was late home. The silence made her uneasy. The place could have been empty except that the atmosphere was charged with tension. She took a deep breath and went into the lounge.

Alex was sprawled on the sofa, a glass of red wine in his hand, a half-empty bottle on the coffee table in front of him. His eyes narrowed with temper when he saw her.

'Where the hell have you been? You know I have a meeting to get to.'

Grace forced a smile. 'I'm sorry. Someone came into the shop just before closing and I'd already told the girls they could go.'

'So complete strangers are more important than me?'

'Of course not,' she retreated quickly, anxious to get away before his black mood escalated into something worse.

In the front bedroom she took off her uniform and put on jeans and a white blouse. Out of habit she replenished her make-up and combed her hair, pulling it through an elastic band and twisting it into a loose knot, her movements automatic.

On her way to the kitchen she hesitated outside Amy's door then pushed it open. Her daughter scrambled off the bed to face her.

'Don't go on at me, Mother. I'm fifteen. If I want to change my image, I don't need your permission.'

Grace stared in dismay. Where was her beautiful little girl? What had the stupid child done? *How would Alex react to this?*

'Aren't you going to say anything?' Amy's tone was belligerent.

An image flickered in Grace's memory; herself as a teenager, challenging her own mother in exactly the same arrogant way – long, mousy hair dyed bright orange. Now she felt her mother's pain. 'It's your hair, darling. If you're happy then I suppose I'll just have to get used to it.'

'So you're not cross with me?' Amy sounded almost disappointed.

'I'm a bit sad. I always loved your curls. But they'll grow again. It's not the end of the world.'

'And it's okay if I go out tonight?'

'As long as you're back by ten o'clock.'

Amy grimaced. 'Mum! I'm not a baby.'

'You're too young to be wandering the streets late at night. Now, I think you should find something more suitable to wear. Dinner will be ready in half an hour.'

'I'm not hungry.'

'Okay. I'll make you a sandwich later.' Grace struggled to hide her anxiety. At least the inevitable confrontation between Alex and Amy would be delayed.

They had their meal at the kitchen table. Alex complained his steak was underdone but he ate it anyway, cutting it precisely, chewing it with relish. Grace moved her food around the plate. She couldn't think of anything to say. When Alex had been drinking even the most innocuous comment could spark an argument and she hadn't the energy to pander to him tonight. With luck, if she kept quiet, he would finish his meal and go. To wherever it was he was going. He put down his knife and fork and pushed his empty plate into the centre of the table.

'Why hasn't Amy honoured us with her presence?'

'She's got a headache,' Grace lied, 'I think the heat's affected her. Do you want anything else?'

'No thanks.' He stood up unsteadily. 'I need a bath. Could possibly drum up a bit of business tonight.'

Grace watched him walk away. Why did he bother with the pretence? She carried the plates to the sink and tackled the pile of washing up, concentrating on removing every tiny bit of grease, deliberately keeping the dark thoughts at bay. When the kitchen was tidy she cut a cheese sandwich for Amy and wrapped it in foil. Alex came to say goodbye as she was making herself a drink.

'Don't wait up for me, Grace.' His fingers stroked her throat. She trembled at the pressure of his lips on her neck and he laughed, mistaking her repulsion for desire. 'Later, Grace. If you're a good girl.'

Abruptly, he released her. She didn't turn round until she heard the front door close behind him.

The trembling wouldn't stop. When she picked up her mug coffee dribbled through her fingers, staining the front of her blouse. She wiped up the mess and leaned against the work top, unable to halt the flow of memories and the terrifying glimpses into the future that crowded into her mind.

What a fool she had been! What a silly, blind, pathetic fool! She had been disarmed by Alex's sturdy good looks and flattered by his attentions. Even the odd outbursts of violence hadn't alarmed her unduly in the beginning – he had been so contrite, so loving afterwards – and it was easier to blame herself for provoking his anger than to contemplate life without him. Now she was trapped, bound to him with no tenable means of escape. If only she had listened to Cassie's warnings. Instead she had argued bitterly with her, severing all contact.

Grace shook her head, appalled at her own stupidity. Last summer Alex had asked to borrow more money for expanding his business and she had loaned him most of her savings. Almost immediately he had encountered difficulties. It had been a terrible time. Alex had become aggressive and moody, turning to drink as a way of dealing with his problems. He had bemoaned the fact that he had no security; no property to put up for sale or re-mortgage. He told her he was a failure, that she would be better off without him and that he intended to sell up, settle his debt to her and leave.

How easily she had fallen for his scheming. She couldn't bear the thought of losing him. Common sense had deserted her. She had offered to take out a second mortgage on the bungalow and, of course, he had pleaded with her not to, which simply made her more determined. She had signed away her independence and her daughter's legacy with barely a qualm.

And then, little by little, Alex had revealed his true colours. Now he no longer made any effort to hide his displeasure when things were not to his liking. He frequently drank to excess and his temper was vicious and unpredictable. At times he didn't speak for days. He made love to her occasionally, without tenderness, using her as if she was a prostitute. And, recently, he had been out several nights a week, ostensibly wining and dining potential clients, returning in the early hours of the morning, his clothes reeking of smoke and perfume. He was not the man she had believed herself in love with. She was afraid of him; afraid to question him; afraid to deny him her body or her home.

But it was her own fault. She had brought this on herself. She had betrayed her husband, forsaken her two older daughters and given the money which had been set aside for her youngest to a man who had fleeced her dry. There were no excuses. She was weak and selfish and she never learned from her mistakes.

Giving way to self-pity, she began to cry silently. What could she do? She had to stay with Alex, hang on to her home somehow, and above all, she had to hide the truth from Amy. Tears distorted her vision. She had failed Amy, just as she had failed Faith and

Hope. Overcome with guilt and remorse, she ran from the kitchen.

In the spare room she knelt to drag an old suitcase from under the bed. Inside, beneath the neatly folded bedclothes, lay an envelope, yellow with age, the corners curled up, the writing on the outside faded. She held it for a moment, her head bent in shame. How long since she last opened it? It must have been when she gave the photograph of Richard to Amy, nearly three years ago.

Why had she hidden them away, her family? Over the years the envelope had been stuffed in a handbag, flattened in the pages of a recipe book, pushed between sweaters in a drawer, and finally, when Alex moved in, hidden under the sheets and pillowcases no longer used. She had sealed up her past, tried to forget her other daughters, forget what she had done to them. But they would never set her free and to look at their faces broke her heart.

She took the photograph out carefully. They smiled up at her – Faith at seven years old, an hour or so before her birthday party, wearing the dark-blue velvet dress bought specially for the occasion; Hope, dressed in pink, nestling in Richard's arms; herself, young and pale, standing slightly apart from the group. *Where were her children now?*

'What are you doing?'

She hadn't heard Amy come into the room.

'Nothing.' She stood up awkwardly. The photograph slithered out of her hand.

Amy picked it up. 'That's you with my father, isn't it? Who's that little girl? And the baby?'

'I can't remember. Children of some friends I think.' Grace prevaricated wildly.

'It says on the back *Tuston Rectory: the four of us on Faith's seventh birthday.*' Amy's voice was sharp.

'Does it?' Grace rubbed her forehead.

'You've been crying. Why has this picture upset you?'

'It wasn't the picture.' Grace sat on the bed, suddenly weary. 'I had a row with Alex.'

'So, what's new?' Amy dismissed the answer. 'I want to know about this.' She waved the photograph in the air. 'Who are these children?'

'I can't tell you,' Grace whispered.

'Are they... are they yours?'

'I don't—'

'They are, aren't they?' Amy grabbed her by the shoulders. 'Tell me, Mum.'

'Yes.' There was no way to hide the truth any longer.

'And you left them?' Amy's features creased in disbelief.

'Yes.'

'How could you? How could you leave your own children? Leave a baby?'

'I did something. Something very bad. I had no choice except to go away. They were better off without me.'

'Don't you ever wonder about them, worry they might be ill? Don't you miss them?'

'I miss them every moment of every day. If I could change things I would.'

'And what about me? I have two sisters I know nothing about. What right did you have to keep that from me?'

'I did what I thought was best for everyone.'

Amy snorted. 'You mean what's best for you! Like bringing Alex here and falling out with Aunty Cass. You don't think about anyone else, Mum. You're a selfish, hard-hearted bitch!'

'Amy— ' Grace reached for her daughter's hand.

'Don't touch me! I'm going out. I can't stand being in the same house as you.'

'Please. Let me try to explain.'

'Tell it to someone who gives a toss.' Amy rushed out of the room, slamming the door so hard that the curtains billowed in the draught.

Grace sat for a long time, exhausted by the encounter. She heard the front door bang and felt the loneliness of the empty bungalow settle round her. Outside the sun was still shining, tinting the walls with a flush of pink, illuminating the dust on the glass-topped dressing table. Somewhere a clock chimed eight. She didn't get up. There was nothing to do. Nobody who needed her.

The five girls waiting on the street corner were rowdy, screeching obscenities at anyone who gave them a second glance. Amy didn't enjoy their company, but the fact that her mother wouldn't approve made them attractive.

'Hiya, Ames. We'd almost given up on you.' Chelsea Turner – dark-haired, thickset, and the undisputed leader of the group – came forward to greet her. 'Got any booze?'

Amy held out the half bottle of vodka she had concealed beneath the jacket she was carrying.

'Good girl.' Chelsea clapped a heavy hand on her shoulder. 'Any fags?'

'No. Sorry.'

'S'okay. How much cash you got?'

Amy handed over two pounds and fifty-seven pence from her purse. One of the girls, older in appearance than her years, was designated to buy cigarettes from a nearby tobacconists. When she returned they headed for the allotment site which had become a meeting place for disaffected teenagers.

They sat under a canopy of trees, eying the boys and making suggestive remarks. Amy made an effort to be part of the group, swigging from bottles of drink, smiling at jokes she only half understood, but her thoughts kept returning to her mother and the implications of their conversation earlier. It meant her whole life had been a lie.

Someone poked her in the ribs. 'You gonna smoke that ciggie, Ames, or just admire it?'

She blinked, startled. 'Got a light then?'

'Here.' Chelsea threw her a silver lighter. 'I nicked it down the shopping centre yesterday. You can keep it if you like.'

'No thanks, you're all right.' Amy lit the cigarette inexpertly and passed the lighter back. She was glad it was growing dark. The talk had degenerated into crude, foul-mouthed reminiscences and she bent her head to hide her blushes.

'How was your first time, Ames?'

'Mine? I—'

'Ames's first time could be now.' Chelsea came to her rescue, pointing to three lads in leather jackets ambling towards them. 'Craig Geddis is always boasting he has a different girl every night.'

Amy swallowed. Surely Chelsea didn't expect her to have sex with someone she had never met?

'I can't.' She met the avid stares timidly. 'It's the wrong time of the month.'

She waited for them to call her a liar and breathed again when they accepted her explanation.

'Tough luck. Maybe next week?' Chelsea winked at her.

Amy looked away as the three boys joined them. She knew it must be after ten o'clock and she ought to be going home. But she wanted to punish her mother. *She doesn't care about me; like she doesn't care about her other two daughters.* The hurt bubbled up inside her, making her reckless. She uttered some risqué comment and was gratified when everyone laughed.

After a while three of the girls wandered off, bored when the boys paid them no attention. A little later a fourth girl left with a thin, greasy-haired youth to the accompaniment of cat-calls and indecent suggestions. Amy began to wish she had gone home earlier.

Craig Geddis stood up, holding his hand out to her. 'How about it?'

She stammered something incoherent.

'Monthly curse,' Chelsea said.

Craig Geddis scratched his nose. 'Want to go for a drive then, the four of us?'

'Might as well, there's not much else to do round here.' Chelsea scrambled to her feet, hauling Amy up with her.

'Okay. Better make a move, before the punters come out of the pubs.'

'Where's your car?' Amy asked.

The other boy, whose name she didn't remember, tittered. 'It's somewhere round here, isn't it Craig?'

They sauntered along a maze of back streets, dumping their empty bottles in garden hedges on the way. As they passed a seedy public house Craig Geddis stopped by one of the old cars parked at the side of the road. At first Amy didn't realise what was happening. He had the passenger door open in seconds and she was pushed in after him while he climbed across to the driver's seat.

'Unlock the back door, quick!' he shouted.

Amy twisted round to pull up the old-fashioned lock. Chelsea and the other boy jumped in, tugging the door shut after them.

'Right, let's get out of here.' Craig Geddis fiddled with the wires under the dashboard and, as he spoke, the engine spluttered into life. He grinned, pressing his foot on the accelerator. 'Here we go.'

He drove at speed through the quiet housing estates, only slowing down when they reached a main road.

'Nobody chasing us, Tod?'

'Nope.'

'Good. Check what's in the glove compartment, Amy, there's a good girl.'

Amy fumbled with the catch. 'There's only a pack of tissues and a notebook.' She was grateful there was nothing of value for him to steal.

'Never mind.' He produced a roll of notes from his pocket. 'I got these little beauts this afternoon. Silly old git had his wallet in his back pocket.'

Amy felt sick. He was so matter-of-fact about it. This was normal; part of everyday life for him.

Craig Geddis drove the car into a twenty-four hour petrol station. 'I'll fill her up and get some drink. You come with me, Tod. There's only a couple of women on the tills. They won't quibble about serving us.'

Within minutes they were on the road again, heading out of the city. Amy gripped the edge of her seat, mesmerised by the blur of neon lights, dreading the inevitable wail of a police car siren.

And then they were in open countryside. The headlights illuminated the straight, grey stretch of road in front, and she saw the needle on the speedometer hit one hundred.

'Where are we going?' she asked faintly.

'Skeggy!' Craig Geddis shouted.

It took her a moment to understand. 'We're going to Skegness? *Now?*'

'Why not?' He took one hand off the steering wheel and ran his fingers up her leg, laughing.

Amy bit her lip, out of her depth. She was different to the others but she had to pretend to be one of them. All she could do was sit tight. The mixture of alcohol she had consumed had given her a headache and when she closed her eyes it only made things worse. The ride was a nightmare. She didn't expect to survive.

But she did. In Skegness they took their stash of wine and beer to the beach. When they had drunk themselves stupid they dispensed with their clothes and ran into the sea, splashing, jumping the waves, pushing each other under the water. For a brief span of time she almost believed she was enjoying herself, until, on the way back to the car, she watched Craig and Tod trampling over flower beds and tearing up plants just for the hell of it.

She was almost sober on the journey home, aghast at the lateness of the hour, terrified at the prospect of facing her mother and Alex. Once again the car sliced through the black countryside, this time swerving dangerously at bends, veering across the white line, sometimes skimming the grass verge at the edge of the road. *What if we crash? What will Mum do if I'm killed?* Horrific scenes played in her head. The endless miles flashed by and she remained mute, rigid with fear.

Craig Geddis slowed down as they approached the city and she saw a blue flashing light in the distance. Another fear surfaced. *What if we're caught?*

'Bloody cops are everywhere.' Tod commented irritably.

'No worries. We're home and dry.' Craig turned into a council estate, weaving his way through street after street until they arrived at the allotments. He drove up a narrow track between the houses. With a grunt of satisfaction he parked in front of a dilapidated shed and switched off the lights. Amy stumbled out of the car.

'Hey, steady on.' Chelsea grabbed her arm.

There was a heavy thud and the noise of wood splintering.

'What are they doing?'

'You don't want to know.' Chelsea answered.

The door to the shed caved in with a crash. Amy put a hand to her mouth, retching. Craig and Tod emerged through the jagged black gash in the wooden panels; swift, grey shadows in the darkness. A sharp smell of petrol filled the air.

'Move it you two!' Craig yelled.

'Come on!' Chelsea dragged Amy down the uneven track. The car was a sudden ball of fire behind them, flames roaring in their ears as they ran.

'Fuckin' hell, Craig,' Tod gasped, 'that was close. You fuckin' idiot. You could've killed the lot of us.'

The explosion cracked open the night. Lights appeared in windows and pale faces peered through parted curtains.

'Run for it,' Craig Geddis shouted, 'before the cops get here.'

Amy couldn't keep up with them. She stopped to pull off the flimsy black mules, her heart thumping so violently she could barely draw breath. Shoes in her hand, she ran on through the dimly lit estate, dodging into an alleyway only seconds before the lights of the first police car scoured the street.

Grace lay awake, every nerve in her body strained. *What time was it?* The sky was becoming perceptibly lighter but she was afraid to reach for the alarm clock in case the movement disturbed Alex. It was hard to lie still. She wanted to be out searching the neighbourhood, phoning the police, doing something. *Where was Amy?* A nagging, pessimistic part of her brain visualised a body in a ditch, raped and disfigured, though she knew staying out all night was more likely her daughter's way of paying her back for the revelations of yesterday evening.

She clenched her hands, wishing she had said nothing about her worries to Alex. He had returned just after one o'clock, surprised, and not best pleased, to find her waiting up for him. She had blurted out her anxiety without thinking. That was her first mistake. The second had been to try and justify Amy's behaviour. She shivered, remembering. He had lost his temper, seizing her by the hair and pulling her into the bedroom, all the time swearing, berating her for being weak and a failure as a mother, calling Amy a little tart who needed a good hiding to teach her to behave respectably. He had ordered her to undress, watching with glazed eyes as she took off her clothes. And when she was in bed he went into the hall and she heard him pushing the bolts across the front door.

Blotting her tears on the sheet, she wondered if he really was asleep. His breathing was steady yet he didn't seem relaxed. Was it imagination or was he, like her, alert and listening for the scrape of a key in the lock?

She heard it at last. Her relief was shot through with dread. *Had Alex heard it too?*

'Mum? Mum, let me in.'

It was only a whisper but she couldn't risk Amy calling again. Slowly she drew back the bedclothes, inching herself upright, pressing her hands down on the mattress to keep it from shifting with her weight, placing first one foot, then the other on the floor.

Alex didn't stir. Carefully, pausing after each step, she walked across the room, feeling her way in the semi-darkness. Once in the hallway she ran to let her daughter in. The noise of grating metal seemed loud in her ears, the hinges creaked as the door swung open.

The light was snapped on.

'What the hell do you think you're doing?' Alex's voice was thick with menace.

Grace spun round. He was coming towards them, pulling on his dressing gown. His face was colourless, his mouth twisted in a sneer, his eyes burning with brutality. Somehow she found the strength to confront him. 'This is my home. Amy is my child. You had no right to lock her out.'

'You bloody bitch!' He lunged at her, smashing his fist into her chest, and she staggered, falling sideways, hitting her head hard against the wall. Amy screamed. Dazed, Grace saw Alex turn on her daughter, grabbing her by the neck, snarling at her like a wild animal.

'What time d'you call this? Some of us have to work in the morning. Don't you think we need a decent night's sleep? Your mother's been worried sick. Look at the state of you. You dirty little trollop.'

He thrust his hand downwards, tearing the black T-shirt from her shoulders.

'Get off me!' Amy struck him with the heels of the shoes she was carrying.

'You'll pay for that.'

His knuckles were white, his fist already raised. Unable to stand, Grace hurled herself at the back of his legs, clinging to them so he couldn't move.

'Go to your room, Amy. Now!' It was hard to speak. Her throat was raw, splinter-sharp.

Alex freed one leg and aimed a savage kick at her stomach. Winded, she let go of him, covering her head with her arms, curling up in defeat as he kicked her repeatedly.

'Mum! I'm going to call the police.'

She was aware that Amy was sobbing. 'No! Please, Amy. Just go to your room.'

'I can't leave you.'

Grace moaned. Everything was growing dim. She couldn't think clearly. There was blood in her eyes and mouth. She summoned the last of her strength. 'For goodness sake, Amy, do as I say before he kills me.'

Amy fled. She crouched on the floor between her bed and the window. The muffled thumps and curses continued for some minutes before a bedroom door slammed. She remained where she was. Outside a thrush began to sing, joined soon after by a chorus of other birds. But she dared not move. She didn't stir until the sky brightened with the sunrise. Then she tiptoed into the hall.

The early light was fast dispersing the shadows, painting everything with a false normality. There was no sign of her mother. She was not dead in a heap on the floor.

Amy returned to her bed and lay on top of the quilt, cold and stiff, her mind frozen with terror.

CHAPTER 33

'Good morning, sweetheart.'

Amy opened her eyes. The remnants of sleep vanished. Her mother was standing by the bed, dressed for work, make-up immaculate, a mug of tea in her hand.

'Mum, are you okay?' Amy sat up, her body cold with sweat. 'Where's Alex?'

'I'm fine.' Her mother smiled, putting the mug on the bedside table. 'Alex has gone to the factory. I didn't want to wake you, but I have to go to work now and I need to know you're all right.' She sat down carefully on the edge of the bed.

'Of course I'm bloody well not all right! Alex is a bloody maniac! He can't stay here, Mum. You have to make him go away. You have to call the police.' Amy clenched her fists. It hurt to speak; it hurt to swallow. And her mother was behaving as if nothing had happened.

'I don't want the police involved.'

'He almost killed you, Mum. If you don't call them, I will.'

'You mustn't do that, sweetheart. We have to make the best of things for a bit longer. Alex owes me a lot of money. If he leaves, I'll never see a penny of it.'

'I don't care. What good is money if you're dead? If he doesn't go then I will. You decide. Alex or me.'

'It's not that simple.'

'It is. It bloody well is!' Amy covered her face, tears hot on her cheeks. 'If you think I'm going to spend another night in the same house as that animal you're mistaken.'

Her mother's arms enfolded her. 'Shush, darling. I promise I won't let him touch you again.'

'Like you can stop him!' Amy pushed her away.

Her mother gasped, holding her stomach, laying her head on the quilt.

'How can you pretend there's nothing wrong? Look at you. You can hardly move.' Amy was beyond sympathy. 'This isn't the first time is it? How often have you covered up for him?'

'Darling, listen—'

'No!' She watched her mother struggle to sit up. 'If you go to work today, don't expect me to be here when you get back'

'Amy, please—'

'I mean it, Mum.'

'Sweetheart, we'll talk this evening. We'll find a way to cope. I need you to help me, Amy.'

'I don't believe this. You think we can all live together after last night?'

'I don't know what else to do.'

'You're pathetic!' Amy choked on the words. 'Just go to work, Mum. Don't worry about me. I can look after myself.'

Her mother stood up with difficulty and kissed her cheek. 'Drink your tea and have a few more hours rest. I'll be home before you know it.'

Amy lay down, squeezing her eyes shut until she heard the bedroom door close. When her mother left for work, she rolled off the bed shivering. The silence frightened her; and the sudden, unexpected noises that ruptured it. *What if Alex came back?* He filled her head. She had to get away. Petrified, she ran to the bathroom, locking herself in before she peeled off the torn T-shirt and washed quickly. There was no time to worry about her appearance. Back in the bedroom she found clean underwear amongst the muddle of clothes in the chest of drawers and, as she did so, caught sight of an old black T-shirt with *Que Lindo Dia* embroidered in shiny pink letters on the front. Aunty Cass had bought it for her three years ago. She hesitated, then pulled it on. Although it was tight, it still fitted, leaving an inch of midriff showing at the top of her skirt. She thrust her feet into a pair of rope sandals and turned to the mirror to drag a comb through her hair. *I wish Aunty Cass was here.*

The decision seemed to make itself. Her panic eased a little as she ran into the hall and picked up the telephone. There was no need to look in the address book; she had no problem remembering the international code and the number.

'Casa Lanca.' The line crackled and then cleared. 'Bom dia.'

'Aunty Cass?'

'Amy?'

'Aunty Cass I need to talk to you. It's about Mum and Alex.'

'What's happened, honey?' Cassie's voice was warm, full of concern.

It made Amy want to cry. Haltingly, she began to recount the events of the night before, beginning with her anger at finding her mother with the photograph of the family at Tuston. Once she started to talk it was impossible to stop. She held nothing back, describing the jaunt to Skegness and Alex's violent reaction, reliving every traumatic moment as she spoke.

'You poor kid. Are you badly hurt? Where's your mother? Shouldn't you both go to hospital for a check-up?'

Amy stared at the floor where a few hours ago her mother had lain like a bundle of rags.

'Amy, are you still there?'

What was Cassie saying? 'Sorry. I didn't catch all that. Mum's gone to work. She says she's fine, but she's lying.'

'And you?'

'I'm okay. I've got a bit of a sore throat. Nothing to worry about.' She moved her neck from side to side gingerly.

'I tried to tell her, Amy. I had a bad feeling about Alex all along. You shouldn't be subjected to such violence. I think you should go to the police.'

'Mum asked me not to.'

'So what are you going to do?'

'I don't know.'

'Will you be safe? Is there anyone you can stay with? A friend or neighbour?'

'I suppose so. I could...' The breath caught in Amy's throat. Of course there was someone. 'Aunty Cass, where's Tuston?'

'It's a village close to Hereford. Not far from the Welsh border. Why?'

'Does my dad still live there?'

'I think so.' Cassie's voice altered. 'Amy, don't do anything rash. Talk things over with your mother, honey.'

'I will, Aunty Cass. I have to go now.' She put the phone down. Almost immediately it rang again. She ignored it.

It took only a short while to pack a small case. By nine o'clock she was ready. She took fifty pounds out of her piggy-bank; money she had been saving to buy some roller skates. Minutes later she was in the street, waiting for a bus to the railway station.

Amy chewed her finger nails as the train sped towards Newark. She had run away to find the father she had never seen, a man who might not even live in Tuston any longer. It was a stupid, risky thing to do, but she didn't care. Her mother had betrayed her. Her mother had chosen Alex in spite of everything, and she would never forgive that.

So far the journey had been easy. She had asked at the booking office for a ticket to Hereford and found there was a direct service. It was ironic. All these years her family had been only a few hours down the line. She pressed her face against the window to see the tracks stretching into the distance, linking town to town, people to people. Herself and her father. This afternoon she would see him! The realisation made her stomach lurch.

She stretched her legs beneath the table in an effort to relax. Plans began to form in her mind. When she reached Hereford she would take a taxi to Tuston and ask the driver to drop her at the rectory. She rehearsed what she would say when she knocked on the door. Everything sounded ridiculous. *Hello, I'm Grace's daughter. Are you my father?* Her courage waned. Perhaps she ought to give up and go home.

But the train rattled on. She closed her eyes, falling almost immediately into an exhausted sleep. She roused, disorientated, in Birmingham, jostled by the press of passengers as the carriage emptied and refilled. Afterwards she dozed intermittently, stirring each time the train stopped. In Worcester there was another mass exit and this time she sat up, eager to see the city she had read about in her history books. *The faithful city.*

Soon they were among fields again. She looked out at hazy green hills, and valleys with glinting streams, at black and white cottages and acres of orchards; all so different to the flat Lincolnshire countryside. Suddenly she felt far away from home. The train passed through several more little towns then, before she could prepare herself, the guard announced they were approaching Hereford. She reached for her case. It was too late to go back now.

* * *

'Dad.'

'Faith? Where are you?'

'I'm at the office. There's been a crisis here – burst pipe on the top floor – so much paperwork destroyed. I won't be able to get home this afternoon. I'm sorry.'

'It can't be helped.' Richard hoped she couldn't detect his disappointment. 'What about Debbie's engagement party?'

'I've asked Rajat to drive me down later. We'll go straight to the hotel. Will it be okay if he stays the night afterwards? We should be home about two.'

'No problem. The bed in the spare room's already made up.' He allowed himself a brief moment of resentment. He wouldn't even have her to himself tomorrow either.

'Thanks, Dad.'

There was a click and she was gone.

Richard replaced the receiver. The house was quiet, almost oppressive. He opened a window in the study, allowing the sounds of summer to filter into the room, along with the smell of newly mown grass. The faint intrusion of the outside world only increased his feelings of isolation. He missed his daughters. And he missed Kate. Their lives had moved on. He was left on his own, grateful for the few hours they could spare him in their busy schedules. With a sigh he straightened the papers on his desk. It was time for a coffee.

In the kitchen, sunlight warmed the atmosphere, lying in bright pools across the work tops, and immediately he felt more cheerful. The water had almost boiled when the doorbell rang. Vaguely annoyed, he switched off the kettle. No one usually bothered him on a Saturday afternoon. It was either an unforeseen emergency, or Gwen Nisbett. Neither of which was a pleasant prospect.

He hurried to open the front door. There was a girl standing in the porch. She looked about seventeen; hard-faced, streetwise, slightly tarty. He had never seen her before.

'Can I help you?' he asked, inwardly reproaching himself for his cursory judgment.

'Are you Richard Lawson?'

'Yes.' He was disconcerted by the way she stared at him.

'I... I think you're my father.'

He stepped back, astounded. The girl must be ill. Or perhaps she had made a genuine mistake.

'I don't think so.' He fought the urge to slam the door in her face. 'What makes you think such a thing?'

'My mother is Grace Lawson. She said... she said it wouldn't be a good idea to try and find you. She's right. I shouldn't have come.' To his dismay, he saw she was close to tears. She picked up her suitcase, about to leave.

'Wait!' *She was Grace's child.* 'I'm sorry.' His voice sounded hoarse. 'This is such a shock. I haven't heard from Grace since she left. Please, come into the house. We need to talk.'

She let him carry her case and followed him inside. He led her into the kitchen.

'I was about to make myself a drink. Would you like something? Coffee? Hot chocolate?'

'Chocolate please.'

She sat by the table, head bowed, and he could see she was younger than he had first thought.

'Biscuit?' He held out a tin.

'Thank you.' She took a custard cream and nibbled the edges.

'So,' he put the drink in front of her, 'where have you been living?'

'Lincoln. I came on the train.'

Grace is in Lincoln. The knowledge bit deep. All these years and she had never had the decency to let him know she was still alive.

'Does your mother... does Grace know about this visit?'

'No.' The girl lifted her head defiantly.

'Won't she be worried about you?' He sat down opposite her.

She shook her head. 'Mum wouldn't care.'

He wondered if this was near the truth. He had no idea what Grace had become.

'I don't even know your name,' he said gently.

'It's Amy,' she replied, 'Amy Charity Lawson.'

Faith, Hope and Charity. He looked at her sharply. 'She has my eyes,' he thought with a start. He observed her as she sipped her drink. There was something about her which lent truth to her claim. Her hair was dark beneath the streaks of red dye; her nose was a much daintier version of his own; her skin was pale, even after the weeks of sunny weather.

'How old are you, Amy?'

'I was fifteen last January.'

A painful memory unfurled. Mentally, he counted back the years and months. Could she have been conceived on the night of Helena's wedding? Was she the result of his unforgivable violation of his wife? Was that why Grace had kept her from him?

'What has your mother told you about me?'

'Not much. Just that you were a priest and that it was an unhappy marriage.'

Her words grieved him. He had done his best to care for Grace.

'That's all? Is that the reason she gave for abandoning me and her children?'

'She said she had done something very bad and she had to leave.'

'Did she?' Richard smiled grimly.

'She did say she misses them – her other daughters – every day of her life.' Amy met his gaze steadily.

'She told you about them?'

'I found her looking at a photograph last night. She was crying. I shouted at her and she admitted the children in the picture were hers.'

'How did you know where to find me?'

'I asked Aunty Cass where Tuston was when I phoned her this morning.'

'She's still in touch with Cassie, then?'

'Not any more. They had an argument about Alex.'

'Alex?'

'Mum's boyfriend.'

Richard gripped the handle of his mug. Of course Grace would have a man in her life. He was silent, wrestling with his conscience, floundering in a morass of guilt and anger. The girl watched him, her eyes – his eyes – wide with apprehension.

'Forgive me,' he said eventually, 'this is difficult for me to accept.'

'You don't believe me?' He heard the misery in her words.

'Yes,' he said. 'Yes, I do.'

Her smile was tremulous and she could no longer hold back her tears. He felt an unexpected tenderness towards her; the tough image she projected was merely a front. Behind it she was a frightened child.

'Here.' He handed her a clean handkerchief. 'Finding each other should be something to celebrate. I'm not such a disappointment, am I?'

She mopped at her face and he could tell by her expression that she didn't know whether or not to take him seriously. He leaned forward and put his hand over hers.

'Amy, why now? What made you come here today? Is something the matter with your mother? Is she ill?'

She looked away. 'It's Alex,' she mumbled. 'I can't live with him any more.'

Her hand shook under his. 'Tell me,' he said.

She spoke quietly, as if she was ashamed, as if she thought she was to blame for whole sordid chain of events she was relating. He listened, appalled, until she finished, the blood pounding in his head red-hot with fury and disgust. *How could Grace allow a child to suffer such an ordeal?*

'Amy, it wasn't your fault.' His fingers tightened over hers.

'But it was. I made Alex angry.'

'Your mother must have known what he was like. She should have thrown him out months – years – ago by the sound of it. She never was much good at picking men.'

Amy withdrew her hand. Perhaps she sensed his bitterness.

'He owes her a lot of money,' she said. 'Mum's always been good to me. We did everything together until she met Alex. But I couldn't forgive her for needing someone else as well as me. My behaviour was selfish and immature. I made things a lot worse for her.'

'Did you know about the violence?'

'Not for sure. Not until last night.' Her face was suddenly stricken with grief. 'I should never have left her alone with him. What if he...?'

'He won't. Trust me.' Richard tilted her chin and dabbed at her wet cheeks with the handkerchief. 'Don't worry. She'll be all right.'

'How can you know that?'

'Because I'm going to get her; bring her back here.' He drew in his breath, wondering what had prompted him to make such an offer. Grace didn't want him in her life. He had no desire to see her again. But she was still his wife and therefore she was still his responsibility.

'When?'

He saw the gleam of hope in her eyes. 'As soon as I've made you something to eat and organised someone to stay with you.'

Her face flushed with sudden animation and he knew he mustn't make her any promises. 'Amy, I can't guarantee Grace will come back with me. I can't force her. All I can say is that I'll give it my best shot.'

'Thank you,' she said.

And he knew she had put her trust in him. He prayed he wouldn't let her down.

* * *

Grace knelt by the fridge, piling fresh vegetables into the salad compartment. Each time she moved a savage pain racked her body and it was all she could do not to cry out in agony. Beneath her clothes she was black and purple with bruises. Her skin felt raw, as if it had been peeled open with a knife leaving the inside exposed and throbbing. She was terrified she might have been damaged internally.

'How much longer are you going to be?' Alex elbowed her aside, reaching for a can of lager.

Grace didn't reply. She was no longer prepared to pander to him. She wanted her money and she wanted him out of her home.

'Still sulking over last night? Where is the little cow, anyway? Shouldn't she be helping you with that?' Alex sat at the table. He poured his drink, watching the creamy head form.

With a struggle, Grace gripped the work top and pulled herself to her feet. She had no idea where her daughter was. Worry nagged her, sharper than pain.

'You can get yourself something to eat tonight. I don't feel well enough.'

Alex wiped his mouth on the back of his hand. 'And whose fault is that? I'll sort Amy out when she comes home.'

Never again. 'No, Alex. I want you to leave.'

His eyes clouded and she saw his lips tighten. 'Bitch! If you think you can get rid of me that easily you're mistaken. I helped pay the mortgage for years. I have a stake in this bungalow whether you like it or not.'

'I thought we could sort something out between us,' Grace stood her ground. 'Can't we at least discuss things?'

'As far as I'm concerned there's nothing to discuss.' He picked up his lager and downed it in one go.

The telephone rang. Glad of the excuse, Grace hurried out of the room.

'Grace. It's Richard.'

'Richard!' Despite the shock of hearing his voice, she spoke in a whisper.

'Amy came to see me. She's at the rectory.'

Had she heard him correctly? *Amy? In Tuston?*

'She told me everything, Grace.'

A shadow fell across the carpet. Alex appeared in the kitchen doorway. 'Don't you dare walk away from me! Get off that bloody phone now.'

'Just a second,' she mouthed. 'It's one of the girls from work.'

'Is it difficult to talk?' Richard queried.

'Sorry, what were you saying?' Grace lowered her head and spoke clearly.

'Listen, I'll be brief. I'm on my way to Lincoln. Can you pack a few clothes without Alex knowing? I'll take you back to Tuston. You'll be safe there.'

'No!' Grace was alarmed.

'Well, the offer stands. I'm coming up anyway. Whatever you decide, I intend to keep Amy with me until I'm sure she's in no danger.'

'I'll see what I can do.' Grace put the phone down, certain Alex could see into her mind.

'What did she want? You've finished work for today. She shouldn't be pestering you at home.' He was barely in control of his temper.

'It wasn't about work. She's got personal problems. She wondered if I could meet her later. Have a chat.'

'Tell her to get knotted. You've got enough bloody problems of your own.'

'You're probably right. But you'll be going out, won't you? And Amy is off with her friends somewhere. I've got nothing else to do.' Grace was amazed at her composure. 'Let's put our differences on hold for tonight.'

'That's fine by me. I'll get something to eat down the pub.' He turned and sauntered down the hall, whistling 'There's no place like home'.

When Alex had gone, Grace wandered through the bungalow, picking up photographs, touching ornaments and furniture, gazing out at the colourful borders in the garden. Richard was asking her to leave all this. Would she ever live here again? Or would she have to sell up; share the proceeds of any transaction with Alex? Wearily she weighed up the odds and made her decision.

She folded clothes automatically, ensuring that she and Amy had enough to wear for a few weeks. When she had packed two suitcases and carried them into the hall, she returned to the kitchen and took the cheque book from the dresser. She didn't want Alex getting his hands on the small amount of money she had left. Besides, she couldn't lodge with Richard indefinitely; she would need to find a cottage or a flat to rent.

It was strange that she could think so rationally when her mind was numb with sadness. Some part of her remained detached, clear-sighted, able to plan ahead. She found notepaper and a pen and sat down at the table to draft a letter to the travel agency offering her resignation, apologising for the lack of notice, explaining that family obligations meant she had to leave Lincoln for a while. Perhaps Richard would drive her to the shop and she could push it through the letterbox.

She glanced at her watch. It was almost nine o'clock. There was nothing more to do. The minutes ticked by and she couldn't settle. She was filled with dread at the prospect of meeting Richard again. His voice had brought the past sharply into focus, reminding her that once she had been loved, a wife, the centre of her family. Richard had forgiven her adultery and she had cheated a second time. How could she face him?

He arrived just before half past nine. She saw his outline through the glass panels before she opened the front door.

'Hello, Grace.'

He had changed. His hair was grey and cut short; there were wrinkles round his eyes, and a slight pouching on his cheeks. He was tall, as she remembered, but thicker round the waist and shoulders.

'Richard.' She stared at him. How stupid to imagine he would still be the same. She was different too.

'So, you're coming with me?' He nodded towards the suitcases in the hall. She realised he found this reunion as difficult as she did.

'If that's all right,' she said tentatively.

'Where's Alex?'

'Out.'

'No goodbyes then?'

'No.' She stood aside while he collected the cases. Then she locked the door and followed him to the car.

As they drove away from the bungalow she closed her eyes. She was leaving her home, the place that had been her refuge for the past fifteen and a half years. But without Amy the place seemed empty. There had been no choice in the end.

The lights of Lincoln slipped into the distance, melting into the mist rising from the fields. Grace braced herself, feeling the vicious pain surge through her body with every bump and ridge, as they negotiated a tortuous length of road works on the A46. Richard had hardly spoken since they left. While she posted her letter he had waited in the car park behind the shopping centre, and when she returned he had driven off without a word before she could even fasten her seat belt. The silence between them was uncomfortable but she could think of nothing to say that wouldn't rake up unpalatable memories. And yet there was so much she needed to know.

She cleared her throat. 'Richard, I know I don't have the right to ask, but I... I would appreciate it if you would tell me about Faith and Hope. How are they? What are they doing now? Do they hate me?'

At first she thought he wasn't going to answer. She touched his sleeve and he moved his arm immediately.

'Where do you want me to begin?' He sounded cold and unfriendly.

'Are they well?'

'Yes.'

'Do they still live at home?'

'Faith lives in London. She works for one of the big publishing houses. Not Calthorpes I hasten to add.'

'And Hope?'

'Do you watch any of the soaps?'

'No. Why?'

'Hope has been appearing in *East Street* over the last few months.'

Hope? On television?

'She's studying at the Lucy Valentine Drama School. They suggested her for the part. She's recording her last episode soon. At the end of next month she's off to Italy to begin filming a new thriller.'

It was too much to take in. Hope was her baby. How could she be a film star?

'Will she come home before then?'

'Yes,' Richard said shortly. 'She'll be back for Kate's wedding in a fortnight.'

'Kate's still around?'

'She's teaching in Hereford. Marrying a chap called Rhys Morgan. Faith and Hope will be bridesmaids.'

Grace bit her lip, overwhelmed by the sensation of loss. Her daughters were strangers. They had made their way in the world without her. 'The girls... have they been happy?'

He laughed, a dry unpleasant sound. 'Happy? You didn't exactly leave them a happy legacy, did you, Grace?'

'No,' she whispered.

'Do you really want to know?'

She bowed her head. 'Tell me.'

He told her in explicit detail. Horrified, she listened to his account of Faith's disturbed behaviour as a child, her truculent teenage years, her unsavoury boyfriends. She was mortified to learn of Hope's distress at discovering her real father; distraught to hear about her pregnancy and the death of her baby; overcome with guilt to learn of her depression during the long struggle to walk again. Richard's words seemed to squeeze every last drop of resilience out of her. She began to cry soundlessly. She could never make up for the damage she had done.

They drove on through the darkness and at some point she fell asleep, tears still wet on her cheeks. When she woke they were almost in Tuston. She recognised the narrow road, remembered each bend before they came to it, imagined the curve of the river as they crossed the bridge, saw the beam of the headlights sweep across the sign at the outskirts of the village. Wide awake now, she was swamped by fears. How could she face people who knew what she had done? What if her daughters refused to meet her? Could she cope with their hostility? She shrank back in the seat wondering if she had the strength to confront the future.

At the rectory Richard parked the car and lifted the cases from the boot. She stood in the middle of the drive, disconcerted. The house and garden hadn't changed. Past and present overlapped, erasing the intervening years from her mind.

'Here we are then. Home sweet home.' Richard said.

His sarcasm wounded her more than Alex's violent blows. She trailed after him like a cowed puppy; an unwanted guest, an extra burden, excess baggage.

* * *

The band was playing the last waltz. Faith felt Rajat's breath in her hair as he steered her expertly round the dance floor. He was the perfect partner, the perfect gentleman; always there when she needed him. Now that he was working for the BBC in London, he lived at his parent's house in Chiswick, only a short ride on the District Line from her own flat near Sloane Square, and it was good to have him nearby.

Her thoughts grew solemn. She had never met any of Rajat's family. His father was a cosmetic surgeon with an exclusive clinic on Harley Street. His mother a high-profile lawyer. They were clever, ambitious people who expected great things of their eldest son and she had the impression they didn't approve of his friendship with her.

'What was that sigh for?' Rajat lifted his head.

'Nothing. I was just thinking how pretty Deb looks. Who'd have thought she'd be marrying little Sam Harris?'

'Little is hardly the word I'd use,' Rajat eyed the burly young farmer with amusement.

'You know what I mean. We all grew up together. He was in the same class as us at school. He and Deb have been friends for years.'

'Perhaps they were in love with each other but just didn't realise,' Rajat suggested softly.

'Perhaps,' she said. 'But I wonder... Maybe it's more of a practical arrangement. Sam's parents are well-off and Debbie's always found it difficult to make ends meet.'

He laughed. 'I don't think so. You can almost feel how happy they are.'

'I suppose you're right. But I always imagined love would be wild and romantic and sweep you off your feet; that you'd just know you had to be with that one person or you'd die.'

'Nobody dies of a broken heart, Faith.'

'Raj, you're so pragmatic.'

'Am I?'

The band finished with a flourish and he gave a little, formal bow. 'Shall we say our goodbyes and thank Mr and Mrs Harris for a lovely evening?'

'In a minute. I'd like a quick word with Deb. I haven't had much chance to speak to her. She's been surrounded by Sam's relatives most of night. And I must say cheerio to Em. It'll be ages before I see her again.'

'Okay. I'll be over by the window.' He smiled, and she knew he was watching as she walked across the dance floor.

Someone grabbed her arm. She tensed, annoyed for allowing herself to be trapped by Wayne Saunders after she had managed to avoid him all night.

'So, how are you keeping, Faith?'

He swayed a little towards her as he spoke and her stomach curdled at the mixture of alcohol and stale smoke on his breath. 'Excuse me. I need to see someone.'

'No time for old friends now?'

She tried to move away but his fingers tightened, digging into her flesh and she could feel the rising panic in her chest.

'Is this man troubling you?' Rajat appeared at her side.

She didn't want to cause a scene. 'He's Debbie's brother.'

'Nice to meet you,' Rajat held out his hand. Befuddled, Wayne released his hold on her arm and she darted past him before he realised he had been duped.

'Fuckin' toffee-nosed bitch!' he shouted. 'Couldn't get yourself an English boyfriend?'

'Don't let him upset you,' Rajat caught up with her. 'I've heard far worse.'

But the evening had been tainted. Rajat was so patient and understanding. She was suddenly sad, knowing he had been hurt by the drunken abuse.

When the party finally broke up, he drove her home along the quiet roads and she rested her head against his shoulder. Outside the rectory he turned off the engine and faced her, his dark eyes serious, deep and lustrous in the faint wash of light from the hall.

'Faith, I have to tell you something?'

'What is it?' She nestled into his jacket, half-asleep.

'I didn't say anything earlier. I didn't want to spoil the evening.'

She sat upright, alarmed. 'Rajat, tell me.'

He brushed a lock of her hair back behind her ear.

'My parents have arranged a marriage for me, Faith.'

For a moment she stopped breathing. She looked down, her mind slowing, the darkness folding in on her.

'Who?' she managed at last.

'The daughter of one of my father's friends in Birmingham. I met her once, a few years ago.'

'Is she pretty?'

'As far as I can remember.'

'You've never mentioned her before. How long have you known? About the wedding?'

'Mum and dad have been discussing it for a while, but I managed to persuade them I needed to establish myself in a career first.'

'How can you marry someone you don't know? You can't love her.'

'I can grow to love her.'

'You don't believe that!' She lifted her head, stung by his words.

He was so close she could smell the clean scent of his skin, feel the heat of his body, see the slight rise and fall of his chest beneath the blue silk shirt. Her eyes and throat were sore, as if she had inhaled a great deal of smoke, and the muscles in her face wouldn't move. She put the palms of her hands to her cheeks and found they were wet.

'Faith, don't cry. We won't lose touch with each other.'

'I'm not crying.' She attempted a smile. 'Congratulations, Raj. I hope you'll be happy.'

He wiped her tears with his fingers. 'Faith, if I thought there was any chance we might ever be more than friends I would go against my parent's wishes. I want you to know that. I've loved you almost from the first time we met.'

He kissed her on the mouth and she clung to him, aching with sadness.

'Go inside, now,' he said. 'There's a light in the lounge. Your father's probably waiting up for you.'

'Aren't you staying?'

'I think it's best if I don't,' he said.

She watched him reverse down the drive, watched the lights of his car illuminate the hedgerows in the lane, watched the blackness creep back. She felt as if part of her had been torn away. Rajat was her friend, but he would belong to someone else now; someone else would have first call on his loyalty. *He would love someone else*. She couldn't bear it. The silence settled around her, chilling and comfortless. She walked to the front door slowly and let herself into the house.

'Faith? Is that you?' Her father called.

It took a few minutes to compose herself; check her make-up in the mirror, blot her eyes with a tissue, smooth her hair. Then she went across the hall and into the lounge. Her father was leaning against the mantelpiece, his expression grave. There was a woman sitting on the sofa, middle-aged, well-groomed, pretty in a jaded sort of way. Beside her was a teenage girl with red-streaked hair. Faith glared at them. Why were they here?

'No Rajat?' her father asked, glancing towards the door.

'He decided to go home.'

She saw his features soften with concern before he spoke again.

'Do you know who this is, Faith?'

'No.' The woman reminded her of someone but she couldn't think who.

'This is Grace. Your mother.'

She was suddenly ice-cold.

'And this is Amy, your sister. The daughter I knew nothing about.'

Even wrapped in her own misery, she was aware of the distress in his quiet words.

The woman stood up and came towards her. 'Faith, if only you knew how much I've missed you.'

But she didn't want to know. This woman with the sallow, pointed face and tragic grey eyes was nothing to her. The woman she had hated for so long wasn't this aging, skinny stranger; this wasn't the smiling young mother whose framed picture she had kept in the bottom drawer of her bedroom cupboard all these years.

'Faith—'

She turned to her father. 'I'm sorry, Dad. I can't deal with this tonight. I don't want to talk to her. I don't want anything to do with her.'

She heard herself sobbing. It was as though she was seven years old again; love and hate raging inside her. Desperate to be alone, she fled from the room.

CHAPTER 34

Hope left the studio just after six. The sun was still high, the air dry and dusty, and the concrete radiated heat. Aunt Helena's chauffeur was waiting for her in the dark-blue Mercedes, his face partly hidden by the newspaper he was reading. He looked up as she approached and leapt out of the car to open the back door.

'Thank you, George.' She smiled vaguely, sliding across the leather seat and putting the canvas bag containing scripts and school assignments beside her. Within seconds they were on their way, leaving the sprawl of buildings behind, the big car purring like a contented cat.

She leaned back, slow to shrug off the emotions of the character she was portraying. She had lived with Natalie Winger's problems for the past ten months, and at times the storyline had come so close to events in her own life that she found it difficult to continue. Impulsive teenager Natalie had believed herself in love with Karl Harper, a brash young man she met on holiday. Days after returning home, she had run away from her respectable, middle-class parents to live with him in his seedy flat on East Street.

Eyes focussed inward, Hope recalled how easy it had been to play the role of Natalie in the beginning. She had drawn on her memories – the joy of being with Russell, the secret afternoons spent together, their first kiss in the snow, the one and only time they made love. Critics had written about her enthusiastically, saying she lit up the screen with her happiness. East Street fans all over the country had fallen under Natalie's spell. But the scripts had grown darker. Natalie became pregnant. Slowly she learned the truth about Karl Harper, learned to fear him. In last week's shocking episodes viewers had seen her pushed down the stairs and watched as she lost her baby on the cold floor of the entrance hall, while her boyfriend drank himself senseless. The memories then had been raw, the scenes harrowing to act out. Yet her performance had received rave reviews.

Hope stared at the London suburbs and tried to oust Natalie from her mind. There were other things to think about. Reality had finally caught up with her. She reached into the bag and pulled out a well-thumbed copy of *Whispers*, the magazine that came free with *The Sunday Vista*. It wasn't a newspaper she usually read – it was more concerned with scandal than news – but one of the cast had given her the glossy supplement, telling her not to worry, that they had all had their fair share of negative press. She turned the pages to read the article about herself for the third time.'*Secrets of East Street's Brightest Young Star Revealed*', the headline proclaimed.

Up and coming young actress, Hope Lawson, must have found her role as Natalie Winger almost unbearable during the filming of last week's heart-rending scenes. We can reveal that, like the character she plays so well, Hope Lawson also lost a baby when she was in her early teens. Former classmate, Vanessa Greaves, spoke about her concern for the pregnant schoolgirl. 'Hope was such a loner, so secretive. She never spoke about any of her boyfriends. We never got to hear who the father was. I'm not sure she knew herself.'

She tossed the magazine aside in disgust, sickened by the implications behind the false sympathy. Her mind sharpened. *How would this affect her career? What could she do to limit the damage?* She closed her eyes, trawling through various possibilities. She could ignore the whole thing and trust it would become yesterday's news, or she could talk to reporters herself – though it was unlikely anyone would be interested when the article in *Whispers* was so salacious, so much more memorable than the truth. And besides, she couldn't divulge the identity of her baby's father, not after all these years. She sighed, pressing a hand to her forehead.

Her thoughts took a different tack. Why not ask Brandon Calthorpe to get his lawyers to sue the *Vista* on her behalf? He had powerful friends in legal circles, as she had found to her cost two years ago when she had been obliged to have a DNA test. It had proved she was his daughter, but then, after all the heartache, he had simply lost interest. Until her recent success. At least he had the decency not to advertise their relationship – perhaps that was Aunt Helena's influence – but he had sent her flowers and taken her out for meals on several occasions. She didn't hate him any more. He would never replace Richard in her affections and he seemed to have accepted that. But he had told her to come to him if ever she needed help.

'Looks like some sort of hold-up ahead.' George's words distracted her.

'What's the problem?' She opened her eyes and looked over his shoulder.

'I can't see. There's a long tailback. I'll turn left at the next junction, find a way round. Do you want me to phone Mrs Calthorpe, tell her we've been delayed?'

'No, it's okay. She said she'd expect me when she sees me.'

George was silent again and Hope resumed her deliberations. The easiest thing would be to talk to her aunt. Since Sir Edward Reece had been diagnosed with diabetes, Aunt Helena had been in London a great deal, looking after his interests and standing in for him at GLP Newspapers. Hope relaxed a little, feeling more optimistic. It was always a treat to stay at the flat in Kensington when she wanted a break from the noisy lodgings she shared with three other girls from LVS. And Aunt Helena would know what to do about the unsavoury article.

It was another half an hour before they pulled up in front of the beautifully restored Victorian house in Sumner Place. Hope said goodbye to George, who would be spending the night in the apartment on the ground floor, which he used when Helena needed him in the city. The uniformed security guard let her into the foyer.

Aunt Helena appeared on the landing as the lift reached the second floor. She looked agitated. 'Hope. Come in. Your father's here.'

'Dad?' Bemused, Hope followed her into the flat. 'He's not cross with me, is he? About the feature in *Whispers*?'

'What feature?' Helena's face was blank.

Hope pulled the magazine from her bag. 'Here.'

Helena took it from her, raising her eyebrows. She flicked over the pages to where Hope had folded down the corners. 'I hardly think your father is likely to read this rubbish!'

'It's not true, Helena. About the boyfriends. I only ever had one.'

'Who is this Vanessa Greaves?' Helena skimmed through the offending text.

'She used to bully me at school. I was running away from her when I had my accident.'

'Give me five minutes. We'll soon have this little rumour scotched. You go and see your father.' Helena lowered her voice. 'He's brought someone with him, Hope. I don't know how you're going to feel about meeting her. Or her daughter.'

'Who are they?'

Helena hesitated outside the room she used as an office. 'I think Richard would like to explain that himself. Go on through; I'll take care of this garbage.'

Hope picked up her bag and walked along the hall, her heart beating rapidly, her mind already replacing one set of worries with another. Why was her father here? Who was the woman with him? Had he found himself a lady-friend? If so, did that mean he was over Kate?

She opened the door of the lounge. For a second she was dazzled by sunlight streaming through the window opposite, and then her father was hugging her. She kissed him, blinking away her tears. 'Dad! Oh Dad, it's so good to see you.'

He stood back, holding her at arm's length. 'You too, sweetheart. Let me look at you. Do you realise you haven't been home for two months?'

'I've been so busy, Dad, with *East Street* and revising for my exams.'

'I know. I know. There's no need to apologise.'

He let go of her and moved aside. For the first time she noticed the woman sitting in one of the huge cream chairs, a silhouette against the brilliant light. A grey shape, like a ghost.

Her father cleared his throat. 'Hope, this is Grace. Your mother.'

The shadowy figure rose and came forward. 'Hope, I can't believe how beautiful you are. I tried to imagine you growing up. I thought of you every day, but I never dared dream I would see you again.'

Hope stared at the woman and felt nothing. So this was her mother? The slender, pasty-faced stranger in front of her could have been anyone. She could have passed her by on the street and walked away with no tug of recognition. She didn't know what to say. What did the woman expect of her? What should she do? Should they shake hands? Embrace?

'How are you?' she asked politely. The question sounded banal.

'Grace has been through a rough patch recently.' Her father came to their rescue. 'She'll tell you in a minute, but there's someone else you should meet.'

He led her across to one of the windows overlooking the quiet, tree-lined street. There was a girl on the window seat, half-hidden by the curtains. She was dressed in black; thin and colourless, apart from her dyed red hair and the splash of scarlet on her lips.

'This is Amy. Your sister.' He smiled at the girl who was twisting her fingers together nervously. 'I didn't know she existed until she came to see me two days ago. Amy, this is Hope.'

'Hello.' The girl lifted her head, brown eyes wide and suspicious.

'Hello, Amy.' Hope shook the outstretched hand and saw, with a sudden rush of sympathy, that the fingernails were bitten to the quick. She looked at her father, her brain seething with questions she couldn't ask until they were alone.

He shook his head. 'Don't worry. I found it difficult to take all this in too.'

Helena came into the room before he had chance to say more.

'It's sorted,' she said briskly. 'Tomorrow morning GLP's biggest-selling tabloid will have your story on the front page and I guarantee you'll have the respect of every reader in the country. I think you can safely forget all about that sordid little item in *Whispers*.'

'Thank you, Helena,' Hope felt the tension in her body ease.

'I'll explain later,' Helena smiled at everyone. 'In the meantime I've ordered us something to eat.'

It was an evening of stilted conversation – politely phrased questions, discreet answers, thinly veiled accusations. Amy said little, answering only when spoken to, but she was alert, piecing together fragments of her mother's past like a jigsaw in her head.

'Tell us about *East Street*. Are you going to miss it?' Her father – it was still a strange notion – dropped the question into one of the awkward silences. Amy heard the pride in his voice. Glancing sideways at Hope, she felt the first cold stirrings of jealousy.

She observed Hope closely, noting the flush on her cheeks, the tilt of her head, the animated use of her hands when she described something. They were all watching her, hanging on to her every word. Yet she wasn't boasting. If anything she was making fun of herself, telling them how inexperienced she was compared with the rest of the cast.

'I'm still a relative newcomer. They make allowances for me.' Hope said modestly and then changed the subject. 'What about you, Amy? What are you planning to do with your life?'

Like you really want to know. Amy scowled.

As if sensing her resentment, her mother spoke for her, telling them about her excellent school reports, her piano lessons and her fluency in French and Portuguese. Amy cringed at the undeserved praise. She was an average pupil. She worked hard but she didn't excel at anything. Not like Faith who had a degree in English or Hope who was going to Italy in September to star opposite Maurizio Quattrone of all people.

Again conversation floundered. Her father stood up.

'We ought to be going. I'm sorry to have taken so much of your time, Helena.'

'Richard,' Helena was by his side in an instant, her hand on his arm. 'It's late. Why don't you stay the night? There's plenty of room. All the guest bedrooms are made up.'

'We couldn't put you to such trouble.'

'It's no bother.' Helena said.

Amy saw the faint flush on her father's cheeks. His features softened and his eyes seemed more lustrous. She remembered a similar look on her mother's face in the early days with Alex. *He's in love with her. My father is in love with Helena Calthorpe.* She was shocked. Surely she had misread the signals? Instinctively, she looked at her mother, wondering if she had noticed. But her mother was staring at Hope as if no one else mattered in the world.

'Which bed do you want?' Hope asked.

Amy shrugged. 'I don't mind.'

'You take the one by the window then,' Hope sank down on the second bed, pulling a shabby pair of pyjamas out of her bag along with a sheaf of papers.

Amy undressed quickly and put on the nightdress Helena had lent her. It was pale blue silk trimmed with lace. In the ensuite bathroom she scrutinised herself in the mirror. With her thatch of red hair she looked ridiculous; the ugly sister, the one no prince would look at twice.

When she came back into the bedroom, Hope was in bed, propped up by pillows, sifting through dog-eared sheets of type written script. 'You don't mind if I read through tomorrow's scenes, do you? It won't keep you awake?'

Amy shook her head. Her mind was too active for sleep. She slid beneath the thin summer duvet, her thoughts muddled and unsettling.

'This has been difficult for you, hasn't it?' Hope put the pile of papers down.

Amy ignored the question.

'I understand how you feel,' Hope wasn't deterred. 'You think nothing will ever be right again. I was like that after my accident.'

'When you lost your baby?' Amy couldn't help her curiosity. Her mother had told her something of Hope's past, warning her not to ask questions.

'Yes,' Hope said. 'I didn't want to go on living for a while.'

'Did you miss having a mum to talk to?'

'I don't think so. I never had anyone to confide in before Ru... before I met the boy who was my baby's father.'

Amy raised herself on one elbow, affected by the sadness in Hope's voice. 'But you had your dad. He's always been there for you.'

'Not always. When I was little he didn't have much to do with me. I think he blamed me for Mum leaving.'

'Why?'

'Didn't you know? I'm not Dad's real daughter. Mum had an affair with his stepbrother, Brandon Calthorpe.'

Amy tried to swallow, gulping in air rapidly, and a strange gurgling sound came from her throat.

'I'm sorry. I shouldn't have told you.' Hope came to sit on the edge of her bed. 'Don't upset yourself, Amy. It all happened a long time ago.'

'Brandon Calthorpe. Isn't he Helena's husband?' Amy felt as if she was suffocating. She had to know everything, even though the answers were shattering her trust, making her uncertain of both past and future.

'Yes,' Hope said. 'Brandon Calthorpe is my father. I was devastated when I found out. Afraid it would change everything.'

'And did it?' Amy pictured her mother with some unknown man.

'Yes. But it didn't change the things that really mattered. I was still the same person and Richard will always be my dad because I love him and he loves me. Your mother will always be your mother. Because you love each other.'

'But she's your mother as well. And she left you.'

Hope evidently had no answer to that. Her expression was thoughtful.

'I feel as if my life has been one big lie.' Amy tasted her own tears.

'I know.' Hope reached over to the bedside table and handed her a tissue. 'But we have to let Mum and Dad sort things out, Amy. We've just got to get on with things, do the best we can. Be ourselves.'

'I suppose.'

Hope giggled. 'I sound like an agony aunt, don't I?'

Amy smiled at her weakly. 'A bit.'

'It's not all bad though, is it? At least we've found each other.' Hope stood up gracefully. 'Now I think we should get some sleep. I'll look at this script in the morning. Goodnight, Amy.'

Amy lay down dutifully and closed her eyes. She felt Hope's lips brush her cheek before the lamps were switched off.

* * *

It was growing light. Russell rolled over, dragging the tangled sheet with him. This was the second night he had slept badly, wrestling with his conscience, agonising over the article his grandmother had shown him in *Whispers*. According to Gran, the whole of the Dalchett Estate was buzzing with gossip, tut-tutting about the morals of Mrs Calthorpe's granddaughter. He couldn't bear Hope's reputation to be smeared so unfairly. He knew the truth.

Should he confess, or write to that awful magazine and tell them what really happened? Yet Hope had insisted they keep their friendship secret. He stretched his legs and lay on his back, staring at the ceiling. What was the right thing to do? If only he could tell everyone that Hope had been an innocent, traumatised by learning the identity of her real father, and that he, Russell Holmes, had taken advantage of her emotional state and made her pregnant. He was to blame. He was the one, not Hope. She didn't know what she was doing.

He pressed his face into the pillow, his skin burning. He had loved her so much. And he still did. Every time he saw her on television he felt the pain of losing her. Watching Natalie Winger's story made him feel physically ill. How could Hope act such a part; make herself re-live the heartache? Maybe she didn't care. Maybe she had never wanted his child anyway. Maybe she never loved him.

His memories mocked him. By the time the alarm clock sounded at half past seven, he was exhausted, unable to think coherently, and no closer to resolving his dilemma. He scrambled out of bed bleary-eyed, washed and dressed like a sleepwalker, and went downstairs. The cottage was cold, even at this time of year. He shivered and scurried into the kitchen to put the kettle on and make himself breakfast. There was no one else to do it for him. His grandfather would already be at the big house and his grandmother stayed in bed late nowadays. She was much better, her behaviour almost normal, but she lived on a knife-edge, keeping her irrational fears at bay with tablets.

The metal letterbox clattered open. Russell collected the newspapers from the hall. He put the *Daily Telegraph* on the settee for his grandfather to read later and carried the *News Breaker* back to the kitchen. As he unfolded it, Hope's picture wavered in front of him. Forcing himself to keep calm, he spread the paper out on the table. His hands shook and at first the print skidded away from his eyes. The headline slipped into focus. *'My Private Hell. Actress Hope Lawson speaks exclusively to News Breaker'*. Russell ran a finger down the page, scanning the text anxiously. *I was very young and naive… I was in love… bullies made fun of me… I saw the van and I knew it couldn't stop in time… they told me I had lost my baby… I wanted to die… life had to go on.*

He went back to the beginning and read the whole page carefully. When he came to the end he was blubbing like a child. There was no need to break his promise to Hope. Anyone who read her story would understand that she had been a tragic victim and not a teenage nymphomaniac. He refolded the paper neatly, leaving it on the table. Then he poured himself a mug of tea and stood by the window watching a sleek blackbird poke its beak into the lawn, searching for worms. *I was in love.* Those had been the words she used. He held them in his heart for the future. Even though he had lost her, he knew now that the feelings they had shared were real.

CHAPTER 35

It was strange to wake in her old room. For a few seconds Kate wondered if she had been dreaming – whether her job at the friendly little primary school in Hereford, and the tiny, two-bedroomed house she had bought with the proceeds from the sale of her flat in Cheltenham had been fabricated in her mind while she slept – and that, in reality, she was still living at the rectory, helping Hope recover from the accident, her own life on hold. She rubbed her eyes, wiping away the mist of sleep.

A shiver of excitement quickened in her stomach. Today was her wedding day! She was marrying Rhys Morgan in Tuston church at one 'clock. Sitting upright, she hugged her knees, picturing the future, relishing the precious few minutes of reflection before the whirlwind of preparations to come. Her wedding dress was hanging on the wardrobe door, a floaty creation of cream chiffon, simple and perfect. The sight of it made her suddenly tearful. She had never been so happy. Her love for Richard, a secret for so many years, culminating in one seductive moment of passion, and ultimately rejected, had brought her nothing but heartache. And yet she had clung to her dreams. When had Rhys begun to supplant Richard in her affections? She couldn't tell. There had been no defining moment. It had happened gradually over the last twelve months and now she couldn't wait to share her life with him. Rhys made her laugh. While Richard was serious, full of compassion, Rhys was fun-loving and passionate, an indisputable romantic. She loved both men, but she was *in love* with Rhys. And he was in love with her. She could hardly believe it. After all the years of pining for Richard, nursing her hopes and her wounds, she had finally found happiness with someone else. She smiled, stretching her arms above her head. She was thirty-eight – thirty-nine in a few days – and she felt like a teenager.

Unable to lie still, she padded to the window and drew back the curtains. The sky was stormy, layered with fast-moving grey clouds. It didn't matter. Nothing was going to spoil the day. She watched a herd of cattle plodding up the lane, their steps measured, their bodies swaying rhythmically. How many times had she witnessed this procession as Kate Emerson; nanny, companion, nurse, housekeeper? But in a few hours she would be Mrs Katherine Morgan. The name sounded odd and she shuddered with sudden apprehension, afraid something would prevent her becoming Rhys's wife.

There was a tap on the bedroom door.

Hope breezed into the room, wearing faded pink pyjamas and carrying a tray of tea and toast. 'Breakfast for the bride. Faith's on her way up. She's bringing the video camera so we can record everything, starting now.'

'You're not going to film me in my nightie?'

'Of course. And with your hair in rollers later. It'll be much more entertaining than a professional version.'

Hope winked at her as Faith, enveloped in an oversized dressing gown, appeared in the doorway.

Kate gave in with good grace. She sat on the bed sharing her breakfast, posing for them, laughing at their enthusiasm.

'Shouldn't Amy be with us?' she asked when they finally put the camera down. She couldn't interpret the look that passed between them. 'It isn't a problem is it, my asking her to be a bridesmaid? I didn't like to leave her out. She is your sister.'

'We know,' Hope flushed guiltily. 'It's just that you've been like a mother to us. We wanted you to ourselves for a while.'

'Anyway, you'd better get up now.' Faith whisked the tray off her.

'You're first in the bathroom,' Hope said, 'and then we'll be back to do your make-up and hair.'

The door closed softly behind them and she heard them giggling as they went downstairs.

The rest of the morning passed in a frenzy of activity and Kate submitted to the unaccustomed pampering without protest. Finally, she stood in front of the mirror in her bridal gown. The three girls fluttered around her like butterflies in their peach-coloured satin dresses, checking her make-up, handing her the bouquet of yellow roses, adjusting the crystal tiara that held her veil in place.

When they were satisfied with her appearance they ushered her out of the room. She walked down the familiar staircase slowly, afraid of treading on the delicate material rippling around her ankles. Behind her the girls were quiet and she could hear the rustle of their skirts as they moved. She saw Grace, pale and insignificant, by the front door, and Colin Marsh – in his best suit and patently nervous at the prospect of having to give the bride away – operating the video camera while his wife stood at his side, whispering instructions.

'You look lovely,' Liz said.

'Thank you.' Kate smiled. 'I have to admit I'm terrified.'

She had nearly reached the hall when Richard emerged from the study, already dressed in his cassock and surplus.

'Kate.' He came to the foot of the stairs. 'You are beautiful.'

He took her hand, helping her down the last step and she noticed the sheen of tears in his eyes.

'I hope you will be happy, Kate.'

She felt her face colour. Her heart began thudding against her ribs. She had known him for so long. Did she still love him? Did he love her? He was saying one thing but his eyes were telling her something else. She froze, uncertain. Could she be making a terrible mistake?

Colin Marsh handed the camera to his wife. 'Are you all set, Kate?'

Hope prodded her gently. 'Time to go.'

It was too late to change her mind. She put her hand on Colin's arm and they followed Richard outside.

The first drops of rain began to fall as she waited in the church porch. Now she wondered wretchedly if the weather was an omen; a sign she was marrying the wrong man. She wanted to turn and run down the path, postpone the wedding, sift through the mayhem in her head, but she heard the opening fanfare of the wedding march and found herself steered forward by Colin, his hand moist beneath her elbow.

A blur of faces watched her walk up the nave. She could see the back of Rhys's head, the dark hair curling above the collar of his grey suit. It was like looking at a stranger. She stood beside him at the chancel steps and the vows she made sounded hollow in her ears. When he put the ring on her finger it felt heavy and cold. Richard's voice filled the church. Richard's touch burned her skin when he joined her hand with Rhys's.

'Those whom God hath joined together let no man put asunder.'

She was faint with panic. Richard was speaking again and the words were reverberating in her head.

'I pronounce that they be man and wife together, In the name of the Father, and of the Son, and of the Holy Spirit. Amen.'

There was a moment's pause and then he smiled at them. 'You may kiss the bride.'

The whole congregation waited expectantly.

She turned to the man who was her husband. His eyes were serious and she saw herself reflected in them. He drew her to him. His kiss was gentle but she could feel his strength, feel the warmth of his arms round her, feel all her stupid fears swept aside by a wild, heady joy. Of course she loved him! She pressed her lips to his, and heard the murmur of approval from their friends.

They knelt at the altar for the blessing; they sang the final hymn. In the vestry they signed the register and then they were walking together down the nave, smiling at everyone as the organist played a medley of popular classical music and the notes soared and danced on the air, echoing their happiness.

The church was crowded, the number of official guests increased by a contingent of parishioners, eager to witness the wedding of their rector's long-time companion. Amy held her head high, walking behind the bride and groom with Faith and Hope, aware that people were staring at her, probably making judgments, remarking on the colour of her hair. She wished she hadn't agreed to be a bridesmaid, but Kate had been so persuasive. It had been a rush to get another dress made at such short notice, to have white satin shoes dyed the right colour, and to find enough silk flowers to create a matching headdress. However, they had all been delivered yesterday. Everything had fitted perfectly and so she was here – the third sister, the runt of the litter, the focus of village gossip.

'You okay?' Hope sounded genuinely concerned.

Amy nodded, looking for her mother, knowing she wouldn't be there, wouldn't want to encounter anyone from the past.

It seemed ages before they reached the back of the church. Once outside, they sheltered from the rain under a dripping canopy of trees while the photographer took what must surely be far too many photographs, grouping and regrouping the guests until everyone was thoroughly soaked.

'At last!' Hope said. 'Come on let's go.'

Amy ran after her sisters to the wedding cars waiting by the gates. Rhys helped his wife into the first car, stooping to tuck the filmy skirt of her dress inside before he closed the door. In the back of the second car the three girls huddled together, shaking the water out of their hair.

'At least Kate had an umbrella,' Faith muttered.

Surprised, Amy saw her sister's face was pinched and surly.

'It's was nice of Grandma to offer Dalchett House for the reception. I think she's quite fond of Kate,' Hope said peaceably as the cars moved off to cheers from the bedraggled knot of spectators.

Amy said nothing. She was looking forward to seeing Dalchett House again. Her father had taken her to meet her grandmother a few days ago and the beautiful old building had intrigued her, rekindling her passion for history. She was unsure about her grandmother though. Ivy Calthorpe was not a comfortable person to be with. She seemed to have an opinion about most things and when she mentioned her daughter-in-law it had been with barely concealed contempt. Amy remembered feeling unwelcome, as if, by association, she had been found wanting. She smoothed the creases in her dress, half-dreading the rest of the day.

As they negotiated the narrow lanes she listened to the swish of the tyres on the wet road and watched the countryside sliding past the window, colours merging into shades of grey beneath the glowering sky. When they turned into the long drive she sat upright, eager for a first glimpse of the chimneys through the trees. But even Dalchett House looked different in the rain, hunched and brooding in its valley. Her spirits fell again. It was going to be a long afternoon.

The great hall was gloomy, despite the wall lights and the huge log fire in the stone fireplace. The caterers had laid out an extravagant buffet and the fifty or so guests filled their plates before sitting at large round tables to eat. Waiters moved among them, refilling glasses with wine as the buzz of conversation grew louder. Amy sat with the bride and groom and the other chief guests. She ate very little, picking at her food, drinking more than she should, longing to escape the sharp eyes of her grandmother.

After coffee, and speeches that were far too long, the guests began to make their way into the winter parlour while preparations began for the evening. Amy lingered at one of the mullioned windows, pretending to study the coat of arms in the coloured panel. She peered through the little panes of clear glass below, almost certain the rain had stopped. No one was taking any notice of her. Careful not to draw attention to herself, she made her way down the hall and into the passageway. The heavy front door had been wedged open for the caterers to carry empty containers back to their vans and she followed them outside, glad to feel the fresh rain-scented air on her face.

Her head was muzzy. Hitching up her skirt, she hurried across the forecourt, staggering inelegantly against some of the parked cars, the gravel sharp beneath the thin soles of her shoes. She walked unsteadily up the drive to the tunnel of trees. Here the ground was drier, though each gust of the warm wind sent a flurry of raindrops skittering through the leaves like small silver coins. They dribbled down her neck, cold as melting ice. When she came to the bridge she leaned on the stone wall watching the rushing water below, her thoughts bleak.

Nobody really wanted her here. Her father was kind, but he had no idea how to communicate with her; they shared no common ground. He knew nothing of the friends and neighbours she had grown up with. He hadn't travelled a great deal and he didn't listen to popular music or watch many television programmes, except, of course, *East Street*. Jealousy gnawed at her. Hope was always the centre of attention. No one else got a look in. And Faith? Faith was just a moody cow!

She stripped the leaves from a stem of bindweed and shredded them absentmindedly. It was hard to make sense of everything that had happened. She was unhappy and lonely. So many things she had taken for granted were no longer the same. She even saw her mother in a different light. Grace was an adulteress, a woman who had abandoned her children to satisfy her own sexual needs. That was the hardest thing to come to terms with.

Now and again the distant beat of music throbbed on the wind. The wedding party would be returning to the great hall, groups of friends chattering and laughing, their voices raised over the blare of the disco. Amy chewed her fingernails one by one. She didn't want to go inside. The solitude of the woods reflected her mood and she breathed deeply, inhaling the damp, sad smell of decaying leaves. The sound of water was hypnotic.

An overgrown footpath straggled alongside the brook as it carved its way through the trees. Without making a conscious decision, she slithered down the bank at the side of the bridge, heedless of her long skirt and flimsy shoes. She found the path was dry underfoot and set off without purpose, stumbling occasionally, her ankles twisting on the high heels.

A sudden roll of thunder echoed round the hills. She hesitated. It was beginning to rain once more, great fat drops, driving through the branches, pattering noisily to the ground. She decided to go on. She would probably be drier here than if she tried to get back to the house.

Another crack of thunder. It was growing steadily darker. The birds had stopped singing and the hiss of the rain intensified, becoming one with the bubbling brook and the restless wind. She headed deeper into the wood. The path looped down into a small clearing where several new trees had been planted. She saw there were piles of logs stacked neatly under a sheet of corrugated iron supported by four sturdy posts. It was a refuge of sorts.

The slope was steep, threaded with brambles. She had nearly reached the bottom when a deafening peal of thunder ripped through the air like an explosion. Unnerved, she lost concentration. Her foot caught on an exposed root and she fell awkwardly, scraping the skin off her hands and knees.

'Hey!'

She sat up, terrified, memories of Craig Geddis and his friends foremost in her mind. Someone was running towards her; a teenage boy in scruffy jeans and a denim jacket. She heard the soft thud of trainers on the ground and shrank back, trembling.

'Sorry. I didn't mean to scare you.' The boy came closer holding out his hand. 'Let me help. I'm Russell Holmes. My grandad works for Mrs Calthorpe.'

Her breathing slowed a little. Ignoring his hand, she stood up shakily. She was soaking wet, both her knees were bleeding, and she could feel tiny pieces of grit embedded in her palms.

'You're Amy Lawson, aren't you? Grandad said you might be at the wedding. He told me about you finding your dad.'

'Great! So now everyone on the estate is talking about me.' Her fear was replaced by anger.

'I shouldn't think so. And if they are, it's nothing to do with me or Grandad. We don't spread tales about the folk at Dalchett House.' He sounded indignant. 'Now I suggest you come into the shelter until this rain stops or you'll catch pneumonia. What are you doing here anyway?'

'I wanted to be on my own.' Amy gave him what she hoped was a withering look, before trailing across the clearing after him, her heels sinking into the ground. Thunder cracked the skies again.

Once under the lean-to she began to shiver.

'Here, have this,' Russell took off his jacket and draped it over her shoulders.

'Thanks,' she said. It was difficult to hold back the childish tears. 'I'm sorry I snapped at you.'

'That's okay. It must have been a shock, seeing me appear out of nowhere.' He grinned.

His grey eyes were bright with amusement, and she wondered how she could have been afraid of him.

'Sit down if you like.' He lifted a grubby haversack off one of the wood piles. 'It's quite dry.'

Lightning flickered eerily. Seconds later, thunder split the silence and the ground seemed to shake. Glad she was not alone, Amy heaved herself on to the logs and sat with her legs dangling over the side, the peach satin dress bunched up above her knees, which were raw and filthy. Russell pulled a folded handkerchief from the pocket of his jeans and held it out beneath the rainwater cascading off the corrugated roof.

'Best mop yourself up,' he said.

Amy accepted the handkerchief and rubbed at the dirt and blood. The trees at the other side of the glen were suddenly illuminated, as if with strobe lighting. She flinched.

'You don't like thunderstorms?' Russell was leaning against the logs, watching her.

'Not when they're this close.' She tensed, trying to hide her reaction to the inevitable thunderclap. 'Thanks for the hanky,' she handed it to him. 'I've made a mess of it, I'm afraid.'

'It doesn't matter,' he said cheerfully, stuffing it into his pocket and producing two sweets in blue foil wrappers. 'Mint toffees. One each.'

He sat beside her and they were quiet, chewing companionably, while the rain drummed on the roof and the thunder rumbled round the hill tops.

Eventually, he spoke. 'It's getting lighter. The rain's easing.'

She was almost sorry. It was cosy in the shelter with this unusual boy. She studied him covertly. He was tall and slim, with broad shoulders and crinkly tight curls like his grandfather's, except that Russell's hair was a rusty brown. She wondered if he had a girlfriend and blushed at the thought.

'You never told me what you were doing here,' she said.

'I come here sometimes to draw.' He picked up a sketchbook which had been pushed between the log piles.

'Can I see?'

416

'If you like. This is what I was working on.' He folded the book open and passed it to her. It was a drawing of a bird in a tangle of wet undergrowth, shaded so skilfully that she could distinguish the different plants entwined around each other and see translucent beads of water on the leaves. The feathers on the little bird were lifelike, ruffled by the wind, the markings subtle yet distinct.

'Russell, it's amazing. It looks so real.'

She began turning the pages, appreciating the quality of his work. There were several sketches of birds and a picture of his grandfather fishing by a lake. The remaining sheets were blank.

'I'd like to go to art college when I leave school.' He sounded wistful, as if he didn't think it would happen.

Amy smiled, returning the book to him. 'You definitely should.' She pushed her fingers through her hair in an attempt to squeeze out the water. 'I wish I was good at something. I'm so average.'

'I don't believe that for one minute.' He put the sketchbook by his haversack and stepped outside the shelter, hands upturned. 'It's almost stopped. Come on, I'll walk you to the bridge.'

She had no alternative. She couldn't say she would rather stay in the woods with him.

'There's no need.' She slid ungracefully off the woodpile and tried to brush the dust from her skirt. Dismayed, she noticed a ragged hole in the front, below her right knee, and two dull red bloodstains which had dried, stiffening the delicate material. The satin shoes were ruined.

'You might need a hand getting up the bank if you don't want to do any more damage to that dress.'

She wondered if he was mocking her but his smile was warm.

Her feet were soon wet through again. She lifted the hem of her skirt, treading in Russell's footprints, avoiding the boggy patches where possible, clutching his arm when her shoes squelched in the mud. The path itself was drier and he helped her up the slope, waiting patiently every time she stooped to free herself from brambles. At the top she stopped, breathless.

'Where does this path go?'

'It follows the brook down to the lake. I'll show you sometime. If you make sure you wear sensible shoes.'

Now he really was teasing, though without any malice.

'Thanks.' She gave him back his jacket and moved ahead of him to hide the stain of embarrassment on her face. 'I'll be okay from here.'

She hadn't expected to be missed but when she came closer to the house she saw a group of people by the front door. Her father broke away from them and ran to meet her.

'Amy, where have you been? I've driven round the entire estate looking for you. Jim Manning's been up to the village. Everyone's been worried sick.'

'I went for a walk.' She was surprised at his concern.

He took her hand. 'What happened? Look at the state of you.'

'I fell over in the woods. Mr Holmes's grandson helped me back to the lane.'

'You look frozen.' Like Russell earlier, he took off his jacket and wrapped it round her shoulders. It was warm and smelt faintly of mothballs.

'I thought you'd run away,' he said gently, and there was something in the tone of his voice that was comforting.

They walked across the forecourt together. She could see Faith and Hope and her grandmother on the doorstep. Kate was behind them, shivering in her wedding dress, and Mr Holmes was standing quietly in the passageway with several of the Dalchett House staff. They were all waiting for her. As if they cared. As if she was part of the family.

When everyone had gone indoors Russell headed back into the woods. The sight of Hope hurt him more than he thought possible. There had been a time when he tried to persuade himself that what he felt for her was just a schoolboy crush – calf love, puppy love, or whatever they called it – yet his feelings were as strong as ever. Now he just accepted his loss. For the last two and a half years he had deliberately avoided seeing her on any of her rare visits, staying clear of the house and its immediate vicinity. On each occasion he sat for hours in the woodland shelter, hoping she would come to look for him. But she never did.

REFLECTIONS

The garden at the back of the rectory was fragrant with the scent of roses and phlox. Amy lay back in the deck chair, closing her eyes and tilting her head so the sunlight lay like a blood-red bandage over her eyelids. The whole village seemed to be asleep but she could hear the little sounds of the countryside – sounds she had learned to recognise over the last six weeks – sparrows squabbling in the bushes, rooks in a distant stand of poplars, the mewling of a buzzard and the soft, steady champing of cattle behind the hedge.

Today these sounds made her sad. They filled her mind with thoughts of Russell. He had taught her so much about birds and animals; about the rhythm of the seasons and the weather; about wild flowers and how to identify trees. And he had shown her there were things to enjoy which had nothing to do with the artificial attractions of the city. With Russell she been able to forget about Alex, to re-discover an innocence she had forgotten. She felt safe with him. He treated her with respect and didn't presume she was eager to surrender her virginity, though sometimes she imagined what it would be like... Her face grew hotter. She was falling in love with Russell Holmes.

And now it was all coming to an end. Her father's lawyers had informed them that Alex had closed the factory, declared himself bankrupt and disappeared. It was assumed he was no longer in Lincoln – certainly he was no longer at the bungalow, which meant that she and her mother could return to their home. Only now she didn't want to go.

She didn't want to lose Russell's friendship. She didn't want to leave her father just as she was getting to know him. Although he was stuffy and reserved, sometimes he looked at her with such tenderness she wanted to fling her arms round him and tell him she was glad he was her dad. If she went back to Lincoln he would be a stranger again. And her sisters too would soon forget her, swept up in the momentum of their own busy lives. She experienced the usual flare of jealousy. Hope was already in Italy, working with the gorgeous Maurizio Quattrone; she had everything – money, looks, fame – yet she had been so friendly, not at all conceited. Amy sighed. She liked Hope. How was it possible to like someone and resent them at the same time? Faith she dismissed with a shrug. Faith was too absorbed with her own unhappiness to care about anyone else.

There were other people also, whose lives had touched hers; people to whom she might have become important in time – Helena Calthorpe and Marcus, Kate and Rhys Morgan, and even her frosty grandmother, who seemed to be thawing a little lately. With sudden, unexpected regret, she visualised Dalchett House;

beautiful, secretive, serene in its valley. It hurt to think she might never see it again.

She opened her eyes and leaned forward, resting her elbows on her knees, chin in her hands, the world hazy for a moment as her pupils adjusted to the light. Why, she wondered, did things never work out as you wanted? Two months ago she would have given anything to be alone with her mother. To have Alex out of their lives. But tomorrow her father was taking them back home and now she longed to stay in Tuston. There was nothing she could do to alter the situation. These few weeks had been an extraordinary interlude. Soon they would be just a memory.

CHAPTER 36

Amy swallowed, suddenly apprehensive. The bungalow looked different. Perhaps it was only because the garden was overgrown, or the curtains closed, or that the mist, which they had run into on their way up, made everything eerie, but she had an instinct something was not right. She imagined Alex in one of the darkened rooms, drunk and violent, waiting for them.

'I'll bring the cases,' her father said. 'You two go in.'

She followed her mother up the drive.

Grace turned the key in the lock and pushed cautiously, as if she too feared what they would find inside. 'Something's stuck!' She set her shoulder against the wood, forcing the door open a few inches. Her muffled cry was half gasp, half sob.

'What is it, Mum?' Amy tried to peer through the gap.

'Problems?' Her father put the cases on the step. 'Shall I go first?'

Without waiting for an answer he lunged at the door, using his weight to make a space wide enough for them to enter. They stood behind him, appalled at what they found.

It was a few seconds before Amy realised the mound of rubbish in front of them had once been furniture. The hall cupboard had been overturned and hacked to pieces, the telephone lay in bits among the debris; the mirror had been pulled off the wall and the glass ground into the carpet; the kitchen chairs and table were heaped on top of the mess, the wood splintered and jagged. There was a strong smell of petrol and piles of screwed up newspaper everywhere.

Her father frowned. 'Looks like someone intended to have a bonfire.'

'It was Alex,' her mother said. 'It's his way of punishing me.'

Amy shivered. She was certain Alex had meant to set fire to the place but at some stage he had changed his mind. He wanted them to witness every little detail of his revenge, to feel his hatred.

They scrambled round the wreckage and walked down the hall. Her father drew back the curtains in the lounge and the extent of the devastation overwhelmed them. The piano had been attacked with a sledgehammer, the sofa slashed and the stuffing dragged out, the television and video player hurled into the fireplace. Pictures had been yanked from their frames and the beautiful cabinet reduced to matchwood, its contents trampled underfoot. Every single ornament had been destroyed.

'I don't know if I can bear any more.' Her mother was trembling.

Amy eyed her without pity. 'You brought the bastard here. You've only got yourself to blame.'

Her father squeezed her arm gently. 'Grace is at the end of her tether, Amy. Don't make things worse.'

She bit back an angry retort. His hand steadied her and she didn't move away immediately.

'Do you want me to check the rest while you stay here?' he asked.

'No.' Her mother made a visible effort. 'I need to see for myself.'

It was the same in every room. In the kitchen their feet crunched on layers of shattered crockery and glass. The cupboards hung off the walls, the cooker and washing machine were cracked and dented, the microwave almost flattened.

'It must have taken him hours,' Amy whispered.

The bathroom resembled a building site. The bath, pedestal and washbasin had been reduced to rubble, the tiles smashed, the shower, mirror and shelves torn down, and shards of plastic and glass covered the floor. The bedrooms were no better. Bed linen had been shredded, feathers from duvets and pillows were everywhere, furniture had been demolished, clothes cut into ribbons, and in the front bedroom Alex had daubed the words *fucking bitch* in red paint across the whole length of one wall.

Amy stood behind her parents, no longer protected by indifference, the callous spark of anger extinguished by horror at the scale of the destruction. Her mother faced them, face pale as sour milk.

'What are we going to do?' The words were hollow with her pain.

Amy turned to her father.

'The insurance will cover the damage,' he said quietly. 'We'll get things put right.'

Her mother stared at him, eyes opaque, looking inward.

'It could take months. And what about afterwards? I don't know if we can afford to live here any more.'

'Think about that when the time comes.' He took a step towards her, as if he wanted to offer her physical comfort. 'I'll do what I can to speed things up.'

She straightened her shoulders. Her hands were clenched, the knuckles white and prominent. 'Thank you. You're right. There's no point in worrying about the future. I need to find somewhere for us to stay and see what we can salvage from this chaos.'

Amy felt a grudging admiration. She spoke impulsively. 'I'll help, Mum.'

Her mother seemed to shrink. She covered her face with her hands and began to cry, horrible, keening sobs.

'I'm so sorry, Amy. So sorry. There's nothing left for you. Nothing!' She staggered, clutching at the air.

Amy ran to her, held her until the storm of weeping died down. 'Don't worry, Mum. Dad will sort it.'

Her father smiled grimly. 'We'll call at the police station to tell them about this and then I'm taking you both back to Tuston. We can deal with everything else over the phone.'

He was calm and matter-of-fact. Amy regarded him with silent gratitude. She schooled her features into a solemn expression and tried to repress the guilty joy that made her want to smile.

* * *

This isn't real. Hope pinched herself surreptitiously. *I can't actually be in Venice, drinking champagne at Florian's with the most attractive man in Italy.* She glanced at Maurizio Quattrone shyly. He looked different, dressed like her in cropped trousers and a plain white T-shirt. His black hair had been pushed under a peaked cap and he wore wrap-around sunglasses which reflected the light. So far no one had recognised him.

Champagne bubbles tickled her nose and she wanted to giggle. It was ridiculous having to conceal her identity from the tourists herding into the Piazza in the late September sunshine. Ridiculous and exciting. She smothered the giggle with a cough.

'You okay?' Maurizio leaned towards her.

'Mmm.' She peered over the top of her dark glasses, absorbing the atmosphere, admiring the elegant facades of the tiered public buildings. It was as though she was on a stage, where, no matter how well the actors played their part, they would always be overshadowed by the magnificence of the set. Lifting her head, she stared at the Basilica, squinting up at the huge domes shimmering against the blue sky. It was exotic, fantastic, and so beautiful it made her want to cry.

Behind her, she heard the murmur of voices and the slow shuffle of footsteps along the arcades. There were hundreds of people in the square and the noise should have been deafening, yet everything sounded hushed, as if they were in a church.

'You like it?' Maurizio touched her hand.

'It's out of this world.' She couldn't begin to explain how the place was weaving its magic into her soul.

They were here purely by chance; an unexpected break in their busy schedule. Less than an hour ago they had crossed the lagoon in a smart little launch, landing at the bustling waterfront. Maurizio, having persuaded their chaperones they weren't needed, had ushered her through groups of exhausted sightseers, past the Doges' Palace, and into the Piazzo San Marco. It was captivating. A fairy tale. And Maurizio was her Prince Charming. She giggled again and hiccupped loudly.

He smiled at her. 'More champagne?'

'No. Thank you.'

'Then we should go. I will take you to the famous *Ponte Di Rialto* and then we will hire a gondola. Yes?' He handed several banknotes to a passing waiter, indicating he required no change.

Hope stretched lethargically. She would have liked to stay longer, listening to the orchestra, watching the kaleidoscope of activity in front of her, but she was too timid to say so. She was unsure of Maurizio Quattrone. He was almost nine years her senior and she never felt entirely at ease in his company. Except when they were filming together.

'Can we go into the cathedral?' she asked tentatively.

'If you wish.' He pulled her chair back with impeccable manners, but she had the notion he was not best pleased.

Inside, the Basilica was shadowy and cool, the aisles crammed with visitors of all nationalities, the echo of movement and conversation muffled. The air smelt of incense and holiness and history. Hope took off her sunglasses. Thousands of candles made the air waver. The mosaics gleamed with gold and the jewel-encrusted altars glittered with an extravagant brilliance. It was breathtaking. She found herself moved along too quickly, jostled by trippers insensitive to their surroundings.

Maurizio was silent. Eventually, becoming aware of his impatience, she allowed herself to be led outside. The brilliant sunshine made her eyes water. She put on her sunglasses as she went along, stumbling a little before the world slipped back into focus. Maurizio put a casual arm round her and she caught herself thinking how well they fitted together, how easy it would be to rest her head against his shoulder. They strolled along a series of narrow streets, each lined with glitzy boutiques and souvenir shops. Once or twice the flash of a camera startled her and she worried they had been discovered, though when she scanned the crowds no one seemed to be paying them any attention.

The Rialto Bridge was teeming with people searching for bargains on the tightly packed stalls. Below, the Grand Canal heaved with the wash from an assortment of vessels, its surface rippled like the scales of a giant grey fish. At the landing stage they climbed into a waiting gondola. Maurizio gave rapid instructions in Italian and Hope leaned back against the faded cushions, enjoying the different aspect on the city, until they turned off the busy waterway and into a forlorn canal secreted between tall, shabby houses. The warmth from the sun vanished. She shivered, her mood changing. Here the water slid beneath the boat, dark and smooth and sinister. The only sounds were the swish as the gondolier propelled them forwards and the melancholy lapping of little waves against damp walls.

Maurizio came to sit by her. 'Are you cold?'

She shook her head.

'Look.' He pointed to a bridge some way in front. Sunlight streamed through a gap in the buildings, reflecting on the water, making patterns on the stone supports. The gondolier began to sing. A cluster of people appeared from nowhere to listen, calling greetings to them as they drifted towards the low arch. Hope smiled, her vague fears forgotten. Again a camera flashed and she waved at the friendly faces peering down at her.

The rest of the journey was over too soon; a sequence of sun and shade and graceful bridges; of peeling, ochre-coloured walls and quiet quaysides. When she stepped out of the gondola she was disorientated, loathe to leave the tranquility of the backwaters.

Maurizio took her hand and they wandered through a maze of deserted alleys. In a peaceful square they discovered a restaurant, with tables beneath an awning in a secluded courtyard.

'I can recommend the risotto alla pescatora,' Maurizio volunteered as she tried to decipher the menu. 'Also, I think, a bottle of Pinot Grigio.'

The meal was delicious. Maurizio was attentive, refilling her glass before it was empty, entertaining her with anecdotes from his past and giving her the lowdown on her fellow actors. Over coffee he described the acrimonious break-up with his last leading lady, an award-winning Hollywood actress. 'It was not my fault,' he finished plaintively. 'Whatever the papers said, I am not the big bad wolf, Hope.'

He reached across and brushed her cheek with his fingers. 'You and I, we are good together.'

Her skin grew hot. She didn't know what he meant. His eyes were concealed by the dark shades and she couldn't read his expression.

'Tell me about yourself, Hope.'

To cover her embarrassment she talked too quickly. Maurizio rested his elbows on the table. After a few minutes he glanced at his watch and she wondered if he was bored. She became anxious, unable to think of anything more to say, and they finished their coffee in silence as the sky changed almost imperceptibly to a deeper, more iridescent blue.

'We must go. It's an early start tomorrow.' Maurizio's chair scraped on the slabs as he stood up, calling to the waiter to bring the bill.

There were few people about when they left the restaurant. The sun was low and the quiet squares full of shadows. Hope had to hurry to keep up with Maurizio and she was relieved when he stopped on a bridge to admire the thin line of a canal caught in the dying rays of the sun. He took off his dark glasses and put them into his pocket.

'See. Nature puts on a show for you, *Mia Ragazza*.' He pulled her to him and they stood side by side. His face was inches away from hers. She tried to ignore the rapid beating of her heart.

'You are very serious, Hope. What do you think of Venice?'

'It's wonderful. I've had a perfect day.' His eyes hypnotised her.

He removed her sunhat and his own, holding them in one hand as he pushed her sunglasses into her hair and bent to kiss her. 'Thank you. It has been perfect for me also.'

For a moment she couldn't breathe. She wanted to run away, wanted to wind her arms round his neck, wanted to deny the cynical voice in her head which told her this was just an adult game.

There were several bright flashes and someone called out. 'Signor Quattrone! Signorina! Per favore—'

Maurizio let go of her. He shouted something in Italian and laughed. Hope noticed figures at the open windows in one of the houses along the canal. There was no doubt they were paparazzi. By tomorrow pictures of her kissing Maurizio Quattrone could be all over the world. She didn't want that. It was something private, not something to be ogled by the masses. Why did he find it so amusing?

Then she realised. 'You set this up? And earlier, in the streets and on the gondola, photographers were there too, weren't they?'

He shrugged. 'It is good publicity. You are not well known. Now everyone will want to hear about Maurizio's new lady friend.'

She was sick with humiliation. He had used her.

Refusing to pose for more shots, she insisted they make their way back to the waterfront where the launch was waiting, its engine throbbing. Maurizio oozed charm, apologising for his deception, telling her he had her best interests at heart. She ignored him.

As the powerful boat cut through the water she leaned against the brass rail, confused and unsettled. How could she have been so gullible? Well she certainly wasn't going to be the next in the long list of Maurizio Quattrone's girlfriends!

Yet there would be so many advantages if her name was linked with his. The thought shocked her. Was this selfish ambition something inherited from Brandon Calthorpe? Had she changed so much? Already she enjoyed the glamorous lifestyle – the parties, the limousines, the plush hotels, the kudos of being a 'star'. 'Worldly trappings', her father would say. She pictured him in his cluttered study and her heart ached for home.

Maurizio came out of the cabin carrying two glasses of wine. Now the charm offensive was over he looked sullen. 'Peace offering.'

She took a glass and moved away, her gaze drawn to the skyline where the city, pearl and mauve in the failing light, seemed to float above a filmy mist rising from the sea. Loneliness gnawed at her, sharp as toothache.

She longed for the people she loved; her father, Kate, Faith... Russell.

Her conscience stirred uneasily. Russell had been her only true friend, the one person she had trusted with her secrets. Yet she had rejected him. Made him hate her.

She drank the wine quickly. But it was impossible to oust Russell from her mind. Fragmented memories surfaced; the way his eyes changed colour with the light, the smile that animated his plain features, his gentleness, the feel of his chapped, roughened hands, the way she could lose herself in his kisses.

Maurizio sighed dramatically. 'Are you going to sulk all night?'

She turned towards him. He was beautiful, like a finely carved statue, yet he no longer made her pulse race. He was all posture and show. She wouldn't be fooled by him again. Russell Holmes was worth a million Maurizios.

CHAPTER 37

The morning had grown steadily darker. Faith stared through the office window at the rain-soaked roof-tops, tempted to cancel her lunchtime appointment. The months since Rajat's engagement had been long and empty, but the dull winter days were even harder to bear. It was as if the gloom had invaded her body, suppressing all enjoyment and enthusiasm. Even her visit home for Christmas had been marred by the presence of her mother and Amy.

Rajat had kept his promise to stay in touch. But it wasn't the same. Why had she never realised what he meant to her? She had thought he was just a good friend; that seeing him was a habit, the security of being with someone who understood and accepted her shortcomings. She was wrong. And now it was too late: he was marrying someone else. Now things were awkward between them and she usually made excuses to avoid him.

Sighing, she shut down the computer and tidied the manuscripts on her desk, checking the one she needed was in her briefcase. As she reached for her coat she resolved, once again, to pull herself together. It was a new year. Time for a fresh start. Rajat would be married soon and there was nothing she could do about it.

The cafe was crowded; a convivial place with dark furniture and art deco lamps. She had chosen it because it was close to the office, not too expensive, and, for some perverse reason she didn't care to analyse, because it was somewhere she and Rajat had frequented in the old days. There was no sign of the woman she was meeting, an author whose first novel they had recently commissioned. Faith was vaguely annoyed. New authors were notoriously protective of their material. She had been hoping to discuss some alterations to the storyline over lunch and be back in the office by mid-afternoon.

A waiter showed her to a table. She ordered a mineral water and surveyed the other diners. There were several couples, snatching time in their lunch hour, talking animatedly, touching hands, absorbed in each other. The sudden jolt of envy made her feel sick. What was happening to her? Why did the sight of other people's happiness hurt so much?

A movement at the entrance caught her attention. Rajat was holding the door open for a tall, olive-skinned girl in a red, padded jacket. He came into the cafe behind her, folding up his old golf umbrella and smiling at a waiter who came to greet them. Faith swallowed, her throat suddenly tight. *What was he doing here?*

She peered through her fringe, hiding her face with the glossy menu. The girl with Rajat was beautiful. Her features were perfect: high cheekbones, a straight little nose, wide, deep-set eyes and shoulder-length black hair with the sheen of satin. She wore the shortest of skirts, exposing smooth thighs above knee-length suede boots, and she moved with an arrogant grace, clearly aware that every man in the restaurant was staring at her. Faith looked away, numb with misery.

'Faith! This is a surprise. How are you?'

She lifted her head. He was standing in front of her. The girl hung on to his arm, a huge square-cut diamond prominent on her left hand. Close to, she appeared very young.

'This is Anshula, my fiancée,' Rajat said stiffly. 'Anshula, this is a friend of mine, Faith Lawson.'

'Nice to meet you.' The girl's handshake was limp.

'Congratulations on your engagement.' Faith wondered if either of them heard the small, sticky sound her tongue made against the roof of her mouth.

'Anshula's in London for the week. I've taken time off work to show her round.' Rajat seemed apologetic.

The girl pouted, tugging at his arm like a spoilt child.

'I've had enough sightseeing for today. My feet are killing me, Raj. Let's sit at the bar until our table's ready.'

Faith wanted to slap her. Instead she made herself smile. 'Don't let me keep you. You look worn out.'

She saw Rajat's lips twitch. 'Take care, Faith,' he said softly.

She couldn't resist watching them, punishing herself with memories until a voice distracted her.

'Excuse me. It is Miss Lawson, isn't it?'

The woman was middle-aged with greying hair and the lined, crepey skin of a heavy smoker. Faith stood up to shake her hand. 'Thank you for coming.'

'Sorry I'm late. I lost my way on the tube. Got off at the wrong station.'

'It's no problem. I haven't been here long. Sit down, please. Perhaps we should order. They're very busy.' Faith handed over the menu, concealing her impatience as the woman fumbled in an oversized handbag for a pair of spectacles and then perused the list of dishes on offer, taking ages to make a decision. Eventually Faith signalled to a waiter, scanning the room as she did so. Rajat and Anshula were sitting at a corner table, dark heads together as they consulted the wine list.

Somehow she ate lunch and conversed pleasantly, forcing herself to concentrate on the task in hand and propose the changes she wanted made. The woman argued her case well and, after a while, Faith found the discussion stimulating, so much so that when she looked across the room again Rajat and Anshula had gone.

It felt like a bereavement. He had left without saying goodbye. She clenched her hands beneath the table, trying to regain control.

'Are you all right, dear?' The woman asked.

'Yes, thank you.' Faith straightened her shoulders. Rajat had a new love. She had to accept that.

***

'Do you believe in Heaven?' Marcus asked.

Amy leaned over the rail above the swollen stream, fascinated by the dark water squirming beneath the rustic bridge.

'I suppose so. Why?' She blew into her gloves to warm her hands.

'Just wondered. I often think I would rather stay here when I die. Like a ghost.'

'Can we talk about something else?' Amy shivered in her warm jacket and anchored the fake-fur hat more firmly on her head.

He laughed. 'Sorry. Don't mind me. I get these weird ideas sometimes.'

She glanced at him. His lips were blue and his face had an unhealthy pallor. 'Shall we go back?'

'We can't go in yet. I promised Raffles a decent walk.' He patted the ten-month-old golden retriever that was tangling its lead around his legs.

'Let's get moving then, before we both freeze to death.' Amy hurried off the bridge and heard him wheezing as he ran to catch up with her.

They trudged along the path at the side of the lake, splashing through the mud in their wellingtons, keeping pace with the eager puppy.

'So are you looking forward to school tomorrow?' Marcus spoke first, his breath forming mist in the arctic air.

'I'd prefer to have a couple more weeks off like you.'

He grinned. 'I'd swap places any time.'

'Don't you like being a boarder?'

'Not much. I miss Mum. And Raffles too.'

Amy noticed he didn't mention his father. She had never seen Brandon Calthorpe, but he seemed to have little time for his only son.

The puppy sniffed at a tree trunk and they waited while it nosed in the undergrowth. Amy stifled a sigh. The cold was beginning to make her feel sick.

Marcus nudged her. 'Cheer up, it may never happen.'

She smiled, appreciating his amiable disposition. He had spent most of the Christmas holiday at Dalchett House while his parents were at work, yet he didn't seem bored or resentful. She thought he looked almost handsome; taller than her now, with the smooth, sensual features of his ancestors which were captured forever in the portraits lining the panelled walls of Dalchett House. He was like Aunt Helena in many ways but he was undeniably a Calthorpe.

They resumed their walk at the puppy's insistence. It seemed even colder when they came out of the trees. The house loomed above the slope, sombre beneath the thick layer of cloud. Amy was glad when the path skirted another area of woodland which offered some protection from the biting wind. They continued in silence, conserving their energy. The roar of water grew louder and further ahead plumes of spray were visible between the trees. Their steps slowed as they approached the makeshift bridge. The brook had become a torrent, creaming over rocks, spitting up stones, churning like a mill race, the colour of sheep's wool where it spewed out into the lake. Marcus put a foot on one of the planks, frowning as the wood shifted. 'It's not safe. The rain's washed some of the bank away.'

Amy stared at the seething water in disbelief. She was chilled to the bone, unable to feel her fingers or toes.

'We'll have to go back.' She plucked at his sleeve, half-afraid he might be foolhardy enough to test whether the bridge would support his weight. They turned to retrace their steps and immediately the wind sliced into their faces.

'Whose idea was this walk?' She tried to joke but it was difficult to speak; the air seemed to freeze in her throat.

'I think we could blame Raffles.' Marcus, too, was striving for breath.

'Why don't we— ' She gasped as the wind snatched her hat and tossed it like a kite towards the lake.

'I'll catch it.' Marcus gave chase, with Raffles cavorting round his ankles.

Amy ran after them, trying in vain to keep the short, flailing strands of hair out of her eyes. 'It doesn't matter,' she yelled. 'Leave it!'

Marcus stopped on a grassy promontory near the mouth of the brook and bent forward, holding his stomach, his shoulders heaving.

'There it is,' he panted, pointing to where her hat bobbed on the choppy water. 'I think I can get it.'

'Marcus, it's not worth the effort. It will be ruined anyway.'

'Well, at least we can give it a try.' He crouched by the puppy to unfasten its lead. 'Hold on to Raffles.'

'You're crazy!' She thrust her fingers beneath the dog's collar as Marcus strode to the edge of the lake. 'What are you going to do?'

'Trust me.' He cast the lead like a fishing line. It fell short, the end landing among the waves with scarcely a splash.

'I need to make it longer.' He unzipped his anorak and removed the belt from his jeans. In seconds he had tied it to the lead. 'This should do it'

'Why bother?' Amy was growing impatient. She didn't want the stupid hat. It was already half-submerged and she couldn't care less. She wanted to be indoors by the fire.

'I'll give it one more go.' Marcus stepped forward gingerly, concentrating while he rolled the combined lead and belt into a coil.

'Be careful!'

'Don't worry, I'm not about to fall in and give myself double pneumonia.' He raised his arm, focussing his attention on the tiny target.

It was all too much for the excitable puppy. Seeing the chance of a game, it sprang to its feet, straining to be free, barking furiously.

'Raffles, no!' Amy shouted.

The puppy paused momentarily, its ears pricked, then bounded towards its master, dragging her in its wake. She couldn't restrain it. The collar was wrenched from her stiff, gloved fingers and Raffles leapt up at Marcus, catching him off balance, sending him sprawling into the lake.

Amy stood by helplessly as he floundered in the deep water, terrified he would drown. Beside her, Raffles yelped, dashing to and fro, his tail wagging.

'Quiet, Raffles.' She pushed the puppy out of the way and lay on her stomach, one arm outstretched. Her flesh was like ice. 'Marcus, hang on to me!'

He was coughing and spluttering, his eyes dilated, his face bloodless, plastered with weed. With a sob of relief, she realised he had pulled himself to his feet and, slowly, like something out of a horror movie, he began to wade through the murky water. She saw his hand seize hers but there was no sensation in her fingers.

'That's it, Marcus. You've nearly made it.' Her voice was hoarse.

He reached the bank and let go of her to grab the twisted roots of a willow. She could see he was exhausted.

'Marcus. You have to get out.' She knelt to hug him, give him what warmth she could.

'I... I can't.' Suddenly he was limp in her arms, his eyes rolling, his face contorted. She couldn't hold on to him and he slumped back into the water.

'Marcus! Marcus, get up. Get up!' Panic-stricken she slid into the lake. The freezing water took her breath away, swirling round her waist, almost lifting her off her feet, but somehow she managed to haul him upright.

'Marcus, help me.'

He was a dead weight, his face a mask. She cradled him to her, eyes blinded with tears.

'Marcus can you hear me? I don't think I can push you up the bank. Please, Marcus, try and help yourself.'

Even as she spoke she knew it was useless. She looked around wildly. Her mind was sluggish. The cold was in her head, in her lungs, creeping through every vein in her body. It would be so easy to give up, to lie down with Marcus and let the water cover them both.

The thought jangled a warning in her brain. She didn't want to die. With a last desperate effort she managed to wedge Marcus's inert form among the roots of the willow and hoist herself up on to the grass. The puppy nuzzled her, its tail between its legs, whining softly when she ignored it. Marcus was still; his eyes closed. She tore the gloves from her swollen fingers and, kneeling again, eased his shoulders forwards so that she could place her hands under his armpits.

At first she didn't think she would be able to lift him. Her chest was raw, her lungs felt as if they would burst and every one of her muscles was stretched to the limit.

'I can't do this on my own, Marcus.'

It was no good. She would have to leave him while she went for help. Sobbing, she renewed her efforts. This time she felt him move. He was free of the snare of roots. Little by little she dragged him up the bank, pausing every other moment to rest.

At last he lay on the grass. She took off her wet jacket and folded it inside out to make a pillow for his head. He wasn't breathing. She couldn't feel a pulse. Raffles came closer to sniff at him, puzzled when there was no response.

'Sit, Raffles. There's a good boy.' Amy patted the dog automatically and then bent over Marcus. Sealing his mouth with hers, she went through the routine she had learned at school: breathe – pause – breathe – pause – breathe – fifteen compressions. She repeated the sequence again and again and again.

She refused to believe he was dead. While she had a trickle of energy left she wouldn't give up. She worked until it was physically impossible to do anything more, until she fell on top of him, too weary even to cry.

It was some minutes before she staggered to her feet and began to stumble along the path, treading in the footprints they had made earlier. She looked round once. Raffles was sitting to attention by the lifeless figure.

The woods were a nightmare world of black and grey and shadow, permeated with the rank, damp smell of rotting foliage. It was all she could do to keep moving. Her clothes were soaked through, tight and cold against her skin, her wellingtons half full of water, her legs leaden. At one stage she resorted to crawling, clawing her way up the slope. When she reached the formal gardens she stopped, disorientated. Across the wide expanse of lawn the house seemed to waver in her line of vision.

'Are you all right, miss?'

She was too weak to respond. The young gardener put down his fork and stepped across the flowerbed.

'Miss?' He touched her arm.

'There's been an accident,' she whispered. The ground had begun to spin in the most peculiar way.

'Steady on. Let's get you indoors.' He picked her up easily and carried her through the walled garden to the kitchen. At the door he set her down, supporting her while he turned the brass knob.

She came round to find herself on the stone floor, a circle of faces peering down at her, each one fuzzy, silhouetted against the light. For a moment her mind remained empty. Then the ghastly memories returned and she sat up, struggling to speak, her brain swamped with shocking images.

'Marcus is... Marcus is down by the lake. He fell in the water. I got him out but I think... he's... he might be...' She gripped her grandmother's hand, digging her fingernails into the skin in her urgency. But she couldn't bring herself to say the word.

'I'll send Jim to fetch him.' Dot Manning was calm and practical as ever.

'Ask Homes as well. Tell them to sort out one of the stretchers from the stables.' Her grandmother took control. 'I'll take Amy upstairs. She needs a warm bath. Trudie fill the hot-water bottles. We'll get her into bed.'

'You don't understand, any of you,' Amy screeched, 'Marcus is dead!'

There was a terrible silence. The three women stared at her and she closed her eyes, unable to bear the sight of their stricken faces. She heard them talking, heard their quick footsteps and someone crying. Then Trudie's plump arms were round her, guiding her to a chair. 'Here, Amy, drink this.'

Her body shook with tremor after tremor. She couldn't hold the glass but she sipped the brandy when it was put to her lips. Afterwards, when her fingers and toes began to tingle and the alcohol had warmed her, she felt dazed, oddly detached from reality, achingly tired.

They wouldn't let her sleep. With Trudie's assistance, she followed her grandmother upstairs to the main bathroom. She submitted without protest while Ivy bathed her and washed her hair and then wrapped her in a towel, rubbing her dry vigorously. Steam clouded the room, condensing on the mirrors, making silvery trails on the glass. Everything had a strange, dreamlike quality.

In the bedroom someone had lit the fire and the thick nightdress was warm when she slipped it over her head.

'In you get.' Her grandmother folded back the sheet.

Amy hesitated, drawn to the window. On the horizon the bruised line of the mountains was almost indistinguishable from the cloud and she could see a veil of drizzle sweeping over the nearby fields. Beneath the lowering sky, the lake resembled a black hole in the fabric of the countryside. She pressed her face against the small leaded panes, scanning the grounds for a glimpse of Holmes and Jim Manning; clinging desperately to the hope that she might have been wrong and Marcus was still alive.

A movement among the trees alerted her. She watched the sad little procession emerge from the woods: the two ageing men, shapeless in their waxed jackets, bearing a stretcher on which there looked to be nothing more than a pile of old tartan rugs. And, a few paces behind, the puppy; forlorn, bedraggled, the unwitting instrument of its master's death.

'Come away, Amy.'

Her grandmother steered her back to the bed and helped her in, tucking the blankets round her. 'Try to sleep, my dear.'

Amy squeezed her eyes shut. But the nightmare played on behind them, flickering in and out of focus like old cine-film.

Sleep. If only she could. If only she could wipe today from her memory and wake up to find it had all been a hideous dream.

The drone of the bombers grew closer and the night sky was arced with lights. She was running along a road of terraced houses, her heart thudding as the sound of gunfire echoed off the walls.

She woke herself with her screams. Terrified, she sat up, pushing aside the jumble of bedclothes. With a sob of relief she identified her surroundings. She was in one of the bedrooms at Dalchett House. The curtains had not been drawn and it was dark outside, but someone had banked up the fire which bathed everything in a rosy glow.

Yet the sound of an aircraft still thrummed in her head. And she could hear shouting. It was hard to separate reality from illusion. Dazed with sleep, she groped her way to the window and peered through. The glass was speckled with rain, but she could just make out a helicopter hovering above a field on the far side of the lake, its landing lights flashing. Along one of the narrow tracks nearby the headlights of a Land Rover pricked the darkness between the hedgerows. Marcus's parents had arrived.

Trembling, she darted back to the bed and huddled beneath the blankets. She lay on her side, alert, waiting for the creak of floorboards in the corridor and the knock on the bedroom door which meant she had to go downstairs and face everyone.

The fire was low, the coal glowing with a bright, steady heat, when she opened her eyes again. The bedclothes had been smoothed, the hot-water bottles refilled and placed by her feet, the pillows fluffed into a softer pile. The air was fragrant with perfume.

'Mum?'

The longing for her mother was instant and intense. She swung her legs out of bed, feeling for her slippers with her feet and snatching up the bathrobe, which was lying on the quilt. She pulled it on, tying the belt as she rushed to the door.

The corridor outside was dimly lit, pooled with shadows. It was empty.

'Mum!' She looked down into the gloomy well of the staircase but her mother was nowhere to be seen.

'Mum!' Her vision obscured by tears, she hurtled down the stairs, losing both slippers in her haste. There was no one about. She could hear no murmur of voices, no clatter from the kitchen, none of the usual sounds of daily life. Alarmed, she ran to the drawing room, hardly aware of the cold slabs beneath her bare feet or the icy draught that ruffled the hem of her nightdress. She pushed the heavy door open.

'Mum.'

The haggard faces were blurred.

'I'm here, darling.' Her mother was sitting in a chair by the hearth. She came across the room quickly. No one else moved. They were like figures in a painting, hunched, frozen with grief, locked within themselves.

'Oh, Mum!' Amy buried her head in her mother's arms. 'It's all my fault. If I hadn't been wearing that stupid hat Marcus would be alive now. If I hadn't let go of Raffles...'

'Hush, darling. You mustn't blame yourself. It was an accident.'

Amy shuddered. 'It was horrible, Mum. I tried so hard to save him but I couldn't. I just couldn't!'

Her voice failed. The man who must be Marcus's father was staring at her, his eyes narrowed and cruel.

'Perhaps you would tell us exactly what did happen.'

'Come and sit by the fire, sweetheart. You're still in shock.' Her mother led her to the armchair and knelt at her feet, ignoring Brandon Calthorpe's request. 'You don't have to talk about things tonight, Amy. We can leave it until the morning.'

'No, we bloody well can't! I want to know how my son died and what part your daughter played in all this.'

'Brandon.' Helena murmured ineffectually. She spoke in little more than a whisper. 'Please, Amy. We need to know.'

Amy nodded, the burden of guilt made heavier by the gentle plea. She dabbed her eyes with the sleeve of the bathrobe, forcing herself to relive the ordeal. 'We took Raffles for a walk, down by the lake. We turned back by the brook because the planks weren't safe — and then the wind blew my hat into the lake, and Marcus... Marcus tried to get it out. I told him not to. I told him it didn't matter but he wouldn't listen.'

Her lips were numb. The words tumbled from her mouth and she didn't know if she was making sense. She couldn't look at anyone. 'He tried to fish it out with the dog's lead, and he fell into the water. I helped him to the bank and then... then he sort of collapsed. I couldn't hold on to him and he went under.'

She covered her face with her hands. 'I tried to save him but I wasn't strong enough. It took ages to pull him out of the water, and by then it was... it was too late. I gave him the kiss of life. I did my best. But it was no use. I'm sorry. So sorry.'

'The doctor who examined him when we arrived told us there was nothing anyone could have done. His heart was always weak. None of this was your fault, Amy. We don't blame you.' Helena sounded strange, as if something was stuck in her throat.

Brandon Calthorpe said nothing.

'I'm glad you were with him,' Helena continued. 'I'm glad you didn't leave him until...' It was a few seconds before she could finish. 'You were a brave girl. I will always be grateful for what you did.'

Amy looked up, Helena's words pouring into her head like a blessing. Her mother squeezed her hand reassuringly.

'What did you mean when you said, if I hadn't let go of Raffles?' There was no hint of forgiveness in Brandon Calthorpe's voice.

'Raffles thought it was a game.' Amy threaded the towelling belt through her fingers, unwilling to meet his hostile stare. 'He broke away from me.'

'And?' The question was like the crack of a whip.

'He... he jumped up and Marcus lost his balance.'

She felt the air move as he leapt from the sofa, heard the tinkle of falling glasses as he struck the wine table with his fist. The door slammed and rattled in its frame behind him. She saw her father and Helena exchange glances; saw her mother grip the side of the chair and her grandmother's thin fingers twisting together. No one said anything, though the tension was almost unbearable.

'No!' Amy stood up unsteadily. Thrusting aside her mother's restraining arm, she dashed out of the room. In the passageway she paused to catch her breath.

Brandon Calthorpe came out of the garden room carrying a shotgun and dragging the wretched puppy by a piece of garden twine tied to its collar.

'Stay out of my way!' he snarled as he passed her.

'What are you going to do with him?'

'What I should have done hours ago. Bloody useless mutt!' He reached the front door and yanked it open.

'You can't kill him. Marcus loved him.'

'Amy!'

She had no idea how long her father had been there.

'Leave it, Amy. Let me deal with him.'

But she didn't listen. She raced up the passage and out into the night. There was a security lamp at the end of the stable block and she saw Brandon Calthorpe tying Raffles to a ring in the wall. He picked up the gun again and stepped back a few paces.

'No!' The gravel was like broken glass on the soles of her feet as she ran. She dropped to her knees by the cowering puppy and wrapped her arms round its neck, feeling its slender body quiver against her, its fur already damp with the fine wintry rain.

'Get out of the way or I'll shoot you along with the bloody dog!'

She heard the click as he released the safety catch.

'Amy, come over here. He's capable of anything in this mood.'

Her father was on the step. She wanted to go to him but she couldn't move.

'You'd better believe it, Richard. That dog killed my son. It deserves to die. And if your daughter doesn't shift I'll blast her to pieces her as well. If Marcus hadn't been with her he'd be alive now.'

Anger gave Amy false courage. 'If you cared about him, he wouldn't have been at Dalchett House in the first place. You couldn't even spare time for him in the holidays.'

'Amy!' Her father's voice was harsh with fear.

'You bloody well asked for this.' Brandon Calthorpe raised the gun to his shoulder, his finger on the trigger. Out of the corner of her eye Amy saw her father running towards him. There was a flash and the explosion ripped through the air, reverberating round the hills.

For a moment she thought she might be dead. Her ears hurt and her head felt as though it was cocooned in layers of wool. Then she heard Brandon Calthorpe's callous laughter.

'Did you think I would throw away everything for that little tart? Just tell her to get the dog out of my sight. I never want to see the thing again.' He strode away and disappeared into the darkness.

Amy slumped on the gravel, her heartbeat so rapid she could scarcely breathe. Her father crouched beside her, held her until the violent shaking eased and she tried to sit up, slowly becoming aware of her surroundings. She saw her mother and grandmother on the doorstep, indistinct figures in the dim light from the passage. One of them was crying.

'I'm sorry, Dad.'

'You're safe, that's all that matters.' He helped her to her feet and lifted her into his arms. 'I couldn't bear to lose you now.'

His words barely registered but the warmth of his body was reassuring. Beside them Raffles whined pitifully.

'Can I keep him, Dad?' Amy tried to push the wet hair out of her eyes but there was no strength in her fingers.

Her father half-smiled. 'How can I refuse? I'll take him for a walk in a while and then put him in our car for the night. He'll be fine, don't worry.'

He carried her to the bedroom. Her mother followed. Together they settled her in the chair by the fire, wrapping a blanket around her and placing a hot-water bottle behind her back. Exhausted she closed her eyes.

She must have dozed for a few minutes. The rush of cold air as the door was opened woke her.

'Your mother's just gone to get you a clean nightdress.'

'Are you angry with me, Dad?' She was alarmed by his grim expression.

'Angry with you?' He sounded surprised. 'Of course not. I'm proud of you. Not many teenagers would have done what you did today.'

'You look angry.'

'Not with you, Amy. I'm angry with Brandon for what he did. But, if anything happened to you, or either of your sisters, I have no idea how I would react. Loss affects people differently. I shouldn't judge Brandon. It's just that we've never seen eye to eye.'

His manner was gentle when he spoke again.

'Marcus's death is a dreadful shock for all of us. He was such a lovely boy; inoffensive, good-natured, completely without guile. I shall miss him.'

Amy folded a corner of the blanket over her dirty hands, tormented by similar thoughts. Her father picked up the poker and began to rake the fire.

'I wonder how his mother will cope.' He seemed to be talking to himself. His face was old with grief.

She remembered the way he had looked at Helena in London and bent her head, overwhelmed by sadness; for Marcus, for her father and Aunt Helena, for her mother, and for the golden-haired puppy outside in the rain.

* * *

The manuscript was making no sense. Faith yawned, stretching her arms above her head, and the sheaf of papers slithered from her lap, spreading into an untidy fan at her feet.

'Drat!' She wriggled off the sofa to retrieve them and stuffed them into a folder. It was impossible to concentrate. She was too low in spirits, unable to banish Rajat and Anshula from her mind.

She looked around disconsolately. The room, with its modern furnishings, seemed soulless. In front of her the pale flames of the gas fire flickered without giving much warmth. The stainless-steel digital clock displayed the seconds in silence.

Determined not to wallow in self-pity, she decided to make a drink and go to bed. She was on her way to the kitchen when the telephone rang.

'Faith.'

It was her father's voice.

'Dad! Is something wrong?' Her heart lurched. 'Is it Mum?'

'No. It's not Grace.'

She had no idea why she felt so relieved; why she even cared.

'I'm at Dalchett House. It's Marcus. There was a terrible accident today. He died, Faith. I thought I should tell you, in case you saw it on the late news.'

A chill crept beneath her skin. She listened, horrified, as he continued. It was hard to believe everything he was telling her. Marcus was so young, so amiable, with all his life ahead of him. How could he be dead? Her own troubles seemed trivial now.

'How's Aunt Helena?'

'In shock. Brandon too.'

'Shall I come up? Is there anything I can do?'

'No, sweetheart. There's not much any of us can do. I'm sorry I had to call tonight but I didn't want you to find out any other way. Take care of yourself, Faith.'

'You too. Bye, Dad.' She put the phone down. The pictures were vivid in her head – the lake at Dalchett House, brooding under the winter sky; the bare trees, the steep-sided banks with their stagnant inlets. She shuddered. Marcus had died while she had been moping over a lost cause, obsessed with her feelings for Rajat, her jealousy of Anshula; indulging herself with the selfish fantasy that they would be so unhappy together he would realise he had made a mistake. No wonder she was on her own. She was despicable.

The flat seemed quieter than ever. She poured herself a large brandy and lay on the sofa sipping it, waiting for the alcohol to dull her senses. But, though her thoughts slowed, the grief was unrelenting. There was a hollow place in her heart. A place that had belonged to Marcus Calthorpe.

Perhaps to punish herself further, perhaps because she could no longer bear the silence, she turned on the news at ten o'clock. She gazed at the colourful images on the screen, oblivious of what was occurring or what was being said. Yet some instinct warned her before the news reader mentioned Marcus's name. She sat upright, tense and alert.

News is just coming in of the death of Marcus Calthorpe, grandson of Sir Edward Reece and heir to the combined fortunes of GLP Enterprises and Calthorpe Publishing. The boy, who would have been sixteen in two weeks' time, is believed to have suffered a heart-attack after falling into a lake in a freak accident at Dalchett House in Herefordshire, the home he inherited from his late grandfather, Quentin Calthorpe. Reports have also reached us of a fire in...

She switched off the television and reached for the brandy bottle, appalled that Marcus's life could be dismissed in a few impersonal words. The digits on the clock flashed relentlessly – seconds, minutes, an hour – enumerating her loneliness. She longed to sleep but she couldn't. Instead she drank more brandy, which made her nauseous.

The doorbell rang just before midnight. She stood up unsteadily. The floor shifted like sand beneath her feet.

The walls seemed to tilt. Her brain wouldn't function properly and it was impossible to walk in a straight line. In the hall she blinked up at the monitor.

'Ras-hjat.' She couldn't pronounce his name.

'Faith, are you all right? Can I come up?'

'I shuphose. She pressed the button to unlock the street door; then, fumbling with the key, opened the door to her flat and waited on the landing, slouched against the banister.

He was breathless when he reached the top of the stairs. Her eyes filled with hot, foolish tears and she went ahead of him, keeping her face averted, concentrating on placing one foot in front of the other. 'Pleash. Come inshide.'

'Can we talk?'

'What about?'

'I've finished with Anshula.'

Her heart began to pump faster, squeezing the breath from her lungs. 'Why?'

'I think you know the answer to that.' He closed the door and followed her into the lounge.

They sat side by side on the sofa. It was like old times except that she was no longer relaxed in his company. The clutter of thoughts in her head slowed. She concentrated her attention on his hands which were clenched, the knuckles like ivory.

He shook the rain out of his hair. 'It's taken me ages to summon the nerve to come here. I thought you might have gone to bed.'

'What did you want to say?'

'You're not going to make things easy for me, are you?'

She shook her head. 'I don't know what you mean.'

'I mean I can't marry Anshula. I've probably always known in my heart. But seeing you today put everything into perspective. Anshula's a spoilt little girl. I don't even like her very much. It was ridiculous to think I could marry her. Especially when I'm in love with someone else.'

Faith sat very still.

He touched her cheek. 'When I saw you in the cafe you were different somehow; you looked at me differently. As if you cared. Was I right, Faith? Do you care about me?'

'No... yes.' She was confused.

'Do you think you could ever love me, Faith?' He took her face in his hands. His eyes were wide and watchful, shining with hope.

'I already do,' she whispered.

And then his arms were round her and she was crying, her cheek against his wet coat, her emotions a volatile fusion of sadness and joy.

CHAPTER 38

What am I doing here?

Grace stood alone by one of the windows in the dining room at Dalchett House. She felt like an outsider. Richard's mother had studiously avoided her all morning and Dot Manning and Betty Holmes had been too busy to spare her more than a few words. Helena, preoccupied with the final preparations for the funeral, had barely acknowledged her. The other women – young wives from the estate presumably – she hadn't met before and no one had bothered to introduce her. Her daughters, on the other hand, had been in great demand; at everyone's beck and call, doing whatever they were asked quickly and efficiently. She envied their involvement. Her own offers to help had been met with indifference. Only Trudie seemed pleased to see her, glad of an extra pair of hands in the kitchen. The tasks were mundane – fetching and carrying, scouring the baking tins, loading the dishwashers – but they had kept her out of the way for a while.

'Well, I think that's about it.' In the centre of the room Ivy folded her arms and surveyed their efforts. Everything was ready – food set out on the long table and covered with cloths, wine glasses and cutlery polished, new candles placed in the elaborate candle holders, napkins folded, flower arrangements finished and the fire already burning brightly. There was nothing more to do. Grace pushed up her sleeve and checked her watch. It was only eleven o'clock. They were far too early. There was still almost an hour and a half to get through before they had to leave. The thought filled her with dismay.

It had been a mistake to come. Despite her concern for Amy, she should have stayed away. She didn't fit in. She wasn't family – she had only met Marcus twice. Helena had insisted on a modest funeral at the village church with only a few mourners; people who had known her son well and loved him. There was to be no fuss. No media coverage, no outside caterers, no extravagant gathering of the rich and privileged. Instead there would be a simple service and Marcus would be buried in the churchyard, like his grandfather, Quentin. Helena didn't want her only child interred in the Calthorpe family vault. And, surprisingly, Brandon had agreed.

Ivy turned to give some further instructions to Dot Manning. The other women clustered together, waiting to be dismissed. Helena moved away from them and began to re-position some of the chairs. She was wearing one of Trudie's aprons over her black skirt, otherwise she was elegant and gracious as ever; only her pallor and the emptiness in her dark eyes revealed her suffering. Grace understood her need to keep occupied, to suppress her grief with relentless activity.

The murmur of voices ceased as Brandon Calthorpe came into the room. Grace eyed him dispassionately. He was no longer handsome. His waist had expanded, the flesh on his face coarsened, and his hair was thinner, receding at the front. She assumed, unkindly, that the lines on his forehead and round his mouth were due to dissolute living rather than any past trauma. He had no power to hurt her any more. But she knew her daughters had reason to fear him.

'Helena, can you spare a minute?' He spoke curtly.

'Yes, of course.' His wife went across to him.

'The florist bought some wreaths. Holmes wasn't sure where to put them...'

Grace was surprised to hear him falter. *Did he have a heart after all?*

'I think we could leave them on the forecourt, in front of the house. It's quite mild outside.'

'Do you want to see them?'

'I'll come now, before I tidy myself up.' Helena followed him out through the great hall.

The tension in the room subsided. Grace looked round anxiously. Hope was chatting to Betty Holmes, apparently unaffected by her father's brief appearance. But Hope was an accomplished actress. Faith was by the fire, her back to the room, and Amy... for a second she couldn't locate her other daughter who was half hidden in the shadows by the door into the drawing room, poised for escape.

What have I done to them? The potent mixture of love and remorse made her light headed. They were strangers, her girls. It was too late to get to know them now. The builder had telephoned yesterday: the renovations to the bungalow were complete. She had no choice but to return to Lincoln. Whether Amy would want to come with her she had no idea. And Richard? She sighed. He would he be relieved to see her go.

I love him. The realisation astonished her. After all the yearning for excitement, the disillusion, the years of unhappiness, she had finally learned to appreciate her husband's worth. There was no joy in the knowledge, only a bitter-sweet regret. He would never return her feelings and she could never reveal them. It was just as well she had to leave.

'I'll ask Holmes to organise refreshments in the morning room before the other guests arrive.' Ivy took charge in Helena's absence. 'We need something to sustain us.'

There was a surge of movement as the women hurried in her wake.

'Are you coming, Mum?'

Grace was surprised to find her youngest daughter at her side.

'Yes, sweetheart.' She put an arm round Amy's shoulder, making herself smile. 'I could do with a cup of tea.'

They were all waiting on the forecourt when Marcus came to Dalchett House for the last time. Amy saw the line of black cars gliding down the drive, windows and mirrors glinting in the winter sunshine, and the dull ache between her ribs sharpened into sudden piercing pain. It was unbearably sad. In front of her Marcus's grandmother, still frail after a bout of influenza, wept quietly, her hand trembling on her husband's arm. Sir Edward Reece, a gaunt figure in his dark overcoat, bowed his head. Brandon Calthorpe stared into the middle distance, shifting his stance from foot to foot, his shoes making a tiny rasping sound on the gravel. Beside him Helena was still, the anguish carved into her face, unflinching as she watched her son come home. All around them, family, friends, and everyone employed on the Dalchett Estate stood in respectful silence, a tribute to the boy who had touched their lives with his natural charm and good humour.

The cars came closer. There was a tall man walking in front, dressed as if he was going to some macabre wedding, in tails and a top-hat with a strip of black silk hanging at the back. Amy looked away, towards the wooded hills. The scent of lilies drifted across to her.

For the second occasion in four months she sat with her sisters in a hired limousine. This time it was different. Her father and mother were with them, perched uncomfortably on the flip-up seats which faced backwards, their expressions bleak. This time there was nothing to celebrate. Except, her father said, the years Marcus had lived and the joy he had brought to those privileged to know him. It was small comfort. She held her breath, trying not to inhale the strong smell of air freshener, which was becoming inextricably linked with death in her mind. Like the white lilies.

At the church, a larger version of the one in Tuston, they followed the bearers, who carried the coffin on their shoulders, through the lych gate, up the broad path to the porch, and through the double doors, which were held open by two elderly parishioners. Inside it was chilly, although Amy could feel heat coming from the grills in the tiled floor as she took her seat in the pew behind Helena's family.

The service seemed interminable. She sang the hymns, knelt for the prayers and listened to the address, but the words were smothered by her own dark thoughts. She kept her eyes focused on the peripheral – the red roses in a wrought-iron stand near the pulpit, the long black feathers on Helena's hat, Reverend Gaskell's glasses winking in the candlelight.

She stood with the rest of the congregation as the ceremony came to an end. The bearers lifted the coffin once more, conveying it, with measured paces, from its lonely place by the chancel steps towards the door.

'Go on, Amy.' Her mother gave her a little push.

It was time. She sidled out of the pew and joined the procession of mourners accompanying Marcus to his final resting place.

Outside the sun was still shining. The distraught group of family and friends spread out somewhat on the narrow path leading to the back of the church. She couldn't control her rising panic.

Her mother frowned. 'What is it?'

'You go on. I'll catch you up.' Amy unzipped her right boot and pretended to shake a stone out of it, letting everyone go past. She noticed Russell with his grandparents among the staff from Dalchett House making their way to the gate, leaving those closest to Marcus to bury him in privacy. She wondered if she could join them. Dismayed by the power of her fear, she pulled the boot back on and waited until there was no one in sight, unsure what to do, hating herself for being a coward.

'Amy, are you okay?'

It was Faith.

'I can't do this. I don't want to watch.'

'I know,' Faith's manner was uncharacteristically gentle. 'I feel the same.'

'I've let Marcus down.' Amy wiped her eyes on her coat sleeve.

'But you haven't. You won't. Neither of us will. If we're not there for him this afternoon we'll never forgive ourselves.' Faith caught hold of her hand. 'We'll do this together. For Marcus.'

She could feel Faith trembling and, strangely, it made her stronger, knowing her sister was terrified too. She managed a feeble smile. 'We'd better hurry then.'

They ran along the path, slowing as they rounded the corner of the building. The churchyard here was green and peaceful, sloping gradually downhill, with a panoramic view of undulating countryside and the welsh mountains. The little knot of people in black clothes were insignificant against the spectacular backdrop. Still holding hands, the girls joined them.

And then all Amy could see was the hideous rectangular hole in the ground. At its edge, Reverend Gaskell was reciting phrases she had only ever encountered in films or on television, his surplus stirring in the breeze, the pages of his prayer-book rustling. The smell of newly disturbed earth made her want to vomit. Faith's grip tightened on her fingers. She shut her eyes as Marcus was lowered into the grave and, in desperation, she prayed for his soul, filling her head with her own words, trying to blot out all other sounds. It didn't work. In her imagination she saw and heard everything.

After an eternity there was a slight movement, as if every person present had begun to breathe again. Faith let go of her hand.

She opened her eyes, giddy with relief. A straggle of men and women were making their way up to the path. Her mother came across the grass.

'It's time to go, girls. Helena and Brandon need a few minutes on their own.' She paused. 'What is it, Faith? Are you ill?'

Amy glanced at her sister. Faith was shivering, her face much paler than usual, a sheen of sweat on her skin.

'I'm...' With a small, choking noise, Faith collapsed into her mother's arms in a frenzy of tears. 'I'm sorry. I didn't mean to do this. I just feel so awful.'

'It's all right, Faith. It's all right.'

Faith's sobs grew wilder. 'I'm desperately sad about Marcus. I really am. But all the time, at the back of my mind I was picturing what could happen to me, or Dad, or...' She shuddered. 'How can I be so selfish?'

'I expect, if they were honest, most people here today would admit to the same thing,' her mother said softly. 'We're all grieving for Marcus. Yet we're afraid for ourselves; for the future. That's human nature.'

'D'you think so?' Faith's voice was thin.

'Yes. You mustn't punish yourself for your fears, Faith.'

The gentle response prompted a fresh spasm of weeping. 'But I am selfish. Look how horrible I've been to you since you came home. And you don't know what I did, all those years ago after you left us. When you phoned...'

'I think I do. But it doesn't matter now. It's all in the past. All forgiven.'

Amy thought she saw the hint of her mother's smile above the tangle of Faith's hair.

A robin flew on to one of the gravestones and began to trill its cheery song. The breeze freshened, intensifying the scent of damp grass. In the distance car doors slammed, engines revved. The church clock chimed the half hour. Her sister's sobs eased.

'Do you feel better now, Faith?' Her mother asked.

'A bit.' Faith raised her head at last.

'We should go then. Your father and Hope will be waiting.'

Amy trailed behind them as they walked up the slope towards the church. It was strange seeing them together.

If her mother and sister could forgive each other was there a chance her mother and father might be reconciled?

The hope flared for a moment. And then she heard Helena crying.

They were quiet on the way back. Amy felt exhausted, as if she hadn't slept for days. As the big car nosed almost silently through the lanes, she leaned against the window, an elbow on the padded arm-rest, her mind empty. When the car drew to a halt she was amazed to find they were at Dalchett House. She remembered nothing of the journey.

In the passageway they took off their coats, handing them to Holmes before they went into the dining room where the rest of the guests were gathered. Amy stayed close to her father. The smell of lilies made her stomach churn.

'Are Helena and Brandon with you?' Her grandmother appeared flustered.

Her father pushed a hand through his hair. 'I think they may be a while yet.'

'Should we make a start on the buffet without them?'

'Wait a bit longer, Mum. People are content with wine and canapes at the moment.'

'I'll ask Sir Edward what he thinks. Some of Helena's relatives may want to leave soon. It's a long drive back to Surrey.'

As her grandmother scurried off, Amy was reminded of a plump brown mouse with its eyes fixed on a tasty morsel of cheese.

She turned away, ashamed of such a mean thought. Her head had begun to ache. The dark-panelled room seemed overcrowded and the flickering candles did nothing to dispel the gloom. The legacy of death was everywhere. She saw it on the drawn, white faces and behind red-rimmed eyes; she heard it in the muffled voices; and it was inside her, in the raw emptiness that was all she had left of Marcus. She longed to escape.

Her chance came when Helena and Brandon returned. Everyone milled around indecisively, some offering condolences, others keeping a respectful distance. Choosing her moment, Amy slipped unnoticed into the drawing room.

Jim Manning was on his knees by the fire, a pile of logs in front of him. He smiled sympathetically.

'Everything all right?'

'Yes, thank you. I just need some fresh air.'

She scuttled past him, heading for the passageway. It took a few minutes to find her coat among the many in the cloakroom and she pulled it on hastily as she ran to the front door. Outside the forecourt was already in shadow, the parked cars empty. She shivered. Perhaps it was not a good idea to be out alone. But she needed to talk to someone. And the only person she could think of was Russell.

Buttoning her collar, she set off up the drive. She looked back once. The sun was low in the sky, soon to be swallowed by a bank of purple clouds, and the lights from the house glimmered faintly through a lacework of branches. At the bridge she hesitated, then, before her resolve weakened, she climbed over the stone parapet and slithered down the slope to the path below.

It was darker among the trees. The rooks carped ceaselessly and their cries made her uneasy. Her pace slowed. What was she doing? Why had she assumed Russell would be in the woods? Wouldn't it be more sensible to go back? But she trudged on, ignoring her misgivings.

There was no sign of Russell when she reached the clearing but his haversack was on the floor in the shelter which meant he wouldn't be far away. Curious to see some more of his work, she took out one of the sketchbooks and settled herself on a stack of logs to examine the drawings.

She saw at once that these sketches were different. There was a portrait of Russell's grandmother as a tormented, skeletal creature with a mad woman's eyes. There was a dismal scene of a man by a field gate – a man who resembled Holmes but much older – hunched with weariness. There was a woman in rags lying in a litter-strewn doorway. Disturbed by the insight into Russell's personal nightmares, she turned over a few sheets together.

The picture seemed to rise up from the page. The book slid from her fingers and lay open on her lap. She couldn't bring herself to touch it. Russell had drawn a young girl staring into a mirror. A baby, its head a ghastly skull, was visible over her shoulder as though she was holding it to her. The reflection showed the girl's face ravaged by tears. But she had no baby in her arms.

There was no doubt the girl was Hope. Amy shuddered. *Could Russell be the father of the child Hope had lost?* Aghast, she let the book fall into the sawdust. Russell and Hope. Surely it couldn't be true.

Richard extricated himself politely from the group of well-dressed women who had been inquiring about the history of Dalchett House and scanned the dining room briefly. He hadn't set eyes on his youngest daughter for some considerable time. She was becoming quite adept at disappearing. He spotted Hope talking to Marcus's former nanny, a vapid young woman in her late twenties, and Grace had taken Faith upstairs to rest. But Amy was nowhere to be seen.

He went through to the drawing room where half a dozen elderly guests had congregated by the fire, drinking coffee and brandy, conversing in lowered tones. Amy wasn't with them. He looked into the winter parlour and found only a huddle of Marcus's school friends. His concern increased. Amy had been traumatised by everything that had happened. He should have watched her more carefully.

It was time to begin a systematic search. She wasn't in the kitchens or the old servants' hall, nor was she in the garden room. The summer parlour on the north side of the house wasn't used at this time of year, but he looked in anyway in case she had fallen asleep on one of the sofas, beneath the dust sheets. Satisfied she wasn't there, he hurried along the passage to the front of the house.

Helena was in the morning room, sitting by the embers of a fire that had been forgotten. She was quite composed yet the expression on her face made his heart ache.

'Do you want me to go?'

She shook her head. He sat down on the arm of her chair and relegated the worries about his daughter to the back of his mind.

'He never liked the dark,' Helena's voice was flat, without emotion. 'I can't bear to think of him alone in the churchyard all night.'

He took her hand. It was icy. 'He isn't there, Helena. It's only his body they buried. His soul is free.'

'I want to believe that. I wish I had your faith, Richard. Yet it wouldn't make losing him any easier.'

'No.'

'He was my baby. My beautiful boy. Always so brave and cheerful, even when he was ill. Brandon never saw that. He never realised just how courageous his son was. Marcus was always trying to prove himself, always trying to make his father proud. Poor lad, he had no chance. He was too kind-hearted. He would never have survived in the business world. And I'm glad he was the way he was. I loved him for it.'

'We all loved him, Helena.'

'Except his father,' she said bitterly.

They were quiet for a while, thinking of Marcus. Then she sat upright, her hand tensing within his.

'I'm expecting another child, Richard.'

The words chilled him.

'I know you think I'm crazy. But I always wanted another baby. And lately Brandon has been more settled.'

He was consumed by a sudden blinding jealousy. 'So you're staying with him?'

'Yes.'

'Do you love him?'

'Not any more.'

'Then, why?'

'He needs me. And I don't want to make a new life without Marcus. Besides, I've never been much good with men; never been sure if they wanted me or the GLP fortune. Let's face it, I wasn't much to look at even when I was young. And now... well... I'm middle-aged. I don't want to start all over again.'

He wanted to say he had always thought her beautiful, but it wasn't the right time. She would think he was lying anyway. She had been schooled all her life to think herself inferior; not the son her parents wanted, not a conventional society beauty, not the woman her husband desired.

'It's funny, I never think of you as middle-aged.'

She gave him a wry little smile. 'I've never met anyone I felt close to, except you. I think you would have loved me for myself.'

'I do. I have for a long time.' He admitted it at last.

She sighed. 'We had our chance. It's too late for us now. We have too many commitments. I have to look after Brandon's heir and my father's company. And your duty is to your family and the church. We wouldn't be happy if we neglected our responsibilities, Richard.'

She was right. He loved her, yet that love had always been forbidden.

He pressed both her hands to his lips. 'God bless you, Helena.'

'Whatever happens,' she said, 'we'll remember what might have been.'

He marvelled at her resilience. She had lost the only thing that really mattered in her life. How could she face the future so bravely?

She seemed to sense what he was thinking. 'I always knew Marcus was living on borrowed time, Richard. Right from when he was a baby. I'm grateful for the years we had together.'

Her words made him ashamed. He was the priest yet he had none of her grace and fortitude. He faced what lay ahead with trepidation – his children moving away, a lonely old age. He was a miserable Christian. His faith had been tested and found wanting.

'Would you do something for me?' She was watching him anxiously.

'Of course.'

'Would you talk to Brandon? Help him cope.'

'If you think it will do any good.' He didn't want to do what she asked but he gave his word.

'Thank you.' She stretched up and kissed him lightly on the cheek.

He sat with her a while longer and then he left to resume his search for his daughter.

A few minutes later he pushed open the library door. Amy was not in there but his stepbrother was sitting at the long table, a pile of exercise books and an almost empty bottle of whisky in front of him.

'He kept diaries. For the last five years. All his visits to Dalchett House.' Brandon looked up. 'I found them behind Dad's old fishing manuals. Helena knew they were there, of course. She told me this morning.'

'I'll leave you to read them in peace.' Richard was taken aback. He had expected a mouthful of abuse. 'I'm sorry. I didn't mean to intrude.'

He made to go out of the room.

'Marcus loved this place you know.' Brandon leafed through one of the thin, dog-eared volumes. 'This is what he wrote a few days before... before the accident.'

Richard noticed he had difficulty focussing on the script.

I think this house understands me. When I'm older I would like to manage Dalchett Estate.' Brandon took a swig of whisky and wiped a hand over his mouth. Richard sat down opposite him.

'He loved your girls too. This is part of the same entry. Listen. *I'm glad Amy's here. She's good fun and she accepts me for what I am. It's hard to believe we never knew she existed until a few months ago.* I had no idea they were friends. Did you?' Brandon glared at him through bloodshot eyes.

'I was aware they spent a lot of time together in the holidays.'

'Ever the vigilant parent, eh?'

'Did he know Hope was his step-sister?'

'Not until recently. He overheard me talking to Helena after that rubbish with Maurizio Quattrone was in all the papers. You needn't look at me like that. I made him promise not to tell anyone.' There was a flash of the old animosity.

'How did he react?'

'He didn't say much. I had to rush off to a meeting and we never spoke of it again.'

Typical. Richard couldn't quite stifle the thought.

'I read this a few minutes ago.' Brandon thumbed through the pages, his hands shaking. He pushed the book across the table.

Richard read the extract unwillingly; the private agony of a boy he loved. *Now I know about Hope, I understand why I've always idolised her. I'm so proud she's my half-sister. She's already a fantastic actress. No wonder my father has no time for me. I can't compete. I'm just a boring schoolboy with a weak heart. I'm not jealous but I wish I could earn his respect.*

Brandon smirked at him. 'I'm a rotten sod, aren't I? I go through life trampling on everyone's feelings. I don't like myself, Richard. I don't like myself at all.'

Richard appraised him silently. It was hard to tell whether his stepbrother was consumed by self-disgust or self-pity.

'It's not all my fault,' Brandon continued, 'I was spoilt rotten as a child. Oh not by Quentin – he was working most of the time – but my mother over-indulged me. When she died, Dad was heartbroken. We came back to the family home and he shut himself away for a long time. I hated it here. And when you and your mother came along I hated you. My father began to enjoy life again. He spent more time with you than with me; you shared the same interests – reading, music, art – all the things that bored me to tears. When he married your mother I thought I might have to share my inheritance with you and I couldn't bear the thought.'

He blinked and drank the last of the whisky. 'Okay. I admit I made life hell for you. But you won in the end. You have what really matters. You have three children who love you. I had a son and I never even took the time to get to know him. Perhaps this is God's judgment on me. What d'you think, Reverend Lawson?'

Richard fought the desire to make an angry retort. There was no mistaking his brother's turmoil. He wondered if Helena had told him about her pregnancy.

'I don't believe God works in that way,' he said.

Brandon disregarded his opinion. 'Hope is my daughter but she will never love me the way she loves you.' For a moment he was quiet, his fingers tapping on the empty bottle. Then his head jerked up. 'Helena loves you too, you bastard! Saint Richard, her knight in shining armour.'

Richard had no answer for him.

'Oh, don't worry. I know you haven't had her. You're far too virtuous. I almost wish you weren't, if only because I could smash your sanctimonious face against the wall. Anything to relieve this awful emptiness inside me.'

With futile rage Brandon hurled the empty bottle across the room. They watched it shatter on the wooden floorboards, the broken glass glinting like chips of ice.

'I want to blame someone. Anyone. Your daughter, that stupid dog, Marcus himself for being so foolhardy. But it won't bring him back. I don't get a second chance. There's no way I can ever make things right with him.'

'No, you can't.' Richard chose his words carefully. 'All you can do is take comfort from the fact that he loved you in spite of everything.'

'How do I know that?'

Richard pointed to the paragraph he had read earlier. 'Why else would he want your respect? Read through his diaries, Brandon. Marcus had such a capacity for love, and he never bore grudges.'

He put his hands on the table and pushed himself to his feet. He was drained emotionally. This was the longest conversation he had ever had with his stepbrother. 'I have to go and look for Amy. I'll ask Holmes to bring you coffee.'

Brandon gave no sign of having heard and Richard let himself out of the room, shutting the heavy door behind him.

Grace was coming along the corridor. He waited for her.

'I've been looking for Amy.'

'She's not in the house. Jim Manning said she went out about an hour ago. Hope's gone to find her.' Grace didn't appear unduly concerned.

'Right.' He made an effort to ignore his nagging worries. 'How's Faith?'

'She's sleeping.'

'Good. We should go back down then.' He couldn't think of anything else to say.

'Richard, can I have a word?'

'What is it?' He was tired. He didn't want any more revelations.

'I had a phone call yesterday. From the builders. The bungalow is ready. I'll be out of your way soon.'

'There's no rush.'

'I've imposed on you for too long. I'm so grateful to you for offering Amy and me somewhere to stay.'

'It was the least I could do in the circumstances.'

She flushed. 'You owed me nothing, Richard. After what I did most men would have said I got what I deserved.'

'What will you do?'

'Sell the bungalow and find somewhere cheap to rent.' She looked down, picking at the skin around her fingernails. 'Could I ask one more favour? Not for me, for Amy.'

'Go ahead.'

'I wonder if Amy could stay with you until I've found somewhere decent. She's happy at school in Hereford. Perhaps if she could stay until the end of term, until Easter?'

He saw how difficult it had been for her to make the request.

'Nothing would make me happier. I've grown to love her, Gracie.'

His skin grew hot. *He had called her Gracie. Why?*

'Thank you, Richard. I know she loves you. I'm sorry I kept her from you all those years.'

She offered no explanation and he didn't ask for any.

'You don't have to stay in Lincoln, Grace. You could come and live in Tuston when everything's settled. The rectory is far too large for one person.'

'I... I don't know.'

He qualified his offer hastily. 'It's okay, Grace. I'm not suggesting we live as man and wife. It would be a practical arrangement. You need a home, I've got spare rooms. And I get to see my daughter grow up. Think about it. You don't have to give me an answer immediately.'

'It's very generous of you,' she murmured.

Her face had lost all animation. Too late he remembered how it had been between them; how quickly her moods would change, how easy it was to upset her. He pushed his hair back wearily. *Why on earth had he given her the chance to come back into his life?*

The light was fading as Russell plodded along the side of the lake, trying to shake off his melancholy. Earlier the sun had set in a blaze of angry colour but now the last of the blue sky had disappeared behind a layer of cloud leaving the landscape grey and featureless. The woods were already dark, the lake black as oil. Apart from the noisy rooks, he might have been the only living creature around. The loneliness suited his mood.

Today his mother had been in his head. Today he had fought the old childish panic as he mourned the boy he had grown to admire over the years; the boy who had become his friend.

And Hope had been there in the church, elegant in her black coat; aloof and unapproachable. She hadn't even looked at him. He kicked a clod of dried mud, his thoughts bitter. She was different. Success had changed her. Perhaps the stories about her relationship with Maurizio Quattrone had been true after all. He walked faster, suppressing his resentment. It was too painful to live in the past. He had to acknowledge the fact that Hope had moved on and he was no longer part of her life.

Nearing the brook his pace slowed. The sharp scent of wood-preservative hung in the air and he noted the two new planks as he crossed the steep-sided channel. He pressed on towards the grassy outcrop, struggling to stifle visions of Marcus and Amy in the icy water. A breeze stirred the undergrowth and his thoughts shifted. He wondered if Amy was looking for him. She often sought him out when she visited her grandmother. But surely she would be with her family today?

He shrugged. Amy was not his responsibility. Nevertheless, anxiety nagged him. The trouble was that he did feel responsible for her. Amy was quick-tempered and reckless, but she was also loyal and brave. And she fancied herself in love with him. She was all fire and ashes. Sometimes she reminded him of Hope. But Hope's mind was full of dreams and secrets while Amy lived for the moment, every fleeting emotion written clearly on her face. Amy was vulnerable, especially today. She might need a friend. He found himself walking faster.

When he arrived at the rustic bridge he was out of breath. As he leaned against the wooden rail, a figure darted out of the trees further along the lakeside, too far away to identify in the gathering dusk.

'Amy, is that you?' He waved his hands to attract attention.

The figure stood still. His heart began to beat erratically. He was almost certain it was Hope out there at the edge of the water. He shouted, 'It's okay. It's only me. Russell.'

She began to walk towards him, slight as a shadow in the half-light. When she came nearer he saw her eyes were wide and startled. She looked thirteen again.

'I'm sorry. I didn't mean to scare you.'

'I was looking for Amy. Have you seen her?'

He was unsure if it was fear or disdain he detected in her clipped tones.

'She's not back there.' He glanced at the path behind him. 'I very much doubt she would come down here.'

'You don't think she might... harm herself?'

He realised what she was thinking. 'No. She probably just wants to be alone, to come to terms with things. Don't worry, she'll be all right.'

'I'll go back to the house then, she may be there now.'

'I have to collect my sketch books from the shelter. If I see her in the woods I'll make sure she gets back safely.'

'Thank you.'

Neither of them moved. They were standing at the place where they first met; where they had made love. His skin prickled with shame. He had taken advantage of her emotional turmoil. He should never have let desire overrule his common sense. No wonder she had rejected him. He had to speak, tell her he was sorry for everything she had suffered because of his weakness.

'Hope...' He stepped closer to her, hand outstretched, pleading silently for forgiveness.

She flinched. She didn't want him to touch her, this stranger who was Russell. For so long she had carried his image in her mind, but it was the image of a skinny, self-conscious youth and not this broad-shouldered, confident man who treated her as if she was a hysterical child. Even his voice wasn't the same. It was deeper, unfriendly. She fiddled with a button on her coat. Her heart was numb with loss, her head heavy with memories of Marcus. She couldn't cope with anything else.

'Hope...'

'What is it? I have to go.'

'I'm so sorry, Hope.'

Sorry for what? For loving her? 'There's no need. What happened between us is history. No sense in raking it up again.'

'Hope, I have to explain how I feel; how ashamed I am of the way I treated you on the night Gran went missing. It's no excuse, I know, but I was angry because you shut me out of your life. You never even told me about the baby.'

'I had no idea I was pregnant until the morning of the accident. I never once thought about the possibility. How naive was that?'

She heard him swallow.

'I didn't know.'

'How could you? It doesn't matter now, anyway.'

'But I shouldn't have been so cruel. You were ill, an invalid. And it was all because of what we did.'

'It wasn't your fault a group of spiteful girls attacked me.'

'Didn't they turn on you because you were pregnant?'

'No. Why would you think that?'

'I just assumed, when you wouldn't talk to me...'

She looked up at him. His face was in shadow, his angular features indistinct, but his eyes reflected the last of the light; the same grey eyes she remembered, clear and compassionate, transparently honest.

'I didn't want to see anyone when I was in hospital, Russ. I wasn't even sure I wanted to live at first.'

'I thought you hated me. But I waited for you, in the shelter, every time you visited Dalchett House.'

Something inside her seemed to soften, as if her heart had been frozen and was melting slowly. She had misjudged him. He hadn't changed, only grown older.

'I did hate you for a while.' She chewed her lip. It was important to be truthful, to set the record straight between them. 'I blamed you for it all at first – the baby, the accident, the fact that I was a cripple. But that hatred didn't last. I was depressed, full of self-pity. I didn't care about anyone or anything except myself.'

'I can understand that.'

'And I felt so guilty.'

'Guilty?'

She was glad it was dark and he couldn't see the colour stinging her cheeks. 'I wished our baby was dead. And that wish came true. But I didn't mean it, Russ. I didn't mean it!'

It was impossible to hold back the rush of tears. She covered her face with her hands, embarrassed by the ferocity of her remorse, the depths of her grief. When he put his arms round her she had no strength to push him away.

He didn't say anything until she was calmer. Then he tilted her chin gently.

'You mustn't punish yourself, Hope. Our baby died because you were injured, not because of any bad thoughts you might have had.'

'Do you forgive me then?'

'There's nothing to forgive.'

She relaxed against him, taking comfort from his words. She had lived for so long with the awful suspicion that she had somehow willed her baby's death and now, at last, she could let it go.

Russell's face was close to hers. The longing in his eyes was unmistakable and she wondered if she could see it mirrored in her own. She hardly dared breathe.

When he bent to kiss her the joy that swept through her body was sharp as physical pain.

The light from the drawing room spilled across the terrace. Careful to keep out of its range, Amy rested her elbows on the balustrade, trying to sort out the conflict in her mind. Her stomach curdled at the idea of Hope and Russell as lovers.

Where was Russell now? She had waited for him until dark and then, desperate for warmth and company, she had hurried back to the house. But at the last moment she couldn't face going inside. Now she was alone, unable to come to terms with what she knew. Her misery hardened into malice. She loved Russell Holmes and she wasn't going to give him up without a fight. Scrubbing the tears from her eyes with her fists, she began to consider her options, taking a perverse pleasure in the process.

She could to drop hints to Russell, say how conceited Hope had become, how she was only interested in her career. Or... she traced a question mark in the lichen on top of the parapet. What if she were to tell Hope about her own relationship with Russell, let her sister think it was something more than just friendship?

But none of this was true. And it wasn't enough. She wanted to expose their sordid little secret, to humiliate them in front of their friends and families.

A cold breeze stirred up the scent of grass and damp earth. She looked down involuntarily. The sweep of lawn merged with the night but she knew that the lake lay at the bottom of the invisible slope. She could smell the black water on the air. Her thoughts turned to Marcus and the weight of grief tugged at her heart. She hadn't expected to miss him so much.

'I often think I would rather stay here when I die. Like a ghost.' His words echoed in her head. If Marcus was a ghost he would be a benign one. She had never heard him utter an unkind word. *And he would be horrified if he knew of her spiteful intentions.*

'Amy?'

A beam of light wavered across the grass and her father appeared out of the darkness.

'I've been looking everywhere for you. Hope's searching the woods. We were worried. Where have you been all afternoon?'

'Just walking.' Her jealousy rekindled. *Hope and Russell both in the woods.*

Her father climbed the shallow steps. He switched off the torch, pushing it into the pocket of his overcoat as he came to stand by her. He put his hand over hers.

'This has been a terrible ordeal for you.'

She felt her breathing grow shallow, her stomach muscles snatch with malicious excitement. *Now was the time to reveal Hope's secret, while she had his undivided attention.*

'I... There's something you should...' The words stuck in her throat. *Why couldn't she tell him?*

Understanding came with sudden clarity. She loved him. She had learned to love them all; all her family.

Whatever their faults, whatever secrets they might have, whatever mistakes they had made in the past, she loved them. And she couldn't bring herself to hurt them. A tear escaped, trickled onto her hand.

In an instant her father's arm was round her, strong and protective. 'You've been under a terrible strain, Amy. I wish I could make it easier for you.'

She gulped, making an effort to stay in control.

He stroked her hair. 'It will take time to get over this. You won't ever forget, sweetheart, but you will remember the good times you had with Marcus eventually. In the spring, when the sun is shining and the wild daffodils are out, the lake won't seem such a terrifying place. You're a brave girl. You'll be able to confront your memories then.'

But I won't be here. By the end of February the bungalow would probably be sold and she would be in Lincoln with her mother, living in some grotty rented flat. It was all coming to an end. She had found a family – her father, her sisters, her grandmother – and now she was going to lose them. Even if they stayed in contact their lives would be separate from hers. The tentative bonds between them would be broken.

'Do you understand what I'm saying, Amy?'

She nodded. His chin was resting on her head. She wanted to hug him, tell him what was in her heart. But she didn't.

He cleared his throat. 'Amy, before this happened, were you happy in Tuston?'

'Yes.'

'That's good because your mother wants you to stay with me until Easter. How do you feel about that?'

It was a reprieve, of sorts, but it would only prolong the agony.

'I'm not sure.'

'Amy, I've asked Grace if she would consider coming to live at the rectory. I rattle about the place like an old tin can on my own. I'd be glad of the company.'

She stared at him in disbelief but his expression was serious.

'You're my daughter, Amy. To tell the truth, I don't want to lose you. I've missed so much of your life already. What do you think? Shall we do our best to persuade your mother?'

There was a roaring in her ears, a sudden fierce happiness welling inside her.

'Oh, Dad, yes!' She turned to throw her arms round his neck.

He kissed her forehead and she felt his lips curve into a smile.

'Come on then. Let's find your mother and sisters and see about getting you home.'

Home.

The word lingered in her mind; a promise. Her father would make it happen, she was sure. She put her hand in his and they began to walk towards the back door of the house.

EPILOGUE

'Quentin James, I baptise you in the name of the Father, and of the Son, and of the Holy Spirit.' The Reverend Gaskell tipped the holy water onto the child's forehead and traced the sign of the cross on his forehead. The baby, resplendent in the magnificent Calthorpe christening robe, kicked vigorously, screwing his face into a comical grimace. His parents and god parents, clustered round the font, gazed at him indulgently. This was the heir to the combined fortunes of the Reece and Calthorpe estates; the heir to Dalchett House.

Richard recalled only too clearly the last time he was in this church. He glanced at Helena wondering if the robust, blue-eyed baby with its fuzz of blond hair would always compete for her affection with a ghost. Quentin James was so obviously Brandon's offspring; there was nothing of Marcus about him, either in appearance or nature.

His thoughts drifted, this time to Kate who was due to give birth in a few weeks. He told himself forty was not so old to have a baby nowadays – after all Helena was nearly forty-six – but he couldn't help worrying. Kate had not had an easy pregnancy. At least he could be reasonably certain her child would have a stable life, with none of the pressures Quentin James Calthorpe would encounter in the future.

He watched Ian Gaskell present Helena and Brandon with the symbolic lighted candle. Behind them, Amy held the baby, a little frown on her forehead as she struggled to keep the flailing limbs covered. He was proud of his youngest daughter, not least for the way she had accepted Russell Holmes's involvement with her sister, even though he was certain she had been infatuated with the boy herself. She had grown up in the last few months. Today she looked almost beautiful, demure in a smart grey coat and ankle boots. The red streaks in her hair had finally grown out and natural dark curls framed her face, softening her features. It was good of his brother, he reflected grudgingly, to ask her to be Quentin's godmother. Brandon had made considerable efforts to atone for the way he had treated her, even depositing a sizable amount of money into a bank account for when she came of age. It was to Amy's credit that she had neither exploited his concern nor rejected his attempts at reconciliation.

Silently, he thanked God for his daughters. They were his greatest blessing. In front of him Faith reached for Rajat's hand, the beautiful cluster of diamonds on her ring finger flashing rainbows in the candlelight. Lately she appeared serene, with none of the dark moods that used to make her so unhappy. He was delighted. Rajat would look after her whatever obstacles the Dasari family placed in the way of their union; whatever problems could still arise, even with today's enlightened attitudes, when two people from different cultures wanted to marry.

Next to them, Hope stood with Russell, the boy who had kept her secret so long and so well. They were still very young. She was not quite eighteen, Russell only a few months older. He had no idea whether their relationship could survive all the separations; all the temptations of their time apart. Hope was leaving for America soon to start work on another film and Russell had just begun a three-year course at the art college in Hereford. They would probably meet at Christmas, but after that it could be months before they saw each other again. However, if they were to marry in a few years' time, he would give them his blessing.

The beautifully embellished service sheet slipped from his fingers, and in trying to rescue it he managed to dislodge a hymn book from the ledge in front. It fell to the floor with a thud. His mother glared at him and he stifled a grin. She was still a force to be reckoned with. At his side Grace retrieved the book, her cheeks scarlet with embarrassment. He noticed that today there was no grey visible in her hair, and for some reason that touched him; the fact that she hadn't quite given up on youth. His heart quickened with a surge of affection for her. Since she returned to the rectory she had been unobtrusive, spending a lot of time in her room, keeping the house clean and cooking his meals. She had taken a part-time job in a supermarket and insisted on paying a regular amount of money towards household bills. There was none of her former restlessness; she lived now for her daughters. He knew she had written to Cassie, hoping to renew the old friendship, and Liz Marsh had called to see her once or twice. Otherwise, she had no one except Kate, who had been a good friend to her since the wedding. It hurt him to see her so subdued. Lately he had begun to wonder if they should give their marriage another chance. She was lonely. He was lonely. And perhaps he had never really stopped loving her...

As the group around the font dispersed to take their seats among friends and family, Grace looked away from the golden-haired baby, the familiar ache heavy beneath her ribs. She had tried so hard to ignore it, this yearning for another child. There was no point in torturing herself. Richard had no interest in her physically and she didn't want any other man. It was ironic; the only two things she craved were the very ones she had rejected years ago. Now it was too late.

She sighed, mentally reproaching herself. Surely it should be enough that her daughters had forgiven her and she was part of the family again? She loved the girls dearly, would die for them if necessary. Yet there was still this guilty hollow inside her; the knowledge that she had left them to fend for themselves. If only she had another chance to prove she could be a good wife and mother.

The final hymn came to a close. Ian Gaskell stepped forward to give the blessing. The choir filed out, guests crowded into the aisles and the sound of the organ grew louder, filling the church with triumphant chords. Grace blinked back tears, hardly aware the service was over. Stepping out of the pew she stumbled and Richard steadied her, keeping his arm round her while they made their way to the door. She leaned against him, glad of his strength, ridiculously aware of his closeness.

Outside, in the thin October sunshine, they found themselves jostled by the crowd. Cameras flashed, women posed in their finery, and journalists collared the rich and famous, desperate for interviews.

'You don't need all this.' Richard steered her between chattering groups of people and along the path to the back of the church.

They sat on one of the seats at the top of the slope. The air was fresh and sharp and she breathed in deeply, the fog in her head clearing.

'You're very pale, Grace. Are you okay?'

She nodded. 'I'll be fine in a few minutes. I should have eaten a proper breakfast.'

'And I should look after you better.'

There was such tenderness in his voice. Tears threatened once more. She was lucky to have him in her life. Why couldn't she be satisfied with things as they were? Silence fell between them and Grace could feel the melancholy of the place cocooning her in misery. There were long shadows across the grass; the reds and yellows of autumn had faded and berries in the bushes hung like drops of blood among the remaining leaves. Beyond the stone wall the vast expanse of countryside seemed forlorn, the mountains almost invisible, veiled in a thin mist. She shivered, her gaze drawn to the brightly coloured wreaths on both Quentin's and Marcus's graves. Instinctively, she turned to Richard.

His expression was bleak, the lines on his face deepened by sadness.

'The two of them had such generosity of spirit,' he murmured. 'They made the world a better place.'

She ached to comfort him. 'Their world was happier because of you. You were like a son to Quentin, and from what Helena told me, you were the father figure Marcus needed. I know how you loved them and how much they loved you.'

And I love you too.

'Yes.' He made an effort to smile.

The intensity of his grief shocked her. Why had she never realised how deeply he was affected by loss? In the early years of their marriage she had seen him return from hospital visits haggard and withdrawn and had never offered any sympathy. How had he coped with his wife's disappearance and losing Quentin on the same day? He had been forced to bring up two of her daughters by himself, to deal with all the traumas in their young lives, whereas she, the woman who should have given him support, had cheated and lied and then simply deserted him. How could she ever compensate for all the suffering she had caused?

A sob caught in her throat. 'Richard, I'm so sorry for all the harm I've done. The way I hurt you and the girls.'

'I forgave you long ago, Gracie.'

'If only I could go back; do things differently.'

He took both her hands in his. 'There's no going back. We can't alter the past. But maybe we should reconsider the future.'

Her mouth was dry. *What was he implying? Did he want a divorce?*

'We can change things now, Gracie. It's not too late to start again.'

Alone or as a couple? Was this his way of ending their relationship or was he suggesting something else? He hadn't mentioned love. But then he had never been good at expressing his feelings.

'I'm not sure. What do you mean?'

His fingers tightened round hers. 'I want you as my wife Gracie; not just the mother of our daughters or some kind of live-in housekeeper.'

For a moment she thought she had imagined the words.

'What do you think? Shall we give it a try?' He prompted her gently.

'Yes.' She found herself trembling. 'Oh, Richard, yes. Yes please.'

'Are you sure? I'm no great catch.' His eyes were wide and anxious, brimming with painful memories. 'Things didn't work out between us first time round. I didn't make you happy.'

It sickened her to see the damage she had inflicted.

'I'm not that selfish young woman any more. For

years after I left, I lived in hope that you'd take me back one day. No one has ever matched up to you, Richard.'

In answer, he drew her to him, enfolding her in his arms, his tears hot on her skin when he kissed her. It wasn't the passionate reunion she had dreamed of, and yet it was somehow sweeter; intense, almost reverent, a silent renewal of their wedding vows.

AUTHOR BIO

Elaine Eleridge lives in Herefordshire. She was a primary school teacher for thirty years until stress forced her to give up the job she loved. Having always been a 'writer', she began to write seriously and obtained an MA in Creative Writing from Bath Spa University.

After the Affair is her first published novel, although there are others languishing in cupboards waiting to be resurrected.

HEREFORDSHIRE AND THIS BOOK

Much of this novel is set in Herefordshire, a beautiful rural county situated between Worcestershire and the Welsh border.

The characters in the book are fictional, but locals and visitors might recognise some of the settings as they are based on actual places.

Tuston is an anagram for Sutton, a village a few miles north-east of Hereford. In Sutton you will find the beautiful little church of St Nicholas and the old rectory next door (privately owned). At the crossroads you can see the public house (no longer painted white) and the 1970s estate where Faith's friend, Emily, lived.

Dalchett house is purely a product of my imagination but there are several historical manor houses and castles in the county. Brinsop Court – a much earlier building – can be found in the area close to the fictional Dalchett Estate. The lake was inspired by that at Berrington Hall.

Hereford itself features in the story. Helena's wedding takes place in the beautiful cathedral which is dedicated to St Mary the Virgin and St Ethelbert, the king murdered by Offa in 794. The cathedral is famous worldwide for the Mappa Mundi, a mediaeval map of the world, created around 1300 by Richard of Holdingham.

It also has a fine chained library and holds a copy (one of only four that survive) of the Magna Carta.

The city's famous May Fair, also mentioned in the novel, has been held since 1121 when King Henry I granted Bishop Richard the right to hold a nine day fair. This was reduced to three days in 1838. The fair usually comes into town overnight on the first Monday of May and fills the streets with music, light and fun for the following three days.

You will still find the little corner café where Hope met Russell in Capuchin Lane, close to the cathedral. Aylestone Hill, the place where Hope had her accident, offers fine views of the city, with its cathedral and church spires, as you approach via the A4103. The white, Victorian house on the outskirts of Hereford, where Deb's engagement party takes place, is still a popular wedding venue.

These are places woven into the story. However, Herefordshire has so much to offer - gentle rolling hills, peaceful winding rivers and lush valleys, orchards, pastureland, picturesque villages and a slower pace of life.

If you are not lucky enough to live here, then do try to visit sometime.